books as a teenager, and now that she remains an avid fan. For her, there is creating romantic stories and engaging plots, and each and every book is a new adventure. Cathy lives in London. Her three daughters—Charlotte, Olivia and Emma—have always been, and continue to be, the greatest inspirations in her life.

USA TODAY bestselling author **Natalie Anderson** writes emotional contemporary romance full of sparkling banter, sizzling heat and uplifting endings—perfect for readers who love to escape with empowered heroines and arrogant alphas who are too sexy for their own good. When not writing you'll find her wrangling her four children, three cats, two goldfish and one dog…and snuggled in a heap on the sofa with her husband at the end of the day. Follow her at natalie-anderson.com.

Also by Cathy Williams

Contracted for the Spaniard's Heir
Marriage Bargain with His Innocent
Shock Marriage for the Powerful Spaniard
The Italian's Christmas Proposition
His Secretary's Nine-Month Notice

Also by Natalie Anderson

The King's Captive Virgin
Awakening His Innocent Cinderella
Pregnant by the Commanding Greek
The Innocent's Emergency Wedding
The Greek's One-Night Heir

Discover more at millsandboon.co.uk.

EXPECTING HIS BILLION-DOLLAR SCANDAL

CATHY WILLIAMS

SHY QUEEN IN THE ROYAL SPOTLIGHT

NATALIE ANDERSON

MILLS & BOON

First Published in Great Britain 2020
by Mills & Boon, an imprint of HarperCollins*Publishers*
1 London Bridge Street, London, SE1 9GF

Expecting His Billion-Dollar Scandal © 2020 by Cathy Williams

Shy Queen in the Royal Spotlight © 2020 by Natalie Anderson

ISBN: 978-0-263-27819-4

MIX
Paper from
responsible sources
FSC™ C007454

This book is produced from independently certified FSC™ paper
to ensure responsible forest management.
For more information visit www.harpercollins.co.uk/green.

Printed and bound in Spain
by CPI, Barcelona

EXPECTING HIS BILLION-DOLLAR SCANDAL

CATHY WILLIAMS

To my supportive children,
and my partner, David,
who has been a huge source of inspiration.

CHAPTER ONE

'WHERE AM I?'

Cordelia swung around and stared at the man lying on the bed. He hadn't spoken for three days. He'd drifted in and out of sleep, as Dr Greenway had predicted he would. He'd opened his eyes and stared around him but in the unfocused way of someone not really taking anything in.

'Keep him on liquids,' the doctor had advised, 'but there's nothing a hospital can do for him that you can't. Less, probably. You know how overworked and understaffed they are there, especially with half of it closed for renovations. The man wouldn't get much of a look-in. As it stands, he must be as strong as an ox to have endured what he has without being the worse for wear.'

So she'd settled him in one of the spare bedrooms in the rambling house she shared with her father, and together they had taken turns keeping their eye on him, relying on the doctor's twice-daily visits for reassurance that a sudden spiral downwards wasn't on the cards. He was roused for his liquid intake and, in the past twenty-four hours, had managed to eat two light meals. Her father had shown him the bathroom and changed him into some of his own clothes.

He had been making progress but, really, he'd still been out of it. Until now.

She stared at him and her heart sped up.

Luca. That was the man's name. Luca Baresi. She knew that because she'd found his wallet in his trousers and had searched for a name and any sort of contact number she could possibly find so that she could notify a member of his family about the accident.

His identity was all she could come up with. God knew, he'd been blown about on the waves long enough for the water to claim his mobile phone, had he been carrying one. The contents of the wallet, which had been wedged in his trouser pocket, had largely been too sodden and waterlogged to prove helpful.

'Well?'

Cordelia blinked and walked towards him. He was propping himself up against the pillow, staring at her, eyes narrowed, head tilted questioningly to one side.

It had been one thing absently admiring the man's striking good looks when he'd been more or less out of it. It felt quite different now, with his green eyes arrowing onto her with laser-like intensity.

'You're in my father's house.' She hovered next to the bed and then gingerly sat on the side.

Eyes as green as the ocean when the sun blazed down on it, she thought distractedly, and the sort of bronzed complexion of someone who definitely didn't hark from Cornish shores. Even the guys she knew, fishermen like her dad, were pale in comparison.

'What am I doing in your father's house and why am I wearing these clothes?'

'Don't you remember anything?'

'I recall being in my boat.' He frowned. 'One minute the sun was shining and the next minute, the sky had turned black.'

Cordelia was nodding sympathetically while thinking how fantastic his voice was, as deep and as rich as the darkest of chocolate. Very distracting.

'That's the weather for you here,' she murmured. 'Especially at this time of year. You'd think summer might be predictable but a storm can erupt out of nowhere.' She gazed at his hand. He was massaging his collarbone, still frowning, trying to get his thoughts together. Understandable, given what he'd been through. He really was, she thought, stupidly good-looking with that dark, dark hair and olive skin and features chiselled with breathtaking perfection.

Or maybe, at the ripe old age of twenty-four and stuck out here, living a life as predictable as the rising and setting of the sun, she was just easily impressed by someone halfway decent.

She stared at him from under lowered lashes and thought that this guy was far from halfway decent. Halfway decent had been Barry, the guy she had dated for eight months before finally admitting to herself that they were never going to get anywhere and certainly not between the sheets, which, as he had implied with ever increasing clarity, was the destination he had had his eyes on and never mind the business of romance and a courtship to get there. Some straggly flowers and the occasional movie or night out at the local pub, had been top of his game when it had come to wooing her.

'That's obviously what happened to you.' She cleared her throat and fidgeted because he was staring at her with such intensity. 'Three days ago. You should have checked the weather report before you decided to go sailing. Most people around here do. They know how unpredictable the weather can be but you're not from around here, are you?'

'What are you doing here?'

'I beg your pardon?'

'Are you a nurse?'

'No. I…no, I'm not. I suppose you're wondering why you're here and not in a hospital, but the local hospital is tiny and Dr Greenway didn't think it necessary to have you taken by ambulance over to the next biggest hospital, which is quite some distance away. He said you would recover just fine here when I called him over. After I found you.'

'You found me?'

'I happened to be looking out of my bedroom window at the time.'

Staring off into the distance and thinking about what it must be like to live out there…in the big, bad world…where adventures happened and the people you met weren't the same people you went to school with when you were five…where excitement lay behind half-opened doors and sadness and loss were no longer her faithful companions…

She blushed because, although he didn't say anything, she got the weird feeling that he knew just what was going through her head, which, of course, was impossible.

'Your boat was just a speck in the distance being tossed around in the storm.'

'At which point you…?'

'Dad wasn't around,' she said bluntly. 'And I'm as confident on the water as anyone else I know.' She saw his eyebrows shoot up and her mouth thinned in a defensive line. She knew nothing about the stranger lying on the bed but she knew enough to realise that, given his staggering good looks and an air of confidence that couldn't be concealed even wearing her father's weathered clothes, he wouldn't be short of female company. And the female company wouldn't, she was thinking, be the sort capable of sailing the high seas in stormy weather.

'Are you, now?'

'Better, probably.' She shrugged. 'I got my captain's licence when I was eighteen and I have every qualification needed to fish at sea. I know everything there is to know about sea survival, including what to do if there's a fire at sea, and I have brilliant first-aid skills.'

'So you rescued me because I was stupid enough to get behind the wheel of my boat without first checking the weather forecast. How did you manage to do that?'

'I used the fastest and most robust boat from my father's collection and headed out. It didn't occur to me to ask anyone for help. I knew that if someone was on the boat and in trouble, then aid had to be immediate.'

'I am remiss in not thanking you. I remember taking the boat out and I remember the storm rolling in but after that…'

'You were out of it. I know. You were in the water clinging to the side of your boat when I got to you. Semi-conscious.'

'And yet you managed to haul me into your own boat.'

Cordelia thought of all those dainty five-foot-nothings she had always longed to be. Fragile and delicate, demanding the adoring attention of boys who had always seemed genetically geared to leap into the protective mode the second they came near.

She'd never been one of those. She was five ten and sinewy. She could swim like a fish and sail with the best of them and it showed in the strong lines of her body.

'You weren't completely out of it,' she muttered. 'You easily helped yourself. Getting back in one piece was a far bigger problem with the storm kicking up a gear and the waves big enough to take us both under.'

'But you never answered my question. Why are you here?'

Cordelia shot him a puzzled frown. 'I told you. I work here. With my father. I help run his business. He owns eight boats. He fishes but also does a rental business to subsidise his income.'

'A challenging life for a young girl.' The green eyes were curious and assessing.

Now she knew what he was getting at. Why was she here? Was that what was going through his head? Instead of living it up in a city somewhere? With a boyfriend and a giddy round of parties and clubs? Doing all those things girls her age did? Nearly all of her friends had disappeared off to university somewhere and those who had returned had all, without exception, had a boyfriend in tow. They'd married and had their first child within the year. They'd had their fun and had chosen to return to the village to settle down because they loved it here.

That option had not been on the table for her and it was why that big world out there seemed so full of possibilities. Possibilities that would never be explored but which she yearned for anyway.

She chose to interpret his remark at face value because her life was none of his business and he certainly wasn't to know that he'd struck a nerve.

'The sea can be very challenging. But it can also be very rewarding.'

A brief and telling silence greeted this remark.

'I should introduce myself,' he said.

'No need.'

'How's that?'

'I know who you are.'

'You know who I am...'

She noted the way he stiffened, the way his face became shuttered, his fabulous eyes veiled. She had no idea what was going through his head but to dispel the sudden tension, she smiled.

'Luca. Luca Baresi. I'm sorry but when I brought you back here, and after you were examined by the doctor, I felt I should see if I could find some form of identification so that I could let your loved ones know where you were.'

'You went through my stuff.'

'There wasn't much to go through,' Cordelia told him quickly. 'Trust me, it was the last thing I wanted to do but I don't imagine you would have thanked me if you'd come to and found that no one could be bothered to try and discover who you were! Everything was unreadable because of the sea water but your identification card was plastic-coated and I managed to make out your name. If you're up to it, I can bring you the telephone and you can call your...family. They must be worried sick about you. Where do you live?'

'I'm not from around here.'

'Further inland?' She nodded thoughtfully. 'Lots of people descend from London in the summer months and lots of them have second homes in some of the more popular towns. They can't bear to be too far away from gastropubs and fancy restaurants.'

'You don't like that?'

'I don't care one way or another,' she said honestly. 'Tourism is great when it comes to renting boats, as it happens, but I'm pretty much the only person around here who thinks like that. If you're close enough, I dare say my dad can drive you back to your wife and kids.'

'Wife and kids? What makes you think I'm married?'

'I…' Her heart fluttered and she could feel the hot burn of colour in her cheeks. 'I suppose I just assumed…'

'Are *you* married?'

'No.'

'Strangely enough, I would have assumed that you were.'

'Why?' Her skin was tingling all over. Her eyes were drawn to his but once there, she was finding it impossible to look away, and something inside her shied away from the notion that he might sum her up and write her off as a country bumpkin, bowled over by his excessive good looks.

So she glanced right past him to the view outside the window of the bedroom, one of swirling clouds and pale grey skies and a drizzle that hadn't stopped ever since she'd rescued him from those stormy waters. Summer had gone into temporary retreat and she had no idea when it planned on returning. Just something else about living in this part of the world.

'You're young,' he drawled lightly. 'You're attractive. How is it that you haven't been snapped up by some local eligible bachelor? Maybe you've just re-

turned from university? Still finding your feet back in
the family home?'

'Not everyone has had the opportunity to go to university, Mr Baresi.' Her voice had dropped a few degrees and her violet eyes were cool when they rested
on his face.

She'd had plans. She'd had her dreams but life and
fate had managed to get in the way of her fulfilling
those dreams.

She wondered whether things would have been different if her mother hadn't died when she'd been a kid.
Mown down by a speeding car in London on one of
her rare shopping trips. Her father had closed so many
doors afterwards. He had become paranoid about her
leaving the safety and security of the village. If she
ventured into one of the bigger towns, he'd wait by the
window for her, even when, at the age of ten, she'd gone
in a gang with one of her friends' parents. School out-
ings had been a nightmare because she'd known that
he would be back at the house, trying hard to quell his
anxiety. A skiing trip at the age of fourteen had been
out of the question. He'd given permission but she'd seen
the fear in his eyes and she'd quietly turned down the
opportunity. She had learnt to support her father but, in
doing so, had continued to carry both their pain on her
shoulders. His fear was a constant reminder of their loss.

Even so…even with all that, university had beck-
oned and she had known that, for both their sakes, it
was something she wanted and needed to do.

When she was seventeen, having been accepted at
her first choice of university in Exeter, which, she had
assured her dad, was only a hop and a skip away, both
their lives had been shattered by the death of her twin

brother. Alex had been her rock, tuned into her feelings in ways that had been quiet and instinctive. He had *understood*. He had given her strength as the pattern of their lives, following the loss of their mother, had changed. He had supported her and encouraged her and fortified her because their father's fears had always seemed to revolve around *her*. The assumption was that Alex could look after himself.

Alex had had no dreams of going to university. He'd always planned on taking over the family business. Fishing was in his blood. It wasn't to be and when he died, all her dreams had been snuffed out and she had resigned herself to taking up where her brother had left off. There were times when it felt as though loss upon loss had piled up on top of her, a weight she could barely carry, with no one in whom she could confide. The carefree joys of being young had never felt within her grasp.

Not a day passed when Cordelia didn't think of the future that had turned to dust before it could even begin, but she had hunkered down, had thrown herself into the business and had proved herself an exceptional sailor. The sea became her haven. It brought her peace and out there, in the open ocean, she could let her thoughts drift and wonder what it might be like to see the world. She could swim like a fish and swimming was always a wonderful escape.

What would this swarthy stranger think were she to confide in him? she wondered.

'Being *snapped up* by some eligible local boy has never been one of my ambitions,' she retorted quickly.

Luca smiled slowly and that slow smile sent a tingle of awareness racing through her body, igniting everything in its path. Her nerves fluttered and the sudden throb between her legs, a sensual reaction that was immediate and intensely physical, shocked her to the core.

Her eyes wide, the thoughts vanished from her head in a whoosh and she stared at him for a few panicked seconds, completely blindsided by a rush of sensation unlike anything she had ever felt before.

He'd hoisted himself higher up on the bed and she subliminally took in the breadth of his shoulders and the raw physicality of his body, which, maybe, she'd subconsciously noticed before but not like this. Then again, he hadn't been addressing her before and engaging with her the way he was now.

She edged off the bed and for the first time in for ever was acutely aware of how she looked.

Faded jeans, faded grey jumper, her waist-long blonde hair pulled back into a lopsided ponytail. As always, she was bare of make-up and as tanned as she ever got from the summer sun, which was hot enough to burn when it decided to show its face. She was barefoot, as she always was when she was in the house, and she shoved her hands behind her back. They were practical hands, used to boats and ropes and the sea.

'Where are you going?'

'I have stuff to do. Work. I only came in here to check on you and refresh your glass of water.'

'You mentioned a telephone.'

'Huh?' She was backing away towards the door, wondering why she was so nervous when, in actual fact, she never was when it came to the opposite sex.

'In the absence of my mobile phone, I'll have to use your landline to make contact with…my father.'

Cordelia blinked. 'I'm sorry I couldn't find any contact numbers in your wallet,' she said in a rush. 'It must feel like an invasion of your privacy, but, like I said, I only wanted to find out who you were and who I might be able to contact to let them know about the boating accident. Your dad must be worried sick.'

'That's not entirely how my life works.'

They stared at one another for a few long, silent seconds.

She was quite stunning, Luca thought absently, and what was almost impossible to credit was the fact that she seemed so unaware of her attributes. She was tall and athletic, her body, from what he could see, sinewy and strong. It should have put him off because he had always been drawn to slight, ultra-feminine women, but it didn't. Her legs, encased in faded jeans, were long and he could detect the fullness of her rounded breasts beneath the drab jumper. Never had he seen any woman so successfully conceal every single womanly trait she might possess. Was that deliberate, he wondered, or did the fashion police patrol the streets of the village, clamping down on anything that wasn't functional?

His eyes drifted up to her oval-shaped face. Her lips were full, her nose short and straight and her eyes a shade of violet he had never seen before. But her hair…

Luca thought of the highly groomed, sophisticated women who flitted in and out of his life. The woman in front of him couldn't have been more different and her hair said it all. She had yanked it back into a ponytail that couldn't seem to quite make its mind up as to which way it should fall, but, even so, the colours were so vibrant that he couldn't drag his eyes away. Every shade of blonde was there, from platinum blonde to the rich hues of pale honey and deeper toffee. A life spent outdoors, he assumed, doing whatever it was she did out there on the high seas. Fishing and rescuing idiots who went out in boats without first having a look at the weather forecast.

He closed down wayward thoughts that suddenly shot into his head at speed. Thoughts about how she would look underneath the workman-like clothes, what that body would feel like under his exploring hands.

Such options, for a multitude of reasons, were firmly off the table.

'I will, naturally, pay you for the cost of the phone call.'

'Why would you do that?' Cordelia asked, bewildered. Did he think that they intended to charge him for his stay at the house? That they wanted money from him? That he had to pay his way the second he gained full consciousness, right down to the cost of a phone call? She bristled. 'We're not the sort of people who would think of charging you for using the telephone,' she said coolly. 'I may have rescued you but I didn't bring you here so that we could start charging you for your stay.'

'The phone call will be to Italy,' Luca said drily.

'Italy?' He was Italian. She should have worked that out for herself going by his name alone, but she hadn't because this wasn't the sort of Cornish village that was invaded by tourists during the height of the summer season. Outsiders were few and far between and yet here was this striking Italian, lying on a bed in her father's house. She felt a buzz of excitement as her imagination took flight. Italy! Just the taste of it on her tongue felt good.

* * *

'It's where I live.' He watched her carefully from under his lashes. He watched to see whether she would make any connections. In Italy, his name would be quickly recognised. Even here, in this country, many people would have heard of the Baresi name, if only because of its association with the wine. The House of Baresi was legendary, as was the formidable wealth of its aristocratic family. Luca Baresi had lived his life in the spotlight of his noble ancestry. His social circle was huge but around it was a protective circle, a dividing line that mere mortals were seldom allowed to cross. It wasn't of his devising. It was the way it was, and if there were moments when he longed to walk out of that circle and never look back, then he was accustomed to quickly closing them down because he knew where his duties lay.

His friends, the members of his extended family—they were all, to varying degrees, as privileged as he was. To the best of his knowledge, the only commoner to have ever broken through those rigid walls had been his mother and that tale had hardly had a happy ending.

This was an avenue of thought he was, likewise, accustomed to shutting down whenever it happened to make an uninvited appearance and he did so now, with ruthless efficiency.

'Tuscany,' he offered. 'Have you been there?'

'I don't often leave Cornwall,' Cordelia admitted and she grimaced at his expression of incredulity.

She met so few people, she realised. Life was so predictable for her and yet she was still young. Twenty-four years old! She should be enjoying all sorts of new and

life-changing experiences. Everyone in the village knew
her back story but now, the urge to confide in someone
new, someone from a faraway and exotic place that she
would probably never visit, at least not in the near future, was overpowering.

'Why is that?'

He paused to look at her and she stared back at him in
silence because suddenly everything, the bits and pieces
and nuts and bolts of her life, seemed so overwhelming.
She thought about all the things that had happened to
her. All the things locking her into this one place. Keeping her there as securely as if she had been trapped in
a cage. How on earth could she unpick all those pieces
of her past and put them into a few casual sentences? It
was crazy anyway. Forget about silly urges! She barely
knew the guy. She wouldn't know where to begin when
it came to answering that simple question he had asked.

He stretched and, in one swift movement, flung aside
the covers and swung his legs over the side of the bed.
'I need to move around,' he threw over his shoulder, as
he headed to the wardrobe and the only place his clothes
could be. 'And change back into my own clothes.'

Cordelia nodded mutely, riveted to him. To start with
he had more or less hobbled, hanging onto her father's
arm to make his way to the bathroom, and even when,
after day one, his strength had begun to resurface, he
had still moved slowly, hesitantly. It was obvious that he
was well on the road to rude health because his movements now were assured and graceful and captivating.

She felt that her mouth might be hanging open. Her
jaw certainly dropped to the ground when, without
warning and with his back still to her, he began stripping off without the slightest hint of inhibition.

She looked away. Her mouth had gone dry and she could feel the hot burn of colour suffusing her face.

'You can look now.' There was amusement in his voice a couple of minutes later and she slowly turned round to face him.

Her cheeks were still pink with embarrassment.

Her body language shrieked her discomfort. Luca had seen nothing like it before. Had there ever been a time in his life when he had been with any woman who had seen his semi-naked body and acted as though the ground would be doing her a favour if it opened and swallowed her up? He couldn't help the spurt of curiosity about her. So beautiful and yet could she possibly be as innocent as she looked?

And what about never leaving this place? How did that begin to make sense?

'How old are you?' he asked suddenly.

'Twenty-four just. Why?'

Luca shrugged. 'You say that you seldom leave here?'

'It's a beautiful part of the world. You'd be surprised how many people who live by the sea find it impossible to stray far from it.'

Not her, though. No, not her, but something inside her felt compelled to defend herself against his curiosity.

He let that non-answer go and instead looked around him. He had no recollection of being brought into the house and he hadn't spared a single second to so much as glance outside the bedroom window. He rectified that now and what he saw was a limitless view of grey sea, a ribbon of road, currently empty, and the tangle of greenery at the side of the road, stretching out towards what seemed to be a gentle incline down, he guessed, to the ocean front. Everything was shrouded in a cloud of fine, persistent drizzle. The remnants of the storm that had capsized his boat.

Then he looked around him, taking in his surroundings fully and for the first time.

Luca rarely noticed his surroundings, at least not the mansion in which he lived or any of the other expensive properties he owned. They were lavish. He knew that. But a lifetime of wealth had made him immune to their impact. Nor did he pay much attention to any of the houses in which his friends or relatives lived. They all ran along the same lines. Some were bigger than others, few more opulent. The town houses and apartments in which the various girlfriends he had had over the years lived had all been expensive, courtesy of rich parents. Such was his life.

The room in which he was standing was far from lavish. It was large, with a wooden floor over which a worn Persian rug tried hard to add a bit of luxury. The furniture was all old but gleaming and highly polished and the walls could have done with a top-up on the paint. But the bed had been incredibly comfortable and he had to admit that there was something seductively cosy about the room, despite its lack of expensive furnishings.

'Show me around?' he heard himself ask her. 'I need to stretch my legs. I feel like I've been confined in one place for far too long.'

'What about the phone call?'

'Ah.' Green eyes met violet and Luca smiled, because it wasn't often that he was in the company of a woman who didn't know his worth. It felt strangely liberating. He could be himself. He was no longer the man who was committed to driving forward the considerable family business he now ran, having hauled it back from the brink thanks to his father. Nor was he the prized aristocrat who couldn't enter a room without being marked as a target by well-bred women with marriage on their minds. Here, tossed up from the sea into the middle of nowhere, he was a man without a predetermined destiny.

He wasn't quite sure *who* he was, shorn of all the trappings that usually surrounded him, but he was willing to have a go at trying the situation out for size.

Especially in the company of a woman who looked the way this one did.

He felt a sudden tightness in his groin and had to stifle a need to groan aloud.

'Like I said,' he murmured, 'no one will have contacted the police to get a search party together just yet.' He commanded complete freedom of movement. He'd told his PA that he would be taking time out for a few days. He hadn't specified how many. She would have cancelled all immediate meetings and would have put nothing in place until told to do so. Likewise, his father would have no real idea when to expect him back. They didn't live in one another's pockets. As for the rest of the world…?

Who was there? He was an only child and a man who did as he pleased without reference to anyone else. He had never believed in the value of teamwork. The only person he had ever relied on was himself. It had served him well. Only now, he was struck by a certain peculiar uncertainty—a feeling that complete independence might not be quite what it was cracked up to be.

He shook his head impatiently.

'Walk me through your house,' he said gruffly, looking forward to immersing himself for a short while in a life that was far removed from his own.

'Only,' Cordelia returned, consumed with curiosity about the life he represented, 'if you tell me about your life in Italy.'

Luca relaxed. There was a lot he could tell her about his homeland. About the rolling splendour of Tuscany, about the beauty of the Alps and the grandeur of the Apennines and the marvel of a climate, caught between the two, that was so perfect for growing the very best grapes, which produced the very best wine in the country. He could tell her about the villages surrounding his estate and the people who lived there, most of whom were employed in some capacity or other by his family and always had been.

Naturally, he would have to tailor all of it because there was even more he had no intention of telling her, starting with the truth of his identity and the position of power he held in the region.

She was leading the way out of the bedroom, onto the broad landing, vaguely pointing out the remaining bedrooms on the floor before heading down the wooden staircase into the body of the house.

Following in her wake, he was half paying attention but mostly looking at her and admiring the spring in her step, the way she half ran down the stairs. He was wondering what her hair would look like unrestrained. She had the longest hair he had ever seen.

They reached the black and white flagstone hall and she spun round to look at him, eyes bright and her expression open and trusting.

Luca blinked to dispel the weird ache that had kick-started inside him.

'I'll tell you everything you want to know about my country,' he said smoothly, 'on the condition that you tell me why you don't get out of here, or have I misinterpreted what you said earlier on?'

'You haven't and that's fair enough.' She smiled hesitantly and pulled the ponytail over one shoulder to distractedly play with it, twirling gold strands of hair between her fingers. She had so many questions she wanted to ask him that she didn't quite know where to begin.

And she could tell him so much about herself and why not? Her father wouldn't be back for another few hours. He was off fishing. And this man who had catapulted into her small, predictable world was so compelling.

Where was the harm in talking to him? It wasn't as though he were going to be around for much longer and it had been such a long time since she had talked, really talked, to a guy, to *anyone*. For ever. Her brother. That was how long it had been. So many years just plodding along, quietly doing what she had to do, without fuss, keeping her loneliness to herself.

Where was the harm in opening up, now, to this stranger...?

CHAPTER TWO

HE DIDN'T PHONE his father or his PA or anyone else for three days and when he did, it was to inform them that he had decided to take a slightly extended holiday. He'd be away for at least another week.

His PA had been a little startled but she was in her sixties, had worked for him for so long that she deserved a medal and had decided a decade ago that sorting out his emails and arranging his meetings was just a small part of her designated role.

'Take as much time out as you want, Luca,' she had soothed. 'You work too hard. You're thirty-four years old and you need to relax more or you'll have a heart attack before you know it. Stress. It kills. Those grapes will keep growing and the machinery will keep working until you decide to get back.'

His father had been largely indifferent. He'd handed over the reins of the sprawling family empire to his son a long time ago and had, since then, devoted his life to marrying and divorcing inappropriate women. Four at the last count although thankfully things had been quiet on that front for the past two years. Luca knew better than to expect that to last. He loved his father but he was far too aware of his failings to assume that a brief respite from unsuitable liaisons could herald anything more than the same old, same old.

And since then...

He looked at his watch. Then at the view spread out in front of him. From where he was sitting, waiting for her at the café on the waterfront, he had a splendid view of the harbour and just at the moment, with the sun shining, it was a picturesque sight. Blue water, the boats bobbing on the surface and people criss-crossing the road in front of him, taking their time getting out of the way should a beaten up car decide to drive past. It was a very far cry from the trendy seaside village where his house resided in a prestigious position on a hill overlooking a marina, which was dotted with expensive yachts and pleasure boats owned by the expensive people who flocked to the Michelin-starred restaurants and chic pubs and quaint tea rooms. The house was the last link to his mother, an expensive youthful present from way back when, when his father had slipped the engagement ring on her finger and led her to a house in the very place where she had grown up, so that she could maintain easy links with her friends and what little family she had left. His old man, even then, had done things in style.

That house summed up, for Luca, the way love and loss were so entwined, and, with everything going on in his life when he had decided to clear his desk and take time out, he had escaped back to it for just such a timely reminder. There was no such thing as love without loss.

He killed pointless musings dead.

As Cordelia had told him when she had shown him round the village two days previously, this was a working fishing village. There were occasional tourists in summer, in search of a more authentic Cornish experience, but largely the place was inhabited by locals, most of whom were involved in the fishing business in one way or the other.

As for Cordelia, Luca had discovered that she was a woman of many talents. Most of her time was spent helping her father run his small business. She did his books and, in summer, oversaw the rental of two of his boats further along the coast at one of the more popular seaside towns. She made sure that everything ticked along.

'Dad depends on me,' she had told him. 'I may not go out there on the trawler with him but I pretty much do everything else. Of course, if needs be, I'm more than capable of helping him at sea if one of the guys is off, but I'm better off staying here and working behind the scenes. He's hopeless when it comes to anything to do with filling in forms or paperwork and forget about computers.'

Luca saw her before she spotted him. She was glorious. Long limbs, arms swinging, her hair, as always, tied back. She radiated vitality and health and he marvelled that he had succeeded in keeping his hands to himself when he'd spent the last three days itching to reach out and touch her. His freedom might be on the brink of disappearing but, right now, he was still as single as the day was long.

But for once, he hadn't dared. There was an innocence about her that kept him at bay. For the first time in his life, he also had no idea how she would react if he made a pass at her. Slap him down? Kick him out of the house? Fling herself into his arms and beg for satisfaction? He had no idea and the uncertainty was paralysing.

He waved when she spotted him and she beamed back at him.

For a second, Luca felt a stab of guilt at the way he had played fast and loose with the truth. He'd talked a lot about his country but had been diplomatically light on detail. He knew that she'd somehow assumed that he'd been over on holiday, maybe chartered a boat for a day out, but the fact that he was hanging around had led her to assume that he was currently jobless and he hadn't disabused her of the notion. Why would he? He would soon be gone and this rare chance to be whoever he wanted to be was addictive.

'I've brought us a picnic.' Cordelia dumped a basket on the table and looked at him.

It was hot. A perfect summer day. This part of the world did perfect summer days like nowhere else. Bright blue sky, turquoise sea, clean smell of the ocean and the soft sound of the water slapping against the sides of the fishing boats.

She shielded her eyes from the glare and stared at him. With only the clothes on his back when she rescued him, he had had to buy a few more things and was wearing a pair of khaki shorts, some loafers and a white tee shirt. He looked magnificent. So exotic, so foreign…so much a vision of everything that was out of her orbit.

'And I've contributed in my own, small way.' He reached down to a cloth bag on the ground and when she looked inside, she saw two bottles of champagne.

'Wow.'

'If you're going to do something, then you don't do it in half measures.'

'But champagne… It must have cost a fortune.'

'I won't worry about the price tag if you don't.'

'I like that,' she confided as they began heading out towards where her boat was anchored just off the jetty.

'What?'

'The fact that you're so carefree.' She slid her eyes across to him and drank in the lean beauty of his face. His hair was longer than when she'd brought him back to the house, curling at the nape of his neck.

'I don't think anyone has ever described me as carefree before,' Luca commented with complete honesty. 'Frankly, it's not a description I would ever have used for myself.'

'Wouldn't you? Why not?' She glanced at him, smiling, then began the business of getting the boat ready for them while he watched and admired her quiet efficiency, doing something she had probably done a million times before. It was compulsive viewing. She was wearing some cut-off jeans and a striped tee shirt. He could just about make out the heavy swing of her breasts as she expertly loosened the boat from its mooring, bringing it into position for them. She had braided her hair into one long plait that fell down the centre of her spine like rope.

'You're here,' she pointed out, steadying the boat and then half jumping on board without really looking where she put her feet because the manoeuvre was so familiar. 'You're not rushing off to do anything. You know how to slow down. So many people don't, although I guess if you're going to slow down, then this is the perfect place to do it and the perfect time, given what you went through.'

Cordelia watched as he hit the deck as confidently as she had. When he suggested he sail the boat, she found herself instantly agreeing because something inside her trusted his expertise, which was contrary to everything she had been brought up to believe.

'Everyone thinks they know what to do when it comes to boats,' her father had told both her and her brother when they were young. 'Don't trust anyone with a throttle, a rudder, a tiller or an engine unless they can produce a captain's licence. It's easy to get out of your depth when it comes to handling a boat, and out at sea, that could be fatal. I'll make sure the pair of you know exactly what to do when you get on a boat. If anyone gets on with you and asks for a go, tell them to get lost.'

She gave directions, sat back and tilted her face up to the sun.

'Do you ever slow down?' Luca murmured, obeying directions, enjoying the speed of the boat as it sliced through the water to the hidden bay she had told him about, enjoying even more the feel of her next to him, her body warmed from the sun, the hairs on her hands white-blonde in the sun.

'Only when I do this,' she replied, eyes still closed. 'Or when I go swimming. I slow right down when I go swimming. Especially if I go swimming at night.'

'At night…and you don't get scared?'

'Of what? I know everything there is to know about the tides around here. I'd never swim if there was a hint of a current, but if the water's calm, then there's something about being in it when it's dark. I can think.'

They'd arrived at the bay. It was deserted and protected by dense shrubbery and tangled trees. The sand was very white and, when they stepped out onto it, already warm from the sun.

'What do you think about?'

Cordelia looked at him and couldn't look away. She'd thought long and hard about what to tell him about herself and, in the end, had said very little. She was ever so slightly in awe of him. He was like a bright, tropical bird of paradise, blown in on the winds, and every time she had felt that urge to confide, she had been overcome by a surge of shyness.

'This and that.' She shrugged and broke eye contact to set up a little picnic area in the shade of one of the overhanging trees. When she turned round to look at him, he had divested himself of his tee shirt and was staring out at the horizon with his back to her.

Her heart sped up. He was a few inches taller than her and perfectly proportioned. Broad-shouldered, narrow-waisted, lean-hipped. He'd shoved his hands into the pockets of his shorts. He'd asked her what she'd been thinking but now she wished she could see into his head, find out what *he* was thinking. His life in Italy sounded idyllic. 'Vineyards,' he had told her, waving aside more in-depth questioning, as though working on a vineyard was something she couldn't possibly find that interesting.

'Grapes…' he had shrugged, when she breathlessly asked for details '…that's pretty much all there is to say on the subject of vineyards. Grapes. You either eat them or you turn them into wine. I'm involved in the latter option.'

She was still shamelessly gawping when he spun round to look at her and she reddened.

'Tell me you're not going to spend the day in jeans and a tee shirt,' he encouraged with a grin. 'Did you bring a swimsuit or do you have plans on skinny dipping?'

Cordelia made a strangled sound under her breath and hastily got rid of her jeans and tee shirt to reveal a sensible black whole piece. Skinny dipping? The thought alone brought her out in a cold sweat.

'Ah, swimming costume. Good. It would be a sin not to try the water on a day like this.' Luca had never seen anyone under the age of eighty in a swimsuit as sensible as the one she was wearing and yet, conversely, had never been so tempted to touch. Her legs were long and shapely, the lines of her body strong and athletic, her skin pale gold.

He averted his eyes but there was a steady pulsing in his groin that was going to prove embarrassing if he carried on giving free rein to his imagination.

Cold water had never looked so inviting. He stepped out of the khakis, down to the swimming trunks he had bought a couple of days earlier.

'Think I need a swim,' he gritted, baring his teeth in something he hoped would resemble a relaxed smile. 'So hot.' He waded straight into the ice-cold water. Felt good. Anything to douse the rise in his body temperature when he had looked at her.

He didn't look back for five minutes and when he did, it was to find that she was striking out in his direction, in long, fluid strokes that ate up the distance between them.

She hadn't been lying when she'd told him that she could swim like a fish. She could. And out here, in the ocean where blue yielded to black because it was so much deeper, she was in her natural element. He could see that as soon as she had caught up with him. There was real pleasure on her face and she was smiling. All the hesitancy and shyness that seemed part and parcel of her personality had disappeared. She looked as though she had barely broken a sweat swimming out to him.

'You're a strong swimmer,' she told him, treading water.

'You're surprised because you thought I was a wimp who could barely man a boat and had to rely on being rescued by a damsel in shining armour because of his own stupidity?'

'Something like that.'

Luca burst out laughing and cast appreciative eyes over her face. She truly had the most amazing eyes, he thought. A shade somewhere between navy blue and bright turquoise with a hint of green and, for a blonde, her lashes were lush and dark.

'Race you back?' Cordelia backed away in the water. The way he was looking at her...she'd caught that expression before, a fleeting glimpse of something heated and *dangerous*, but she had told herself that it was her imagination playing tricks on her. She lacked the sophistication to interpret those kinds of games and she didn't trust herself to even try. It was a lot easier to pretend there was nothing there, that any wayward expression she might have glimpsed in him was all in her mind. Why would a man like Luca look at a woman like her? He was so beautiful, so exotic, so compelling while she...was a country girl who worked her fingers to the bone in the fishing business. Vineyard versus fishing. Even if all he did was pick grapes and do whatever people did to grapes when they were picked, it was still impossibly glamorous as far as she was concerned.

She didn't wait for his response. She began swimming and all the thoughts left her head as she felt the cold water sluice against her body and the exertion of the swim heating her up until the sea was warm against her skin.

He kept pace and then increased it so that he hit the shoreline before she did.

She was laughing when she emerged from the water. Her hair was still in the braid but she tugged the elastic band off and rifled her fingers through its length so that it spread over her shoulders and down her back, reaching all the way to her waist.

Luca felt as though he'd been punched in the gut and he was breathing heavily as he turned away to open the bottle of champagne. Hell, she might be fine with this scenario but he was in desperate need of a drink. He only wished he'd thought to bring something a little stronger. A bottle of whisky would have done the trick. Instead, he popped the cork on the champagne, which was still cold thanks to the sleeve into which it had been put, and he extended one of the two plastic glasses to her.

'Are there rules about drinking and sailing?' he asked, sitting on a rock while she tidily spread an oversized rug on the sand.

'I've brought lots of water.' She smiled and sipped some champagne. 'And lots of food. That should take care of the alcohol.'

'If it doesn't, we could always spend the night on the beach.' Their eyes tangled and he slanted a smile at her. 'I guess living here, that's something you must have done a million times…?'

Luca knew that he was shamelessly fishing for information but he wanted to find out more about her, dig a bit deeper, which was something he was seldom inclined to do when it came to the opposite sex. He'd long discovered that the women he dated were all largely gifted in the art of talking about themselves. There was almost no need to ask questions.

'Not once,' Cordelia murmured thoughtfully. 'Although there are loads of bays and coves around here and, yes, there were always parties during the summer holidays.'

'But you didn't go to them.'

She swallowed some more champagne and grimaced. 'When I was twelve, one of my friends had a birthday party on a cove not far from this one. Of course, adults were there. Since then, I've only ever sailed to one of these coves on my own.'

'No reckless teenage parties with contraband alcohol and furious parents hunting down their wayward offspring to drag them back home?'

'Not for me.'

'Why not?'

'Because…' The sun was beating down but the rug was under the shade of a tree and there was just enough of a balmy breeze to make her feel sleepy. He'd left the rock at some point and was on the rug with her, sitting up, but then he lay flat, staring up at the cloudless blue sky, and she followed suit. 'Because my father was very protective. My mother died when I was young. I told you that, but after she died, Dad, somehow, developed a crazy fear that if I ventured too far, something bad would happen. Of course, I didn't notice it at all when I was young, but the older I got…the more I realised that I didn't have the same freedoms as loads of kids my age. But then, my brother died and everything got…so much more difficult.' She paused and gathered herself.

'You had a brother? I had no idea.'

'Why would you? Dad never talks about Alex. In fact, when he died, Dad made sure that all the framed photos of him were taken down. Alex was my twin.'

She was surprised and then moved when she felt Luca link his fingers through hers. Her mind was engaged in the past, but she still felt a jolt of electricity run through her body. The warmth of his fingers was so good, so reassuring and it was the first physical contact they had shared since she looked after him. Excitement leaped inside her but she told herself that this was just the normal gesture of someone empathising with what she had just said. The equivalent of a hug. Hugs weren't sexual. A brotherly hug from a friend didn't end up in a steamy kiss. But she still liked the touch of those fingers...and the thought of a steamy kiss was... well...in her head before she could take defensive measures to keep it out.

'Your twin!'

He levered himself into a half-sitting position and leaned over her, to stare at her with startled, concerned eyes.

Cordelia dealt with that by closing her eyes. His fingers were still linked with hers and having him so close to her, close enough to feel his warm breath on her cheek, was too much to handle.

'Everything changed after Alex died,' Cordelia said. 'I'd planned on going to university, even though I knew that Dad would have to resist phoning twice a day to make sure I was all right. I think he always felt, deep down, that he should have been able to protect my mum, that he should have been there with her when she went to London, then she wouldn't have been hit by that car and everything would have been all right. If he couldn't protect Mum, then he would devote his life to protecting me. But going to university?' She sighed. 'I'd worked out that it was just something I had to do. Alex was destined to help Dad in the fishing business and eventually take it over. It was all he'd ever wanted to do whereas I...'

'Whereas you...?'

'I had dreams of leaving here, seeing what was out there. It would have been the right thing to do for me and for my dad. Instead, those dreams died with Alex. I had no choice but to step into his shoes. Don't get me wrong, it's not a bad life, but there's a big world out there and I've resigned myself to the fact that I'll never get to see it.'

She opened her eyes to find that he was still staring down at her and she smiled.

'I'm not about to start weeping and wailing on you,' she said.

'I have no objection to a weeping and wailing woman,' Luca lied. He could have expanded. He could have told her that weeping and wailing set his teeth on edge. He'd had his fill of watching the antics of his father's ex-wives, the emotional dramas played out for public consumption when the marriages began to unravel. He could remember one memorable occasion when one of his father's birthday celebrations had descended into full-blown farce when an inebriated wife number three had decided to spill the beans on everything she hated about men, and about his father in particular. So weeping and wailing? No chance.

'Liar.' But the smile was more heartfelt this time. 'Men hate women crying on them.'

'You speak from experience? Some guy turn on you because you cried?'

'No!' She couldn't resist any longer and she reached out and stroked the side of his face and noticed that her fingers were trembling. It was only a stroke, but it felt as daring as if she'd done a striptease. Her nipples were pinched into tight, sensitive buds and heat had bloomed between her thighs.

The warm sun, the champagne, the sharing of these confidences…and this enigmatic stranger. The mix was heady and combustible.

'No guys?' He held still her hand and then opened it and, eyes still on her, he kissed her palm, then licked it, the delicate trace of his tongue on her skin.

She sighed and trembled, caught between an urge to pull back because this was dangerous territory and a need to go further because she'd never done a dangerous thing in her entire life and the temptation was overpowering.

She felt as if she'd spent so long looking through a pane of glass at a world filled with exciting possibilities that the chance to go past that glass and actually have a taste of that excitement was too much to resist.

She shifted, her breathing quickening, invitation playing on her parted lips.

'I've told you all about myself,' she whispered shakily. 'It's your turn to tell me all about yourself.'

'I've done nothing but tell you about myself for the past few days…' *How to redefine the truth?* That was the thought that ran through Luca's head, but he swept aside that momentary discomfort.

'I guess the work is seasonal, which is why you can afford to take time off and stay here…'

When are you going to go?

She found that the prospect of him leaving made her feel weirdly hollow inside.

'There are more optimum months for harvesting the grapes...that's true...'

'And what do you do when you're not picking them? Do you travel? Visit family? Who do you live with in Italy?'

'That's a lot of questions, *tesoro*...'

'I'm curious about you. For so many reasons, I'm stuck here. You can't blame me for asking questions.' She looked at him wistfully, imagining his world, which would be so different from hers. A world without obligations and responsibilities, where work was something that could be picked up and dropped on a whim. Maybe he did other, odd jobs, aside from the grape picking, although she doubted it because his knowledge of the wine industry was so detailed. He obviously loved what he did.

'No, I can't,' Luca told her honestly. 'But guilt is no way to lead your life, *cara*. You're too young to think that you're stuck somewhere without hope of escape, looking at places on a map and assuming you'll never get to visit any of them.'

'You've met my father. You've seen for yourself that I can't just waltz off in the sunset...'

Luca shrugged. Yes, he had met Clive Ramsey, a weathered man in his sixties whose life revolved around his daughter and the sea. He'd lost his wife and he'd never really moved on. Just another example of what a waste of time love was. It got its hooks into you and from that point on, you were on a road to nowhere.

Luca struggled to think of a single example of all that starry-eyed, fairy-tale rubbish soppy movies promoted.

In fairness, Clive hadn't been around much. The fishing season was at its height and he was gone most days and many nights, trawling for crab and lobster, leaving the running of the house and his business to the daughter he clearly couldn't do without. Luca was sure things would have been different had her brother lived, but now, as she'd told him, she'd had no choice but to step up to the plate.

He suddenly had an overwhelming urge to take her away and show her all those faraway sights she had only ever dreamed about.

'We're talking too much,' he murmured, bringing things back down to familiar terrain. 'Let's just enjoy being here.'

Cordelia smiled, heart swelling with excitement. There was nothing she yearned for more than to enjoy the moment for what it was. She wanted so much for him to touch her, really touch her, but her lack of experience was crippling.

He was attracted to her. She knew he was, unbelievable as it was. That was a start in the right direction.

'No one ever comes to this cove,' she confided nervously. 'At least not during the day...'

'Shame. It's exquisite.'

'It's because you need a boat to get here. It's inaccessible from land. Not that many people have boats that they can just take out for the fun of it.'

'Lucky you.'

'I feel it. Right now. Lucky, I mean...' she said breathlessly. She shifted onto her side and shuffled a bit closer in what she hoped were movements barely visible to the naked eye.

She fought down a wave of nervous nausea and ran her hands softly over his stomach, enjoying the feel of muscled strength under her fingers.

She saw the look of astonishment in his eyes and was tempted to pull her hand away, but she didn't because something inside her knew that if she didn't seize this moment, it would never be there for the taking again.

'Cordelia...' Luca said in a roughened undertone, shifting but not doing what he knew he should be doing, namely removing himself from temptation. He hadn't been able to resist touching that satiny smooth skin but alarm bells in his head were louder than the church bells in his local village.

'I really like you...' she admitted, blushing furiously but maintaining eye contact.

Luca groaned and clenched his jaw hard. He was rock hard. If he glanced down, he knew that he wouldn't be able to miss the sizeable bulge underneath the still slightly damp trunks. Nor would she. If she'd been more brazen, it would have been easy to pull away, however attractive he found her, but her innocence, the courage to say what she had, which he could tell was costing her dear, her damned *back story*, was lethally persuasive.

She reached out for his hand and he felt the tremor in her fingers. He heard himself say something softly under his breath when she placed his hand on her breast and then, shockingly, reached to stroke his thigh.

Not courageous enough to touch what clearly needed touching, but it didn't matter because what she was doing was sending his body into explosive overdrive. Those little circular motions with her finger, gentle and delicate. They made him wonder what it would feel like to have her tongue there, and that elicited another guttural groan of desire.

'This…' He struggled to sound normal. 'Not a good idea…'

She immediately removed her hand. 'I was wrong. You don't fancy me. I understand.'

Luca couldn't answer. Instead, he grasped her hand and returned it to his thigh.

'I've never wanted any woman more in my life,' he confessed shakily. 'But…'

'But I guess you're more accustomed to sexy, dark-haired Italian women…'

'You need to look in the mirror a little more often, *la mia bellezza*.'

He drew her close, pressed her against him while the sun poured down like honey and the impossibly blue sea stifled all the perfectly sound thoughts in his head, hypnotising him into wanting one thing and one thing only. Her.

By way of response, Cordelia nuzzled his neck and then tentatively covered his thigh with her own. She could feel his hard erection pulsing against her belly and she desperately wanted to put her hand over it, feel it moving, but when she actually thought of doing that, she felt faint.

She had zero experience when it came to men. At least, none of her fumbling adventures, such as they'd been, were worth writing home about.

She hadn't avoided sex. She'd never had any puritanical ideals to turn it into some kind of prize to be handed to the right guy. No, as luck would have it, she'd just had the one semi-serious boyfriend and they hadn't ended up in bed. Now she knew why. She hadn't been turned on. She hadn't had the foggiest idea what being turned on *was all about*. Because *this* was what it felt like to be turned on. *This* was what had been missing from the equation.

This and so many other things.

This was excitement. Heart-stopping, pulse-racing, nerve-jangling excitement and if he wanted her, then she couldn't begin to describe just how much *she* wanted *him*.

CHAPTER THREE

SHE FELL BACK compliantly when he pushed her gently so that he could lever himself up to stare down at her. His breathing was a heavy rasp and his eyes were dark with passion, unfocused, as though he had been transported to another world.

He ran his hand along her side and then up along her ribcage. The almost dry swimsuit was an irritant, a scratchy barrier between them that Cordelia wanted to yank off but, again, her lack of experience was paralysing. She didn't have the confidence to take the reins and she wondered whether that lack of confidence and experience would be a turn-off for him.

He was so...*sexy*. So dark, so exotic, so unbelievably, sinfully *compelling*. You didn't have to let your imagination wander too far to realise that he wouldn't have lived a life deprived of adoring women and it wasn't just about his looks. Over the past few days, she had seen the three-dimensional man who had not been in evidence when he'd been in and out of sleep for the first couple of days after she had rescued him.

He was dry, witty, funny and a brilliant listener. He had painted such vivid images in her head of the bright Italian sun streaming down on acre upon acre of carefully cultivated vineyards. He could describe the colour and texture of the fat, juicy grapes with the detail of a poet and his adventures…the places he'd visited! Cordelia could only assume that he used the pay he made working in the wine industry to travel the world when the harvesting season came to an end.

In every way, shape and form his life was a window to a faraway world she could only dream of.

And here he was, with her, and the need to have this man and enjoy this moment was overpowering.

She tentatively drew his hand to her breast and felt him shudder against her.

When he made a half-hearted motion to remove it, she held it fast and was filled with a sense of reckless daring.

'Cordelia,' he groaned under his breath. 'Like I said…this isn't a good idea…'

'Why? If you fancy me and I fancy you, why isn't it a good idea?'

'A million reasons,' he murmured, but he was touching her, massaging the full weight of her breast in his big hand and then slipping a finger under the strap of the swimsuit so that he could slowly draw it down.

Her eyelids fluttered shut and she sighed and then arched up as the swimsuit was pulled down. She twisted and moaned and linked her fingers behind his head and drew him lower. She could feel the conflict inside him but she knew that temptation was stronger than the voice of reason. Inexperienced she might be, but she *knew* that with unerring, feminine certainty. He wanted her and he couldn't help himself and that filled her with a sense of heady power.

Everything about this man was an eye-opener and she was loving it.

His mouth circled her nipple and he flicked his tongue over the stiffened bud and began teasing it into such fierce arousal that a hum of sensation began between her thighs, growing in intensity until she was rubbing her legs together in an attempt to control it.

She was desperate for his hand to be there and, as if reading her mind, he cupped her between her legs. When she wriggled against the palm of his hand, he obligingly and gently pressed down.

Her body was behaving in all sorts of wild and wonderful ways.

Not knowing what she was supposed to do with *him*, she slid her hand over his muscled thigh and shuddered.

'All in good time.' Luca's voice was husky and only just the right side of controlled.

He nuzzled her breast and then moved to the other and laved it with his tongue.

It was unbearable. She parted her legs and trembled when he immediately slid his hand under the stretchy Lycra of the swimsuit, distorting it as he began to rub her there.

He removed his hand and then began easing the swimsuit off her, all the while licking her nipple and suckling on her breast. She couldn't think straight. Couldn't think *at all*.

She just wanted him on her and in her and she wanted it in a hurry.

Her hands scrabbled at his swimming trunks.

Luca stilled. There was enough common sense still left in him to realise that this was not in the plan. Yes, he'd looked at her and discovered that his libido could reach heights he could never have anticipated, but he'd fast worked out that that was only partially to do with the fact that she was attractive.

Maybe more than *just attractive.*

He'd worked out that it was due to a combination of things, not least the fact that he was away from normality, away from the trappings of power and wealth that had always defined him and away from the people who lived in that rarefied world. He was a free man here and so everything was heightened, including the mystifying power of his attraction to the woman lying in this slice of empty paradise.

So many responsibilities awaited his return that freedom had never tasted sweeter.

Was it, therefore, so surprising that he could barely string two coherent thoughts together when he was around the woman?

He'd replaced his computer on day four when he'd headed out to get himself a handful of new clothes to replace the ones he had borrowed from her father. He'd hit the nearest town, headed for an Internet café and re-booted his working life, but even the pressing emails and endless reports and the lucrative deals with companies abroad awaiting his attention couldn't quite manage to distract him from whatever spell had been weaved on him.

Luca was loving it all. Accustomed as he was to a life of staggering control and predictability, he was thoroughly enjoying the sensation of letting himself go.

Which didn't mean that he'd turned into the village idiot! He always used protection but right now, right here…

For the first time in his life, the thrill of the gamble was greater than the pull of common sense. He knew what he should do and what he shouldn't but there was a weakness inside him, driving him on to take a chance, *just this once.*

She was still naked and so, so beautiful and he still had an erection as hard as a rod of steel.

He felt the slickness between her legs because he just couldn't *not* go there.

'Okay.'

'You're a siren.' His groan was unsteady. 'I can picture you sitting on a rock out there, calling to sailors. They wouldn't stand a chance.'

He levered himself down, trailing his tongue along her body and tasting the salt from the sea. Her breasts and stomach were paler, emphasising the rich pink of her nipples, each tipped with stiffened buds the colour of claret. He played briefly with one nipple, teasing it between two fingers, but then he moved to circle her slender waist with his hands. He stroked her hips with the pads of his thumbs, then he moved even lower to gently peel apart the groove between her thighs that sheathed the pulsing of her clitoris.

He licked it, tasted her honeyed sweetness and felt himself swell even more at her little whimpers and soft, startled moans and the way she moved against his mouth, bumping up and down and wriggling, keeping his head in place because her fingers were curled into his over-long hair, and panting.

'Please…' she breathed and that simple plea scattered that well-intentioned voice of reason to the four winds.

He couldn't resist.

Not when she was like this, her slender legs spread

apart, open to him like a flower, inviting him to come inside. Reason, logic, forward-thinking… His brain shut down, leaving him at the mercy of sensation.

Shaking with desire, Luca stood up to rid himself of his swimming trunks, pausing only to smile at the rapt attention on her face.

Cordelia smiled back. Was it an alluring, siren-like smile, or a nervous I've-never-done-this-before smile?

She desperately hoped that he would think the former. She wanted him so badly.

'You're right,' she whispered with gut-wrenching disappointment because this felt like a do-or-die situation. They would not relive this opportunity, not when they were back in the house and she was busy once again with the accounts and phone calls and making sure everything was okay with the house and the various things that needed to be done in it.

'This is crazy.' She blushed and looked away and felt the gentle touch of his finger under her chin.

'Everyone needs a little crazy now and again. Don't talk. I can't talk. I just…want you…'

Her whole body was trembling. So was his. He'd never felt anything like it before. He'd never felt this *need* before. It was like being in the grip of a tornado.

He came inside her in one deep, satisfying thrust. Her tightness encased him perfectly and he groaned and moved, deeper, feeling his shaft sinking into her wetness.

The sensation was so intense he wanted to pass out. There was no artistry in this lovemaking. It was frantic, driving and mind-blowing. She bucked underneath him, arching and stiffening and her short nails dug into his back. He came fast and hard. He could feel the swell and release as he pumped into her, sucking the wild energy out of him and leaving him breathing hard and deeply, shockingly sated.

'Oh, God,' he groaned. He lay flat on his back and shielded his eyes for a few seconds from the glare of the sun. Breathing normally was still a problem as his body came down from its high. 'I've never been like that before.' It was a struggle to think. 'Was it…okay for you?'

'More than okay,' Cordelia whispered under her breath and he turned onto his side to look at her. She angled her body so that they were facing one another.

It was so beautifully warm and the sound of the water lapping against the sand was hypnotic.

'If I could bottle this,' she confessed with honesty, 'then I would.' She stroked his cheek and edged closer to kiss his chin. Her whole body was still thrumming from where he had entered her. She'd felt a twinge of discomfort but her body had been ripe and ready for his entry and the bigness of him inside her, the way he'd moved, had taken her to places she'd never dreamed existed. She'd felt the surge of his orgasm meshing with her own. Their bodies had been as one, united. She couldn't wait to touch him again, to make love again.

How could they not when it had felt so good?

There were no alarm bells ringing in her head. She was on cloud nine and it was only when their eyes met that she wondered whether too much honesty about how much she'd enjoyed what had just happened between them might not be such a great idea.

'Cordelia,' Luca murmured, clasping her hand between his and pensively stroking her chin with his thumb. He sighed. 'That was better than great.'

She beamed.

'You have a smile that could light up a room,' he said, distractedly.

'Thank you. I don't think anyone's ever said that to me before.'

'Maybe because there aren't sufficient eligible men around here to notice it. But trust me, you have.' He looked at her in silence for a few seconds. 'What we did...we shouldn't have done,' he said bluntly, because beating round the bush had never been his thing. 'I don't know what happened. Things got out of hand. I... wanted you, wanted to feel myself in you. I was in the grip of...something bigger than common sense. I still don't understand... It's unheard of, if I'm being honest.' He shook his head, genuinely bewildered. 'I'm usually in control of...everything. I don't get it.'

'Of everything?' Cordelia smiled, because what he was saying was music to her ears. 'Is that possible?'

'God, yes. I certainly have never lost control when it comes to sex, but I did this time and for that I apologise.'

'Luca...don't apologise. I...' *I absolutely adored it, loved it, was blown away by it...* 'I really enjoyed what we did.'

She'd never thought about what sex might *feel* like. She'd vaguely assumed that it was something that would happen sooner or later, when she found someone she actually wanted to date, someone she could envisage sharing her life with. That such a person hadn't come along yet had not filled her with any sense of disappointment. Frankly, looking around at the nearby talent, she'd felt relieved that marriage and everything it entailed wasn't high on her agenda because the choice of candidates for the post of potential life partner was lamentably non-existent.

Dreaming of the great, big world out there was a lot more fun.

And now…the great, big world had landed on her doorstep!

'It's not just about losing control,' Luca said roughly. 'I'm no good for you.'

'What are you talking about?'

'That was good sex.' He decided that bringing it down to basics would kick the conversation off to a good start, put things in perspective for her. 'Better than good,' he amended. He thought back to the urgings that had prompted him to throw caution to the winds and taste, just for one wild moment, what it felt like to be inside her. *Better than good* didn't come close to an adequate description. She'd been so unbelievably, fantastically tight around him. He frowned and focused.

'But I need to remind you that this isn't the start of… any kind of relationship. I'm not one of the local lads who's going to come knocking on your father's door to take you out on a date.'

'I know that.' She broke eye contact. The pulse in her neck was racing madly, and for some reason what he'd just said stung. She sat up abruptly and drew her knees up to her chin and stared out to sea. It was empty. No passing boats. No ship on the horizon. Nothing to make you think that you were anywhere but alone on an island in the middle of the ocean. When she glanced over her shoulder to him, it was to find him looking at her with pensive, brooding intensity.

It was a ridiculous conversation to have when they were both naked, she thought with a spurt of anger.

She felt suddenly vulnerable even though, lying there, he obviously couldn't give a hoot whether he was clothed or not. She glanced down and immediately diverted her eyes. Erect or not, he was ridiculously impressive.

She felt her body jerk into uninvited reaction and clicked her tongue with annoyance because she'd just been given the brush-off, in so many words, and the last thing she should be doing by way of response was getting worked up all over again.

'Do you?'

Cordelia gritted her teeth and ignored him completely as she sprang to her feet and hastily donned the swimsuit that had been shed with such enthusiasm less than an hour earlier.

Much better.

'Of course.' Her voice was a lot more normal when she looked at him now, as were her pulse rate and the general state of her nervous system.

'If you hadn't ended up half drowning...' she said.

'Don't remind me. Men have fragile egos when it comes to that kind of thing.'

'We would never have met. But here you are and I don't think, for a second, that this is the start of any kind of relationship. I'm not on the lookout for a relationship! But I don't get to adventure much and this is *fun*.'

'Good. So we understand one another.'

'Does every woman you happen to sleep with need a warning just in case they start thinking that you're interested in a long-term, full-time relationship?' She folded her arms and stared at him. He raised his eyebrows, amused, and she blushed scarlet when she had visible proof that he was getting aroused once again.

He idly took himself in his hand while he continued to look at her, and she reddened further.

He took his time standing up but even then he didn't put on the discarded swimming trunks, choosing instead to saunter down to the water, whereupon he turned to look at her.

'Another swim? Or food?'

Cordelia frowned. She was fairly certain that this was a serious conversation that should be afforded a suitable amount of gravitas. Instead, that crooked half-smile of his held just the hint of an invitation, and she found herself walking towards him, pulled in his direction by invisible strings.

She pictured him sitting on that rug in all his glory, tucking into the sandwiches she had made and wearing nothing but his birthday suit, and she strode into the water.

'Well?' She turned to him and folded her arms. 'Do you always think that you have to warn women off in case they start expecting more than you want to give?'

'More than I'm capable of giving,' Luca surprised himself by saying.

'What do you mean? What are you talking about?'

'I'm talking about me, Cordelia. Me, women and my experiences with them.' He turned away and began swimming out, his strokes long and clean, and she followed until they were both out in the deep blue ocean, their bodies adjusted to the cold, cold water, which felt good in the burning heat of the midday sun.

She flipped over onto her back and felt the sun pouring down over her. When she glanced across it was to find that he had done the same.

For one fleeting second she questioned what she had got herself into. This wasn't the boy next door. This wasn't one of the local lads who drank at the same pub every weekend and followed their dad into the same family business. Those were the boys she knew and was accustomed to.

This guy was all dark and dangerous and out of her league and if he was also funny and sharp and challenging, she knew that she should still never forget that there was a lot more to him than that.

Maybe that was part and parcel of the tingle that rippled through her as she feasted her eyes on his averted profile.

She'd never had a single experience with any man. He'd been her first.

He'd obviously had so many experiences with women that he had built up a portfolio on their behaviour patterns and expectations when it came to relationships.

Mingled with simmering excitement, a certain amount of unease nudged its way through but she blithely shoved that aside because, as he'd just reminded her, he was just passing through. People who were passing through didn't cause problems. It was the ones who stuck around and made a nuisance of themselves you had to be wary of.

'You sound like an old man,' she half joked.

'There are times I feel like one,' Luca said heavily.

'Don't you believe in love?'

'Strangely, I don't believe anyone's ever asked me that question directly before.' He sounded surprised. 'But now that you've asked, I don't. I don't believe in love, I don't believe in the fairy tales people insist on telling that there's such a thing as a happy-ever-after. You're young, *mi tesoro*, which is why I felt that I should warn you off me.'

'And like I've told you, there's no need. Why don't

you? Believe in love and marriage, I mean?' She thought of herself in a white dress floating down the aisle on her father's arm, to meet the man of her dreams. Instantly, a few pedestrian details jarred the dreamy image. Firstly the thought of herself in a dress, which was an item of clothing she didn't possess, and secondly the thought of what this man of her dreams would look like.

Tall, dark and handsome.

Like the one lying next to her floating on the gently rolling water.

But, she hurriedly amended in her head, clearly *not* the one next to her. Maybe one similar.

'Oh, but I do believe in marriage,' Luca said wryly. He thought of Isabella, waiting for him back in Italy, and a sharp tug of guilt drove into him with the force of a serrated knife cutting through skin. There was nothing to feel guilty about. He knew that. At least, the cold, logical side of his brain knew that. He was on the same page as the woman floating alongside him so what if, besides the fact that he wouldn't be sticking around, another very valid reason for him being the least suitable man on the planet for her lay in the fact that he was practically engaged to someone? Did that matter? No, of course it didn't because a relationship wasn't on the table and he'd been brutally honest in making that clear.

Aside from which…he was fond of Isabella and she was perfect for him because she would never ask for what he couldn't give. They would marry and two great families would unite and, of course, they would be careful about their outside interests because, under the guise of marriage, they would be as brother and sister. She and her girlfriend, Ella, would carry on seeing one another and he…he would discreetly do what any red-blooded man would have to do to satisfy his libido. For a man who did not believe or trust in love, it would be the ideal marriage.

And yet…

Suddenly restless, he began swimming back to shore, making sure that Cordelia was following him and then slinging his arm around her shoulders as they stepped out of the water. He retrieved the swimming trunks and put them on.

'You just haven't found the right woman? Is that it?' Cordelia returned to the conversation as she began unpacking the picnic, carefully putting the contents of Tupperware containers on the rug and not looking directly at him.

'There's no such thing as the *right* woman. There is, however, such a thing as a *suitable* woman. I want to have a family as much as the next person,' he confided with utmost honesty. 'I also want to have a successful marriage and, as far as I'm concerned, those two things are perfectly possible provided there are no unreasonable expectations on either side.' He paused and Isabella flashed into his head once again. For all her sexual proclivities, they would produce the requisite heir. A discreet consultant would easily facilitate that. The signatures weren't exactly on the paper yet, but they would be by the time he returned to Italy.

The business of love would never complicate matters. Luca wondered whether that was why he had returned to Cornwall, to remind himself of what he already knew. Love had destroyed his father and Cornwall was a symbol of that love. You could almost say that that was where the story began.

'I don't suppose that's exactly your cup of tea, is it?'

He looked at her, appreciating, yet again, the white-blonde tangle of her hair flowing down her back and over her shoulders...the healthy gold of her skin, so much darker than where the sun didn't touch...the intense violet of her eyes...the athleticism of her strong body. Jesus, was he hardening *again*?

'Not at all,' Cordelia admitted lightly. She passed him a chunky ham and cheese sandwich on a paper plate and sat back on her haunches to look at him for a few seconds. The glare was sharp and she was squinting into the sun. 'Not many women would accept that sort of situation.'

'You'd be surprised,' Luca murmured in response. It felt as if he'd already said too much. Sitting here, talking about this touchy-feely stuff...made him vaguely uneasy. Something about her lulled him into feeling just so damned *comfortable*. 'Nice sandwich.' He changed the subject, steering firmly away from dangerous ground. 'Generous.'

Cordelia burst out laughing at his expression. 'I've spent too many years making sandwiches for my dad and some of the other fishermen to switch from sandwiches like these to delicate little cucumber ones.' She sobered up and settled into a more comfortable position. 'Why don't you believe in love? What happened?'

Luca looked at her. Her expression was open and quizzical. No agenda there. She was so much a part of this wild, beautiful, Cornish slice of land and yet as trapped in it as he was trapped in his own privileged, rarefied world, if only she knew.

He experienced a moment of such perfect *oneness* that he had to clear his throat and make a conscious effort to gather himself.

'I don't...' *Don't talk about my private life to anyone, ever.* 'I don't know what happened, but I've figured out over the years that my father's disastrous personal life had something to do with it.' He paused. There was an odd, swooping sensation in the pit of his stomach that he had never experienced before. She was quietly working her way through her sandwich and thoroughly enjoying it. He'd brought champagne but he figured she would be the sort of girl who wouldn't mind a pint now and again. He had an insane desire to introduce her to his wines, watch her taste the soft subtleties on her palate and, again, he had to shake himself back into the moment and remember, *with relief,* that in the blink of an eye he would walk away, back to reality, never to see her again.

'I know how that feels.' She smiled ruefully, prompting him to do the unthinkable and continue.

'My mother died when I was young.' His smile matched hers. 'We may have more in common than you think because her death blew a hole in my father's life and he was never the same since. Unlike your father, though, he didn't emotionally retreat from the world and he certainly didn't become overprotective of me. The opposite. My father has made a career out of trying to find a substitute for what he lost. Never succeeded.'

'Do you have siblings?'

'No. There's just me.'

No twin, as you had, to share the loneliness and grief, just a father walking away as he tried to carve a life of his own to fill his own void, leaving his only son to work things out for himself.

'Holding the fort, so to speak.' He thought of those vast acres of vineyards and the incomparable wealth, growing daily under his studious, watchful eye. Her idea of the fort in question would bear no resemblance to reality, that was for sure.

'Working to keep things ticking over. Like me.' She had a vision of him, so strong, labouring under the sun, watching out for his father the way she watched out for hers. 'Do you live with your dad? You should count your blessings that your father has allowed you to get on with living your life. An overprotective dad can be more of a curse than a blessing sometimes.'

'He lives nearby,' Luca murmured.

'Close enough to be a problem?' She raised her eyebrows and grinned.

'Close enough for me to keep an eye on him.' Luca's mouth twitched and he smiled back at her. The sandwiches, he thought, were bloody good. Wholesome. 'The truth is life might have been better if he'd done what your father did, and retreated, at least for a decent amount of time. Instead, my father has entered into marriages with alarming regularity and none of the endings have been good ones.'

'I'm getting the picture.' No wonder he was jaded, she thought with a spurt of sympathy. She rested her hand on his wrist and gave it a little squeeze. The feel of that touch sent an electric charge racing straight from his wrist to what was visibly stirring underneath the swimming trunks. He shifted uncomfortably, adjusting himself in the process.

Whatever picture she was getting, it certainly wasn't a complete one.

'It must have been a lonely time for you.'

Luca shrugged. 'I've never been lonely in my life.' He thought back with some fondness to the English boarding school he had attended for so many years. No, there had been no shortage of people in his life. Had he been lonely? He frowned, unwilling to give house room to that notion, which smacked of the sort of weakness he despised.

'Were you close to any of your...er...stepmothers? How many were there?'

'A few and no.' He settled back on his elbows and stared up at a blue, blue sky. 'I don't believe there was a stepmother who didn't turn out to be a piece of work. It's a blessing my father's been on his own for a couple of years now, although it might be a bit premature to say that he's seen the light.'

'You really love him, don't you? For all his failings. Just something else we have in common!'

Luca looked at her thoughtfully. 'Amazing,' he murmured, 'given the circumstances, that you are as upbeat and romantic as you are.'

'You think I should be cynical and jaded?'

'I've seen the trail of misery love has a habit of leaving in its wake. You call it cynical and jaded but I call it realistic. As far as I'm concerned, you look at life with your eyes wide open and you can escape most of its predictably unpleasant fallout.'

'Which is why you like the thought of an arranged marriage...'

'A suitable union between two people whose outlook on life is similar. Remind me why we're talking about all of this...?'

'Because it's nice getting to know someone else. I *know* you won't be around for much longer, but it's still nice getting to know you.'

When was he actually going to go? He'd extended

this visit far longer than was technically acceptable. He was a workaholic and, of course, this unforeseen break in the normal course of events had been fun, but it couldn't continue.

And yet…he remembered the feel of her against him and his explosive reaction to her body, and the thought of jumping ship when he knew he should, which was just as soon as he could shove his clothes in a plastic bag and order a cab to the nearest airport, held little appeal.

'And believe me,' he murmured with heartfelt sincerity, 'I would certainly like to get to know you better as well.' It was a sign of creativity and a willingness to go with the flow that he was prepared to take a few more days out of his hectic schedule. In life, if something presented itself as a once-in-a-lifetime opportunity, you grabbed it with both hands. This was a once-in-a-lifetime opportunity.

He smiled slowly.

'Another week here isn't going to hurt…is it?' He reached forward and she leaned into him. He kissed her long and slow and Cordelia melted.

'Another week,' she sighed breathlessly, 'would be great.'

'And then we'll bid our fond farewells. Deal?'

Something inside her stirred and she tore her eyes away from the puzzling void that opened up when she thought about him leaving.

She smiled. 'Deal.'

CHAPTER FOUR

'OF COURSE IF you want to go, if you feel you need to leave me when things are so busy here, then I can't stand in your way. You're a grown woman, Cordelia. You can do whatever you want to do and I understand that you need to get away for a while. Don't blame you. What young thing wants to be cooped up with her old fool of a father?'

Under normal circumstances, Cordelia would have wilted under this flagrant emotional blackmail. Sitting across from her father at the pine table where they had just finished sharing a fraught supper, she took a deep breath, the sort of deep breath typical of someone determined to power on whatever the obstacles.

These were not normal circumstances and she didn't have the luxury of succumbing to Clive Ramsey's mournful blue eyes.

'One week at the very most, Dad.'

She glanced down to the chips slowly going cold on her plate. She'd barely eaten. She shoved the plate to one side and leaned forward, elbows planted on the table.

Once upon a time, her father had been gloriously good-looking. A strapping man with the same white-blond hair as hers and light blue eyes. Time, grief and disappointments had changed all that and now, at the age of sixty-two, he was still lean and strong, but his face was lined, his hands gnarled from all the manual work he did, and his once erect frame was stooped. A tall man hiding away from life and it showed in the way he carried himself.

'One week?' He sighed and attempted a smile, which tugged every heartstring she had.

'I know you think that once I'm gone, I'm never going to come back, but that won't be the case.' Cordelia thought of the trip she was about to make. If she lasted five minutes there, then she would be amazed. Nausea swamped her again and she shoved the plate with the now cold chips further away from her because the sight of the slowly congealing food was doing nothing for the state of her stomach.

Pregnant. How could it have happened? Her period, as regular as clockwork, had been ten days overdue before it had even occurred to her to do a pregnancy test. She had been living on her nerves ever since.

Luca had stayed on for a further week and then he had gone. The impact of his departure on her had been something she hadn't foreseen. Yes, she had assumed that she would miss him because they had shared such a wonderful three weeks together. He had blown a hole in her orderly, predictable life and she'd known that it would take a while for normality to paper over his absence.

But she hadn't expected the depth of those feelings of loss and wanting. She physically *ached* for him. She saw him in every room in the house and on every corner of every street in the little village, where he had become such a familiar sight that people asked after him when he'd gone.

And when she closed her eyes, his image took shape in her head with such clarity that she felt that if she tried hard enough, she would open her eyes and he would be there. Standing in front of her, so tall and so bronzed and so sinfully sexy.

He'd gone, though, and he hadn't looked back. Not a text, not an email, not a phone call. Nothing. He'd warned her that he was just passing through and he'd cautioned her about getting emotionally involved with him and she'd nodded and agreed and said all the right things and had promptly done just the opposite of what he'd asked.

She'd laughed in the face of common sense and flung herself into a one-sided relationship with a guy who didn't believe in love.

And now she was pregnant and it was like walking in a dense fog with her feet in treacle. Every thought about *what happened next* required such effort that she had spent the past few days just wanting to crawl into her bed and close her eyes and sleep for a hundred years.

As it had turned out, fate had had an excellent way of galvanising her into action. No taking time out to think things over! Or hiding under the duvet and pretending to be an ostrich!

'And I don't want you fretting that something's going to happen to me,' she said briskly, sweeping aside her fear of the big unknown and plastering a reassuring smile on her face.

Her father knew nothing about the pregnancy and that was something that she would broach in due course.

When she reached the right levels of courage. That time was certainly not now.

'Things happen,' her father responded morosely. 'We both know that.'

'And we have to move on, Dad.' God, she missed having her mum. She adored her dad, with all his endearing, frustrating, lovable little ways, but, Lord, what she wouldn't have given for the emotional support of a mother, a hand to reach out and hold hers right now when she so desperately needed it.

'You're young. The wisdom of youth is fleeting. Take it from me. I'll say no more except that I'll miss you. Maybe you could leave a list of what needs to be done while you're away.'

'Ah.' She paused and waited until her father was looking at her. 'There won't be any need for you to worry about anything while I'm away, Dad.'

'I'll be out fishing all day.' He frowned. 'The haul is good just at the moment. I won't have time to sort out that business with the rentals. And food. No, forget I said that. I can buy in some tins. Baked beans. Soup. You go and enjoy yourself, Cordy. You deserve it.'

Cordelia thought about the enjoyment lying in wait for her and shuddered. 'Dad—' she inhaled deeply '—you won't have to worry about food or the rental because Doris is going to take care of all of that for you.'

She waited for the explosion. She almost closed her eyes. Doris Jones was her father's arch enemy. Buxom, blonde and with a personality that could send strong men scurrying for cover, she had had her eye on Clive Ramsey's business for as long as Cordelia could remember.

'We could be a team,' she had ventured years ago.

'My three boats with yours. We could have ourselves a proper little business.'

Clive had been incandescent with rage at the barefaced cheek of the woman. There and then, she had become his nemesis. As fate would have it, nemesis was going to be taking charge while Cordelia was away, whether her dad liked it or not.

Of course, if he refused to oblige, she told him once he had finished ranting and raving, which made a change from his stoic, barely concealed gloom, she would ditch her plans and stay put...because he certainly wouldn't be able to cope on his own and she had no intention of spending her one week of the year when she should be relaxing worrying about him.

Cordelia knew that she was taking a gamble. If her father dug his heels in, then what was she going to do? Her ticket was all booked and even though this trip to Italy filled her with sickening apprehension, it was something that had to be done. For better or for worse, the guy who had vanished out of her life and hadn't looked back would have to be told about the baby he had never expected to father.

Her father caved in.

'It'll be fine.' She hugged him.

It'll be fine for at least one of us, at any rate.

'Don't think I haven't noticed you and Doris having a laugh now and again at the pub over a pint.'

Clive Ramsey flushed and he glared at his daughter. 'A man can't be rude all the time,' he countered defensively.

She'd won this round. There was no way she intended to let on to her father that she had found herself between a rock and a hard place when it came to

Doris. If life were a fairy tale, she would laugh at the crazy coincidence of being caught red-handed emerging from a bathroom clutching a pregnancy-testing box by the one person who shouldn't have been anywhere near the area. But Doris had been there, larger than life and bursting with curiosity and she hadn't given up asking questions until she'd got the truth. Cordelia could only console herself with the thought that at least her father would be well fed, if nothing else. Doris was well known for her pies.

'So it's agreed, then...' She looked at him anxiously and she saw him visibly soften.

'I don't like it...'

'Those rentals need to be sorted. I know the timing's awful, but I had no idea...'

No idea that I was going to find myself carrying a child...that all that longing to see new places would end up as a nightmare journey to deliver a message that was definitely not going to brighten Luca Baresi's day...

'I had no idea that that problem would blow up like a squall, just after I'd booked to go away on the spur of the moment.'

'Well, Ireland isn't a million miles away, I suppose. And I know you've been wanting to do a little research into your mum's family tree.'

Cordelia didn't say anything but her fingers were tightly crossed behind her back.

She never ever lied and certainly would never have dreamt of lying to her dad, but the truth, laid bare, would have turned his already grey hair even greyer.

There was only so much she could deal with just at the moment and telling her father the whole truth and nothing but the truth, and then having to deal with the fallout, had felt like a step too far.

She smiled weakly. 'I promise it's going to be all right.' She was tempted to burst into manic laughter because from where she was sitting there was very little chance that anything was going to be all right in the foreseeable future. 'I'm going away and maybe we should both see that as the start of a changing future. For both of us. Maybe it'll do you good to not have me around. Now, I'm going to pack. I have a taxi booked to take me to the airport and it'll be coming very early, so I'll say goodbye now and poke my head in your bedroom in the morning if you're not already up.' She could see tears gathering in the corners of his eyes and her heart restricted.

She had to go. She'd meant what she'd said about changes. Everything was changing and for someone who had spent a lifetime harnessed to the yoke of duty and responsibility, the changes were terrifying.

The future was sprawled in front of her with a frightening lack of certainty. She'd spent her life yearning for what lay out there, beyond the small confines of the village where she lived, and now a door had been opened but for all the wrong reasons and what lay behind that door was not, she felt, going to be the wonderful adventure she had always hoped for.

One week, though, and she would have had the conversation she had to have, then she would be back, and at least she would have seen somewhere different, breathed in different air, looked at a different landscape.

She would have to keep her fingers crossed that she could handle everything that came in between.

* * *

'There's someone here asking for you.'

Luca looked up from where he had been scrolling through his emails on his computer to the elderly man who had ambled into his office without knocking and was now in the process of straightening everything on his desk, clucking disapprovingly under his breath.

'Roberto…' Luca controlled a sigh because the man had been a loyal retainer since the dawn of time and if he was now in his early eighties, with a meandering mind and prone to forgetting that there was an army of stalwart help paid to do what might once have been part of his job, then so be it. 'There's no need to tidy the desk. I know where everything is. At any rate, I'm busy so anyone wanting to see me will have to make an appointment through the usual channels.' He had two PAs. One handled matters of a more confidential nature, the other handled anything that required interfacing with non-Italian clients, of which there were very many.

PAs…hired help…three-course meals that appeared as if by magic…a social life that left very little free time, especially now that the presumption of nuptials with Isabella lay thick in the air, even though nothing had been formally announced. Recently he'd felt as though he had to make time in his packed diary to breathe.

He frowned and restlessly pushed himself away from his desk and waited until Roberto had straightened everything to his satisfaction.

'Never used to be that way,' Roberto responded, shaking his head sadly. 'There was always time for a face-to-face meeting. A chat. Everybody knew everybody. It was a family.'

'Times change.' Luca had heard all this before. Naturally, he couldn't interface with everyone who worked for him! His winery employed very many people, kept two villages in employment, practically! There wasn't a human being who could keep track of every single person who might show up unannounced on the doorstep. 'I haven't got time to see anyone at the moment. Now, is that all?'

'So I'll show her in, shall I?'

Luca flung both hands in the air and gave up. He had zero curiosity as to the identity of his visitor. Theoretically his door was always open to any of his employees. In practice, the door was largely shut and, when ajar, was ferociously guarded by PA number one, who made sure that his time was uninterrupted by anything of a remotely trivial nature. If it could be sorted outside the hallowed walls of his office, which sprawled across one of the wings of his grand house, then it was. Rosa saw to that. Sadly, Rosa was on a one week vacation and, for some reason, Luca had not wanted the annoyance of a temp because there was no way Sonya, his tri-lingual PA, could be spared to waste time for a week doing bits of grunt work.

Unfortunately, without Rosa around, Luca could see that irritating interruptions were not going to be headed off at the pass. At least, not if Roberto happened to be unofficial gatekeeper.

'Five minutes,' he huffed, all but tapping his watch to make sure Roberto got the message loud and clear. 'And then you're to come and remove whoever I happen to be with.'

'Very rude, sir, when someone is kind enough to call by for a chat.'

'But essential. *Five minutes*, Roberto!'

Luca had doubts as to whether these instructions would be obeyed. He would have to control the urge to snap were they to be ignored. His temper, always ruthlessly controlled, had been far too much in evidence ever since he had returned from that brief sojourn on the Cornish coast and he had no idea why.

What he *did* know was that the lack of control infuriated him.

He waited until Roberto had shuffled off and then he swivelled his chair to face the massive bay window, frowning and staring out towards a vista that was impressive by anyone's standards.

He barely noticed the mansion in which he lived. It was there. Ancient, beautiful, vast, handed down through the generations. Huge tracts of it were unused simply because there were so many rooms. Walls were adorned with exquisite paintings that were seldom seen. There were priceless rugs upon which no feet ever trod and windows were flung open in rooms simply to let in a bit of fresh air before they were shut again and those very rooms remained silent and empty until they were aired again.

His own quarters, done to the highest of standards, were far more modern, as was the four-bedroomed annexe in which his father lived when he wasn't travelling, as he was now, hopefully not on the lookout for another unsuitable wife. Personally, Luca couldn't abide the heaviness of all that traditional décor that characterised most of his estate but he didn't care enough to do anything about it.

It was his ancestry and that was the end of it.

He barely noticed any of it, but through this window...
that was what he noticed.

The rolling acres of carefully cultivated grapevines,
marching in lines towards a distant horizon, punctuated
by tall, elegant cypress trees...the backdrop of hazy
purple mountains rising so high in the distance that the
peaks were blurred by cloud...the villages clinging to
the sides of the hills, white squares against lush green.

He was staring out at the scenery when the door was
pushed open and, with a sigh of resignation, he slowly
spun round to address whatever needed addressing.

For a few seconds, Luca only registered Roberto,
who was hovering, eyeing up the desk with intent, resisting the urge to do a bit more tidying, then he stepped
aside and...

He'd been relaxed back in the deep leather chair.
Now Luca leant forward and every nerve and muscle in
his body slowly stretched to breaking point. The woman
was, naturally, registering in some part of his brain
but even so his eyes were telling him that he couldn't
possibly be seeing the leggy blonde with whom he had
spent three weeks of unadulterated carefree pleasure.

It wasn't possible. For once in his life, Luca was
rendered speechless and, in that brief period, Roberto
pushed an obviously reluctant Cordelia into the room.

'Will tea or coffee be taken, sir?' he queried without a hint of irony, even though he had been banned
from fetching and carrying three years previously after
he had managed to drop an eye-wateringly expensive
vase, which he had been lifting from its podium to dust.
'Some wine, perhaps?' His watery eyes glinted.

'Just close the door behind you, Roberto,' Luca managed to say. 'And no tea or coffee and certainly no wine at four in the afternoon. Thank you.'

He couldn't tear his eyes off the woman who was now pressed against the closed door. He was barely aware of drawing breath. His thought processes had been temporarily suspended and the most he could do was take in the rangy body that had been his undoing for three sensational weeks.

She was dressed in a pair of faded jeans and a loose red and white checked shirt. Her long hair was pulled back into a plait.

Luca's nostrils flared at the memory of that vibrant hair spilling over her shoulders, a tumble of gold and vanilla and every other shade of blonde imaginable. He recalled the electric charge that had raced through his body every time he had curled his fingers in its length, held her heavy breasts in his hands, nuzzled the soft down between her thighs and felt her writhe with passion under his touch.

'Well,' he drawled, lazing back in the chair, 'this is certainly a surprise.' And, he thought, an unwelcome one, never mind the trip down memory lane, which had the annoying effect of reminding him that he had a libido.

Luca was a pragmatist. He had known from the very first time he had touched her that what they had was not destined to go anywhere. Those three weeks had been enjoyable—no, that didn't come close to describing it, but it had been life lived in a bubble. He'd been completely free for the first time in his life and freedom had tasted sweet.

But this was his real life and never the twain should have met.

Displeasure flared inside him, partly because she had shown up here unannounced and now he would have to firmly but politely turn her away, and partly because there was a treacherous side of him that was *pleased* at her unexpected appearance. He realised that he'd been thinking about her, in a dark, subconscious sort of way, his thoughts titillating and illicit.

'How can I help you?' he pursued into the lengthening silence as she continued to hover.

Of course he knew why she was here and he wondered how she would broach the inevitable conversation. It was disappointing that it had come to this but not really that surprising. People were lamentably predictable in the ways they reacted to money.

Even her, and if it made his gut twist to wise up to the fact that she was no different from the next person, then that was his deal.

'Is it all right if I sit?' There was an empty chair in front of the desk and her legs were like jelly. If she didn't sit soon, she would end up crumpled in an undignified heap on the floor and she could tell from the lack of warmth on his face that he wouldn't be offering her tea and sympathy should that be the case.

Indeed, from the expression on his face, the last person he wanted to see at all was her.

The man staring at her with cool, assessing eyes was a stranger. He bore no resemblance to the guy who had swept her off her feet and taken her to places she had never dreamed possible with his fingers, his hands, *his mouth*.

But then this guy bore no resemblance to the man she'd thought she'd find when she'd set off. He worked in a vineyard. He picked grapes. Then when the season was over, he travelled. He wasn't an itinerant, but neither was he...*this*.

She'd known where he worked and lived because he'd told her. She'd expected a modest dwelling, maybe shared with his father. Something modest but pretty. One of those whitewashed Mediterranean houses she'd seen in pictures over the years.

But when she'd asked after him, she'd been directed to this mansion. A lovely old woman with a crinkled face and black eyes as lively as a sparrow's had walked with her up the hill, with carefully tended vines falling away from them in rows down towards fields and trees. There had been no conversation. Cordelia didn't speak a word of Italian and the old lady, smiling and friendly as she was, spoke no English, so there had been no opportunity to ask what the heck was going on and why was she being taken to a vast stone fortress complete with turrets and surrounded by cypress trees.

The heat had been sapping and the pull-along had felt as heavy as lead by the time they had trudged in silence up the hill to stand in front of the fortress, which, on closer inspection, wasn't quite as coldly unwelcoming as she'd first thought.

There were shutters in the windows and colourful flowers spilling out in borders at the front.

And now here she was and if she didn't sit soon...

She didn't wait for him to signal the seat in front of him. She walked towards it, her troubled blue eyes skittering away from his closed, unwelcoming face.

He didn't want her here and it was beginning to dawn on her why that was the case.

Luca Baresi wasn't an ordinary guy. This wasn't the

house of an ordinary man. Luca Baresi was a multi-millionaire, and she wished that she'd had the common sense to look him up on the Internet before she'd packed her bag and made the trip to Italy.

But why, she asked herself feverishly, would she have done that?

She'd thought that he was a simple guy who worked in a vineyard in Italy. Simple guys didn't have profiles on the Internet.

'I guess you're surprised to see me,' she opened, clearing her throat.

'Less surprised than you might think.' Luca's voice was cool.

'I would have contacted you...phoned...but...' Her voice trailed off. She noticed that she was plucking compulsively at the checked shirt and she sat on her hands to stop.

'No phone number. I know. I didn't leave you with one.'

Cordelia flushed. He couldn't have made it any clearer that she was not welcome. She tilted her head at a combative angle and reminded herself that this trip had been voluntary. She was pregnant and she could very easily have not bothered to tell him. She was here for a reason and she'd be gone within the hour. Lord knew, a week seemed like a long time but maybe she would see a bit of Tuscany before she headed back home.

'No,' she said with equal cool. 'You didn't. Why would you when you spent three weeks lying to me? Of course, the last thing you would have encouraged would be any further contact from the country bumpkin you used for your own amusement and dumped. Heaven knows, my showing up here on your doorstep must seem like the worst of your nightmares.'

Luca had the grace to flush but he didn't say anything because there was no point launching into self defence.

'You said you weren't surprised to see me here,' Cordelia prompted icily. 'What did you mean?'

He shrugged eloquently and sat back, steepling his fingers under his chin, then clasping his hands behind his head to look at her from under thick dark lashes.

'You looked me up on the Internet,' he said flatly. 'Curiosity, no doubt. You discovered that I was not quite the person you thought I was.'

Cordelia could barely conceal her snort of disgust. She thought back to just how elegant, arrogant and self-confident he'd been. She'd naively put it down to his *foreignness*. Instead, those had just been the telltale traits of a man who lived in a castle and owned a million acres of vineyards. Lack of experience had not been her friend when it had come to making sense of his personality.

'Really?' she said, tight-lipped.

'Really. You would have struck jackpot on the first hit and I guess that got you thinking that what we'd enjoyed might have come to something of a premature end. Were you dazzled at the thought of continuing a relationship but this time with a man worth billions instead of a guy with only the clothes on his back and a seasonal job?' He paused, watched carefully for signs of guilt and embarrassment, and saw neither.

Luca raked his fingers through his hair and vaulted upright. The chair suddenly felt confining, the room too small.

'I'm a rich man,' he said, striding towards the window and looking out to everything he owned for a few seconds, before turning to face her. 'I know how the game is played.'

The sun was no longer high in the sky and its rays through the window emphasised the pale hue of her skin and the sprinkling of freckles across her short, straight nose. His lips thinned as he felt a familiar ache in his groin.

'So you think I've come here to offer myself to you because you have all *this*...'

'Of course you have!' He heard the softness of her laughter in his head, the lilt of her voice when they were in bed, talking quietly while he stroked her face. He clenched his fists because he didn't welcome those memories. They didn't belong here. 'But you've made your trip in vain, Cordelia. Naturally, I will compensate you for your travel. But return to Cornwall you must, because you don't, for a thousand reasons, belong here...'

CHAPTER FIVE

'A THOUSAND REASONS?' Cordelia enquired icily. She didn't think so. One reason and he had just said it in four simple words. *You don't belong here.*

Was this the opening she needed to take? Should she nod mutely and leave? Let him think that he had struck jackpot with his insulting, offensive and sweeping assumption?

She thought of her father. An honourable man. She'd inherited his sense of right and wrong. To walk away now without explaining why she had come in the first place...

What would that make her? In his eyes and in her own? She would know the truth and, of course, that should be all that mattered, but the very idea of leaving him with the mistaken impression that she was a seedy gold-digger willing to sacrifice herself for cash was too much to take in.

'Cordelia.' Luca's voice softened. 'You really don't understand...'

'I really think I do,' she returned, without skipping a beat. 'You think I've come here with a begging bowl. You think that the only reason I might have wanted to get in touch with you would be because I've found out how rich you are and what a catch you would be for a poor fisherman's daughter like myself.'

'Maybe that's just a part of the equation,' Luca murmured, simultaneously knowing that he should gently but firmly usher her to the door, see her on her way, yet, stupidly, finding that he couldn't quite bring himself to do it. Not just yet. 'And I mean no insult.'

'That's wonderful of you,' she said tightly. 'You mean no insult and yet you just happen to have insulted me in the worst possible way.'

'Of course I don't consider you a poor fisherman's daughter. As a matter of fact, I have a great deal of respect for your father. He is an honest man making an honest living. Believe me, I have spent my adult life seeing the corruption that all this can buy.' He gestured to encompass the vastness of his house and the enormous wealth it represented. 'Your father... I respect him...'

'Thank you,' Cordelia said politely, while, inside, she raged with the force of an erupting volcano at what she could only interpret as his smug contempt for everything she stood for. How on earth could she not have seen through him? 'I'll make sure I tell him.'

'Perhaps,' Luca murmured, watching the satiny softness of her skin, the tinge of colour spreading across her high cheekbones. He had to stop himself from staring. Worse, from closing his eyes and remembering the supple strength of her beautiful body, the fullness of her breasts, the smoothness of her inner thighs. 'Perhaps...' he dragged his thoughts away from those dangerous zones and back to the matter at hand, which was the necessity to show her to the door '...you really haven't come here because you'd sussed who I was and what I'm worth. It beggars belief that you would have taken this length of time to make your move, but were I to give you the benefit of the doubt…' he sighed and raked his fingers through his hair, annoyed because for once in his life the logical way forward with the conversation was not one he felt comfortable taking '…then the outcome would be the same. *Cara*, we had our moment in time, and believe me when I tell you that I will cherish it for ever, but it was no more than a moment in time.'

His words slithered through her like shards of glass, destroying every rose-hued memory. She felt sick. The ground seemed to be spinning under her feet and she took a few deep breaths and balled her hands into fists.

'My life here is prescribed,' he said softly. 'More than I can begin to explain. These vineyards…' he signalled to the window, beyond which lay all those rows of carefully tended vines, heavy with grapes '…they are my legacy and I can no more escape my destiny than you can escape yours.'

'My destiny to remain where I was born? You mean *that* destiny?' Of course, that was what he meant. She'd told him all the ins and outs of her life, had lain in his arms and mused on all those doors that had been solidly closed for her. She'd laid bare her heartfelt wish that she could see the world, see what was out there. God, was it any wonder that, with her having shown up on his doorstep, he'd instantly jumped to all sorts of conclusions?

'You have always wanted to see the world. If you have not researched me, if you truly arrived here thinking that you would find the impoverished manual worker you imagined me to be, then you have my most sincere apologies. It would make sense that you might find yourself tempted to cross the ocean to make contact with someone who might represent an escape from your life, which is as prescribed as my own...'

Cordelia tilted her head to one side. She was curious to see how far he would run with this particular theory. It wasn't quite as offensive as theory number one, but nevertheless it still felt like a kick in the teeth after all the things they had shared.

After all the things, she mentally amended, *she* had shared. He'd just sat back and done the taking. And, of course, *the lying*.

'But, as I said, for very many reasons, what we have is no more and cannot be resurrected.' He looked down, lush dark lashes concealing his expression.

'Of course,' Cordelia expanded coolly, 'as you mentioned, I don't belong here.'

'Cordelia, it's slightly more than that.'

'What more could there be, Luca?' She paused and looked at him in stony silence. 'If I'm not a gold-digger, then I'm a sad, love-struck ex who was so desperate to live a little that she decided to show up, unannounced, on the doorstep of a guy who walked away from her without a backward glance. I don't know which is worse. Oh, no. I *do* know. They're both bad.'

'I am destined to marry a woman I have known from my childhood.' Why bother going round the houses? He watched as the colour drained away from her face.

'You're *engaged*?'

'Not as such.' Luca flushed darkly and looked away from her accusing gaze.

'What does that mean?'

'It is an understanding.'

'I see.' It was a mistake coming after all. He was engaged to be married. The outcome couldn't have been worse for her. To be faced with a baby bombshell would be his ugliest nightmare and she couldn't do that to him. The giddiness was growing and the spinning in her head made her want to close her eyes but she gritted her teeth together and remained present.

'I don't think you do.'

'You're going to be married and yet you led me to believe...you let me think...'

'No rings were exchanged. You misunderstand.'

'I don't believe I do.'

'It was always an understanding between families. A marriage of convenience. Isabella belongs to a dynasty like mine and the union would secure an estate of unimaginable wealth.'

'Right. What could be better than that? Who, in their right mind, would refuse unimaginable wealth?'

Luca shook his head in frustration. 'You're not getting it. I...when you met me, I was in a weird place. I knew that the time for this marriage was fast approaching but I was reluctant to commit to that final step. I needed to think.' He pressed the pads of his thumbs against his eyes and then looked at her wearily.

For a second, just a second, Cordelia could sense his confusion and she felt a tug of sympathy for a man trapped by his elevated birth, more trapped than she had ever been, then her sympathy vanished and she hardened her jaw because she was in an impossible situation and he had lied to her.

'And do you...love her?'

'Love? What are you talking about?'

'I'm just asking a question.'

'Love has nothing to do with this arrangement,' Luca said matter-of-factly.

'Poor woman.'

'Isabella?' His voice held surprise.

'Does she know what she's letting herself in for?'

'We are tremendously well suited.' They were. They looked the part and they certainly belonged together. That was a given.

Yet his thoughts sped back to those heady three weeks when he had been just an ordinary person with no expectations weighing on his shoulders, free to enjoy life in all its wonderful simplicity. Free to enjoy the woman staring at him as though she didn't quite recognise the man sitting in front of her.

Cordelia was hearing him but she had stopped taking in precisely what he was saying.

He was getting married. There were no rings on fingers yet, but he was getting married and he'd known that when they had slept together. He had truly only seen what they'd enjoyed as something passing and she knew that, while she had said all the right things, while she had assured him that she, likewise, knew the rules of the game, in her heart she had started hoping for more.

Maybe he didn't love the woman whose finger was destined to wear his ring, but they were tremendously well suited. Cordelia wasn't sure quite what that meant, but there had been affection in the tenor of his voice and affection was only a heartbeat away from love.

At any rate, it was a heck of a lot more than he felt *for her*. She thought of the baby she was carrying.

In her enthusiasm to get to Italy and tell Luca about the pregnancy, Cordelia had not been thinking straight and she could see that now. She'd never, of course, thought that Luca might have been lying to her. She'd also, she now realised with dismay, nurtured a certain excitement about seeing him again, even though he hadn't glanced back in her direction. She'd cherished the wild hope that they might recapture what they'd had, that he might actually *want* the baby she was carrying. She'd been swept away by happy-ever-after fantasies and now that all those fantasies had been exposed for what they were, she was desperate to leave.

She was going to keep this secret to herself. She would never hide his identity from the child they shared and in due course, if he or she wanted to meet him, then she wouldn't prevent it. By that time Luca would be happily married and a child he had sired as a youthful mistake before getting married would not be the catastrophe it would be now.

She stood up, keen to leave, thoughts in a confusing, sickening muddle, and felt the ground sway gently under her.

She held the back of the chair to steady herself and was vaguely aware of him shooting to his feet as she turned away, eyes fixed on the door.

'Cordelia…!'

When she looked up it was to find him standing right in front of her, his eyes filled with concern.

'You're as white as a sheet.' He placed his hands on her arms and she shrugged them off but she didn't say anything because her mouth was refusing to co-operate. 'Look at me,' he commanded, tilting her head so that she had no option but to do as he'd asked although her eyes, when they met his, were mutinous. 'I want you to sit back down. Have you eaten anything in the last few hours? I get that all this will be a shock to you but there was no point in keeping anything back, in giving you false hope.'

'Leave me alone, Luca. I just want to go. I should never have come here in the first place.'

'If things had been different...' he said roughly.

'If things had been different...*what*, Luca?'

'The time we spent together was special to me.'

'I'm thrilled to hear that,' Cordelia told him acidly. The swaying had stopped but she still felt giddy, as though she'd been flying on a roller coaster and now the ride had stopped but her head was still spinning.

He had softened his hold on her and as their eyes tangled he gently and absently began to massage her shoulder with his hand, slow rhythmic motions that shot straight to every nerve ending in her body with devastating effect. Her eyes widened in horror at her treacherous body and she began to take a step back to break the connection that had sprung up between them, but she just couldn't seem to do it. Her feet were nailed to the ground. It was a struggle to do anything. Breathing was proving a problem, never mind anything else.

'I have never been the man I was with you, with any other woman,' he said in a roughened undertone. 'I have never *wanted* any other woman the way I wanted you.' His eyes dropped to her full mouth and the connection she was desperately trying to sever took on a life force of its own.

He traced the outline of her mouth with the tip of his finger and she breathed in sharply.

He was going to kiss her. She could feel it in the simmering intensity of his gaze. It was the last thing she wanted! She opened her mouth to protest and her whole body shuddered as his lips touched hers, gently at first but then with increasing hunger.

Cordelia curved against him. His lean, hard muscularity felt so wonderfully familiar. He'd been her first and only lover and she had traced the contours of his perfect body with such awe that he used to laugh at her enthusiasm.

It took more willpower than she knew she even possessed to flatten her palms against his chest and detach herself from his devouring caress.

She was shaking when she stepped back. She could barely look him in the eye and he seemed to have as much of a problem holding her gaze. As he should, she thought bitterly. She'd succumbed to a moment of uncontrollable desire but she was free, single and unattached. It went utterly against the grain but she wasn't the one about to go shopping for engagement rings!

'I have to go,' she half muttered.

'I still want you.'

'You're practically married!' She flung him a look filled with accusation.

What did his fiancée-to-be look like? she wondered. It was an arranged marriage, if he was to be believed, and who could believe a guy who'd lied once? She drew some comfort from the thought that the woman in question might just be nothing much to look at and then hated herself for allowing her thoughts to travel down that uncharitable route.

Since Luca could hardly deny that reality, he maintained a tactful silence. The taste of her mouth was still on his, though, sending his thoughts into wild disarray. He didn't want to notice anything about her but he was noticing everything, from the slight tremor rippling through her long body to the strands of white-blonde hair escaping to brush against her cheek. He wanted to touch so badly that he had to bunch his hands into fists to stop himself from reaching forward.

'Are you in love with her?' Cordelia whispered, hating the way she wanted an answer to that question, even if the answer might be as painful as having a knife twisted in her gut.

Luca remained silent. Where was the point in going down this road? It was as it was.

'That question is inappropriate,' he finally said, when she continued to look at him with huge, accusing, wounded eyes.

Cordelia shrugged. The giddy feeling was sweeping over her again. Of course he loved the woman. He just didn't want to come right out and admit it because to do so would have been conclusive proof of the cad he really was and there wasn't a man in the world who would voluntarily have chosen to hang that description round his neck if he could avoid doing so.

The picture building in her head was not an attractive one.

He'd gone sailing in his expensive toy on one last adventure as a free man before he tied the knot. She'd happened to walk slap bang into his path and he'd thought... *Why not?*

She'd utterly and completely misread him. She knew that she could no longer weakly try and give him the benefit of the doubt. The fact that he refused to deny that the woman he was betrothed to marry was more than just a convenient wife said it all.

She had to get out of his great big palace of a house

because it was pressing down on her, making her feel nauseous.

She thought of the baby inside her and the utter mess she had walked into and suddenly, without warning, she could feel herself falling and it was the most peculiar sensation.

It was as though she had left her body and was looking down at herself. Looking at the way her legs began to weaken and her eyes began to droop and her shoulders slumped and then her whole body went limp and slowly, oh, so slowly, she crumpled to the ground like a marionette whose strings had been cut.

He caught her before she hit the ground. Even as she briefly lost consciousness, she was aware of his arms around her waist and of him carrying her urgently over to a sofa.

Her eyes fluttered open and she shrank back because he was so close to her that the smell of him filled her nostrils and made her feel faint all over again.

'You're in shock,' he said. She began sitting up and he gently kept her still, his eyes anxiously scanning her face. 'You're not going to be getting up just yet. I don't want you fainting again.'

'I never faint.'

'I'm going to argue with that statement, considering I've just caught you before you hit the ground. Wait here. I'll be back in five.' He vaulted to his feet but stayed where he was for a few seconds, as though making sure she obeyed him.

Much as Cordelia wanted to run as fast as she could to the door and then make a bolt for it, she felt as weak as a kitten.

She was in shock. He was right. She sighed and lay

back, closing her eyes and blocking out the sight of his tall, commanding figure.

She only opened her eyes when she heard the soft pad of his returning footsteps. In his hand he carried a glass of amber liquid and he positioned himself on the very edge of the sofa and gently placed his hand under the nape of her neck.

'You need to drink this.'

'What is it?' she whispered.

'Brandy. It'll do the trick.'

Cordelia whipped her head to one side.

'Drink it, *cara*. It'll make you feel better and then I'll make sure you have a bed here for the night. I know this is probably not the outcome you envisaged when you began your trip over here, but…like I said…'

'I'm not drinking any of that stuff.'

'For God's sake. I'm trying to *help* you. You're deathly white!'

'I can't drink it!' The words were out before she could claw them back and he stared at her, puzzled.

'Why not?'

'Because…it wouldn't be a good idea…'

'Why not?'

'Because I'm pregnant.'

She hadn't meant to say that. She'd decided, just as soon as she'd heard about his soon-to-be engagement to the woman who came from the same background as him and was his perfect match, that silence was the only option, but here, on his sofa, with legs like jelly, staring at a glass of brandy, the admission could not be stopped.

Maybe in her heart, she thought, she'd come to tell him about the pregnancy and she would have ended up doing so, whatever the circumstances.

A silence, thick with unspoken questions, settled between them as he stared at her with narrowed, incredulous eyes.

He wasn't taking any of it in and she could hardly blame him. In all those scenarios he had concocted explaining why she had travelled to Italy, none of them had touched on what should have been a likely contender.

'I'm sorry. I don't think I heard what you just said.'

'I'm sorry, Luca. I didn't come over here to try and resurrect a relationship with you because I discovered you had money and I didn't come to resurrect it because I stupidly decided that I just couldn't live another minute without you. I apologise if I've dented your ego. I came because I found out that I was pregnant a few days ago and I thought I owed it to you to tell you that you were going to be a father.'

The silence continued to coalesce. She couldn't look at him. She didn't want to see the horror there.

'You're lying,' Luca said hoarsely. 'That can't be... true.'

Cordelia sneaked a glance. He was ashen. He was also staring at her but she could tell that he wasn't really seeing her. He was seeing the nightmare scenario in his head. She watched as he sprang back to begin pacing the room, his movements, for once, lacking their usual grace.

Still muggy, she heaved herself into a sitting position and took a few deep breaths to steady herself.

His restless pacing was making her dizzy and yet, while he was walking, he wasn't talking and she dreaded hearing the dark, disbelieving and horrified timbre of his voice.

'I don't believe you,' he finally said, pausing to stand in front of her, then dragging a chair towards the sofa so that he could sit, interrogation style, directly in her line of vision. 'You can't be. We...were careful. We took all the necessary precautions. This can't be true.' He narrowed his eyes and stared at her and she could almost see the way his mind was working, shying away from the truth, finding other paths to follow.

She wasn't entirely surprised when he said, bluntly, 'Is this some kind of ploy to get money out of me? Because if it is, then it's not going to work.'

'We're back to that, are we?'

'A fake pregnancy is the oldest trick in the book.' But she wasn't lying. Luca knew that in the very depth of his being. She wasn't like that. She was achingly honest and if she had travelled all this way to tell him that she was carrying his baby, then carrying his baby she was.

Right in front of him, the world was falling apart at the seams.

'Remember that first time?' Cordelia asked. She felt too tired to argue with him about whether she was pretending to be pregnant or not. It was ridiculous that he would even allow his thoughts to travel along those lines but, then again, who was to say how he really thought? Who he really was?

'I remember.'

'We were on the beach. Well, we weren't exactly careful then, were we?'

'I... Jesus... I... We... No, I took chances. I took a chance.' He flushed darkly as he relived every second of that mind-blowing experience. He'd been so turned on—and she'd been lying there, as tempting as a siren and he'd thought…that he would get away with it. No, that was a lie. The truth was that he hadn't thought at all. Her tightness had wrapped around his erection, rubbing it into a frenzied state of arousal, and he had exploded inside her.

His groin ached as he thought about it and he could feel his libido shoot into the stratosphere without warning.

Utterly inappropriate.

'You show up here, out of the blue…naturally, I would want confirmation…'

Cordelia shrugged. 'Why would I come all the way over here to lie to you about something like that? Don't you think that it's something that could be easily disproved if I were making it all up? One trip down to the local chemists would be all it would take.' She sighed and cast her eyes around the lavish room, so in keeping with the lavishness of the house and the stunning splendour of the limitless vineyards stretching into the blue horizon.

The giddiness had eased and her mind felt clear for the first time since she had found out that she was pregnant.

'What happened between us was a mistake,' she told him quietly. He was so ridiculously good-looking that she could barely allow her gaze to settle on him for too long. Look for too long and her mind started playing cruel tricks on her, started travelling down memory lane, and that was never going to do. 'You swept into my life and I guess it was just the extraordinary nature of the circumstances that brought you there, and the fact that you were so…so different from everyone and everything I'd ever known, that combined to undermine all the principles I'd lived by. I'd longed for adventure and, suddenly, there you were, just about as adventurous as they came. I admit that I was a little sad when you left, Luca…' she paused and took a deep breath, making sure that, whatever happened, she left with her dignity intact '…but not sad enough to come all the way over here in an attempt to seduce you back into a relationship.'

Luca scowled. Contained in that explanation was an insult although he couldn't quite put his finger on it, or on why he should feel so piqued.

'So you said.'

'It's understandable,' she mused softly. 'You were my first lover.'

'Your *first lover*?' Luca wanted to scoff, because, in his world, virgins were as rare as hen's teeth, but then he remembered the feel of her, that tightness. And more than that, he remembered what she had been like, skittish and shy, giving and then retreating, at once eager and timid. 'I would have known.'

'There's no point talking about that.' She waved aside his interruption. 'I came here because I thought you ought to know. I never expected to find what I did and I certainly never thought that I would be sitting here, explaining this situation to a guy about to tie the knot.'

Luca shifted uncomfortably. He thought of Isabella and the neatly parcelled future that had been lying in store for him.

'This is a mess,' he muttered.

Cordelia reddened. 'Not for you,' she said coolly.

'How so?'

'I'm not asking anything of you. I plan on going back to Cornwall and, of course, if you ever want to come and see your child, then you would be welcome, but that's as far as it goes when it comes to my expectations of you.'

'You're kidding, right?' he said incredulously.

'No, Luca, I'm not. In fact, the minute I heard that you were about to get married…'

'No one's bought a hat yet! Isabella has always been destined to be my wife. I am now thirty-four years old and the time has come. At this point it is an understanding rather than an arrangement with a fixed date.'

'Whatever. The fact remains that the minute you told me about…about… Isabella…' she could barely get the name out '… I made up my mind to leave without saying anything at all, but then I fainted and when you offered me that brandy, I thought of the baby and out it all came.' She shifted. 'But I don't intend to stick around here, *messing up* your life. I'm going to head back home and, like I said, you can do whatever you want to do.' She began getting to her feet.

'You're not going anywhere,' Luca gritted.

'I'm fine. I won't be fainting again, trust me. I'm as strong as an ox.'

'Repeat, you're not going anywhere. You don't get to drop a bombshell in my life and then tell me that you're going to walk away as though nothing's happened.'

'I don't like the word *bombshell*.'

'And I'm not particularly in love with the notion of being a daddy in nine months' time, but there we have it. You're going to sit back down and we're going to discuss what happens next in this scenario.' His eyes involuntarily flickered to her stomach.

Fatherhood had always been something vague on the horizon. Naturally, he would have a child, preferably a son. It would all be part of the destiny lying in wait for him. Marriage to Isabella and the uniting of two great Italian families. Then a child, an heir to the throne, so to speak. Like him, Isabella would do what was expected and nothing beyond that. They were both very well aware of the circumstances of their individual situations and accepting of it. They were on the same page when it came to their future.

All pre-planned, laid out with precision. No room for emotion. It was the way he liked it anyway. He didn't believe in getting carried away. Love, and all the disorderly chaos it entailed, had never been for him. He'd seen too much and witnessed too much. Nothing good ever came from yielding to emotion and allowing it to carry you away until you became a helpless object, drifting wherever it decided to take you. His father had allowed emotion to dictate his life. His ex-wives...the constant upheavals...the shouting and crying and then the vindictiveness born from relationships gone sour. Too much.

And then his mother. He thought of his mother. He thought of the hole she had left in his father's life. And in his own. He would never revisit any situation that could put him in that distressing and vulnerable place again. If he could control his emotions, he could control his life. Control. That was what Isabella would bring to the table. He knew where he stood with her.

The woman looking at him in stubborn silence was the very opposite of Isabella. She'd brought out something in him that had been free and reckless and unchained and there was no place for that man here, in Italy. That man belonged back in Cornwall.

Did she think that she would find that man again? If so, she was very much mistaken. The Luca Baresi who lived here was not that man, which didn't mean that he could cheerfully send her on her way, not now that she had lit that fuse under him, a fuse that would spark a fire that would gobble up everything he knew and every plan he had ever made.

'I told you—' Cordelia began.

'I heard every word you said,' he murmured smoothly, 'and now you're going to hear every word I have to say.'

CHAPTER SIX

'FIRST OF ALL I will need to have the pregnancy confirmed. I have a trusted doctor.'

'I don't see the point. I'm not lying and I don't want anything from you. If you choose to disbelieve me, then that's okay. I will have done what I came to do and I'll leave here with a clear conscience.' She burned with curiosity about this woman he had chosen to be his future wife. Were they lovers? She didn't want to let her mind drift down those disturbing paths but she couldn't block out images of him with another woman. Her hormones were all over the place and just thinking those thoughts brought the sting of tears to her eyes.

'Provided there is a confirmed pregnancy, the announcement of our marriage will…not be a straightforward affair.'

Cordelia's mouth fell open and she stared at him in astonishment. He didn't notice. He was frowning, thinking, calculating. She realised that he was working out how to deal with the mess that had landed on his lap.

But *marriage*?

'I will have to convene a family meeting,' he continued, still seemingly oblivious to her gaping incredulity. He was thinking aloud and she could have been a potted plant in the corner of the room for all the attention he was paying to her. She was a problem that had to be addressed and he was in the process of addressing it.

'"Convene a family meeting"?' she asked, when in fact the question on the tip of her tongue was, *Marriage? Are you insane? What on earth are you talking about?*

'Firstly, I will, of course, have to break the news to my father.'

It struck Luca that his father was probably not going to hit the roof, contrary to what everyone else might expect. He knew his father. Giovanni Baresi, like the entire Russo clan, of whom Isabella was one of four daughters, expected him to marry into the other great Italian winery. Celebrations might not be afoot just yet but once the expected announcement was made, and everyone knew that that time was just round the corner because neither he nor Isabella were getting any younger, then preparations would move swiftly and smoothly. The wedding of the decade would be arranged with the exquisite perfection of a highly organised military campaign.

His father had talked about this arranged marriage recently, before departing on his extended holiday. There had been pressure but the pressure had been slight.

An arranged marriage. What suited him from an emotional point of view, not to mention financial point of view, was, deep down, anathema to a man like Giovanni Baresi, who had always enjoyed the highs and lows of an emotional-roller-coaster personal life. His great love had died too young but that had not stopped him from searching for its replacement in every unsuitable nook and cranny.

It had been enough to turn Luca off the whole messy business of falling in love for ever, which was something he suspected his father had never really understood.

So to have the news broken to him that his son had got a girl pregnant because he had been careless, had behaved out of character, would probably bring a sheen to the old man's eyes.

Luca would have to quench any romantic visions his father might have with brutal finality.

Then he would have to break the glad tidings to Isabella and finally to her parents.

Then the whole world would know and another, different life would begin for him.

He thought of Cornwall and the free, wild girl without make-up and he wondered how she would cope with life in Italy. He concluded, before that thought could go anywhere, that she would cope just fine because she would have limitless supplies of money and that always oiled the nuts and bolts of any discomfort.

He focused on her and narrowed his eyes because she was hardly looking as though she'd won the lottery.

'This won't be running along the normal lines,' he informed her with clipped gravity. 'There is a lot of unravelling that will have to take place. Unpicking expectations will always be a nightmare and expectations about my eventual nuptials with Isabella have long been embedded. Naturally, there will be disappointment all round. Tell me, how did your father take the news?'

Cordelia hadn't managed to squeeze a word out. Her head was buzzing. She felt as though she'd been whipped into some other parallel universe, the rules of which she didn't know and the scenery was not one with which she was familiar.

'My father?' she parroted weakly, clinging to the one thing he'd said that made any sense.

'Was he…surprised? I don't suppose…' Luca had the grace to flush '…it was what might have been expected of you.'

'He…he doesn't know.' She blushed and looked away.

'I'm sorry,' Luca said gruffly and her eyes shot towards him.

She heard the rough sincerity in his voice and for a split second remembered the guy she had given herself to. He hadn't been this cold-eyed stranger. He'd been the guy who had just told her that he was sorry.

'Don't be. Things happen. You can't always predict the future.' She cleared her throat. His gaze on her was making her uncomfortable, reminding her of sensations that were no longer appropriate. She sternly told herself that it was precisely because of how he had made her feel that she had ended up here.

'Actually,' Luca confessed, 'I've always prided myself on being able to do just that.'

'In which case, I should be the one apologising.'

'For leading me astray?' His eyebrows shot up and the taut cast of his features relaxed into something approaching a smile. 'As they say, it takes two to tango and I was very much a willing dance partner.'

A sudden sense of danger rippled through her. The hairs on the back of her neck were standing on end and there was a tingle between her legs, a shameful feminine awareness that felt utterly inappropriate given the circumstances.

'I...' She cleared her throat to get a grip and directed her thoughts to her poor dad, who had been handed over to the safekeeping of his arch nemesis, Doris. 'I plan on telling him when I...get back...'

'This situation is pretty messy for both of us, isn't it?' Luca said quietly. 'How did you manage to get away? I was under the impression that he had quite a hold over you.'

Cordelia shot Luca a wry look from under her lashes. When they weren't talking about the pregnancy, she could feel herself noticeably relax even though asking about her father wasn't so much changing the subject as circling around it.

'I...it's a long story.'

'I'm all ears.'

'One of the women in the village happened to be in the very same chemist's a million miles away from home where I went to buy a...er...test. I didn't want to be spotted by anyone I knew and there was no way I could go to the local pharmacy, not unless I wanted the news to be shouted from the rooftops before I got to the end of the street.'

'And as luck would have it...?'

Cordelia nodded. Their eyes met and for a few seconds, neither looked away. Her heart was thumping like a sledgehammer and a fine perspiration had broken out all over her. She wanted to tear her eyes away but she couldn't and, in fact, he was the one to break eye contact, a dark flush spreading over his high cheekbones as he did so.

'As luck would have it,' she repeated breathlessly.

She sucked in some air and steadied herself. 'The thing is, Doris isn't just any old nosey parker. She's had her eye on teaming up with Dad for ages, years, and she used the opportunity when she realised what was going on to nudge her way past the front door.'

'Surely you could have laughed and told her that it was for someone else.'

'I could have but I guess I just wasn't thinking straight at the time. I was so nervous. Petrified, as a matter of fact.'

Luca didn't say anything. He'd made a deal of his own life being irrevocably altered. He'd used expressions that she had found objectionable. Yet she, likewise, was facing the same life-changing event but had risen above the negativity to a place of acceptance.

Right now, he didn't feel great about himself but how was he to suspect, when she walked through that door, the reason for her sudden appearance? And it was perfectly understandable, surely, if he happened to be a bit tactless in his summary of the situation, given the fact that he had had zero time to digest what she had come to tell him.

And yet...

Something about the purity of her gaze and the wrenching honesty of her approach shamed him.

'There's no need to be petrified,' he murmured as he settled into the idea of a different life from the one to which he had resigned himself.

For one split second, he felt something that almost resembled elation, then it was gone, replaced by a far more prosaic take on what was unfolding in front of him. The horror, he had to admit, had subsided. He could only conclude that this was what was meant by thinking on your feet and adapting to a situation that had sprung from nowhere and wasn't going to go away. There would be consequences, not least the financial ones that would have benefited the union of two great wine-producing houses, but he would face those down and, more importantly, he would do so without grudging resentment. He would man up. He was good at that. He'd been doing it since he was a kid, when his mother had died and he'd been left in a wilderness.

'At least, not now.'

'You mean...' The weird marriage conversation began replaying in her head and she stared at him.

'Tomorrow, I will begin the process of breaking the news to all parties concerned.'

'Luca, no.' Cordelia felt that she had to interject before he got carried away. 'I didn't come here looking for...for that kind of solution.' She thought of the mysterious, wonderfully suited fiancée he had conveniently failed to tell her about and, just in case he started getting all the wrong ideas, added, 'We both agreed that what we had was just something that happened in the moment. We both agreed that we weren't, fundamentally, suited to one another. I know things have changed with this...situation...but it doesn't mean that we have to start thinking about getting hitched, because we don't. I am very happy for our child to have an ongoing relationship with you, which doesn't mean that *I* have to as well. And marrying you isn't going to do anything for my apprehension levels. You're not a knight in shining armour riding in on a white stallion to save me.'

'*Cara*, there is no option, I'm afraid.'

Cordelia stared at him and wondered how she'd managed to miss just how old-fashioned he must be, because no one in this day and age thought that a pregnancy had to be accompanied by a walk down the aisle.

Even in the village where she lived, Marsha Hall had had her baby out of wedlock and not too many eyebrows had been raised.

'What do you mean?'

'Maybe in your world,' he said gently, 'it is acceptable for a woman to have a baby while simultaneously relegating the father of the baby to the nearest wayside bin, but that's not how it works in my world.'

'Whoever said anything about wayside bins?' Cordelia questioned faintly.

'Provided, of course, that everything checks out, you will be having my baby and my baby will become the heir to...' he looked around him in the manner of a warrior casually surveying the fruit of his many conquests '...all of this. As an only child, it fell upon me to take up the mantle of responsibility, to do as duty dictated, and so it will be for my son. Or daughter, of course.'

'Sorry, but there are two of us involved in this equation, Luca. This child isn't exclusively *yours* and it's not a given that his or her future is to patiently do as told because that's what duty demands! Besides...' she narrowed shrewd eyes on his lean, handsome face '...weren't you trying to run away from all that wonderful duty of yours when you got caught out in that storm?'

Luca had the grace to flush. 'I don't like the term *run away.*'

'You know what I mean.' Cordelia clicked her tongue impatiently.

'I was having a bit of time out from my responsibilities. Everyone needs a holiday now and again.'

'It wasn't *a holiday*, Luca. Holidays are those things

people take when they want to kick back and, most of the time, they don't involve doing a disappearing act from the rest of the world and then faking their identity so that they don't get caught out. Holidays are things that are booked in advance and everyone knows about them.'

'Since when did you get so argumentative?'

'Do you want to think about any child of yours being so harnessed to a yoke of responsibility that the only way to escape it is to disappear on a boat in the middle of the ocean where there are no prying eyes and no one telling them what needs to be done next?'

'There is a lot of exaggeration in that statement,' Luca said stiffly.

'I don't have the same aims as you, Luca, and I don't like to think that any child of mine would have the same aims as you.'

'We're going to be married, Cordelia. My child... *our* child is going to be born into the Baresi family.'

'You're not being reasonable.' Cordelia could hear the slight tremor in her voice. She had come here to deliver a message. She hadn't dwelled on what the outcome of that message might be. Maybe, deep down, she had romantically dreamed of him telling her how much he'd missed her, welcoming the news about the baby, seeing it as an opportunity to resume what they had so prematurely brought to an end. She would, naturally, express misgivings. After all, he *had* walked away from her without looking back, but he would persist and she would succumb.

Admittedly, the daydreams had been unbelievably rosy hued, but even in those rosy-hued daydreams she had never thought that he would propose to her and certainly not a proposal as an arrangement, not unlike the nature of the one he had earmarked for his childhood sweetheart, if that was what she had been. He had been ready to marry for money, whichever way you looked at it, but then she had come along with news of a pregnancy and now he was ready to marry for the sake of the baby.

Luca Baresi did marriages of convenience but he didn't do marriages based on love and that was what her hungry, romantic heart craved. Since when had it ever been her dream to be someone's convenient bride?

'When I marry,' she murmured huskily, 'I want it to be for love.'

'Life is full of unfulfilled dreams.' Luca shrugged. 'I find it pays to adhere strictly to reality. You will have to break the news to your father and I will understand if you want to do so face to face, but can I trust you to return to Cornwall and not refuse to come back here? Probably not, which is why I will be more than happy to make arrangements for him to join us out here.' Luca paused. 'Rest assured he will travel in the very best possible style.'

'He can't leave his work!' Cordelia gasped. 'Nor would he want to!'

'Then you'll have to relay the news over the telephone.'

'You can't hold me prisoner here.'

'Is that what you think I would be doing?'

'What else, Luca?'

'Let's focus on one thing at a time, *cara*.' He flipped his mobile phone out and dialled, speaking in rapid Italian, not a word of which Cordelia understood. That, in itself, only served to make her feel even more disoriented. When the call was over, he sat back and looked at her with a shuttered expression.

'Tomorrow,' he announced, 'we will visit my consultant. Only then will any serious conversations begin...'

Within twenty-four hours, Cordelia realised that by *serious* Luca had actually meant *boardroom-formal*.

She had shown little resentment at having to prove to Luca what she knew to be the case. She was pregnant. She could have suggested taking a simple test— another one—but if he wanted to involve a consultant, then he would whether she did a thousand tests or not.

Along with the fact that he was not the man he'd said he was, she was discovering all kinds of sides to his personality that had not been at the forefront when they had had their brief, heady affair.

He was stubborn, proud, ridiculously traditional. He was also a man who expected to get exactly what he wanted and what he wanted was his child, with her as the price he would pay to achieve that.

The second the pregnancy had been confirmed, he had ushered her out into the fading sunshine, straight into the passenger seat of his low, sleek sports car and from there directly back to his mansion. Nothing had been said on the drive. He'd been thinking. She could sense that. As for the direction of his thoughts... Cordelia could only guess but, whatever she'd come up with, she had a suspicion that it would only cover part of the ground.

She'd reminded herself that it didn't matter what he was thinking because he couldn't force her to do anything she didn't want to do, and what she didn't want to do was marry a guy for all the wrong reasons.

Still, her stomach had been tightly clenched with nerves by the time they had arrived back at his house and he'd ushered her through the front door and into a kitchen that was as big as a ballroom and just as grand.

Had she decided about her father? he'd asked. Bring him over or deliver the news via phone? He would give her a night to mull it over and to digest the direction her life would now be taking. She was free as a bird to explore every nook and cranny of the house. It was, however, late. He would instruct the resident housekeeper to deliver her food to her bedroom. He, meanwhile, had phone calls to make but he would see her first thing in the morning for breakfast and they would begin their discussions about the future they would now be sharing.

If he had hoped to soothe her frayed nerves, he'd definitely gone about it the wrong way. She had barely been able to enjoy the lavish pasta meal that had been delivered to her door at a little after eight by a shy young girl who had practically genuflected as she'd revealed the elaborate meal she had wheeled in on a super-sized trolley.

Cordelia had tossed and turned, thinking about how she was going to handle the forthcoming conversation.

Now, here she was, summoned by the very same shy young girl who had delivered her meal the previous evening and taken through the vast, echoing mansion to a sitting room where a selection of breads, cold meats and cheeses were waiting, on a highly polished sideboard, to be sampled.

The appetite that had deserted her the evening before enthusiastically responded to the tempting spread and she was slapping way too much butter on some sourdough bread when she heard the door behind her being pushed open.

She spun round as though yanked by invisible strings and inhaled sharply at Luca, who was standing by the door, one brown hand resting light on the doorknob.

He looked stunning. When did he ever disappoint on that front? she reflected a little sourly.

On every other front, he had come up short, but when it came to looks, he continued to deliver with a punch.

'Good,' he opened, strolling towards her and looking at her plate with satisfaction, 'you're eating. Better than last night.'

'What are you talking about?' Strings cut, her legs remembered what they were there for and she walked towards the small circular table by the bay window, which overlooked the swathes of grapevines.

It was the most relaxing view she had ever had. The sea, in all its glory, was fascinating and ever changing, roaring with black anger one minute, as flat and as calm as a sheet of glass the next. But this was so still, so perfectly peaceful.

It was a reminder of just why she had always craved escape from the narrow confines of her life. To taste all the different things the world had to offer. It was unfortunate that her first taste had been offered to her in the way it had.

She looked at him with guarded eyes as he sat opposite her with a plate of breads and cheese. It was a small table. She could reach out and touch him if she wanted.

'Sylviana reported back to me, as duly requested.'

'You're now spying on my eating habits?'

'You're carrying my baby. Everything you do now is of importance to me.' He paused and looked at her, taking everything in. Luca wasn't a fool. He knew he had to tread gently, manoeuvre the situation with the agility and expertise of someone navigating a minefield.

She wasn't like any other woman he had ever known. She was like quicksilver. Money didn't interest her, which was something he had found incredibly appealing and frankly still did, it would seem. She had laughed off his marriage proposal because love wasn't on the table. Cold logic dictated that he pay close attention to that line of reasoning. Women always wanted more than he was prepared to give on the emotional front and, even though she had made it perfectly clear that she had never seen them as anything other than a couple of people who'd had a bit of fun, an enjoyable no-strings fling that had escalated into the unthinkable because of the pregnancy…who knew…?

Was the silent rider to his proposal that she would accept if there was a courtship involved? Did she think that the only way for them to have a permanent relationship would be if they aimed for the fairy-tale ending where he looked soulfully into her eyes and promised her the earth? Did she secretly crave what every other woman craved, aside from Isabella, which was what had made her so suitable a marriage prospect? That gradual breaking down of all defences until you were left as raw, vulnerable and exposed as a mollusc without its shell?

It wasn't going to happen and Luca knew that he had to work his way carefully around that while still getting her on board with the marriage idea, because married they were going to be.

His eyes lingered for a few seconds on her and he found himself staring.

That face of hers. Strong-boned, free of make-up,

healthy and without artifice. Her hair was plaited. Just
the one plait, which she had dragged over her shoulder.
The vibrancy of her blonde hair stood out even more
over here in a country where most of the women were
brunettes.

He felt his pulse pick up speed and a dragging in his
groin. He'd spent the night thinking of her, working out
a future that he hadn't bargained for. He'd thought of
her and had felt the same ache, reminding him that his
libido was all present and intact and had not been sated
since he had last slept with the woman now carefully
working her way through the various fresh breads she
had taken. He'd had a lot on his plate workwise and,
with Isabella looming on the horizon, he had not been
tempted to immerse himself in any kind of dating scene.

Marriage, he reflected, was not going to be all bad.
They would naturally share a bed and, while love in
all its nauseating complications wouldn't be part of the
equation, sex most definitely was going to be on the
menu, and the menu looked very tempting from where
he was sitting.

But, he reminded himself with baffled frustration,
nothing was going to be on any agenda until vows had
been exchanged. Right now, he would do well to keep
her at arm's length until the details had been sorted.

'I have already apprised my father of the situation.'

Cordelia looked at him in consternation. 'He must
have been devastated. All those plans made...' The
enormity of what Luca was prepared to sacrifice for
her made her suddenly uncomfortable with her stubborn refusal to play ball. Her head was pointing her in
one direction but her heart...what it wanted...

'Have you decided when you will tell your father?'

Cordelia shifted uneasily. Would a simple *'No'* sound too abrupt? It was so complicated, but then she thought of arrangements made from birth, a marriage understood, a future planned, the twinning of great fortunes and everything that came with that…all gone in a whoosh. For Luca, there would be devastation all round and not just for him, but for everyone associated with a marriage that would now never happen.

To his credit, he hadn't raged and stormed and if he'd used the vocabulary of shock, then who could blame him? He certainly didn't seem to be dwelling on the downsides of the situation and she could only reluctantly admire him for that.

'I plan on phoning him later…' she said vaguely.

'But you're not sure.'

'He needs to find out, of course he does.'

Luca sat back and looked at her thoughtfully, gauging the atmosphere, his antennae picking up on things that weren't being said, sensing her doubts and confusion and sympathetically understanding the reason behind them.

She was an innocent. She didn't have the tools at her disposal to deal with some of the things life decided to throw at you. He did. He knew the value of working with what couldn't be changed and then adding the upsides to the situation. It was the difference between winners and losers and he had always been a winner.

He winced. Unlike his father, who had actually congratulated him on living life properly for the first time.

'You have enough money for a thousand lifetimes,' Giovanni Baresi had bellowed down the phone, drowning out the disturbing sound of music and laughter in the background. 'Time you started really finding out what life's all about!'

That had been before he could tell his father that it wasn't the exalted love affair he seemed to believe it was, but an honest mistake that carried consequences. After that bracing, booming, slap-on-the-back response, Luca had held his tongue, and the weird thing was that there was a part of him that had been secretly pleased to have heard genuine admiration in his father's voice.

He had made more money for the family than could be counted in gold coins...he was respected and held in awe by financiers the world over...and yet, telling his dad that he had had a three-week fling with a girl in Cornwall, had got her pregnant and was going to marry her, had elicited more joy and pride than anything he had ever done in his life before.

'I want us to be married,' Luca began with rough sincerity. 'You think it's because I'm a dinosaur. You think I'm mired in pointless tradition that's past its sell-by date because who needs marriage these days when a baby is involved? There are countless single mothers bringing up kids while fathers get a look-in now and again before moving on to have their own families.'

He paused and Cordelia looked at him as his words sank in. Single mothers. Visiting fathers. And then, naturally, those visiting fathers would move on to per-haps have another family. She thought of Luca having children with another woman, Isabella. Children who would be born to roam on these vast estates while on the other side of the ocean...

Her heartbeat sped up and she gulped.

'And maybe,' he continued quietly, 'I *am* a little old-fashioned when it comes to family. Maybe it's beyond the pale to see duty and responsibility as things to be worn proudly on one's shoulders. Yes, I have sometimes yearned to be free to do whatever I want to do but, mostly, I have been content and proud of my heritage and my legacy. Is that a bad thing?'

Luca allowed the rhetorical question to hover in the silence between them.

'I will love our child with everything in me. I will protect him from every sling of every arrow and he, I feel, will learn to love his inheritance the way I have. You tell me that you can't consider marriage without love. Love you may not have, but respect you will, and in abundance.'

But he would never love her. He had just confirmed that, in case she started getting any ideas. She could see the way his brain was working. But was the search for love, if it ever happened anyway, enough to compensate for their child being torn apart from a father who dearly wanted him?

And what about *her* feelings for Luca? They ran deep. Deeper than he could ever imagine and it was no use pretending otherwise. Who would catch her when she was falling hard for a guy who wasn't going to be truly emotionally available to her? The balancing act between her head and her heart made her dizzy.

'And think of that one thing you've always wanted, Cordelia. To see the world. That would be what our child would have were we to marry. There would be no corner of the globe left unexplored. Great wealth, I'm driven to say, can buy travel to the four corners of the world...'

'I... I'll think about it,' Cordelia said helplessly, knowing that he had struck below the belt but unable to resist the glorious image of planes and ships and foreign lands and her child—*their* child—being exposed to all the adventure that went along with that, adventures she had never had.

'Say yes,' Luca urged, leaning forward and taking her fingers in his hand, an absent gesture that made her skin tingle with forbidden pleasure.

'But surely you would eventually resent me? Resent the fact that I had stopped you from marrying Isabella?'

'You haven't stopped me from doing anything,' Luca murmured. 'This decision is my choice. How could I resent you, that being the case? Say yes and here is what will happen next. I will tell Isabella and her family. Tomorrow. And then we will get your father over, tell him face to face. Together. But not just yet. In the meanwhile, I will show you my land, show you my country, show you…what our child will enjoy. What do you say, *mi tesoro*?'

Caught on the horns of a dilemma, she breathed in deeply and sank into the earnest intent in his eyes.

'Okay. I'll say yes—even though…'

'Shh.' He placed his finger over her mouth. 'Yes is enough. No need to qualify it.'

CHAPTER SEVEN

THE FOLLOWING DAY Luca had had his chauffeur drive him the lengthy three-hour round trip to Isabella's parents, where he'd presented the situation as a *fait accompli*, no questions asked, no room for manoeuvre.

He had sat in a living room as grand and as formal as his own, where he had been served delicate morsels and strong coffee in china cups and watched his hosts' disappointment as he'd broken the news. There had been no formal engagement but, between families, the unspoken understanding had been almost as strong, and, while they had politely congratulated him on a marriage no one had foreseen, they could scarcely contain the fact that they had been badly let down.

'It would have been so good for Isabella,' Maria, her mother, had said, shooting a glance at her husband, who had looked away. 'She...'

'Maria!' Alberto had said sharply. 'We do not need to trouble Luca with our regrets. It is as it is. Naturally, we will continue to work harmoniously together. Our great wines benefit from this close relationship, not to mention the other avenues for development that are in the making.' At which point he had ushered Luca to the cellar where he had shown him his addition of rare reds to the collection he already had.

Both Maria and Alberto were far too well bred to show any emotion and neither had he. It was as it was.

He was more concerned about Isabella. This marriage would have suited her but maybe, he'd thought, on his way back to his villa, it was fate. Perhaps she needed to find the courage to tell her parents about her sexuality instead of trying to hide behind a façade of a happy marriage.

He had, in fact, spoken to Isabella at length on the telephone on the way to her parents'. A face-to-face meeting was out of the question as she was holidaying with friends on the Riviera. He had smiled wryly at the relief in her voice when he had broken the news of his upcoming marriage to Cordelia. Let off the hook for the time being. Her congratulations had been sincere and heartfelt and when he had hung up, it had flashed through his head that neither Isabella nor Cordelia were what might be considered orthodox candidates for walking up the aisle.

One was relieved not to be doing so and the other was doing so only because all alternative exits had been barred. Money, it had to be said, definitely didn't buy love. Just as well, considering it wasn't something he was looking for.

That job over, here he was now, at ten the following morning, waiting at a chic café in the stunning city of Siena. He'd returned late the previous night to find Cordelia dead to the world in one of the guest bedrooms. He had left orders for her to be given whatever she wanted for breakfast and, at a little after six in the morning, he had taken himself off to his head office, where he had powered through key emails and filled various CEOs in on what might prove a temporarily disjointed work schedule.

A makeover for his reluctant wife-to-be was on the cards.

Then, once they were back at his house, a jeweller would be personally escorted on Luca's private plane so that a ring could be chosen.

She had taken some persuading to agree to marry him and he wasn't going to sit on his hands and hope she didn't change her mind. Speed was of the essence and he intended to put his foot on the accelerator until she was bound to him, with all i's dotted and t's crossed.

Woolly nonsense about love not being on the agenda was not going to be a spoke in any revolving wheels.

His father had offered to return to Tuscany immediately so that he could meet the lucky bride and Luca had only just managed to dissuade him, pointing out that it would be far better to wait a couple of weeks until she was fully settled before bombarding her with yet more stuff to confuse her.

'She's from another...er...' Luca had thought of her, her sinewy, purposeful body, her lightly freckled face bare of make-up, her hair hanging down her back in a riot of tangled curls, and the word *planet* had sprung to mind.

However, any such description wasn't going to do, he'd acknowledged, because his father truly thought that at long last his hard-nosed son had traded his head for his heart, and Luca had been strangely reluctant to disillusion him on that front.

'It's like me and your mother,' Giovanni Baresi had murmured in a trembling, emotional voice down the end of the phone line. 'Same part of the world, even. Oh, my dear, dear son...'

Luca had found it astonishing that, after the many conversations they had had over the years on the subject of relationships and Luca's outspoken disapproval of his father's antics, his father could still be swept away on a tide of emotion at the unrealistic assumption that his son had somehow managed to dispatch his brain on a long-distance holiday, leaving him vulnerable to the one thing he had always declared he didn't believe in.

Having allowed his father to think the wildly improbable, he had had to go with the flow. Likewise, for better or for worse, Isabella and her parents also nurtured thoughts of a love match. Isabella should have known better, considering they had discussed the suitability of a marriage of convenience, but there you had it.

Luca sighed and glanced at his watch.

Who believed what didn't matter anyway, so dwelling on it was a waste of time.

She was late.

He dialled her number and opened, without hesitation, 'Where are you?'

'I'm sorry,' Cordelia responded breathlessly. Sitting in the back seat of Luca's plush four-wheel drive, she could barely take in the splendid sights bypassing them as his driver whizzed along the deserted roads. Her head was moving left to right, her senses darting frantically so that she didn't miss a thing. 'I'm afraid I asked your driver to pull over a couple of times...well, maybe more than a couple, actually...'

'You were sick? Is there a problem?' Luca jerked into an upright position and wondered whether to video call her instead of talking down the end of a phone. So much more could be deciphered from looking at someone and Cordelia was certainly one of those people whose faces were as transparent as a sheet of glass. She wasn't the complaining sort but was there some kind of medical problem happening? He wondered how fast he could get his consultant over to his house.

'Oh, no,' Cordelia responded airily. 'It's just that the scenery is so breathtaking that I wanted to take some pics on my phone.'

Luca sagged with relief, then he clicked his tongue impatiently.

'My PA has set up appointments with the couturier,' he drawled.

'You never said.'

'I didn't think you would waste time stopping on the way for Kodak moments.'

'I still don't understand why I have to…have a change of wardrobe, Luca.'

'You're marrying me, *cara*. You will be entering a world that's far removed from the one you have always been accustomed to. It is just a question of assimilation.'

Cordelia didn't say anything. She had made her decision and she knew that he had a point. She could no longer hang around in jeans and tee shirts because she was no longer going to be living the life she had always lived. Close to the sea, barefoot on a beach, interacting with people who built lives around the ocean. She had dreamed of faraway adventure and now she had got what she'd always wanted, but that dream came at a price and it was too late to start quibbling about how high or low that price should be.

At least when she had earlier spoken to her dad, he hadn't sounded as anxious as she'd expected.

Lord knew, his anxiety levels would shoot through the roof when she broke the news to him about the pregnancy, but that was a bridge she was happy to cross a bit later.

She could only hope that Doris would keep quiet, but there was nothing she could do about that.

She resisted the urge to make Luca's driver stop again when they entered the city because it was so unimaginably beautiful.

The colours of sand and taupe, buildings that seemed to be carved from the earth, ornate, majestic and breathing an ancient history.

It felt as though, literally, she was entering a different world. She wanted to hop out of the car and begin exploring immediately. Instead, she poked her head through the window and tried hard to take it all in.

Regrettably, they were at the designated meeting spot all too soon for Cordelia's liking.

She tipped into the most amazing open space, a fan-shaped central square ringed by ancient medieval buildings with the occasional modern shop front as a token nod to the twenty-first century. A thin bell tower dominated the vast circle of old buildings and she took a few seconds out to gaze at it.

Luca was sitting outside the café, the name of which he had texted her. He was lounging back in a pair of grey chinos, a white short-sleeved linen shirt and dark designer sunglasses that inconveniently concealed his expression as she walked towards him.

He looked the very essence of sophisticated and laid-back, with an elegance that only money could buy.

No wonder he wanted her out of her uniform of jeans as fast as possible, she thought. He might have found that charming in Cornwall but it was definitely off limits here in his rich life and all that that rich life entailed.

She had a twinge of doubt. Was this really her? She had agreed to marry a guy who didn't love her. She had signed up to a life the rules of which she didn't know. Then she thought of the baby inside her and swallowed back all her fears and misgivings. She had to settle in one camp and put the pull-push feelings away. She also had to stop hoping for the impossible.

Their marriage might not be what she had had in mind for herself but, then again, neither had she ever contemplated the prospect of a pregnancy she hadn't planned and, while Luca might not love her, he had been prepared to sacrifice the direction of his own life to accommodate a situation that would have hit him as hard as it had hit her. That spoke volumes. That was enough because it would have to be enough.

She just couldn't deny their baby the huge advantages of inheriting a lineage that was rightfully his.

Step one would be to accept the path she had chosen without fuss. She wouldn't argue about everything and she wouldn't look further than what Luca could put on the table. She would also stop thinking about the woman he had walked away from, speculating on what he might or might not have felt for her, on what she might or might not look like.

Her future was starting this very moment and glancing over her shoulder wasn't going to do.

'You worried me when you told me that you'd asked Roberto to stop on the way here,' he opened, getting down to business straight away but unable to overlook the tug at his groin when he looked at her. Luca had never had a problem when it came to women and moving on, and he absently wondered whether the fact that she was pregnant with his child somehow accounted for the ongoing effect she seemed to be having on him.

'I'm sorry,' Cordelia parried stiffly as she sat on the chair next to him and facing out onto the square, which was great because it meant she didn't have to look at him, which was a disaster zone for her when it came to thinking clearly. 'I couldn't resist. I've never travelled abroad. It was all too much.' That admission of just how wildly different their worlds were brought a tinge of colour to her cheeks. 'If we're going to be late for...for whatever it is that you've arranged, then perhaps we should leave now.'

'They'll wait.' Luca shrugged. 'I thought all women enjoyed shopping and having things bought for them. You're acting as though I'm punishing you by getting you a new wardrobe. Whatever you want. You name it and it's yours.'

'We're so different, you and I,' Cordelia couldn't help but murmur, glancing across at him and then finding her gaze helplessly locked to his sharp, aristocratic profile.

'We are,' he agreed without hesitation. 'You're not going to start using our differences to return to the discussion about love and marriage, are you?'

'Of course not.'

'Good.' He removed the sunglasses to dangle them on one finger and glanced sideways at her.

So different.

Yet she had taken the plunge and was about to enter a world she would never have envisaged for herself. She would be buffed, polished and primed for life in the luxury lane and he felt that she might be scared stiff at that unknown future ahead of her. It was one thing to talk about exploring different shores. It was quite different when you found yourself dumped on one of those shores with the signposts all in a foreign language, far from everything that might feel familiar.

'This is going to work,' he told her firmly, voice low, waving aside a hovering waiter and standing because there was a lot to do.

'You can't say that.'

'Of course I can. I intend to be an excellent father and an excellent husband.'

'You don't love me.'

Luca cupped her elbow so that he could usher her into the square, away from the café and towards a corner in which was nestled an array of high-end shops, all peeking out from their grand façades of weathered, ochre-coloured brick.

'I will, however, respect you as the mother of my child. Likewise, you will find me a faithful husband.'

Looking at him, Cordelia sighed at the confident, cocky smile he shot her. God, he was so different from her yet he got to her in ways no one else could.

'That's another sweeping statement,' she murmured, although she couldn't help but breathe a sigh of relief that some of her darkest doubts were being addressed.

Not love, but fidelity. It was an exchange that would have to do. Many unhappy relationships ended up with far less.

'I've never approved of my father's search for love,' Luca confessed as they strolled towards the small but exquisite boutique with which he was vaguely familiar. 'He loved once and when that was prematurely ripped away from him, he thought that he could replace it. Love was always just round the corner. Marriage always

followed and heartbreak was always the eventual outcome. Not to mention vast drops in the family coffers
thanks to greedy exes and expensive lawyers. A wise
man can avoid all of that nonsense by making sure he
doesn't start picturing a life of happy-ever-afters. So if
I'm cynical about the therapeutic powers of love, then I
have every reason to be so. That said...' He paused and
looked at her with a frown. He was still dangling the
sunglasses but now he stuck them on and she shielded
her eyes from the bright glare of the sun.

'That said...?' Cordelia prompted.

'That said,' he drawled, shaking himself free from
whatever weird hold she'd temporarily exercised on him
with those gently questioning, impossibly blue eyes, 'he
was always a great believer in the value of monogamy.'

'That's important.' Cordelia fell into step with him
as he moved off, heading towards the far corner of the
piazza.

Luca laughed under his breath. 'His values were always in the right place. It was his heart that couldn't
stop hiving off in all sorts of undesirable directions.
We're here. Clothes and whatever else you might see
that takes your fancy. You'll need everything from shoes
to bags to jewellery. Then my PA has arranged for you
to hit one of the beauty salons around here. I have the
address.'

'It's a comprehensive overhaul.' Cordelia valiantly
tried to laugh that off rather than see it as some kind
of implied insult.

'You'll thank me for it in the long run. I have an important charity gala to attend in a couple of weeks and
you will be on my arm as my wife-to-be.'

Sudden nerves plucked at Cordelia's tummy and she

spun round to stride in front of him, stopping him from marching onwards by dint of placing her hand on his chest.

'Why am I only hearing about this now?'

'Does it matter?'

'Luca, I have no experience when it comes to…to that kind of thing…'

'What kind of thing?'

'I don't even know what a charity gala entails!'

'Lots of important people meeting up to have fun while raising money for one or more designated charities. The women will all be dressed to the nines, hence one of the reasons for this shopping trip taking place today.'

'I'm never going to fit in!'

'Don't be negative, Cordelia. You have a fortnight to get used to the idea. These things may be tedious but we're not talking about water torture.'

'The closest I've come to anything like that in my life before,' she protested in a high-pitched voice, 'were the monthly do's at the village hall! I'm thinking that a charity gala isn't going to be in the same league.'

'I would never have taken you for someone so lacking in confidence.'

'I feel out of my depth.'

Luca paused, hitched his sunglasses to the top of his head and looked at her so seriously and so intently that Cordelia could feel hot colour race into her cheeks.

Now he's seeing what he's let himself in for, she thought miserably. *I'm just an ordinary girl from a Cornish village and no amount of fancy dress can ever change that. Is this the point when he decides that marriage might not be such a great idea after all?*

She was astonished at the gaping hole that opened up inside her at the prospect.

It was one thing for him to hitch his wagon to the mother of his child, but quite another to hitch it to a woman who could never possibly live up to his exalted lifestyle.

She stared down at the wildly unfashionable sandals she had brought over with her and started when she felt the graze of his finger against her burning cheek.

'Don't worry,' Luca murmured. He tilted her chin upwards and their eyes met and held. 'You can lean on me. I have no intention of letting you flounder.'

Cordelia blinked.

Every straining muscle in her body was propelling her forward, one small step then another.

She was barely aware of herself leaning up or of her mouth parting, inviting more than just a casual touch.

She closed her eyes and sighed with pleasure as Luca's mouth descended.

What was going on here? Luca despised public displays of affection. Since when did he do stuff like this? But he was in the grip of something far more powerful than common sense and he plundered her mouth with scant regard for who might or might not be watching.

It was the least cool thing he had ever done in his life before.

But the feel of her lips, her darting tongue, the soft shudder of her body so close to his...

Irresistible.

He drew apart with reluctance and stared down at her.

'We...have things to do...' He raked his fingers

through his hair and shifted restlessly. The only thing he wanted to do was grab her hand, head for his car, which was parked less than ten minutes away, and take her back to his house and straight into his bed. 'Clothes to buy,' he muttered thickly.

'My makeover. I know. Sorry. I got…' She couldn't keep looking at him because she would just want to kiss him again. 'I got a little carried away…'

'I think that getting a little carried away is allowed.' He held her hand, linking his fingers through hers in a gesture that felt strangely intimate. 'After all…' he smiled raggedly '…it's not as though we aren't in the most intimate place two people could be in. Yes, getting a little carried away…' he breathed deeply, getting a grip '…is definitely allowed, don't you think?'

Sex, Cordelia thought pragmatically. That was what it was about. That chemistry between them was still alive and kicking and it wasn't all on her side. He wanted her as much as she wanted him. She had felt it in that kiss.

There would be passion and he would be faithful and he would protect her from the slings and arrows of this new life she had to get used to. He'd made that pledge and somewhere deep inside she believed him.

And if there was no love, then three out of four would be good enough.

As he had predicted, they were welcomed into the wonderfully air-conditioned boutique like royalty. The *closed* sign was put on the door and she was invited to take a seat so that clothes could be brought out for her inspection.

She was downright intimidated by the cool grey walls, the marble floor, the clothes hanging on the rails. There was no comforting pop music in the background. Choosing these clothes was serious business. There weren't thousands of items on each rail but she figured that each one would cost a small fortune. It was a minimalist, coldly clinical boutique that only opened its doors to the uber-rich.

She had never felt more uncomfortable in her life before.

A model of similar height but remarkably skinny, with long dark hair and sultry dark eyes, paraded a selection of outfits while Cordelia sat and tried hard to look riveted by the experience. Ever so often, she murmured and nodded, very much aware of Luca next to her, sprawled on the white leather sofa with his laptop to one side, flickering and demanding attention.

'Okay,' he announced, 'I think we've seen enough.'

The sultry-eyed, dark-haired model looked visibly disappointed at this pronouncement.

Cordelia had scrambled to choose a few things and was already dreading step number two in the makeover. Did she really want to be buffed and polished?

'We'll take…the red dress, the long one and…' he carelessly pointed to the pile that had been set aside to be reviewed '…that lot.' Then he stood up and held out his hand to her.

'You don't have to come with me to the beauty place,' Cordelia said as soon as they'd left the cool boutique and stepped out into the baking summer air.

'I've decided you don't need the spa experience after all.'

'What? Why? I thought I had to have a complete makeover before I could be let loose into high Italian society.'

Luca flushed because, put like that, it didn't seem to say much about him and his values.

Since when had he ever cared what other people thought? He'd been protecting her, but watching that catwalk model parade those clothes had made him realise that she didn't need protecting, at least not when it came to whether she would fit into his world or not.

Naïve and ingenuous she might be, but on the looks front she was head and shoulders above all those women who looked exactly like the dark-haired model. He would guide her through the labyrinth of all those tedious social niceties he had grown up with but, for the rest, she could more than hold her own.

And besides...

It had surprised him to find that he didn't like the thought of her dolled up in all those designer outfits that had been on show.

He was positively turned off at the thought of her in extravagant black outfits or small, intricate dresses that showed off everything and screamed *haute couture*.

'I made a mistake,' he muttered gruffly. He reached for her hand and they began walking away from the stunning *piazza* down one of the many streets that fanned outwards from the main circle.

The impressive architecture didn't stop in the *piazza*. It continued down the side roads—ornate and magical. Legend had it Siena was a city founded by Senius, the son of Remus who was suckled, along with Romulus, by a she-wolf—hence its emblem.

Cordelia had managed to look up some historical facts on the drive and had lapped them up thirstily.

She would have loved nothing better than to have played tourist and seen all the sights but there would be time for that in the future and, for the moment, she was too intrigued by Luca's change of mind to start talking about city tours.

Also, her hand was tingling where their fingers were entwined.

That kiss had lodged in her head and she wanted more. *Man and wife...*

How could she ever have imagined that the chemistry between them wouldn't supercharge given the circumstances? He hadn't looked back when he'd left after those heady three weeks. He had had his life neatly packaged but now here she was and if this was called making the best of a bad deal, then she was going to take it, because she wanted him more than she could ever think of wanting anyone.

'What do you mean?' They were at the car and she stood with her hand on the door, looking at him across the width of the Lamborghini. It was black, sleek and just the sort of high-powered sexy car that needed an alpha male like Luca at the wheel.

'Maybe,' Luca drawled, watching her with his head tilted to one side, 'you awakened a taste in me for everything that's natural.'

'Because I live half my life barefoot and don't own any make-up?' But her heart was leaping all over the place because that sounded a lot like a compliment.

'Who would have thought that shoes could end up being a highly overrated commodity?' He grinned and raised his eyebrows and she shivered with a sexual awareness that made the hairs on the back of her neck stand on end. 'Besides,' he continued in a lazy drawl, 'I couldn't stand the thought of hanging around in Siena any longer.'

'It's a bore for you,' she agreed, glancing down and then slipping into the passenger seat of the car. It smelled of soft leather. 'I guess you probably thought that it was a waste of time, especially when you probably have lots of work to do.' She turned to him with apologetic eyes because caretaking her really had to be the last thing in the world a guy like him needed or wanted. He was used to expensive women who didn't need to be escorted to the right shops to buy appropriate clothing.

Although hadn't he just said that he liked the thought of her *au naturel*…?

A rush of pleasure surged through her body.

'It would have been a bore for me,' Luca murmured, swivelling so that he was looking at her. He carelessly had one hand by her headrest and he lightly stroked her hair, running one lazy finger through its vibrant blonde curls, 'because I could have thought of a million better things I would rather have been doing with my time.' He paused and then traced her mouth with his finger, tugging on her fuller lower lip until she wanted to faint. 'No, I tell a lie. I would have been thinking of just the one thing I would rather have been doing with my time…'

'What's that?'

Luca laughed, amused. 'Will it turn you on if I spell it out?' He looked at her with satisfaction when she nodded. 'I won't spell it out. I'll show you just as soon as I get you into my bed…'

CHAPTER EIGHT

CORDELIA STRETCHED OUT on the bed and sighed with contentment.

The past week had been a whirlwind. Much of it had been spent in bed, the rest on a voyage of discovery. The day after their visit to Siena, Luca had announced that he intended to keep to his word and show her a bit of his country before she broke the news to her father.

There was work he had to do in Milan, some deals that needed fine tuning. He would arrange for a guide to take her on a personal tour of the city and then they would drive to his house on Lake Como, so that she could see a different countryside from the one she had glimpsed in his Tuscan home.

Vineyards, of course, but also olive trees, oleanders and palm trees and, along with that, incomparable stretches of exquisite villas, their gardens dipping down to the lake shores.

'Italian aristocracy at its very best,' he had wryly informed her, and when she had asked him whether his house might be amongst those villas, he had laughed and returned, 'But of course. Would you expect otherwise?'

His tone had been one of amused irony but, actually, Cordelia had thought that, no, she wouldn't have expected otherwise. The more she glimpsed of his eye-wateringly privileged life, the more she acknowledged the gaping differences between them.

She was forever telling herself that if he could shrug off those differences, then so would she.

'I want you to feel a little more at home in my country before your father gets here,' he had confided as they had boarded his private jet that would take them to Milan. 'I want you to show him that this is a country that you can love, as I love it. I would not want him to leave with any...doubts that you are doing the right thing.'

Still warm after a bout of passionate lovemaking, Cordelia had thought that that was the nicest thing Luca could have said because it showed that, beyond the baby, he was also thinking about her and her well-being. That counted for a lot.

Milan had been a wondrous place. For someone who had never been abroad, it was mesmerising. Busy but small, it had offered a variety of riches and Cordelia had paid close attention to the charming young guide who had taken her on her whirlwind tour of the city, starting with Piazza del Duomo with its towering cathedral, followed by a visit to see the paintings of the old masters, all of whom were familiar to Cordelia via the many books she had devoured over her lifetime.

This wasn't like Siena with its feeling of medieval splendour and laid-back charm. This was hectic and busy. There were chic cafés everywhere, dotted in between the historic splendour of the *piazza*. The young people all seemed ridiculously good-looking.

She had enjoyed every minute of it and now here

she was, enjoying every second of a completely different environment.

From the window of Luca's fabulous villa, she could see the placid waters of the lake in the distance. When the car had first swerved onto the long drive leading to the villa, Cordelia had been gobsmacked. She hadn't bothered to hide her awe. The square white building with its evenly spaced rectangular windows and its formidable symmetry reeked of opulence. From the front of the villa, gardens led down to an archway that opened out onto the lake via a series of shallow stone steps. It was, put simply, breathtaking.

That, however, was a sight that had been taken in several days ago and now, lying here in bed while Luca showered in the fabulous en-suite bathroom, Cordelia could only marvel at the speed with which she was becoming accustomed to this extraordinary life.

'Penny for them.'

Cordelia's eyes shot to the bathroom door where Luca was lounging against the doorframe with a towel slung round his waist. They had already made love that morning and yet she could already feel herself getting turned on all over again. One look at him and stuff inside her ignited and exploded, leaving her wet and weak and at the mercy of his clever mouth and hands and fingers.

'I was just looking out of the window and thinking how beautiful this all is,' she confessed truthfully, watching as he moved from doorway to wardrobe to extract a white linen shirt and a pair of loose trousers, which he dumped over the back of the chair.

Slowly Luca began to dress.

She was, of course, right. It was beautiful, although

in truth he rarely noticed the scenery here. In fact, he couldn't think of the last time he had visited this particular property. For Luca, downtime wasn't something he enjoyed very often. The last time, he now mused with some surprise, was when he'd vanished off to Cornwall to get his thoughts together, and look at where that had got him.

A baby on the way and…his eyes roved over the delectable sight of his wife-to-be, pink-faced and tousled, her white-blonde hair spread across the pillow, one long leg draped over the duvet, the other tucked away underneath.

Even when she was relaxing, even when his libido was at rest and sex wasn't on the menu, there was something intensely appealing about her. He was finding that he couldn't keep his hands off, which was just as well considering the situation.

And that situation, he had to admit, was doing very well. He had never, not once, having found out that she was carrying his baby, contemplated not making her his wife. Anything else would have been out of the question, and when she had turned his offer down flat with all that talk about 'love' and 'finding the one' he had momentarily been disconcerted at the notion that she might, actually, walk away from him.

That instant of panic was something he had never experienced before and certainly never in connection with a woman, but she wasn't like anyone else. She was unique insofar as his money was immaterial.

He had appealed to her longing to see the world. It had been, first and foremost, a deliberately well-considered plan to open her eyes to what richness lay in store for her and for their child, and the funny thing was that he had begun to see his own country in a slightly different light.

Had begun to view his own possessions through different spectacles and was appreciating what he had spent a lifetime taking for granted.

He couldn't offer her love, but he could offer her a lot more besides and he could tell that all those bonus extras were weaving their magic.

'This is just the tip of the iceberg,' he murmured, moving to perch next to her at the side of the king-sized bed. 'You have yet to see the splendour of Rome and Florence, although we will try and visit those two cities when there are fewer tourists. Then there is the Riviera...' He couldn't help himself. He drew down the duvet exposing her breasts, bountiful orbs tipped with ripe pink, pouting nipples that begged to be suckled.

'Don't,' Cordelia sighed weakly, relaxing back against the pillow and instinctively arching her naked breast to his mouth. 'We have a lot to do today. Sailing...oh, Luca...oh, yes...' She clasped her hand behind his head as he took her nipple into his mouth and sucked and licked until she was panting and writhing helplessly on the bed.

'The things you do to me,' Luca groaned, vaulting up to strip off the shirt with unsteady hands while his eyes burned into her.

He had work to do. At least a couple of hours before the day could be theirs and yet...he couldn't resist her.

Nor did he intend on shortening the time he had with her, which meant that work would have to take a back seat, which was a first for him and would have been hugely disconcerting if his mind had actually been able to focus on anything other than the woman looking back at him with a helpless yearning that mirrored his.

Their lovemaking was fast and hard and he came with such intensity that the breath left his body for a few wild moments.

It took him a while to come down from the high. Goodbye any work at all, he thought. Emails would have to be handled later. At some point.

He lay back and flung one arm over his eyes and Cordelia wriggled against him. Warmth spread through her at the feel of his arm heavy across her back and shoulders.

His body was slick with perspiration and she flattened the palm of her hand on his chest.

She loved him. It was as simple as that and the realisation barely shook her because it was something that had crept up slowly but surely, sinking into her consciousness until it was just a fact of life.

She was in love with this guy and that was why she had agreed to marry him. Or at least, it had been a very strong motive, underneath all the very logical reasons she had told herself.

If she had truly felt nothing for Luca but bone-deep indifference, then she would have walked away. Yes, she would have made sure contact was maintained for the sake of their child, but she could never have borne living with someone she didn't care about.

Curiosity and recklessness had propelled her into doing something she would never have dreamt possible given all the principles she had always lived by and, bit by bit over those three weeks, she had fallen for him and fallen hard.

The past week and a half had only made that love

deeper, because she had seen him for the good guy that he was underneath the power and the wealth.

All this time he'd taken to show her around, to introduce her to his beautiful country. There was no need for him to have done that!

Surely that meant something?

He was no longer the flint-eyed stranger who had made her want to disappear into the ground when she had first shown up in his office.

She had caught him on the hop, crashed slap bang straight through all the plans he had made for himself, and of course he had been knocked for six, but he had recovered and she wondered whether he wasn't now finding himself at the mercy of feelings he couldn't really express. He gave every semblance of enjoying her company. He was tender and considerate with her, making sure she ate all the right stuff at all the right times. He was the guy she had rescued from the stormy ocean...the guy with no background, no past and certainly no vast fortune to his name.

And they were lovers once again.

Passion was a powerful force and, accompanied by genuine affection...well, how far were those things from love? Not very. There was no point to viewing the future with anything but optimism and, right now, Cordelia was happy to put on rose-tinted spectacles that made the world look so much better.

She snuggled and closed her eyes and enjoyed his nakedness against her.

'Sailing,' Luca murmured drowsily into her hair. 'It awaits us.'

'I thought you were going to try and get through some work before we left...' She ran her fingers along his chest and felt him shudder in instant response, before he absently covered her hand with his. 'You wanted to nail your guy about that project with the refined olive oil...you said he seemed to be digging his heels in on the quality-check front and you were going to push him where you wanted him to be...'

Luca frowned. He must have told her about Giuseppe without even thinking about it.

Disturbed for some reason, he edged off the bed and headed for the shower.

He was gone for a handful of minutes and when he re-entered the bedroom, he was all brisk business as he got dressed.

'You shouldn't have reminded me, *amore*.' He was concentrating on his mobile, only looking up to glance quickly in her direction with his hand on the doorknob. 'Now I'll have to deal with him or my guilty conscience will get the better of me. The great outdoors might have to be put on hold until tomorrow.' He watched her disappointment with a veiled expression.

This was all going swimmingly but it was fair to say that disappointment was part and parcel of life. He should know. His father, embroiled in his own emotional world, had largely been a bystander in his life. Luca had learned from an early age to expect little from a guy who never attended sports days and had shown scant interest in the personal goings-on of his son. Disappointment, he had long ago concluded, did wonders for developing tough independence.

And she would need it because she would realise soon enough that long days doing nothing were not the norm and weren't going to last for ever.

He frowned and restlessly raked his fingers through

his hair, because her attempts at a bright, sympathetic smile were worse than outright annoyance that plans had changed.

'Sure,' she said cheerfully. 'I get it.'

'I will arrange for someone to show you around.'

'No need. I can explore on my own. I might even do a bit of sailing. I could probably give a few courses to the instructors out here. You keep telling me to take it easy but that's not what I'm used to. A little exercise will do me the world of good.' She waited for a light-hearted response, which didn't come so she shuffled off the bed, for some reason self-conscious of her body because of the sudden drop in temperature between them.

Freed to do what Luca knew he did best, namely bury himself at work, which would be a timely reminder this mini break was a means to an end, he found himself hovering and watching her through narrowed eyes as she took herself off to the en-suite bathroom, making sure to lock the door behind her.

'Don't take any risks,' he warned gruffly, as soon as she was back in the bedroom, fully clothed in some khaki shorts and a white tee shirt.

'Risks like what?' She looked at him, perplexed.

'You're pregnant.'

'I know. Go slow.' Cordelia's smile felt forced. Of course she was. It was a simple statement of fact but it felt like cold water being dashed over her. That shift in atmosphere—the sudden need to attend to work... Had Luca sensed something in her? Something tender and vulnerable? Something that wasn't part of the package deal? Had she transmitted feelings to him by osmosis and had he reacted by pulling back the way he had?

It made sense.

'I'm strong. I'll manage and, don't worry, I won't take any risks. I may just have a nice stroll and explore what's around.' The smile broadened and felt more forced. 'What time shall I aim to be back here?'

'I would rather you had a personal escort.'

'And I would rather do my exploring on my own without someone trailing behind me to make sure I don't trip over any paving stones.'

'Why are you suddenly being difficult?'

Tension spiked and, for a second, Cordelia was sorely tempted to come right out and tell him what was on her mind. Was he worried that she might be getting too emotionally involved with him when he'd specifically told her that love wasn't on the menu? Was he afraid that she might start making demands he wouldn't be able to meet?

Fear at where such a conversation might lead gripped her and she backed away from it fast.

'Nothing. I guess I'm just a little disappointed that I'll be spending a whole day without you.'

Luca visibly relaxed. He strolled towards her and smoothed his hand over her arm. She had skin as soft as satin.

'Me too.' He was tempted to dump the work but that wouldn't do. Behaving out of character when he was around her was becoming a career choice and he didn't like it, even though he could rationalise it well enough. She was having his baby so of course he was going to treat her differently! 'I'll meet you mid afternoon. I should have had everything wrapped up by then. Keep your mobile handy and I'll call you. We can have tea.'

Cordelia thought that this was how awkward moments were navigated. Was this a prelude of things to come? Small, emotional inroads always taken under cover? Her love hidden away for fear that if he sensed it, he would back off? There was no point dwelling on it, she decided. She would go and have an enjoyable day. When she smiled this time, it was genuine.

'Sure. No rush. If I don't hear from you, I have the address and I can make my way back. Everything feels pretty close so I'm sure I'll be able to walk where I want to go. See you later!'

She headed for the door and knew that he was following her through the villa to the imposing front door overlooking the lake. She didn't want to do anything silly and tempting like spin round and fling her arms around him because she hated the way things had suddenly and inexplicably gone frosty, but instead she slipped on her boat shoes, glanced over her shoulder without making eye contact and gave a little wave.

She had her map.

She'd spent a lifetime longing to leave the Cornish coastline, to see the world. She was seeing it now and she couldn't afford to live off her nerves, letting her imagination get the better of her and letting all the considerable wonders at her fingertips pass her by.

She would have to obey the rules of the game and if that meant keeping her love hidden away like a shameful secret, then she would do that.

Luca wanted to go to one of the windows to follow her progress to the shore.

Perhaps he had allowed that temporary blip in his good humour to show through, but wasn't the occasional mood allowed? She'd also laughed off his concerns about her safety but, hey, wasn't a little paranoia allowed on his part? She was carrying his child and accidents happened!

Luca was not accustomed to worrying about a woman. He wasn't accustomed to imaginary scenarios about unlikely things that might or might not happen on a simple walk by a lake.

He repeated the mantra about this not being a normal situation because she was the mother of his baby. It worked for a while but when he discovered that he had been staring at the same page of the report he had been reading on his email for fifteen minutes, he was forced to concede that the mantra, while it made sense, wasn't having the desired effect.

Like it or not, his head was crammed with a variety of possible dangers she might encounter because she felt she needed some exercise and fresh air.

He couldn't squash his fears even though there was nowhere on earth safer than the shores of this stunning lake. For a start, there were endless tourists around. It wasn't one of the smaller, quieter lakes. If she slipped or fell or fainted or urgently needed to lie down, there would be people around to help and she'd call him, but none of those things would happen anyway because all she would do was stroll and maybe stop and have something to drink at one of the cafés. You couldn't walk five metres without colliding into a packed café.

Not that she was going to slip. Or fall. Or faint. Or urgently need to lie down.

But what if she did?

He would never forgive himself. Protecting her was his duty. The place for him right now wasn't in front of his computer trying to focus. It was by her side…making sure she didn't slip.

Mind made up, he left his villa at speed. He hadn't been to the villa for a hundred years, or so it seemed, but he knew this lake like the back of his hand. Just one of the many exotic destinations he had frequented in his early days. It was muggy outside. Grey skies and the lake wearing an angry look, as though thinking about getting choppy.

Luca ignored the crowds. How far had she walked? He was approaching at pace by the time he spotted her, laughing on one of the rental boats, of which there were many. This one was a small, sleek, mahogany little number, your basic speedboat made for two.

And she was with a guy, which made him pull up short.

Blond hair in a ponytail, tanned, wearing a shirt that was stupidly unbuttoned all the way down and surfer shorts.

Something wild and primitive ripped through Luca and he had to take a few seconds to gather himself.

They were laughing.

He thought back to that tight smile she had given him before stalking out of the villa earlier and he saw red. Fists bunched, he breathed in deep and by the time he made it to the boat, he was in control.

'Having fun?'

In the midst of trying to make herself understood, in Italian, to the very pleasant guy from whom she was trying to rent the boat, Cordelia took a few seconds to register that Luca had shown up, far earlier than she had expected.

She turned around and, smile fading as she took in his glowering expression, she tentatively said, 'You're early. I didn't think you'd be here for a couple of hours.'

She was standing on the deck of the small outboard motorboat, and she leapt off with the surety of a gazelle.

She knew boats as well as she knew the changing moods of the ocean.

Shading her eyes with one hand, she turned around and offered a very poor goodbye in Italian to Elias, the young guy who was now not going to get the rental he wanted.

'What are you doing?' Luca enquired coolly, having restrained himself from being just too aggressive for no reason towards a perfect stranger.

'What do you mean?'

'I thought you were going to have a stroll and maybe grab some lunch somewhere. Instead, you've decided that that's all too tame and you'd rather risk life and limb on a speedboat...'

Cordelia's mouth dropped open. 'Luca, there's no need for you to be overprotective! Are you forgetting that I rescued you from the sea? I've been handling boats faster and bigger than this since I was ten.'

'You're pregnant. You shouldn't be thinking of doing anything as reckless as sailing. Of course, if I'm with you, then that's a different story.'

They were heading towards the centre of the village, a charming honeycomb of small winding streets jam-packed with attractive, expensive shops, cafés and restaurants. Tables set out on the pavements were filled with tourists playing people-watching.

Luca veered off the main thoroughfare down one of the smaller avenues and eventually they managed to find themselves a quiet corner in one of the restaurants.

'And who was that boy you were laughing with?' he asked with a scowl.

'Elias?'

Luca nodded and shrugged and looked away for a few seconds before scrutinising the menu and ordering nothing more than a double espresso from the waiter who had sidled up to the table.

'He was the guy in charge of the boat rentals.' Cordelia broke off to order a selection of little cakes, irresistible, before returning her gaze to his face with a frown. 'Why?'

'No reason. Should I have one?'

'I have no idea what you're getting at.' The coffee and the cakes arrived and Cordelia gazed at them, marvelling at how perfectly formed each one was. Almost a shame to eat them. She wasn't looking at Luca at all.

'You seemed a little familiar.'

Her eyes flew to meet his.

'Luca, were you...*jealous*?'

'Jealous?' Luca sat back and drummed the tabletop with his fingers while he looked at her with a brooding expression. 'I have never been jealous in my entire life.' He gestured in a way that was exotically Italian and gave a bark of laughter. 'I don't believe in jealousy. It's a corrosive emotion.'

Cordelia didn't say anything because what he really could have said was that he didn't do jealousy because to be jealous you had to have some kind of intense emotion inside you for someone, and intensity on that level wasn't something he was capable of feeling.

Suddenly deflated, she fiddled with the small fork that had been placed in front of her.

'However,' Luca gritted, 'I'm an old-fashioned man with old-fashioned principles. I don't care for the idea of my woman flirting with other men.'

At that, she met his steely gaze with a look of out-raged incredulity. *His woman?* That level of posses-siveness seemed to beg for a far deeper connection than business arrangement for the sake of a baby with some-one you had a fling with, but she decided to let it pass. Was it a case of a business arrangement and keeping her at arm's length except when his arrogance kicked in, at which point she turned into *his woman*?

'I wasn't flirting,' she said in a low voice.

'You were laughing.'

'Since when is laughing the same as flirting?'

'It's a damn sight more than I managed to get from you today,' Luca gritted in immediate response.

Uncomfortable with a show of feeling that was so far removed from his usual calm, cool and collected responses to anything that asked for an emotional re-sponse, Luca concentrated on drinking his espresso. There was no point continuing a conversation that seemed mired in abstract nonsense.

So what if he'd been jealous? It was only natural. A wife-to-be was quite different from a passing conquest.

Jealousy had never been an issue with Isabella. Per-fect.

'A person can't be in a happy mood all the time,' Cordelia pointed out, finishing the last of the tasty deli-cacies and licking the very last of the icing sugar from her finger while she thought about how he had changed earlier on, gone from light-hearted and warm to sud-denly as cold as the Arctic sea. From wanting to spend time with her to needing to spend time on his computer.

'I get that,' Luca growled. When it came to happy moods, he hadn't, after all, written the book. 'But I want you to be. I… I'm going the extra mile… I'm *trying*.'

'What are you talking about?'

Luca didn't want her to feel tempted to return to the life she was going to be leaving behind. Showing her his country was a labour of love, more so because he seemed to be seeing so many beautiful parts of it for the first time himself, but he knew that it was also his way of getting her on board. He didn't see anything devious about that. It seemed perfectly fair and reasonable.

Luca tightened his jaw and reminded himself that, first and foremost, he was a man who never allowed any part of his body to govern his behaviour except for his head.

The feathers that had been stupidly ruffled by that admission of jealousy smoothed back into their normal position and not a second too soon.

'I'm showing you my beautiful country.' He gestured around him but his fabulous eyes remained pinned to her face. 'I am putting work concerns on the back burner so that I can bring you to a place like this!'

'And so I should be smiling all the time?' An unwelcome picture began to form, one that killed off any romantic notions that what he felt for her might, actually, have legs.

She could read between the lines as good as the next person.

He was putting himself out to entertain her and it wasn't because he was necessarily enjoying it or even really wanted to. Everything had changed for Luca the second he had found out that she was carrying his baby and he had rolled with the punches because that was the kind of guy he was.

He had sussed the situation, known the direction he

wanted it to go in and had altered his programme accordingly.

Did he think that if he'd handed her over to a tour guide and returned to his work schedule, she might have reconsidered the marriage option?

Had it occurred to him that, as a husband in the making, it wouldn't have done to have given her the wrong impression? She'd turned down his marriage proposal to start with…it made sense for her to have a visible demonstration of what she would be getting if she took him up on the offer after all. He'd won her with his persuasive arguments and maybe he thought that, yes, he would go the extra mile in making sure she didn't change her mind.

'Of course, I appreciate all the hard work that's gone into making me feel welcome,' she concurred coldly, pushing away the flowered plate and sitting back to rest her hands on her lap.

Luca had the grace to flush. 'That is not what I meant.'

'Sounded like it to me.'

He glared and dumped his serviette on the table with a flourish and summoned the waiter to pay the bill.

'Let's move on from this conversation.' He offered his hand to help her and she took it readily enough but then dropped it the second she was on her feet. 'I feel it's one that could end up going round in ever-decreasing circles and getting nowhere fast.'

'Sure.' She was going to have to look at the bigger picture. She was going to have to see this upcoming union for what it was and look for no more than what was on the table.

She would enjoy the last couple of days in this wonderful place because, all too soon, she would have to tell her dad about the pregnancy and break it to him that she would not be returning to Cornwall, but making her home on the other side of the ocean.

'We will be back in Tuscany in no time at all.' Luca mirrored what she was thinking with uncanny accuracy. 'Let's try and relax here. Stress is no good for a pregnancy. There will be much to do when we return.'

So factual, Cordelia thought, so well-mannered, and if she wanted more then that was her problem and nothing to do with him.

CHAPTER NINE

HER FATHER WOULD be coming over for the charity gala.

'It makes sense,' Luca had pointed out in the sort of voice that implied that anyone who didn't agree with that sweeping statement was clinically insane.

'He'll be walking into something he hasn't banked on and he's not the kind of man who would know what a charity gala is.' Cordelia's voice had been laced with scepticism. 'He doesn't even own a suit. Or if he does, it will be the one he was married in and it probably won't fit. And that's the kind of thing he would want me around to help him with. Choosing a suit.' Her eyes had welled up.

'He won't be walking into it unprepared,' Luca had returned equably. 'He has already accepted that you've looked me up over here and he probably suspects that the very reason you left Cornwall in the first place was to get in touch with me. He's already overcome the disappointment that you didn't tell him the truth in the first place. So we tell him that there will be an event taking place. Who knows? He might look forward to it.'

Cordelia had maintained a healthy silence on the matter. What did Luca know? She hadn't cared for his remark about the disappointment her father had had to overcome but she hadn't been able to argue the logic behind the remark. Luca, she had discovered, didn't pull his punches. If something had to be said, then he said it. End of story.

Heaven only knew what her father thought of her now, lying to him about this trip.

There was no way Luca could understand how she was feeling and, even though she didn't want to sound vulnerable and needy, she hadn't been able to stop herself from confiding in him when the plan had been hatched up.

That was how he got to her. One minute her head was telling her to look for nothing, to play it cool, to accept the conditions that had been imposed on this relationship. It was a situation that had been forced on him and there was nothing offensive in the fact that he was rising to the occasion and doing whatever was within his power to make her feel comfortable about the choice she had made. He was proud that he had gone the extra mile. So what right did she have to be upset about it?

She should be able to maintain a stalwart and adult silence on all things personal, but then the second something began weighing on her mind, like the thought of her father coming over to Italy, leaving his beloved Cornwall behind, and being confronted with the sort of over-the-top event he wouldn't know how to cope with, she instinctively turned to Luca to hear what he had to say.

Even though he was the instigator of the whole thing! How did that begin to make sense?

Love, she had thought with helpless desperation.

'Don't underestimate the power of change,' he had advised her in that calm, utterly reasonable voice of his. 'You may find that you've kick-started something you hadn't foreseen. He might have discovered that he can manage just fine without you around. Might prefer it, even.'

Now, with her fancy dress laid out on the bed and a bath run, Cordelia thought back to what Luca had said. There was a knot in her stomach. Her dad would be arriving at Luca's villa in under three hours, before the charity gala was due to begin. He was walking into a rolling estate the likes of which he had never seen before and he would quickly realise the set-up and just how magnificent it was going to be. She had gaily told him that Luca, despite what they had both originally assumed, was pretty well off. She'd played down the extent of his wealth because somehow it seemed okay for 'pretty well off' to be a simple oversight on Luca's part, something that might not have reasonably come up in conversation, whereas, 'billionaire who owned vast vineyards and half of Italy' wasn't quite such an acceptable oversight. And something in her resisted the thought of denigrating the guy she was so hopelessly and foolishly in love with.

'You just don't know what you're going on about,' she announced out of the blue.

Standing in the doorway to the en-suite bathroom with just his jeans on, because he had discarded his white linen shirt on the ground, Luca paused and looked at her with a frown.

There were times when she was so utterly illogical that he was reduced to complete speechlessness.

Who'd have thought? She could swim like a fish for miles, could handle a boat like a sailor and could talk to fishermen as if she were one of them, making them obey her orders without complaint, and yet, out of the blue, she said something like this that left him scratching his head and wondering what the hell she was talking about. Unpredictable. He'd never cared for unpredictable but he'd had to get used to it and fast.

Whatever she was now trying to say, his gut feeling told him it was going to be a convoluted conversation.

'Trust me,' Luca said smoothly, deliberately going for what he knew she wasn't talking about, but seeing it as a safe port in what could be an uncomfortable gathering storm, which was the last thing either of them needed hours before a gala where their engagement was going to be officially announced to all and sundry. 'That dress is going to look amazing on you, *tesoro.*'

Cordelia was sufficiently distracted by that random comment to look down at the dress laid out on the bed by the young housekeeper. She'd tried it on the one time a hundred years ago in that shop, forgotten what she looked like in it, and now quailed at the thought of appearing in it in front of a bunch of people she didn't know.

It was long, which was reassuring. But it was tight, which most definitely was not.

And then there were the shoes. Several inches of nude into which her feet would have to be squeezed.

'I'm going to look like a clown,' she muttered.

Luca raked his fingers through his hair and half smiled. This was what he liked, this connection that ran like a current between them. It felt, suddenly, as though a signpost that had been there all along was staring him in the face, pointing him in a direction, and he frowned, in the grip of something he couldn't quite grasp even though, deep inside, he felt that he would be able to if he thought a bit harder about it.

All he knew was that he missed her easy laugh when it wasn't there and the way she would look at him, those slanting glances that always turned him on as no one else had ever been able to. He missed the way he occasionally felt taken for granted and didn't seem to mind all that much. He missed the essence of her, although he wasn't really too sure what that essence was. He just knew that in some low-level way, he missed it.

Hearing the uncertainty in her voice relaxed him now because she sounded more normal, more like the girl he'd so quickly become reacquainted with ever since she had appeared on his doorstep with her bombshell revelation.

'You could never look like a clown.' Luca strolled towards her, a slow smile transforming the harsh contours of his beautiful, lean face.

'I can't tell you the last time I wore a dress.' Annoyingly, Cordelia was finding it hard to hang onto what she had meant to say to him. He was so close now that she could smell the late summer warmth on his skin and see the ripple of muscle in his chest and shoulders. He always knew that the rough edges could be smoothed like this, with a touch.

The second he got just a little too near her, she couldn't seem to help herself. She could be cross, angry, dejected or plain frustrated to within an inch of her life, and her body would still do its own thing, would still curve towards him like a plant turning towards the sun, searching for nourishment.

'What about those dances you tell me you used to go to…?'

'Dances?'

'Where all the local talent would strut their stuff once a month in the village hall.'

'A lot of people found the love of their lives at those dances,' she pointed out. 'Maybe if I'd worn dresses instead of trousers, I might have been one of the lucky ones.'

Luca lowered his eyes. He didn't say a word and she had a sudden urge to prod him into something more than tactful silence, but what would be the point of that? They were where they were.

'Before you distracted me with the whole dress thing,' she said, although impetus had been lost, 'I was going to tell you that you just don't know anything about Dad.'

Temporarily lost, Luca looked at her with bewilderment. She wasn't going to clarify. She was going to wait until he clocked on with where she was going with this and woe betide if he missed the turning.

He felt something shift inside him, some illogical feeling that made him vaguely uncomfortable even though it was a feeling that he perversely liked.

'You mean,' he said slowly, thinking on his feet, 'the bit about him not being as nervous about being here at the gala this evening as you think he might be?'

'That's exactly what I mean.'

Luca breathed a sigh of relief. He cupped the side of her face with his hand and looked at her solemnly. 'I meant every word of it, *cara mia*. You've clung to one another over the years and I am sure he has built up a dependency on you because of that, has been fearful of you striking out because past experience has taught him that striking out can end in tragedy, but you have cut that tie and don't be surprised to find that he's more resilient than you think he will be. I mean, did he express any hesitation about making the trip over here?'

'Not as such.' She shrugged.

'There you go. Point proven.'

'Because he felt badly about complaining down the end of a telephone doesn't mean that he actually wants to be over here. He's going to be gutted when I tell him…what I have to tell him.'

'We could break the news together,' Luca suggested and she laughed shortly.

'You mean like the happily loved-up couple we're not?' She regretted the words as soon as they left her mouth. She'd made it sound as though this were a black-and-white situation. Her voice had been tart and sarcastic and bitter.

'I'm sorry,' she muttered indistinctly, and Luca looked at her with suddenly cool eyes.

'I don't know what's going on with you, Cordelia, but, whatever it is, you need to put it on hold, at least for the duration of this gala. Do you think you could do that?'

Cordelia wanted the ground to open up and swallow her because what had he done but try and deal with what had landed on his lap in the most gentlemanly way possible? He was right when he said that that had been an unnecessary outburst. More to the point, it wasn't true. He might not be in love with her, but what they had was certainly not the cold, emotionless relationship of two people forced into an arrangement against their will.

They talked, they laughed, they made love and there was sufficient affection there for her to really believe that he would do his utmost to be a good father and a good husband.

'I'm just nervous.' She lowered her eyes, hating the drop in temperature between them. She needed his support and driving a wedge between them just at this moment seemed an incredibly stupid thing to have done.

She took a couple of faltering steps towards him and looked at him hesitantly.

She felt rather than saw some of the icy tension ease out of him and it flashed through her mind that if he could touch her and banish all thoughts from her head, then she could do the same for him.

It was the power of sex and, while it certainly wasn't love, there was something vital and fierce about it and she should be very happy that it was still there, like an electric charge always running between them.

'We'll be late.' Luca raked his fingers through his hair and fidgeted on his feet, suddenly restless.

'I don't know what you're talking about,' Cordelia murmured and he looked at her with a wicked gleam in his eyes.

'I'll bet.' He pulled her towards him. His breathing had thickened and he was already smoothing his hands over her waist, hitching up the shirt and then tugging down the zip of her trousers. 'It's a low trick to use sex to change my mood,' he growled, with rampant amusement in his voice. 'I like it.'

Their lovemaking was fast and hard and mind-blowingly passionate.

By the time they hit the bed, clothes had been scattered on the ground. There was none of the usual foreplay. He kissed her urgently, hungrily, and she was wet and hot when he slid one expert finger into her, stoking her moisture and sending her pulses shooting off in all different directions.

She curled her fingers into his hair and arched back as he drove into her and all it took was one thrust for her to feel the exquisite rising pleasure of a soaring orgasm.

Her groan was long and guttural as her whole body stiffened against his rigid shaft. He came as fast as she did, rearing up and thrusting deeper into her.

'Jesus, woman,' he said in a shaky voice, when they were both back on planet Earth, 'what was that all about?'

'Don't you know?' she breathed.

His head was buried against the nape of her neck and he was limp against her. She stroked his shoulders and was overwhelmed with a feeling of complete tenderness. There were times when he seemed so vulnerable. Times like right now.

'We need to get ready.' His voice was muffled and he tilted his head to one side and their eyes met, a long, steady gaze that made her hold her breath because it felt *loaded*.

He levered himself up and stood, staring down at her. 'Your dad is going to be here in a couple of hours. I don't think he'll be too impressed if he finds us in bed, do you? Although he would have a pretty vivid picture of how we ended up where we have, with a baby on the way.'

With which, he vanished into the bathroom to emerge less than twenty minutes later, giving her plenty of time to get into her finery.

Clothed, Luca was impressive. Naked, he was mind-blowing, but now was certainly not the time to hang around appreciating his masculine athleticism and perfectly toned body.

Sylviana, the young girl who had made her appearance on day one, was going to be helping her get ready and Cordelia didn't wait to watch Luca change.

There was nothing for her to do because an army of hired help had been brought in to prepare the house and grounds for the event. Nothing would be left to chance. From the food to the decorations—everything would be the epitome of perfection.

'It's a well-run machine,' Luca had informed her a couple of days previously. 'Same faces with the only changes being some VIPs I'm hoping to do business with from the Far East and their various assorted family members and professional colleagues.'

The only snag was the fact that his father would not be able to make it because, with first-class ticket in hand and ready to depart from the small Caribbean island where he had ended up after a couple of months of travelling, a world-class hurricane had decided to put paid to his plans.

Privately, Cordelia had been relieved. One father at a time was plenty enough.

Her nerves were all over the place as she got ready. When Sylviana had entered the bedroom, as sweet and as helpful as ever, Cordelia had heard the distant sounds of things happening downstairs, but as soon as the bedroom door was shut, there was complete silence save for their low murmurs as Cordelia dressed.

The redness of the dress was a direct challenge to that tomboy side of her that only ever felt comfortable in jeans, and she hesitated for a few seconds before Sylviana laughed and informed her, in very broken English, that she was going to look beautiful in it.

Really? Cordelia wanted to say. *Even though I'll be the tallest woman there, and that's without the five-inch heels?*

Italian women were dark and dainty and impossibly pretty, she had discovered, and she didn't think that this charity gala was going to prove otherwise.

She didn't glance at herself in the mirror as she got dressed. Sylviana was keen to do the make-up and Cordelia could think of nothing she wanted more because her ability to don warpaint was minimal.

She sat at the dressing table, closed her eyes and let the young housekeeper do her thing.

Her thoughts drifted. There was so much she had to tell her father. She had spoken to him several times on the phone but he was no good when it came to lengthy conversations on the telephone and she, for her part, had felt that there was too much she couldn't tell him for their conversations to be natural and easy.

She hadn't asked how the Doris connection was working out and he hadn't volunteered any information. He'd talked about his catches for the day.

She dreaded to think what would happen when he learned that she, Cordelia, would be spending the majority of her time in Italy. Her brain ached from thinking about it all.

She was on a different planet when Sylviana told her to wake up.

'Is ready, Signorina Cordelia.'

The reflection staring back at her in the mirror was a woman she didn't quite recognise.

The contours of the face were the same, but the subtle

application of make-up had given her aristocratic cheek-bones and…were her lips really so full…her eyelashes quite so thick and long?

Her curls hadn't been tamed but they *had* been styled to ripple down her back in a far more orderly fashion.

But the most amazing thing was a figure she had always taken for granted.

Tall, rangy, not particularly curvy had been transformed into six feet of elegance once the nude heels were on.

Cordelia turned round and giggled a little nervously as she reached for the gold clutch bag, which was completely empty save for her mobile phone in case her dad called while she was busy bustling downstairs.

She towered over Sylviana but she was still walking on air as she got accustomed to the heels and made her slow way down the staircase in the general direction of the noise.

Vast areas of the house had been transformed and when she glanced outside, she could see that the same applied to the grounds, with tiny lights everywhere, and lanterns hanging from the trees.

When it was completely dark, it would make a marvellous sight.

This was going to be her home. This magnificent, palatial house was going to be where their child grew up. If they stayed together, who knew? There might very well be other children.

They would have all of this at their disposal. The world would be their oyster. When Cordelia thought of the lovely but narrow life she had lived, when she thought back to her yearning to see what was out there, she knew that she had done the right thing in agreeing to marry Luca.

How could she have, in good conscience, denied their child this birthright?

She paused to glance at the frenetic activity in the hall. It would be chaos in most of the other rooms.

Where was Luca?

She didn't think he would be found tasting the food to see whether any further tweaks were needed.

In fact, the thought of him doing that brought a smile to her lips because if there was one thing he had zero interest in, it was what went into the production of all those fine meals that were brought to him by his very talented and loyal staff. Food was always an amusing accompaniment to the main event, which was the wine.

She headed away from the kitchens and the fuss happening in that expansive wing of the villa.

She headed in the direction of his office because she knew that he would probably be working.

It got quieter. She thought of their lovemaking and that, too, made her smile and fired up something proprietorial inside her. He'd made that remark when he had surprised her chatting to the guy with the boat for hire at the lake. *His woman.* There were times when she had a similar feeling, which was that Luca was *her man.*

The office door was ajar when she got there. Where the rest of the sprawling mansion was floored with a mixture of wood and marble, a combination of cool and warm, the long corridor with the far more comfortable rooms leading off it, including Luca's office, was carpeted.

Her steps were soundless. She couldn't hear anything

inside but she pushed open the door just to make sure he wasn't there and froze.

Literally, she could feel a coldness washing through her, turning her to ice.

She was numb with it as she looked, open-mouthed, at Luca and the woman in his arms.

They didn't see her. The office was in semi-darkness, as was the corridor down which she had walked, so there was no back light behind her as she watched and stared.

They were standing and they were...entwined. That was the only word for it. Entwined. He had his hands in the woman's hair and Cordelia could hear the sound of quiet, muffled sobbing.

Isabella.

She didn't know how she knew that, she just did. The small, fragile woman curled against Luca was the woman he had been destined to marry, and of course the reason there was so much sobbing going on would be Isabella's distress that she was not going to be the name announced as the lucky fiancée.

She would not be the one flashing the enormous diamond on her finger and accepting congratulations.

What Cordelia was looking at was a love that would never be fulfilled because of her and a pregnancy Luca had never banked on.

She felt sick. She also couldn't move because her feet seemed to have become cemented to the square foot of carpet on which she was standing.

Luca was the first to notice her presence and she saw him still, and his body language must have transmitted something to the woman in his arms because she, likewise, looked up, and now they were both looking at her in complete silence.

'I'm guessing—' at long last she found her voice, and she was pleased that it didn't shake or wobble or worse '—that I've interrupted a special moment between you two?'

'Cordelia…'

Luca's voice was hoarse, emotional in a way she had never heard him be emotional before and, more than anything else, that brought the sting of tears to her eyes.

Isabella was untangling herself from his embrace, making a move to come towards her, and Cordelia, horrified at the prospect of having to listen to some love-struck platitudes, was suddenly galvanised into action.

She began backing away. The high heels were an encumbrance. She wanted to run as fast as she could, but all she could manage was a fast-paced hobble, one hand lifting the long red dress, the other clutching the little bag so tightly she suspected it wouldn't survive the vice-like grip.

She was aware of Luca saying something in Italian behind her but she was oblivious to his approaching steps until she felt his hand circle her arm, pulling her to a stop.

Heart beating like a sledgehammer, Cordelia swung around to look at him and spied Isabella standing hesitantly in the doorway of the office, as dainty and as fragile as spun glass. Her eyes were red from crying but, even so, she remained a beautiful woman, with dark, chocolate-brown hair upswept and a long black dress accentuating a gamine figure. There was a glittering choker at her neck, a string of diamonds that would have cost the earth, befitting the woman who, as Luca had once told her, was his appropriate match.

It was obvious that, along with that understatement

of the year, there were a million other things he had failed to mention.

'Cordelia…'

'I don't want to hear, Luca.' Her eyes were dark with disappointment, anger and hurt. 'How could you?'

'How could I *what*?'

'I don't know…' Her voice was laced with biting sarcasm but underneath the acidity she was all too aware of the gathering storm as her mind flew off in all sorts of directions. 'Hmm…let me think…how could you *what*, I wonder? Abandon your own stupid gala so that you could have a final intimate moment with the woman you always wanted to marry? Is that a good beginning to your question, Luca?'

'This is ridiculous.'

'No, Luca…' She tugged at the exquisite diamond on her finger, remembered when it had been chosen and what she had felt when, only a couple of days ago, after it had been sent away for refitting, it had been slipped onto her finger. '*This*…' she handed him the engagement ring '…is ridiculous.'

'I can't believe I'm hearing this. You've got to be joking!'

'Take the ring, Luca, because I don't want it.'

'You're overreacting and interpreting something in completely the wrong way.'

'Am I? I don't think so. Correct me if I'm wrong, but that *was* Isabella, wasn't it? The old family friend you were always destined to settle down with? One wealthy family marrying conveniently into another wealthy family?'

Luca remained silent.

He was put on the spot, all the years of never explaining himself coming to the fore. He clenched his jaw. He wasn't going to take the ring, which was lying in the palm of her outstretched hand. Intense frustration washed over him.

'You're wrong in whatever assumptions you're making, Cordelia. You need to trust me on this.'

His words hovered between them. For a second, Cordelia stopped to consider what he had just said, but only for a second because, as far as she was concerned, if she'd misread the situation, then it was up to him to clarify.

How hard was that? More to the point, was this what marriage to Luca was going to be? What had she agreed to take on? What would be the role of a convenient wife? Exactly?

Part of her wanted to curl her fist round that ring and shove it back on her finger because when she projected to a future without him, she literally quailed with fear.

But a greater part was forced to ask the question— would marriage mean hugging to herself a love that could never be brought out into the open? A love that turned her into someone so emotionally dependent on Luca that it was okay for him to do exactly as he pleased without explanation? Would she be facing a life of having to take his word *for everything*?

He'd reassured her that he would be faithful, but then he would have, wouldn't he? It would be in his interest to tell her what he knew she would want to hear.

But she had seen what she had seen and if her interpretation had been off target, then he wouldn't be standing there in front of her now, still as a statue, with eyes as cool as an Arctic blast, expecting her to just blindly believe him. He would be defending himself.

She shoved the priceless diamond at him.

'I can't go through with this. I'm sorry. When Dad comes, we'll leave. Right now, I'm going to pack my bags, and don't worry. I won't be taking anything I didn't come here with.'

CHAPTER TEN

Would she skulk out of the house? Slip back into her jeans and tee shirt? Shimmy away from the clutter of guests, excitedly sipping their expensive drinks and tucking into expensive canapés and exchanging notes on what had happened since the last annual charity gala had brought them together?

Everyone in the neighbouring towns would be there, from the great and the good to those way down the pecking order. No discrimination, as Luca had told her with some satisfaction a few days previously, when she had been fretting about it.

She shuddered when she thought about running away. The guests would not have started arriving if her father arrived on time but if his flight was delayed, then she ran the risk of doing a runner in the most awkward of situations.

How on earth was Luca going to deal with it? What would he say?

She closed her mind off to any weakness and focused on flinging clothes into her suitcase, the one she had brought with her.

When everything was packed, she stood back, breathing hard, and stared at her reflection in the mirror. She didn't see herself. Instead, she saw Luca in that darkened office with his arms around Isabella, comforting her, his face soft with affection.

Without stopping to think too hard, she climbed out of the designer dress that had made her feel like a million dollars, and crept back into the loose leggings she had adopted ever since her stomach had started expanding and a baggy white tee shirt.

These were the clothes she belonged in.

She sat on the bed and waited. Eventually, her mobile pinged with a text from her father that he was in the taxi and would be with her in under an hour, at which point she agitatedly paced the room, only emerging to head downstairs when she was sure that he would be about to arrive.

There was no sign of Luca.

She wondered whether he had disappeared back into the office with Isabella. Perhaps he was explaining the situation. Maybe he had decided that he would revert to his original plan and marry the girl he had been destined to marry in the first place. It wouldn't take him long to realise that joint custody worked.

Cordelia didn't think there would be any begging by him for her return. He was a proud man and she couldn't have dented his pride more successfully if she'd spent a year planning it.

The fact that he hadn't bothered to find her said it all.

For a moment, she'd stepped into a world as dazzling as a fairy tale. Her prince had stepped forward and, okay, so it might not have been ideal happy-ever-after material but, deep down, she'd figured that there was enough love inside her for both of them. Deep down, when she looked close enough, she'd flirted with the tantalising hope that, with a ring on his finger and a baby on the way, the love he claimed he could never give her would find a way out.

For all she had told herself that the only way to deal with what was on the table was to apply cold logic and reason, she had still succumbed to the notion that things might change because nothing ever remained the same.

She'd been a fool.

Leaving the suitcase in the bedroom and with no clear plan as to what she would tell her father or how, exactly, she would make her exit, she headed down the stairs, slipped into the sitting room closest to the front door, and waited by the window for the taxi bringing her father to arrive.

She wasn't going to do it. Not really. Surely not. The world would be gathering at the villa in under two hours. There was no way she was going to rock the boat at the eleventh hour. She'd reacted with all the emotionalism he knew her to be capable of but she would cool down.

Wouldn't she?

'Go and find her,' Isabella had urged, her pretty face anxious and distressed.

Luca wasn't going to do any such thing.

She would calm down. At any rate, he refused to go down the road of explaining himself to anyone. Surely it wasn't too much to ask for trust in a relationship? He had told her that there was nothing going on between Isabella and himself and he didn't see why she couldn't take him at his word. Had he ever, since she had shown up, given her any reason to think that he was the sort of guy who couldn't be trusted? No, he had not!

Skewered with uncertainty, Luca thought of her, her open, trusting face clouded with doubt and accusation. Something inside him twisted and, like a dam bursting, thoughts that had been pushed to the side now broke through in a tumultuous rush.

A rapid succession of images darted through his head, images from the very first time he'd laid eyes on her in that little room in the cottage she shared with her father to that mind-blowing moment when they had made love for the first time.

And along with those images came other things, feelings he had stashed away, emotions he had never thought he would have.

Galvanised into action, Luca took the stairs two at a time, up to the bedroom, where he saw her packed suitcase on the bed.

It was small, a relic from her dad's days in all probability. The sight of it made him feel sick.

At least he knew she hadn't left the villa.

Heart hammering, he raced through the rooms, impatiently brushing aside several employees who wanted to talk to him, ask his advice on something or other. He barely noticed the way the house had been transformed. He certainly had no time to stop and make polite noises about all the work that had been put into turning his mansion into a wonderland of lights and candles.

He'd started his search in the vast hall but the room she was in was the last he actually looked in. She was gazing out of the window with her back to the door. She hadn't turned on the light and she was a shadowy figure, perched on the window seat.

For a second, Luca had a vivid image of the girl she

must have been over the years, sitting just like that, gazing out of a window, dreaming of adventure.

'Cordelia,' he husked, moving quickly towards her. 'No, please don't turn me away. I've come…you're right…'

Luca, she thought, heart leaping, an instinctive reaction to seeing him, to hearing the deep, velvety tone of his voice.

'What do you want?' She edged away from him because he'd perched right next to her, crowding her and sending her nervous system into frantic free fall. She wished she'd turned the lights on because it was too dark in the room. It had, somehow, felt more comforting to be in the dark when she had entered the room half an hour previously.

'I've been looking everywhere for you.'

'Forget it.'

'You surprised me. I… I wasn't expecting you… when you walked into my office…'

'So I gathered,' Cordelia said icily. 'As you can see, I don't want to have anything to do with you or this gala. I just want you to leave me alone. Dad is going to be here pretty soon and I shall tell him about the pregnancy and then I intend to get a taxi to the nearest hotel for the night. You want to have fun with your ex? Then, by all means, go ahead, but don't think that I'm going to be hanging around in the background, putting up with unacceptable behaviour. I'm very sorry if this means you're going to have to do what most modern-day couples do who share children but aren't together. You're going to have to arrange visiting rights and get a lawyer to sort out maintenance payments. Apologies

for putting you in the terrible position of having to behave like a twenty-first-century man, but that's life.'

'I... I'm sorry, *mi tesoro*.'

'Don't call me that.'

'But it's what you are,' Luca said softly. 'You're my
treasure.'

'Don't!' She looked away quickly and made a determined effort to staunch her foolish desire to burst
out crying.

'Look at me. Please.'

'Go away, Luca.'

'You think I was doing something in there with Isabella?'

'Why would I think that?' Her voice dripped sarcasm. It hurt. It hurt looking at him and it hurt not looking at him. Everything hurt but she knew that this was
a turning point. She had to stick to her guns and walk
away or else get lost in a relationship that would eat her
up and spit her out.

'What you saw...'

'I don't want to hear.'

'I was comforting her, my darling.' He reached for
her hand and, predictably, she snatched her hand away
and he couldn't blame her.

He honestly couldn't blame her if she walked away
and never looked back. He had lied to her about his
identity when they had first met; he had questioned
her arrival on his doorstep, immediately suspecting the
worst. He had lectured her with monotonous regularity
on his inability to give her anything beyond what was
demanded by duty. He had held himself aloof when
he had known that what she wanted and what she de-

served was a guy completely committed to her for all the right reasons.

He had presented her with marriage, a union shorn of all the things that should define it, and he had blithely expected her to fall in line.

And then tonight...

When Luca thought about what she must have felt when she'd walked into that room, he wanted to punch something.

And his reaction when she'd pinned him to the spot? He'd brushed aside her very valid concerns because he hadn't seen why he had to explain himself.

On every level he had laid down the rules and expected her to fall in line because that was what everyone did. What he'd seen in her was an opportunity for getting hurt. He'd fallen for her but, instead of facing up to it, he'd rejected it and pushed her back because he'd been afraid.

How could he now expect her to hear him out and give him one last chance?

Why would she not react the way anyone would react and assume that he was fabricating a story simply to get things back to where he wanted them to be?

Why wouldn't she treat whatever he had to say with the cynicism he so richly deserved?

Luca went from pale to sickly ashen as his mind began running away with possible outcomes.

She'd wanted love and marriage and all that stuff he had spent a lifetime writing off as unreasonable nonsense. It was hers for the taking now, but would she believe him or would it be too little, too late?

'I wouldn't blame you if you refused to listen to a word I have to say,' he told her with wrenching honesty. 'And even if you *did* hear me out, I wouldn't blame you if you sent me packing, but I really…need…to… explain myself.'

'But I thought you *never* explained yourself to anyone, Luca,' Cordelia said coldly. 'I thought that if you said "believe me" it was my duty to ask no more questions.'

'Once upon a time, I may have thought like that. I gave orders and people followed them without question,' Luca said quietly, 'but then I met you and it seems that everything changed. I don't know when and I'm not sure how, I just know that I am not the man I once was.'

'Oh, please.' She turned to look away because she could feel his words dragging her back to a place she didn't want to revisit, but he placed one finger on her chin and tilted her back to look at him and she couldn't resist.

'You are the best thing that ever happened to me and I was an idiot for not realising that sooner.' He looked at her and breathed in deeply. This was foreign territory and he had to grope his way to find the right words. 'I met you and I was a different man with you. I was the man I was meant to be and not the man I had been conditioned into becoming. You freed me, my darling, but I didn't pause to analyse why that had happened or what it meant. I just assumed that I acted differently with you because you didn't know me as the billionaire who could have whatever he wanted. I left but my mind kept returning to you and, again, I never asked myself why. I simply ploughed on because that was what I did and what I'd always done. I faced my destiny and my destiny was to marry Isabella and I didn't question it because…that was how it was.'

Cordelia stiffened. The mention of Isabella was a timely reminder of what she had witnessed and, as if sensing her withdrawal, he leaned forward, his body language imparting a searing sincerity that held her spellbound against her better judgement.

'Then you came. You showed up. In all your stunning glory.'

'Don't, Luca,' she whipped back.

'Don't what?'

'Try to get under my skin again. I've had it with you doing that.'

'You thought you walked in on me sharing something intimate with Isabella and, yes, you did, but not in the way you think. Isabella is gay. I've known that for a long time and that's why the marriage made sense. I didn't believe in love. It wasn't for me. And Isabella wanted the cover of a traditional marriage to hide her sexuality from her parents. Not ideal and I tried to persuade her to come out, but she refused, and I suppose, in a way, the arrangement suited me as it stood.'

He sighed, wondered where doing what was right stopped and doing what was convenient began. The lines had become blurred over time when it came to Isabella. 'She was crying because she'd finally decided to tell her parents so that she could be with her partner of eighteen months. She was a wreck and I was trying to comfort her and tell her that it would be okay. That was the scene you interrupted and I was a fool for not explaining myself immediately, for telling you that you had to trust me. Who the hell did I think I was?'

'Isabella is gay? But you were planning on getting married...'

'And who knows? Maybe we would have if she

hadn't met the woman she's in love with. Or maybe, if I hadn't broken it off, the worst would have happened and she would have married me because it would have been what tradition demanded. We would have both been miserable in the end.'

'Luca… I wish you had said something. Told me the situation from the start. You have no idea…what's been going on in my head.'

'Old habits die hard.' He grimaced. 'And besides,' he admitted, 'I might have been forced to recognise what I'd been hiding from myself.'

'What's that?' Cordelia asked breathlessly.

'That I'm in love with you. That you were the woman I have been waiting for all my life.'

Afterwards, everything happened very fast. It was a blur. He loved her. She'd questioned him, of course she had. He could be making it up! But she knew he wasn't because it just wasn't something he would ever make up.

He'd never believed in love, he'd told her. Love had destroyed his father. He had lost his only love and then worse had followed when he had reacted by hurtling from one ghastly and costly mistake to another. And he, Luca, young and grieving the loss of his mother, had been a casualty.

What was there to admire about that lifestyle? Only a fool, Luca had confided, would have chosen to emulate it. Only a fool would have blithely believed in the restorative power of love, having witnessed first hand its ability to destroy.

Not for him, and that was the rule he had lived his life by. He would marry for convenience and that way he would never risk getting hurt.

Every word had been music to her ears.

She had had to pinch herself several times because she couldn't believe that the man she had given her heart to had given his heart back to her, not when she had spent so long bracing herself for just the opposite.

Now, back in the gown but on cloud nine, she slipped her hand into his and gazed at him at the top of the stairs.

Her father was due any minute. Preparations were well under way. Noise levels had escalated. As she gazed down, she could see that the hall was festive with lights and flowers and the smell of food was wafting through the house, making her mouth water.

'I love you.' She smiled at Luca and reached up to kiss him very lightly on the mouth. 'I feel I've spent my life sitting there by the sea, looking out at a horizon and imagining what might lie beyond it. I never, ever thought that I would find everything I could ever hope for and more.'

'The mermaid who found her legs,' Luca murmured, curving his hand against her cheek. 'Mine for ever.'

His eyes slid past her and he smiled.

'Your father is here,' he said, 'and I'm guessing that the buxom blonde clinging to him is none other than the woman he didn't want around because he was too set in his ways?'

Cordelia stared and then burst out laughing because that was Doris, all right. Her case was bulging and Cordelia could only guess at what outfit might be inside. Doris had never been known for her modesty when it came to dress code.

'I don't believe it,' she breathed as they headed down the stairs. She gave a little wave to her father and braced herself for the conversation that would soon be taking place, although, now, it was a conversation she wouldn't be having with a heavy heart.

'Didn't I say?' Luca murmured into her ear. 'All's well that ends well, wouldn't you agree?'

Yes, she would.

There could be no better endings, in fact. She thought that as she looked down at the softly breathing baby in the basket next to the bed.

Three weeks ago, her contractions had kicked in, sending Luca into frenzied panic, even though he had been as cool as a cucumber as the time for the birth had drawn ever closer, wisely telling her when she should pack her bag for the hospital and assuring her that it was all probably going to be far calmer than she feared.

He had stayed with her for the duration of the ten-hour labour, had even helped to deliver their daughter and had only admitted afterwards that he had been close to passing out several times.

He was the most devoted father Cordelia could have hoped for. Now, she felt his arms around her as he shifted against her, levering himself up to gaze at their daughter, breathing softly in her basket, her tiny hands balled into fists. She had a mop of curly dark hair and was pale gold. She was the most wonderful thing they had ever seen and they never tired of admitting it.

Her father had flown over three days after Giulietta was born, along with Doris, and, after fussing over his granddaughter, he had shyly announced that he and Doris would be joining forces to expand the business.

'When you say *joining forces*…' Cordelia had encouraged and he had gone a deeper shade of scarlet.

'Woman's only gone and proposed,' he'd said gruffly, while Doris had looked at him with such tenderness that Cordelia had wanted to rush over and give her a huge hug.

The solitary man who had spent a lifetime mourning the life that had passed him by was finally waking up and Cordelia couldn't have been happier.

There would be another wedding in three months' time and Luca was already making noises about having a proper honeymoon afterwards. Somewhere hot and sunny, with a private beach, where they could re-live good times, specifically the good times that had brought their beautiful baby into the world.

'She's a miracle,' Luca murmured, wrapping his arm around his wife and nestling closer to her. 'In case I haven't mentioned it, you girls are the two most important people in my life.'

'I think you've mentioned it before.' Cordelia smiled. She wriggled until she was facing him and their bodies were pressed against one another.

'Have I mentioned, in that case, that I am already thinking that when it comes to family numbers, four seems a far more rounded number than three?'

Cordelia laughed, eyes gleaming. 'Is that a fact?'

'I never thought I'd hear myself say it, my dearest love, but loving you is the best thing that ever happened to me...'

* * * * *

SHY QUEEN
IN THE ROYAL
SPOTLIGHT

NATALIE ANDERSON

For my own Prince Charming
and the four delightful sprites we've been blessed with.
I love you.

CHAPTER ONE

'Fı?'

Hester Moss heard the front door slam and froze.

'Fifi? Damn it, where the hell are you?'

Fifi?

Hester gaped as it dawned on her just who the owner of that voice was. As Princess Fiorella's assistant while she was studying in Boston, Hester had met a few of the important people the Princess consorted with, but she'd been in the Princess's *brother's* presence only once. That one time there'd been many present and she certainly hadn't spoken to him. But, like everyone, she knew he was outrageous, arrogant and entitled. Not surprising given he ruled the stunning Mediterranean island kingdom that was the world's favourite playground.

She'd had no idea he was coming to visit his sister. It wasn't in the immaculate schedule she kept for the Princess, nor in any correspondence. Surely it would have been all in caps, bold, underlined *and* highlighted if it had been planned? Perhaps he was trying to fly beneath the radar—after all, he attracted huge publicity wherever he went. But if that were the case, why was he *shouting*?

'Fifi?'

No one spoke with such familiarity to the Princess, or with such audible impatience. For a split second Hester considered staying silent and hiding, but she suspected it was only a matter of seconds before he stormed into her bedroom. With a cautious glance at the corner Hester sped to the door and quickly stepped out into their living room.

And there he was. Prince Alek Salustri of Triscari, currently turning the lounge she and the Princess shared into a Lilliputian-sized container—one that was far too small to hold a man like him. Not just a prince. Not just powerful. He was lithe, honed perfection and for a moment all Hester could do was stare—inhaling the way his jet-black suit covered his lean muscled frame. The black shirt beneath the superbly tailored jacket was teamed with a sleek, matte-black tie and he held his dark-lensed aviator sunglasses in his hand, totally exuding impatience and danger. It was more than the bespoke clothing and luxurious style. He was so at ease in his place in the world—monstrously self-assured and confident because he just owned it. Everything. Except right now?

He was angry. The moment his coal-black gaze landed on her, he grew angrier still.

'Oh.' His frown slipped from surly all the way down to thunderous. 'You're the secretary.'

Not for the first time Hester found herself in the position of not being who or what had been hoped for. But she was too practised at masking emotion to flinch. No matter what, she never let anyone see they'd struck a nerve. And being the source of irritation for a spoilt playboy prince? Didn't bother her in the least.

'Your Highness.' She nodded, but her knees had locked too tight to perform a curtsey. 'Unfortunately Princess Fiorella isn't here.'

'I can see that.' He ground his teeth. 'Where is she?'

She kept her hands at her sides, refusing to curl them into fists and reveal any anxiety. It was her job to protect Princess Fiorella from unwanted interruption, only Prince

Alek wasn't just higher up the ladder than most of the people she shielded the Princess from, he was at the very top. The apex predator himself.

'At a bio lab,' Hester drew breath and answered. 'She should be back in about half an hour unless she decides to go for a coffee instead of coming back here right away.'

'Damn.' Another stormy emotion flashed across his face and he turned to pace across the room. 'She's with people?'

Hester nodded.

'And no phone?'

'Her bodyguard has one but the Princess prefers to be able to concentrate in class without interruption. Would you like me to message—?'

'No,' he snapped. 'I need to see her alone. I'll wait for her here.'

He still looked so fierce that Hester was tempted to send a quick message regardless. Except blatantly disobeying his order didn't seem wise.

She watched warily as he paced, brusquely sidestepping Hester's scrupulously clean desk.

'Is there anything I can help you with?' She was annoyed with how nervous her query sounded. She was never nervous dealing with Princess Fiorella. But she wasn't quite sure how to handle this man. Any man, actually.

He paused and regarded her, seeming to see her properly for the first time. She stared back, acutely aware of his coal-black bottomless gaze. Whether those beautiful eyes were soulful or soul*less*, she wasn't sure. She only knew she couldn't tear her own away.

With slow-dawning horror she realised the inanity of her question. As if she could ever help him? He was Prince Alek—the Prince of Night, of Sin…of *Scandal*.

His phone buzzed and he answered it impatiently. 'I've already said no,' he snapped after a moment.

Even from across the room Hester heard the pleading tones of someone remonstrating.

'I will not do that,' the Prince said firmly. 'I've already stated there will be no damn marriage. I have no desire to—' He broke off and looked grim as he listened. 'Then we will find another way. I will not—' He broke off again with a smothered curse and then launched into a volley of Italian.

Hester stared at the top of her desk and wished she could disappear. Clearly he wasn't concerned enough by her presence to bother remaining polite or care that she could hear him berating the ancient laws of his own lands.

The world had been waiting for him to be crowned since his father's death ten months ago, but he hadn't because 'Playboy Prince Alek' had so far shown little interest in acquiring the wife necessary for his coronation to occur. None of those billion *Ten Best Possible Brides* lists scattered across the world's media had apparently inspired him. Nor had the growing impatience of his people.

Perhaps he'd been taking time to get over his father's passing. Hester had seen Princess Fiorella's bereft grief and had tried to alleviate any stresses on the younger woman as best she could because she knew how devastating and how incredibly isolating it was to become an orphan. She'd been pleased to see the Princess had begun spending more time with friends recently. But Prince Alek hadn't retreated from his social life—in fact he'd accelerated it. In the last month he'd been photographed with a different woman every other night as if he were flaunting his refusal to do as that old law decreed and settle down.

Now the Prince growled and shoved his phone back into his pocket, turning to face her. As she desperately tried to think of something innocuous to say a muffled thud echoed from the bedroom she'd stepped out of. Hester maintained her dispassionate expression but it was too much to hope he hadn't heard it.

'What was that?' He cocked his head, looking just like that predator whose acute hearing had picked up the unmistakable sounds of nearby prey. 'Why won't you let me into her room?'

'Nothing—'

'I'm her *brother*. What are you hiding? Is she in there with a man or something?'

Before she could move, the Prince strode past her and opened the door as if he owned the place.

'Of course you would think that,' she muttered crossly, running after him.

He'd halted just inside the doorway. 'What the hell is that?'

'A terrified cat, no thanks to you.' She pushed past him and carefully crept forward so as not to frighten the hissing half-wild thing any more than it already was.

'What's it doing in here?'

'Having dinner.' She gingerly picked it up and opened the window. 'Or at least, it was.'

'I can't believe Fi owns that cat.' He stared at the creature with curling cynicism. 'Not exactly a thoroughbred Prussian Blue, is she?'

Hester's anger smoked. Of course he wouldn't see past the exterior of the grey and greyer, mangled-eared, all but feral cat. '*He* might not be handsome, but he's lonely and vulnerable. He eats in here every day.' She set him down on the narrow ledge.

'How on earth does he get down?' He walked to the window and watched beside her as the cat carefully climbed down to the last available fire escape rung before practically flying the last ten feet to the ground. 'Impressive.'

'He knows how to survive.' But as Hester glared at the

Prince her nose tingled. She blinked rapidly but couldn't hold back her usual reaction.

'Did you just sneeze?' Prince Alek turned that unfathomable stare on her. 'Are you *allergic* to cats?'

'Well, why should he starve just because I'm a bad fit for him?' She plucked a tissue from the packet on the bedside table and blew her nose pointedly.

But apparently the Prince had lost interest already, because he was now studying the narrow bedroom with a scowl.

'I'd no idea Fi read so many thrillers.' He picked up the tome next to the tissues. 'I thought she was all animals. And how does she even move in this space?'

Hester awkwardly watched, trying to see the room through his eyes. A narrow white box with a narrow white bed. A neat pile of books. An occasional cat. A complete cliché.

'Where's she put all her stuff?' He frowned, running a finger over the small wooden box that was the only decorative item in the room.

Hester stilled and faced the wretched moment. 'This isn't Princess Fiorella's bedroom.' She gritted her teeth for a second and then continued. 'It's mine.'

He froze then shot her a look of fury and chagrin combined, snatching his finger from tracing the carved grooves in the lid of the box. 'Why didn't you say so sooner?'

'You stormed in here before I had the chance. I guess you're used to doing anything you want,' she snapped, embarrassed by the invasion of privacy and her own failure to speak up sooner.

But then she realised what she'd said and she couldn't suck it back. She clasped her hands in front of her but kept her head high and her features calm.

Never show them you're afraid.

She'd learned long ago how to act around people with

power over her, how to behave in the hope bullies would get bored and leave her alone. With stillness and calm—on the outside at least.

Prince Alek stared at her for a long moment in stunned silence. But then his expression transformed, a low rumble of laughter sounded and suddenly Hester was the one stunned.

Dimples. On a grown man. And they were gorgeous.

Her jaw dropped as his mood flipped from frustrated to good-humoured in a lightning flash.

'You think I'm spoilt?' he asked as his laughter ebbed.

'Aren't you?' she answered before thinking.

His smile was everything. A wide slash across that perfect face that somehow elevated it beyond angelically beautiful, to warm and human. Even with those perfectly straight white teeth he looked roguish. That twist of his full lips was a touch lopsided and the cute creases in his cheeks appearing and disappearing like a playful cupid's wink.

'I wouldn't think that being forced to find a bride is in the definition of being spoiled,' he said lazily.

'You mean for your coronation?' She could hardly pretend not to know about it when she'd overheard half that phone call.

'Yes. My coronation,' he echoed dryly, leaving her room with that leisurely, relaxed manner that belied the speed and strength of him. 'They won't change that stupid law.'

'Are you finding the democratic process a bitter pill to swallow?' she asked, oddly pleased that the man didn't get everything his own way. 'Won't all the old boys do what you want them to?'

He turned to stare at her coolly, the dimples dispelled, but she gazed back limpidly.

'It's an archaic law,' he said quietly. 'It ought to have been changed years ago.'

'It's tradition,' she replied, walking past him into the

centre of the too-small living room. 'Perhaps there's something appealing about stability.'

'Stability?'

There was something impish in his echo that caused her to swiftly glance back. She caught him eyeing her rear end. A startling wave of heat rose within—exasperating her. She knew he wasn't interested, he was just so highly sexed he couldn't help himself assessing any passing woman. Her just-smoking anger sizzled.

'Of having a monarch who's not distracted and chasing skirt all the time,' she said pointedly.

His lips curled. 'Not *all* the time. I like to rest on Thursdays.' He leaned against the doorframe to her bedroom.

'So it's a rest day today?'

'Of course.' His gaze glanced down her body in a swift assessment but then returned to her face and all trace of humour was gone. 'Do you truly think it's okay to force someone to get *married* before they can do the job they've spent their life training for?'

There was a throb of tension despite the light way he asked the question. He cocked his head, daring her to answer honestly. 'You think I should sacrifice my personal life for my country?'

Actually she thought nothing of the sort but she'd backed herself into a corner by arguing with him. 'I think there could be benefits in an arranged union.'

'Benefits?' His eyebrows lifted, scepticism oozing from his perfect pores. 'What possible benefits could there be?'

Oh, he really didn't want his continuous smorgasbord of women curtailed in any way, did he?

'What if you have the right contract with the right bride?' she argued emotionlessly. 'You both know what you're heading into. It's a cool, logical decision for the betterment of your nation.'

'Cool and logical?' His eyebrows arched. 'What are you, an android?'

Right now, she rather wished she were. It was maddening that she found him attractive—especially when she knew what a player he was. Doubtless this was how every woman who came within a hundred feet of him felt, which was exactly why he was able to play as hard and as frequently as he did. When a man was that blessed by the good-looks gods, mere mortals like her had little defence against him.

'Perhaps when you're King you can lobby for the change.' She shrugged, wanting to close the conversation she never should have started.

'Indeed. But apparently in order to become King I must marry.'

'It's quite the conundrum for you,' she said lightly.

'It has no bearing on my ability to do my job. It's an anachronism.'

'Then why not just make an arrangement with one of your many "friends"?' she muttered with frustration. 'I'm sure they'd all be willing to bear the burden of being your bride.'

He laughed and a gleam flickered in his eyes. 'Don't think I haven't thought about it. Problem is they'd all take it too seriously and assume it was going to be happily ever after.'

'Yes, I imagine that would be a problem.' She nodded, primly sarcastic.

He straightened from the doorway and stepped closer. 'Not for someone like you, though.'

'Pardon?'

'You'd understand the arrangement perfectly well and I get the impression the last thing you'd want is happily ever after with me.'

Too stunned—and somehow hurt—to stop, she answered back sharply. 'I just don't imagine it would be possible.'

Those eyebrows arched again. 'With anyone or only with me?'

She suddenly remembered who it was she'd just insulted. 'Sorry.' She clamped her lips together.

'Don't be, you're quite right,' he said with another low laugh. 'The difficulty I have is finding someone who understands the situation, its limitations, and who has the discretion to pull it off.'

'Quite a tall order.' She wished he'd leave. Or let her leave. Because somehow this was dangerous. *He* was dangerous.

He eyed her for another long moment before glancing to survey the neat desk she'd retreated behind. 'You're the epitome of discretion.'

'Because my desk is tidy?'

'Because you're smart enough to understand such an arrangement.' He lifted his chin and arrogantly speared her with his mesmerising gaze. 'And we have no romantic history to get tangled in,' he drawled. 'In fact, I think you might be my perfect bride.'

There was a look on his face—a mischievous delight tempting her to smile and join the joke. But this wasn't funny.

So she sent him a dismissive glance before turning to stare at her desk. 'No.'

'Why not?' The humour dropped from his voice and left only cool calculation.

Definitely dangerous. Definitely more ruthless than his careless façade suggested.

'You're not serious,' she said.

'Actually, I rather think I am.'

'No,' she repeated, but her voice faded. She forced her arms across her waist to stop herself moving restlessly, to stop that insidious heat from rising, to stop temptation escaping her control.

She *never* felt temptation. She never *felt*. She'd been too busy trying to simply survive for so long…but now?

His gaze didn't leave her face. 'Why not take a moment to think about it?'

'What is there to think about?' she asked with exaggerated disbelief. 'It's preposterous.'

And it was. He'd walked in less than five minutes ago and was now proposing. He was certifiable.

'I don't think so,' he countered calmly. 'I think it could work very well.'

He made it seem easy, as if it were nothing.

'You don't think you should take this a little more seriously instead of proposing to the first woman you see today?'

'Why shouldn't I propose to you?'

Hester breathed slowly, struggling to slow her building anger. 'No one would ever believe you'd want to marry me.'

'Why?'

She mentally begged for mercy. 'Because I'm nothing like the women you normally date.'

His gaze skidded down her in that cool and yet hot assessing way again. 'I disagree.'

She gritted her teeth. She didn't need him to start telling her she was attractive in a false show of charm.

'It's just clothes and make-up.' He stole the wind from her sails. 'Fancy packaging.'

'Smoke and mirrors?' She swallowed the bitterness that rose within her because she just knew how little the world thought of her 'packaging'. 'I meant I'm not from your level of society. I'm not a *princess*.'

'So? These "levels" shouldn't matter.' He shrugged carelessly.

'I'm not even from your country,' she continued, ignoring his interruption. 'It's not what's expected of you.'

He glanced beyond her, seeming to study some speck on the wall behind her. 'I'll do as they dictate, but they don't get to dictate *everything*. I don't want to marry anyone, certainly not a princess. I'll choose who I want.' His gaze flicked back to her, that arrogant amusement gleaming again. 'It would be quite the fairy tale.'

'It would be quite unbelievable,' she countered acerbically. She couldn't believe he was even continuing this conversation.

'Why would it, though?' he pondered. 'You've been working for Fi for how long?'

'Twelve months.'

'But you knew her before that.'

'For three months before, yes.'

Hester had been assigned as Princess Fiorella's roommate when the Princess came to America to study. Hester was four years older and already into her graduate studies so it had been more of a study support role. It turned out that Fiorella was smart as, and hadn't needed much tutoring, but it hadn't been long before Hester had begun helping her with her mountains of correspondence, to the point that Fiorella had asked her to work for her on a formal basis. It had enabled Hester to reduce her other varsity tutoring, she'd finished her thesis and now focused on her voluntary work at the drop-in centre in the city.

She scheduled Fiorella's diaries, replied to messages and emails and organised almost everything without leaving their on-campus apartment. It was perfect.

'Then you've passed all our security checks and proven your ability to meet our family's specific demands.' Prince Alek took another step closer towards her.

Hester stared at him, unable to believe he was still going with this.

'Furthermore it's perfectly believable that we would know each other behind palace walls,' he added. 'No one knows what might have been going on within the privacy of the palace.'

'Sorry to poke holes in your narrative, but I've never actually *been* to the palace,' she pointed out tartly. She'd never been to Triscari. In fact, she'd never been out of the country at all. 'In addition, we've been in the same airspace only once before.'

Prince Alek had escorted Fiorella to the university in lieu of the King all those months ago.

'And this is the first time we've actually spoken,' she finished, proving the impossibility of his proposal with a tilt of her chin.

'I'm flattered you've kept count.' His wolfish smile flashed. 'No one else needs know that though. For all anyone else knows, the times I've called or visited Fi might've been a cover to see you.' He nodded slowly and that thoughtful look deepened as he stepped closer still. 'It could work very well.'

Hester's low-burning anger lifted. How could he assume this would work so easily? Did he think she'd be instantly compliant? Or flattered even? He really was a prince—used to people bowing and scraping and catering to his every whim. Had he ever been told no? If not, his response was going to be interesting.

'Well, thank you all the same, Your Highness.' She cleared her throat. 'But my answer is no. Why don't I tell your sister you'll be waiting for her at your usual hotel?'

She wished Princess Fiorella would hurry up and get home and take her insane brother away.

'Because I'm not there, I'm here and you're not getting rid of me...' He suddenly frowned. 'Forgive me, I've forgotten your name.'

Seriously? He'd just suggested they get married and he didn't even know her name?

'I don't think you ever knew it,' she said wryly. 'Hester Moss.'

'Hester.' He repeated her name a couple more times softly, turning it over in his mouth as if taking the time to decide on the flavour and then savouring it. 'That's very good.' Another smile curved his mouth. 'I'm Alek.'

'I'm aware of who you are, Your Highness.' And she was not going to let him try to seduce her into complying with his crazy scheme.

Except deep inside her something flipped. A miniscule seed long crushed by the weight of loss and bullying now sparked into a tiny wistful ache for adventure.

Prince Alek was studying her as if he were assessing a new filly for his famous stables. That damned smile flickered around his mouth again and the dimples danced— all teasing temptation. 'I think this could work very well, *Hester.*'

His soft emphasis of her name whispered over her skin. He was so used to getting his way—so handsome, so charming, he was utterly spoilt. Had he not actually heard her say the word no or did he just not believe it was possible that she meant it?

'I think you like a joke,' she said almost hoarsely. 'But I don't want to be a joke.'

His expression tightened. 'You wouldn't be. But this could be fun.'

'I don't need fun.'

'Don't you? Then what do you need?' He glanced back into her bedroom. 'You need money.'

'Do I?' she asked idly.

'Everyone normal needs money.'

Everyone normal? Did he mean not royal? 'I don't, I have sufficient,' she lied.

He watched her unwaveringly and she saw the scepticism clearly in his eyes.

'Besides,' she added shakily, 'I have a job.'

'Working for my sister.'

'Yes.' She cocked her head, perceiving danger in his silken tones. 'Or are you going to have me fired if I keep saying no to you?'

His smile vanished. 'First thing to learn—and there will be a lot to learn—I'm not a total jerk. Why not listen to my proposition in full before jumping to conclusions?'

'It didn't cross my mind you were really serious about this.'

'I really am,' he said slowly, as if he didn't quite believe it of himself either. 'I want you to marry me. I'll be crowned King. You'll live a life of luxury in the palace.' He glanced toward her room before turning back to her. 'You'll want for nothing.'

Did he think her sparse little bedroom was miserable? How dared he assume what she might *want*? She wanted for nothing now—not people or things. Not for herself. Except that wasn't *quite* true—and that little seed stirred again, growing bigger already.

'You don't want to stop and think things through?' she asked.

'I've already thought all the things. This is a good plan.'

'For you, perhaps. But *I* don't like being told what to do,' she said calmly. And she didn't like vapid promises of luxury, or the prospect of being part of something that would involve being around so many *people*.

But the Prince just laughed. 'My sister tells you what to do all the time.'

'That's different. She pays me.'

'And I will pay you more. I will pay you very, *very* well.'

Somehow that just made this 'proposal' so much worse.

But, of course, it was the only way this proposal would have ever happened. As a repellent job offer.

He looked amused as he studied her. 'I am talking about a marriage *in name only*, Hester. We don't need to have sex. I'm not asking you to prostitute yourself.'

His brutal honesty shocked her. So did the flood of heat that suddenly stormed along her veins—a torrent of confusion and…other things she didn't wish to examine. She braced, struggling to stay her customary calm self. 'An heir isn't part of the expectation?'

He stiffened. 'Thankfully that is not another onerous legal requirement. We can divorce after a period. I'll then change the stupid law and marry again if I'm ever actually willing. I've years to figure that one out once I'm crowned.'

Hester swallowed. He was clearly not interested in having kids. Nor ever marrying anyone for real. He didn't even try to hide the distaste in his eyes. Too bad for him because providing an heir was going to be part of his job at some point. But not hers.

'We'll marry for no more than a year,' he said decisively. 'Think of it as a secondment. Just a year and then back to normal.'

Back to normal? As the ex-wife of a king? There'd be nothing normal after that. Or of spending a year in his presence as his pretend wife. She was hardly coping with these last ten minutes.

He hadn't even thought to ask if she was single. He'd taken one look at her and assumed everything. And he was right. Which made it worse. Another wave of bitterness swept over her even though she knew it was pathetic. Hester Moss, inconsequential nobody.

'Can you use your country's money to buy yourself a bride?' she blurted bitterly.

'This will be from my personal purse,' he answered

crisply. 'Perhaps you aren't aware I'm a successful man in my own right?'

She didn't want to consider all that she knew about him. But it was there, in a blinding neon lights, the harsh reality of Prince Alek's *reputation*. She couldn't think past it—couldn't believe he could either.

'There's a bigger problem,' she said baldly.

'And that is?'

'You've a very active social life.' She glanced down, unable to hold his gaze as she raised this. 'Am I supposed to have just accepted that?'

'I didn't realise you've been reading my personal diary.'

'I didn't need to,' she said acidly. 'It's all over the newspapers.'

'And you believe everything you read?'

'Are you saying it's not true?'

There was a moment and she knew. It was all *so* true.

'I've not been a monk,' he admitted through gritted teeth. 'But I didn't take advantage of any woman any more than she took advantage of me.' He gazed at her for a long moment and drew in an audible breath. 'Perhaps you've held me at bay. Perhaps I've been hiding my broken heart.'

'By sleeping with anyone willing?' she asked softly, that anger burgeoning again.

'Not *all* of them.' He actually had the audacity to laugh. 'Not even my stamina is that strong.'

Just most of them, then? 'And can you go without that… intimacy for a whole year?'

He stilled completely and stared fixedly at her. 'Plenty of people can and do,' he said eventually. 'Why assume I'm unable to control myself?'

That heat burned her cheeks even hotter. 'It's not the lifestyle you're accustomed to.'

'You'd be amazed what hardships I can handle,' he retorted. 'Will *you* be able to handle it?'

He was well within his rights to question her when she'd done the same to him. But she didn't have to speak the truth. Provoked, she brazenly flung up her chin and snapped, 'Never.'

But he suddenly laughed. 'You're so serene even when you lie.' He laughed again. 'Marry me. Make me the happiest man on earth.'

'If I said yes, it would serve you right,' she muttered.

'Go on, then, Ms Moss,' he dared her softly. 'Put me in my place.'

A truly terrible temptation swirled within her and with it came a terribly seductive image. She shook her head to clear it. She couldn't get mesmerised into madness just because he was unbearably handsome and had humour to boot. 'It's impossible.'

'I think you could do it.' His eyes gleamed and she grew wary of what he was plotting. 'If you don't need money…' he trailed off, his voice lifting with imperceptible disbelief '…then give it to someone who does.'

Hester froze.

His gaze narrowed instantly. 'What's your favourite charity?' He sounded smoothly practical, but she sensed he was circling like a shark, in ever-decreasing circles, having sensed weakness he was about to make his killer move.

'I'll make a massive donation,' he offered. 'Millions. Think of all those worthy causes you could help. All those people. Or is it animals—cats, of course. Perhaps the planet? Your pick. Divide it amongst them all, I don't care.'

'Because you're cynical.' But her heart thudded. Because she'd give the money to people who she knew desperately needed help.

'Actually, I'm not at all,' he denied with quiet conviction. 'If we find ourselves in the position to be able to help others in any way, or to leave the place in a better condition than which we found it, then we should, shouldn't we? It's called being decent.'

He pinned her with that intense gaze of his. Soulful or soul*less*? Her heart beat with painfully strong thuds.

'You can't say no to that, can you?' he challenged her.

He was questioning her humanity? Her compassion? She stared back at him—he had no idea of her history, and yet he'd struck her with this.

'If you don't need it,' he pressed her, 'isn't there someone in your life who does?'

There were very, very few people in her life. But he'd seen. He knew this was the chink in her armour. And while she really wanted to say no again, just to have it enforced for once in his precious life, how could she not say yes?

At the drop-in centre she'd been trying to help a teen mother and her toddler for the past three weeks. Lucia and her daughter, Zoe, were alone and unsupported having been rejected by family and on the move ever since. If someone didn't step in and help them, Lucia was at risk of having Zoe taken and put into care. Hester had given Lucia what spare cash she could and tried to arrange emergency accommodation. She knew too well what it was to be scared and without security or safety or a loving home.

'You're emotionally blackmailing me,' she said lowly, struggling to stop those thoughts from overwhelming her.

'Am I?' He barely breathed. 'Is it working?'

He watched her for another long moment as she inwardly wrestled with the possibilities. She knew how much it mattered for Lucia and Zoe to stay together. Her parents had fought to stay together and to keep her with them and when they'd died she'd discovered how horrible it was to be foisted upon unwilling family. With money came resources and power and freedom.

Prince Alek sent her a surprisingly tentative smile.

'Come on, Hester.' He paused. 'Wouldn't it be a little bit fun?'

Did she look as if she needed 'fun'? Of course she did. She knew what she looked like. Most of the time she didn't care about it, but right now?

'You like to do the unpredictable.' She twisted her hands together and gripped hard, trying to hold onto reality. 'You delight in doing that.'

'Doesn't everyone like to buck convention sometimes? Not conform to the stereotype others have put them in?'

He was too astute because now she thought of those bullies—her cousins and those girls at school—who'd attacked her looks, her lack of sporting prowess, her lack of *parents*...the ones who'd been horrifically mean.

'I *really* don't want to be used as a joke.' She'd been that before and was sure the world would see their marriage that way—it was how he was seeing it, right? Nothing to be taken seriously. And she was too far from being like any woman he'd make his bride.

'Again, I'm not a jerk. I'll take you seriously and I'll ensure everyone around us does too. I'll make a complete commitment to you for the full year. I promise you my loyalty, honesty, integrity and *fidelity*. I only ask for the same in return. We could be a good team, Hester.' He glanced again at her desk. 'I know you do a good job. Fi raves about you.'

Hester's pride flickered. She did do a good job. And she knew she was too easily flattered. But this was different, this was putting herself in a vulnerable position. This was letting all those people from her past *see* her again. She'd be more visible than ever before—more vulnerable.

But hadn't she vowed not to let anyone hurt her again?

'Working for Princess Fiorella is a good job for me,' she reminded herself as much as informed him. 'I won't be able to come back to it.'

'You won't need to,' he reasoned. 'You'll be in a position to do anything you want. You'll have complete independence. You'll be able to buy your own place, fill it with cats and books about serial killers. All I'm asking for is one year.'

One year was a long time. But what she could do for Lucia and Zoe? She could change their lives *for ever*. If someone had done that for her parents? Or for her? But no one had and she'd spent years struggling. While she was in a better place now, Zoe wasn't.

Hester squared her shoulders. If she could survive what she already had, then she could survive this too. And maybe, with a little change in 'packaging', she could subvert that stereotype those others had placed on her— and yes, wouldn't that be a little 'fun'?

That long-buried seed unfurled, forming the smallest irrepressible bud. An irresistible desire for adventure, a chance impossible to refuse. She couldn't say no when he was offering her the power to change everything for someone so vulnerable. And for herself.

'I think you'll like Triscari,' he murmured easily. 'The weather is beautiful. We have many animals. We're most famous for our horses, but we have cats too...'

She gazed at him, knowing he was wheedling because he sensed success.

'All right,' she said calmly, even as she was inwardly panicking already. 'One year's employment.'

Predatory satisfaction flared in his eyes. Yes. This was a man who liked to get his way. But he was wise enough not to punch the air with an aggressive fist. He merely nodded. Because he'd expected her acquiescence all along, hadn't he?

'It'll cost you,' she added quickly, feeling the sharp edge of danger press.

'All the money?' His smile quirked.

'Yes,' she answered boldly, despite her thundering heart. 'So much money.'

'You have plans.' He sounded dispassionately curious. 'What are you going to do with it?'

'You want your privacy, I want mine,' she snapped. 'If I want to bathe in a tub full of crisp, new dollar bills, that's my prerogative.' She wasn't telling him or anyone. Not even Lucia and Zoe, because she didn't want any of this to blow back on them. This would be a secret gift.

'Wonderful. Let me know when you want them delivered.' He looked amused. 'Shall we shake on it?'

Gravely she placed her hand in his, quelling the shiver inside as he grasped her firmly. He didn't let her go, not until she looked up. The second she did, she was captured by that contrary mix of caution and curiosity and concern in his beautiful eyes. She had the horrible fear they were *full* of soul.

It didn't seem right for him to bow before her and, worse, she couldn't make herself respond in kind, not even to incline her head. She couldn't seem to move—her lungs had constricted. And her heart? That had simply stopped.

'Let's go get married, Hester,' he suggested, his lightness at odds with that ever-deepening intensity of his gaze. 'The sooner the better.'

CHAPTER TWO

ALEK COULDN'T QUITE believe what he'd just established.
But that reckless part of him—that sliver of devilishness—
felt nothing but euphoria. Here she was. The method by
which he'd finally please the courtiers and parliamentar-
ians who'd been pestering him for months. The means by
which he'd find his freedom and fulfil his destiny at the
same time.

Ms Hester Moss.

Personal assistant. Calm automaton. Perfect wife. Yes,
he was going to give his country their most inoffensive,
bland Queen. In her navy utility trousers, her crisp white
tee shirt, her large-rimmed glasses and her hair in that
long, purely functional ponytail at the nape of her neck,
she looked least like any royal bride ever. Not tall, not especially slender, not styled and definitely not coated in
that sophisticated confidence he was used to. In that sense
she was right, she was nothing like the women he usually dated. And that was perfect. Because he didn't want
to date her. And she definitely didn't want to date him.
This would be a purely functional arrangement. No sex.
No complications.

She had something better to offer him. She was self-
contained, precise, earnest, and—he'd bet—*dutiful*. She'd
be efficient, discreet, courteous and they'd co-exist for this

limited time in complete harmony And she wasn't a dragon or a bitch; she seemed too bloodless to be either. Actually, now he thought about it, she struck him as *too* controlled, too careful altogether. Irritation rippled beneath his skin. He knew she judged him—hell, who didn't? But he wanted to scratch the surface and find *her* faults. After all, everyone had flaws and weaknesses. Everyone had something that made their blood boil. He'd seen it briefly when she'd referenced his 'lifestyle', when she'd called him out for being 'spoiled', when she'd felt the need to snap *no* at him.

But he'd just got her to say yes to him and damn if it didn't feel good. Only now he was wondering *why* she wanted the pots of gold.

He could pull her file from security but immediately rejected the idea. His father would never have allowed Fiorella near someone unsuitable, so there could be nothing in her past to cause concern. He'd satisfy his curiosity the old-fashioned way. Face to face. The prospect of breaking through her opaque, glass façade and making her reveal the snippets of herself that she seemed determined to keep secret was surprisingly appealing. The only question was *how* he'd go about it.

Now he had her hand in his and he was gazing into her eyes—a breath away for the first time. Even behind the large-framed glasses, he could appreciate their colour— pure gold, a warm solid hue—and it seemed she wasn't averse to a little smoke and mirrors because she had to be wearing mascara. Her eyelashes were abnormally thick. Heat burned across the back of his neck and slowly swept down his spine, around his chest, skimming lower and lower still. Startled by the unexpected sensation, he tensed, unable to release her cool hand, unable to cease staring into her amazing, leonine eyes.

'Alek?'

He blinked and turned his head. 'Fi.'

His sister was gaping at their linked hands.

He felt a tug and turned back to see awkwardness swarm over Hester's face. Slowly he obeyed her wordless plea and released her hand.

'What are you doing here?' Fiorella stepped forward, her astonishment obvious. 'What's going on?'

He drew a sharp breath and slammed into a snap decision. He would do this with supreme discretion. No one but he and Hester would know the truth and if they could pass the Fifi test here and now, they'd be fine with the rest of the world. 'We didn't intend to surprise you this way,' he said smoothly. 'But Hester and I are engaged.'

'Engaged? To *Hester*?' Fi's eyes bugged. *'No way.'*

'Fi—'

'You don't even *know* each other.' Fi was clearly stunned.

'That's where you're wrong. Again,' he muttered. 'We know each other far better than you think.'

'But…' Fi looked from him to Hester and that frown deepened on her face. 'No way.'

He glanced at Hester and saw she'd paled. She shoved her hands into the horrendously practical pockets of her cotton drill trousers and stood eerily still, her façade determinedly uncrackable.

'Hester?' Fiorella gazed at her assistant, a small frown formed between her brows. 'I know you've been distracted lately and not as available…'

Alek glanced at Hester and saw she'd gone paler still. His instincts were engaged—what had been distracting her? The whisper of vulnerability prickled his senses.

'She works for *me*.' Fifi pulled his attention back with her quiet possessiveness. 'And I don't want you to…mess her around.'

Hester's eyes widened and colour scurried back into her cheeks. But to his astonishment, a pretty smile broke through her tense, expressionless façade. His jaw dropped and for a moment he had the oddest wish that he'd been the one to make her smile like that. She'd suddenly looked luminous and *soft*. But then the smile faded and her self-contained neutrality was restored.

'I'm a big girl, Princess Fiorella,' Hester said in that careful, contained way she had. 'I can take care of myself.'

Alek realised Hester had feared Fi disapproved of *her*. And she was hugely relieved to discover she didn't.

'I know you had no idea,' Hester added as she gestured towards him. 'But we had our reasons for that.'

Instinctively he reached out and clasped her hand back in his. A stunningly strong ripple of possessiveness shimmered through him. Again acting on instinct, he laced his fingers through hers and locked his grip. For the proof in front of Fifi, right?

His sister now stared again at their interlinked hands, her eyes growing round before she flashed a hurt look up at Alek. 'Is this because of that stupid requirement?'

'This is because it is what both your brother and I *want*.'

Hester's faintly husky emphasis on the 'want' tightened his skin.

'I'm so sorry to have kept this from you, but it's been quite…tough.'

'And I'm sorry for the short notice,' Alek added as Hester faltered. 'But I'm taking Hester back with me immediately.'

'To Triscari? Now?' Fi clasped her hands in front of her chest. 'You're for real? Like really for real?'

That light flush swept more deeply across Hester's face as Alek confirmed it with a twinge of regret. His sister was young and unspoiled but he found himself watching Hester more closely for clues as to what was going on beneath her still exterior.

'It's like a fairy tale,' Fifi breathed. 'Oh, Alek, this is wonderful.'

Hester's hand quivered in his and he tightened his hold.

'You're really leaving right away?' Fi asked.

'It's been difficult,' Alek said honestly. 'It's best we get back to Triscari. There's a lot for Hester to take in.'

Worry dulled the delight in Fi's eyes.

'It's okay. Everything's in your diary and you can always text me with any problems,' Hester said earnestly. 'I can keep answering your correspondence—that's the bulk of what I do for you and there's no reason why I can't continue.'

Alek bit his tongue to stop himself interrupting with all the reasons why she wasn't going to be able to keep working for his sister.

'Are you sure?' Fi's relief was audible.

'Hester can help train someone up to take over from her quite quickly.' He sent Hester a shamelessly wicked smile. 'After all, you'll be busy managing your own mail shortly.'

A mildly alarmed look flickered in her eyes before she smiled politely back.

'Well.' Fi drew breath. 'I have to go, I'm late to meet my friend. I only called in to tell Hester I need her to…never mind. I can do it. I'll leave you to…go.' She glanced again between him and Hester. 'I still can't believe it.'

Fi stepped in and Alek gave her a one-armed hug.

He met Hester's gaze over the top of Fi's head and saw the glint of amusement in her eyes. She was very good at managing her emotions and at managing a volatile Fiorella. A volatility he knew he had in common with his sister on occasion.

When Fi left, he released Hester's hand—with a surprising amount of reluctance.

'Thank you,' he said. He needed to focus on the important things. Like fabricating their story. 'You're good at lying.'

'I'm good at saying what's necessary for self-preservation,' she replied. 'That's a different skill.'

His senses sharpened. Self-preservation? Why was that?

'You really want us to maintain this "relationship" in front of Princess Fiorella?' she asked too calmly.

'For now.' He nodded. 'I don't want to risk any inadvertent revelations and I don't want her to worry.'

'She's your sister, she's going to be concerned about your *happiness.*'

'I thought she seemed more worried about you than me.' He shot her an ironic glance.

'She doesn't need to worry about me.' Hester gazed down at her desk. 'I'm fine. I can handle anything.'

He had the odd feeling she could but that didn't mean that she *should.* 'It seems the pretence is under way, Hester. This is your last chance to back out.'

She was silent for a moment, but then lifted her serene face to his. 'No, let's do this. You should be crowned.'

Really? He didn't think she was in this for *his* benefit. She'd become rich; that was the real reason, wasn't it? Except he didn't think it was. What did she plan to do with the money?

He frowned. It shouldn't matter, it wasn't his business.

But what had she been so 'distracted' with lately? Not a man, or she'd not have said yes to him. He'd bet it was someone else, someone she wanted the money for.

He huffed out a breath and willed his curiosity to ebb. He didn't need to know any more. She was palace employed, therefore palace perfect. Contained, aloof, efficient. She even maintained a polite distance from Fi, who he knew was physically demonstrative. He now realised part of Fi's shock—and reason for her eventual belief—had been because he and Hester were *touching.* Fiorella hadn't hugged Hester when she'd left. He was sure the re-serve came from Hester—strictly observing her role as employee, not confidante or friend. Doubtless she was all about 'professional boundaries', or something. It was evi-dent in the way she dressed too. The utilitarian clothes and sensible black canvas shoes were almost a services uni-form from the nineteen-forties. But her hourglass figure couldn't quite be hidden even by those ill-tailored trousers. Her narrow waist and curving hips held all the promise of soft, lush pillow for a man…that *stability* she'd made him think of.

But she made him think about other things too—like why did she live in that prison-like cell of a bedroom? Why was it so lacking in anything personal other than a mangy stray cat, a broken wooden box and a pile of sec-ond-hand books?

She was like a walled-off puzzle with several pieces missing. Happily, Alek quite enjoyed puzzles and he had a year to figure her out. Too easy—and there was no reason they couldn't be *friends*. He could ignore the unexpected flares of physical interest. If his desperate speed-dating of the last month had proven anything to him, it was that the last thing he wanted was anything remotely like a real relationship. Definitely not a true marriage. Not for a very long time. As for that vexed issue providing his kingdom with an heir…that he was just going to put off for as long as possible. Somehow he'd find a way to ensure any child of his didn't suffer the same constraints he had.

'We should make plans.' He moved forward to her desk. 'I need to contact the palace. You need to pack.' He glanced over to where she stood worryingly still. 'Or…?'

'How are we going to end this?' she asked pensively. 'In a year. What will we say?'

He was relieved she wasn't pulling out on him already. 'I'll take the blame.'

'No. Let me,' she said quietly. 'You're the King.'

'No.' He refused to compromise on this. 'You'll be vilified.'

Double standards abounded, wrong as it was, and he wasn't having her suffer in any way because of this. He'd do no harm. And she was doing him a huge favour.

'I don't want to be walked over,' she said a little unevenly. '*I'll* do the stomping. Keep your reputation. Mine doesn't matter.'

He stared at her. She stood more still than ever—defensively prim, definitely prickly—and yet she wanted to be reckless in that?

'You'd sacrifice everything,' he tried to inform her gently.

'Actually, I'll sacrifice nothing,' she contradicted. 'I don't care what they say about me.'

No one didn't care. Not anyone human, anyway. And he'd seen her expression change drastically when Fi had returned, so Hester was definitely human. She'd been terrified of his sister's reaction—of her disapproval. Which meant she liked and cared about Fi. And she cared about doing the stomping.

Now he studied her with interest, opting not to argue. He'd had all the wins so far, so he could let this slide until later because he was totally unhappy with the idea of her taking the responsibility for their marriage 'breakdown'.

'We'll finalise it nearer the time.'

She softened fractionally.

'You know they'll want all the pomp and ceremony for this wedding.' He rolled his eyes irreverently, wanting to make her smile again. 'All the full regalia.'

'You really don't think much of your own traditions, do you?'

'Actually, I care greatly about my country and my people and *most* of our customs. But I do find the feathers on the uniform impede my style a little.'

'Feathers?' She looked diverted and suddenly, as he'd hoped, her soft smile peeked out. Followed by a too-brief giggle. 'So, you really mean smoke and mirrors?'

'It's a little ridiculous, I'm afraid.' He nodded with a grin. 'But not necessarily wrong.'

'Okay. Smoke. Mirrors. Feathers.' But she seemed to steel herself and shot him a searching look. 'You don't think everyone will know the wedding is only for the coronation?'

'Not if we convince them otherwise.'

'And how do we do that?'

'We just convinced Fi, didn't we?'

'She's a romantic.'

'So we give them romance.' Fire flickered along his limbs and he tensed to stop himself stepping closer and seeing what kind of 'romance' he could spontaneously conjure with her. What he might discover beneath her serene but strong veneer. 'Trust me, Hester. We'll make this believable. We'll make it brilliant.' He cocked his head. 'I think with some work we can look like a couple in love.'

Her eyes widened. 'But there's no need for us to *touch*.' She sounded almost breathless with horror. 'Nothing like that. We'll be very circumspect, won't we?'

Alek suppressed his laugh. His officials were going to love her, given how much they loathed his usual less than circumspect affairs. And if she presented this shy, blushing bride act to the public, she'd melt all hearts.

'You mean no public displays of affection?' he queried more calmly than he felt.

'That's right.'

Was she serious? 'None at *all*?'

He keenly watched her attempt to maintain her unruffled expression, but tell-tale colour surged over her skin and ruined her proud attempt. But she didn't reply and he realised she was utterly serious. So what about *private* displays of affection?

The fierce desire to provoke her came from nowhere and astounded him. The ways he'd make her blush all over? To make her smile and sigh and *scream*?

The immediate cascade of thoughts was so hot and heady, he tensed all over again. It was just the challenge, right? She'd initially told him no with unapologetic bluntness, while excoriating his social life. Now she reckoned she didn't want him to touch her?

Okay, no problem.

Yet surely he wasn't the only one feeling this shocking chemistry? The magnetic pull was too strong to be one-sided. Her colour deepened as the silence stretched and thickened. Of course she felt it, he realised, feeling a gauche fool. It was the whole reason for her complete blushathon.

Hester stared as he hesitated for what felt like for ever. Her whole body felt on fire—with utter and absolute mortification—but this was something she needed not just to clarify, but to make certain—iron-clad in their agreement. It suddenly seemed *essential*.

'Okay,' he agreed, but amusement flitted around his mouth. 'I wasn't about to suggest we practise or anything.'

'Good.' She finally breathed out. 'That would just be stupid.'

'Indeed. I don't need to practise. I know how to kiss.'

Hester didn't quite know how to respond. She wasn't about to admit how totally lacking in kissing experience she was. That heat beat all over her body, but she counted breaths in and out, to restore outward calm at least. Inside she was still frying.

'Because, just so you know, we will have to kiss. Twice, if you can bring yourself to agree.' He gazed at her steadily. 'During the wedding service, which will, of course, be live-streamed. We'll need to kiss after the commitment during the ceremony and once again on the steps outside the church afterwards.'

'Live-streamed?' Her lungs constricted. 'From a church?'

'In the palace chapel, yes. It's just the part we're both playing, Hester.'

The palace chapel? It really was the stuff of fairy-tale fiction. As long as she remembered that was all it was, then she could go through with it, right? As long as she remembered what she could do for Lucia and Zoe.

'Two kisses,' she conceded briefly.

She was sure they'd be chaste pecks, given they were going to be live-streamed and all. Not even the outrageous Prince Alek would put on a raunchy show for the world with his convenient bride. There was no need for him to ever know she'd never been kissed before.

'Do you think I can hold your hand at the banquet afterwards? Look at you? Smile?'

He was teasing her so she answered with even more determined seriousness. 'Depending on the circumstances, I might even smile back.'

'Depending on the circumstances?' he echoed idly. 'There's a challenge.'

But he sat down at her desk, grabbed a blank piece of paper, borrowed one of her favourite pens and began writing. She watched, fascinated as the paper filled with small squares and a task or reminder beside each. Efficiency, list-making and prioritising? Who'd have thought? After a few moments he studied the list and nodded to himself before pulling out his phone and tapping the screen.

'Good news, Marc. I'm to be married after all. I know you've had the wedding plans in place for months so now you can press "go",' he said with a bitter-edged smile. 'We'll journey home this afternoon.' He paused for a long moment. 'You think that's achievable? Is that long enough for—?' He paused again. 'You flatter me, Marc, but if you're sure.' A few moments later he rang off. 'We're getting married in ten days and the coronation will take place in the week after.'

'Ten days?' Hester echoed.

'I know, sooner than I'd have thought too. But it seems to have been planned since before I was born. It's going to be a state holiday apparently.' He scribbled more items on his ever-increasing list. 'They've got plans for everything—processions, funerals, baptisms.' He glanced across at her with a laughing grin. 'My obituary is already written. They just update it every so often.'

'You're kidding.'

'No. They're prepared for everything. I think they thought I'd get killed in a plane crash or something a few years ago.' He suddenly chuckled. 'Don't look so shocked.'

'It just seems…' She trailed off, wary of expressing her thoughts. But it seemed sad somehow, to have your life so meticulously planned, documented, constrained. Was it so surprising he'd rebelled against it?

'Don't you have every eventuality covered in your management of Fi's correspondence?' He gestured at her immaculate desk. 'I'm assuming you're a lists and contingencies person.'

'Well, yes, but—'

'They just have more lists than you.' He gazed down at his list. 'You'll need a wedding dress. It would be diplomatic if you choose a Triscarian designer. Would that be tolerable?'

'Of course,' she mumbled, but a qualm of panic struck. What had she been thinking? How could she pull off a live-streamed wedding with millions of people watching? Every last one would pick apart, not just her outfit, but every aspect of her appearance. She wasn't a leggy beautiful brunette like Princess Fiorella. She was on the shorter, wider sides of average—as her aunt had so often commented when comparing her to her gazelle-like, mean cousins.

She took a breath and squared her shoulders. She *didn't* care. She'd resolved long ago never to care again. Because the simple fact was she could never live up to the expectation or never please all of them, so why worry about *any*?

'My assistant will arrange for some samples to be brought to the palace.' He wrote yet another item in his harsh scrawl.

'There's not much time to make a dress or adjustments in ten days.' There wasn't much time to get her head around anything, let alone everything.

'They'll have a team. We'll do some preparation as well, how to pose for photos and the like.'

How to *what*? 'You mean you're going to put me through some kind of princess school?'

'Yes.' He met her appalled gaze with laughter. 'There'll be lots of cameras. It can be blinding at first.'

'Perhaps Princess Fiorella can guide me,' she suggested hopefully.

'*I* will,' he replied firmly. 'Fi needs to meet her obligations here. She'll join us only for the ceremony.'

'But it's okay for me to walk out on her right away?'

'Your obligations to me and to Triscari now take precedence.' He added something else to his endless list.

Hester glanced about the room, suddenly thinking about all the things *she* was going to need to achieve. 'I'll have to—'

'Find someone to feed the cat.' He nodded and wrote that down too.

'Yes,' she muttered, internally touched that he'd remembered.

'At my expense, of course,' he added. 'Do you have other work obligations we need to address?'

'I can sort it.' She didn't flatter herself that she was indispensable. No one was. She could disappear from the college and very few people would notice. She'd disappeared before no trouble at all. But she was going to need to sort out Lucia. 'Um…' She cleared her throat. 'I'm going to need…'

'The money?' He lifted his head to scrutinise her and waggled his pen between forefinger and thumb. 'You want your first bathtub full of dollar bills?'

The intensity in his eyes made it hard to keep her equilibrium.

'A few bundles would be good,' she mumbled.

He tore another piece of paper from the pad and put it on the opposite side of the desk in front of her. 'Write down the details and I'll have it done.'

He didn't ask more about why she wanted it. She half hoped he understood it wasn't for her.

'What family would you like to invite?' he asked. 'You can have as many as you like. Write the list and I'll have them arrange invitations, transport and accommodation.'

She froze, her pen hovering just above the paper. Family?

She eventually glanced at him. He'd stopped writing and was watching her as he waited for her reply with apparently infinite patience. She wanted to look away from his eyes, but couldn't. And she'd said this so many times before, this shouldn't be different. But it was. Her breathing quickened. She just needed to say it. Rip the plaster off. That way was best. 'My parents died when I was a child.'

He didn't bat an eyelid. 'Foster parents, then? Adoptive? Extended family?'

She swallowed to push back the rising anxiety. 'Do I have to invite them?'

His gaze remained direct and calm. 'If you don't invite anyone, there will be comment. I'm used to comment, so that doesn't bother me. But if it will bother you, then I'd suggest inviting but then keeping them at a distance. That would be the diplomatic route that the courtiers will prefer.'

'What would you prefer?' Her heart banged against her ribcage.

'I want you to do whatever will help you get through the day.'

That understated compassion shook her serenity and almost tempted her to confide in him. But she barely thought about her 'family'. She couldn't bear to. And she hadn't seen them in years. 'If they do come, will I have to spend time much with them...?'

He looked thoughtful and then the corners of his eyes crinkled. 'I can be very possessive and dictatorial.'

'You mean you'll abuse your power?' She couldn't supress another giggle.

'Absolutely.' His answering grin was shameless and charming and pleased. 'That's what you'd expect from me, right?'

Her heart skipped. 'The perks of being a prince...'

But her own smile faded as she considered the ramifications. She'd never wanted to see those people again, but this was an extremely public wedding. If she didn't invite them there'd be more than mere speculation: journalists would sniff about for stories. If they dug deep old wounds might be opened, causing more drama. Anyway, her extended family liked nothing more than status, so if she invited them to the royal wedding of the decade, they'd be less likely to say anything. They'd never admit they'd disowned her father, spurned her pregnant mother, and caused her teenage parents to run away like some modern-day Romeo and Juliet. They'd never admit that they'd only taken her in after the accident for 'the look of it'. Or that they'd never let her forget how she was the unplanned and unwanted 'trash' who'd ruined the perfect plan they'd had for her father's life.

'Do you have someone you'd like to escort you down the aisle?' he asked.

She noted with a wry smile that he didn't suggest she be given away. 'It's fine, I'll do that alone.' She looked at the paper in front of her. 'But perhaps Princess Fiorella might act as bridesmaid?' She wasn't sure if it was appropriate, but there really wasn't anyone else she could think of.

'That would work very well.'

'Perfect for your pining heart narrative,' she joked to cover the intensity of the discussion.

'The media will seize on this as soon as they hear anything,' Alek said solemnly. 'They will pry into your private life, Hester. Are you prepared for that?'

'It's fine.' She went back to writing her own list to avoid looking at him. 'They can say what they like, print what they like.'

'No skeletons in the closet?' he queried gently. 'It wouldn't bother me if there were. Heaven knows I have them.' She heard his smile in his voice before it dropped lower. 'But I wouldn't want you to suffer.'

She shook her head and refused to look up at him again. 'It's fine.'

'There are no ex-boyfriends who are going to sell their stories about you to the press?'

Her blush built but she doggedly kept looking down. Why did he have to press this? He didn't need to know.

'They're harder on women,' he said huskily. 'Wrong as that is.'

'There are no skeletons. I was lonely as a teenager. I wasn't really close to anyone.' Uncomfortable, she glanced up to assure him and instantly regretted it because she was caught in the coal-black depths of his eyes. 'My life to date has been very boring,' she said flatly. 'There's literally nothing to write about.'

Nothing in her love life anyway. She couldn't break free of his unwavering gaze and slowly that heat curled within her—embarrassment, right? But she also felt an alarming temptation to lean closer to him. Instead she froze. 'Is it a problem?'

'Not at all.'

She forced herself to focus on listing the details he'd asked for, rather than the strange sensations burgeoning within her.

This marriage was a few months of adventure. She had to treat it like that. If she'd been crazy enough to say yes to such an outlandish, impulsive proposal, she might as well go all the way with it. 'Will your assistant be able to find me a hairdresser?' She pushed past her customary independence and made herself ask for the help she needed. 'And maybe some other clothes...'

'You'd like that?'

She glanced up again and saw he was still studying her intently.

'All the smoke and mirrors?' she joked lamely again. 'I'd like all the help I can get to pull this off.'

'Then I'll have it arranged. Write down your size and I'll have some things brought to the plane.'

Heat suffused her skin again but she added it to her list before pushing the paper towards him. 'I think that's everything.'

'Good,' he said briskly. 'Start packing. I have several calls to make.'

Relieved, she escaped into her small bedroom. With an oblique reference to 'a family matter', her volunteer coordinator at the drop-in centre expressed regret but understanding. It took only a moment to open an anonymous email account from which she could make the arrangements for her support for Lucia. Packing her belongings took only a moment too. She picked up the antique wooden box Alek had touched and carefully put it into the small backpack she'd used when she'd run away all those years ago. Her clothes fitted easily into the one small suitcase she'd acquired since.

'That's everything?' He stared in frank amazement at her suitcase when she returned to the lounge.

'I don't need much.'

'You're going to need a little more than that.' He reached out to take the case from her. 'It's probably good that we leave before Fi gets back. Saves on all the questions she'll have been stockpiling over the last hour.'

But Hester didn't follow him as he headed towards the door. 'Are you absolutely certain about this, Your Highness?'

He turned back to face her. 'Of course I'm certain,' he said with absolute princely arrogance. 'And you need to call me Alek.'

'Okay.' She hoisted her backpack and walked towards the door.

But he blocked her path. 'Do it now. Practise so it slips off your tongue naturally. Call me Alek.'

'I will.'

He still didn't move to let her past. A frisson of awareness, danger, defiance, shivered within her as she defiantly met his gaze.

'Say, *Alek is wonderful*. Now,' he commanded.

She glared harder at him. 'Alek is bossy.'

'Good enough.' He stepped back, the distance between them enabling her to breathe again. But his slow smile glinted with full wickedness. 'For now.'

CHAPTER THREE

SWIFT WASN'T THE word for Alek's modus operandi. When he'd decided something, he moved. Fast.

'You're very used to getting your own way,' Hester said as she followed him downstairs out of the campus residence she'd called home for the last three years.

'You think?' He shot her a look. 'I have the feeling I might not get everything quite on my terms for a while.'

'Is that such a threat?' Without thinking, another small smile sparkled free.

'Not at all,' he denied with relish. 'I enjoy a challenge.'

Oh, she wasn't a *challenge*. She was never going to be some kind of toy for this notorious playboy. But she forgot any flattening reply she was mulling when she saw the entourage waiting outside. Large, almost armoured vehicles were staffed by a phalanx of ferociously physical suited and booted men armed with earpieces and dark eyewear and who knew what else beneath the black fabric of their jackets. Alek guided her directly to the middle car. She was absurdly glad of its size and comfort, air conditioning and sleek silence. Her pulse hammered as they drove through the streets and she tried to stop herself snatching looks at him.

Lucia and Zoe will be secure and together.

That was what she needed to focus on. *Not his dimples.*

But her nerves mounted. The fluttering in her tummy was because she'd never flown in a plane before, that was all.

That's not all.

This whole thing was insane. She needed to tell him she'd made a mistake. Back out and beg him to help that family—surely he would once he heard about Lucia's struggle?

'Okay?' Alek was watching her with astute amusement.

She thought about Lucia and Zoe again. She thought about living on a warm island for a while. She thought about full financial freedom and independence for the rest of her life.

'Okay.' She nodded.

They went through a side door of the airport terminal. A uniformed woman escorted them directly to the plane.

'Everyone is aboard?' Alek asked.

'Yes, sir. We're cleared for departure as soon as you're seated.'

Hester paused in the doorway and frowned. This wasn't a small private jet like ones she'd seen in the movies. This was a commercial airliner. Except it wasn't. There weren't rows of cramped seats and masses of people. This was a lounge with sofas and small armchairs around wooden tables. Accented with back-lit marble and mirrors, it was so beautiful, it was like a *hotel*.

She gaped. 'Is this really a plane?'

He smiled as he gestured for her to sit in one of the wide white leather armchairs and showed her where the seat belt hid. 'I'll give you the tour once we're in the air. Can I take your bag?'

'Can I keep it with me?' Her box was in there and it contained her most precious things.

'In this compartment, here.' He stowed it and took the seat opposite hers. 'I've arranged for a stylist to fly with us, so you can make a start, and I've had an assistant pull together a report on some key staffers so you can get ahead of the game on who's who at the palace.' He pulled a tablet from another hidden compartment. 'I don't find the palace intimidating, but I was born there so it's normal for me.' He shrugged his shoulders.

She nodded, unable to speak or smile. It was enough effort to stay calm. Was she really about to leave the country? About to marry a man who was destined to become a king? About to launch into the air in a giant tin can?

'Nervous?'

'Of course,' she muttered honestly. 'But once I've done some preparation I'll feel better.'

His pilots would have years of expertise behind them. She breathed carefully, managing her emotions. After a while she could glance out of the window. They'd climbed steeply and now the plane levelled out.

'Follow me,' Alek said, unfastening his seat belt.

She fumbled and he reached across and undid her belt for her.

'Are you—?'

'I'm fine,' she interrupted and quickly stood, taking a pace away from him. He was too close and she was unable to process the spaciousness. 'Are all private planes this big?'

'No,' he smirked. 'Mine's the biggest.'

'Of course it is,' she muttered. 'Your ego could handle nothing less.'

'Miaow.' He laughed. 'I see why you're friends with that grumpy cat.'

Beyond the private lounge he pointed out a bedroom suite—with more marble and mirrors—then led her through another lounge to another cabin that was more like the business-class seating she'd seen in the movies. Half the seats were full—several of those suited bodyguard types, then others who looked like assistants. As she and Alek neared, they all scrambled to stand.

'Please.' Alek smiled and gestured for them to remain seated. 'Is your team ready, Billie?'

'Of course, Your Highness.' A slim jeans-clad woman stood, as did another couple of people.

'This is Hester,' Alek said briefly when they were back in the second lounge. 'I'll leave you to introduce your team. Please take good care of her.' He sent her a small mocking smile and headed back to the front of the plane.

That was it? There were no instructions? She had no idea what she was supposed to do.

'We're here to help you, Ms Moss,' Billie said confidently.

And there was indeed a team. A hairdresser, a make-up artist, a beautician and a tailor. They were doing a wonderful job of hiding their curiosity but it was so strong she could almost taste it.

'Would you mind if we untie your hair?'

Hester paused. She had to trust Alek's choice, and in their professionalism. 'Of course.' She pulled the elastic tie to free her ponytail. 'I just need you to make me presentable as consort to the King.'

All four of them just stared at her, making her feel awkward.

'That's not going to be a problem,' Billie replied after endless seconds. 'Not a problem.'

She didn't pretend she could reach for anything more than presentable. But she'd been around Princess Fiorella long enough to understand a few tricks. Tailored clothing and some polish could make her passable.

'We have some dresses,' Billie said. 'Would you try them on first so I can make alterations while you're with the beautician?'

'Of course, thank you.' Hester watched, stunned, as

Billie unzipped several garment bags while Jon the hair-dresser began laying out his tools on the table. 'You must have run to get all this together so quickly.'

'An assignment like this?' A huge smile spread across Jon's face. 'Once in a lifetime.'

Once in a lifetime was right. And it was an assignment for her as much as it was for them. She could learn to do what was necessary, she could even excel in some areas. But she definitely needed help with this. She'd never had the desire to look good before; frankly she'd never wanted people to notice her. Blending in was safer. Hiding was safer still.

But now people were going to be looking so she needed armour. That was what clothing and make-up could be, right?

Hester spent the best part of an hour turning this way and that and holding still while Billie pinned her waist and hem. The fabrics were so soft and sleek, slowly her trepidation ebbed and she actually began to enjoy herself.

'Now I have your measurements, I can get you some more when we land in Triscari,' Billie said.

Hester glanced at the pile of clothes laid out on the table. 'Do I need more?'

'Much more.' Billie swiftly hung the dresses. 'It's not all photo shoots and public engagements. You'll still have day-to-day life at the palace.'

Hester bit back a nervous giggle. It sounded fantastic and her usual navy utility trousers weren't exactly palace proper. 'Okay, some more casual items would be wonderful. And...' she fought back her blush '...perhaps some new underwear.'

'Leave it with me.' Billie smiled.

Hester smiled shyly. As the beautician waxed, plucked, buffed and massaged her, hours of flight time passed by and she was able to avoid conversation by studying the information on the tablet Alek had given her. Wrapped in a white fluffy robe, she sat in one of the chairs in the boardroom while Jon settled a towel around her shoulders.

She'd never coloured her hair or had any sort of stylish cut because she'd never been able to afford it. So now she sat still for hours as Jon and his assistant hovered over her while Billie hand-sewed alterations to the stunning dresses.

'Okay,' Jon said. 'Take as long as you like in the shower and then we'll get to drying it.'

'Shower? Seriously?' On an airplane?

'Apparently so.' Jon grinned. 'I've been in some planes…but this?'

The biggest and the best. She bit back her grimace.

As she dressed, Hester tried not to wonder what Alek would think of her make-over. He didn't need to find her *attractive*. She just needed to pass inspection.

But inside, she felt oddly different. There was something sensual about her smooth skin, rendered silky by the luxuriant lotions the beautician had rubbed in. For the first time in her life she felt pampered—almost precious.

Alek sprawled back in the recliner, absurdly satisfied with the day's events. He'd gone from frustrated and angry to being in complete control of the situation. Flying off last minute to vent to Fi after another monster row with his chief advisor, Marc, had turned out to be the best idea he'd ever had.

He'd forgotten all about his sister's prim secretary but she was perfect for this assignment. It didn't matter if she wasn't the most beautiful bride the world had ever seen because she was, after all, the one student his father had approved of. Back when Alek had been fighting to get his irascible control-freak father to allow Fiorella to study overseas, he'd come up with the idea of having an approved older student act as a mentor. His father had selected Hester from the pile of student records. So what better temporary wife could Alek produce now? The irony of it delighted him. And not having any emotional entanglement would make this 'marriage' wonderfully straightforward.

Though her determined reserve still fuelled his curiosity. He suspected she was more inexperienced than he'd first realised, but she had a smart head on her shoulders and it was insulting of him to think she couldn't handle this. She was a tough, brave little cookie.

His curiosity deepened as he wondered what personal fire she'd been through to make her so. Because there had to have been something. Why else had she been less than enthusiastic to invite what little family she had left?

He thought again about that barren little bedroom. There was minimalist simplicity and there was plain sad. He knew she had no education debt because she'd been on a scholarship and worked her way through her degree. She was clearly frugal and knew how to live on only a little. Yet she'd wanted a bundle of money in a hurry. Maybe one day she'd tell him why. Though he had the extraordinary inclination to make her tell him sooner. How would he get her to do that? She was so reticent he'd have to tease it out of her. He eased further back in the chair, enjoying the possibilities when the door opened. He glanced up as a goddess walked into his lounge.

Hester Moss.

At least he thought it was Hester. His brain had suddenly been starved of oxygen and he had to blink a couple of times and force his slack jaw actually to suck in a hit of air before he could quite believe his eyes.

'Do I pass?' She gestured to her outfit in an offhand way, her gaze not quite meeting his. 'Am I ready for the media onslaught?'

Her glasses were gone. Her hair was loose. Her baggy, boring clothing had hopefully been consigned to an incinerator because he only wanted her to wear items that fitted her as gorgeously as this dress did. He noticed all these things, but somehow he couldn't actually *think*. He could only stare.

Her expression pinched. 'That much of a difference, huh?'

'We're arriving early—they won't get much in the way of pictures,' he muttered almost incoherently before clearing his throat and reaching for his glass of water.

'Are you saying I just sat through an hour-long hair-drying session for nothing?' She finally looked him directly in the eyes.

'Not for nothing.' Oddly breathless, he detangled the tie in his tongue. 'I think it looks lovely.'

'Oh, that makes it so worth it.' She sat down in the recliner next to his. 'Lovely.'

He grinned, appreciating the lick of sarcasm in her tone. He'd deserved it with that inane comment, but he could hardly be honest. He didn't even want to face that raw and uncontrollable response himself.

Her unruffled composure had swiftly returned and he ached to scrape away that thin veneer because the leonine spark in her eyes a second ago had looked—

'Can you see without the glasses?' he muttered.

'Well enough. Just don't ask me to read my own handwriting,' she quipped.

He stared, leaning closer. 'Your eyelashes are—'

'Weird. I know.'

Her increase in visible tension was so small you'd have to be paying close attention to notice. Fortunately, Alek was paying extremely close attention.

'It's a genetic thing,' she said dismissively, but intriguingly her fingers had curled into fists. 'Don't pull an eyelash out to check they're real.'

As if he'd ever think to do that. Whoever would? 'I believe you.' He forced his stiff face into a smile.

Had someone done that to her in the past? He blinked in disbelief. They really were the thickest, most lush lashes he'd ever seen. 'And your transformation hasn't been a waste of time. We need a portrait shot to go with the media release.'

'You want to take that now?' She looked startled. 'You have a professional photographer on board too, don't you?' She nodded to herself. 'Unreal.'

He chuckled, appreciating the light relief. 'You'll get used to it.'

He buzzed for the photographer, who bounded in with more enthusiasm than usual and keenly listened as Alek explained what he wanted.

'Okay, we can use the white background over here,' the photographer said. 'What about the engagement ring?'

'We'll display that later,' Alek answered swiftly. 'Work around it for now.'

'We can do head and shoulders, but then some relaxed shots—more modern, arty, from the side—'

'Whatever you think,' Alek interrupted. 'Just get them as quickly as you can.'

Hester looked so stiff and uncomfortable, Alek had to suppress both his smile and frustration. He could think of one way of helping her relax but he didn't think she'd appreciate it. Besides, he'd ruled that out, hadn't he? He'd glibly assured her that of course he could be celibate for a year.

A *year*. The term hit him with the force of an asteroid.

'You *will* get used to it, Hester,' he repeated to reassure her.

But he was the one facing the grim reality of his impetuous decision. No sex. No touching. Just a measly two kisses—what did he think he was, twelve? And did he really think he was in 'complete control' of the situation? Because somehow, something had changed. It had only been a few hours and he was already seeing Hester in a new light. Was he so shallow it was all about the make-over? Or, worse, was it a case of wanting what was off limits—as if he were some spoilt child?

But as he stood next to her his temperature rose. He never sweated through photo sessions; he was too used to them. But she was close enough for him to catch her scent and she seemed to be glowing and it wasn't just the make-up. His fingers itched to touch and see if her skin was as silky soft as it looked.

'Can we try it with you looking at each other?' The photographer sounded frazzled. 'Um…yes, like that.'

Alek gazed at her upturned face. He couldn't think for the life of him why he'd thought her anything less than stunning. She wasn't just beautiful, she was striking. Her golden eyes with those incredible lashes? Her lush pouting lips? That infuriating serenity and stillness of her very self? He couldn't resist putting a careful hand on her waist and drawing her a little closer. He heard the slight catch in her breath but she didn't frown.

'Better,' the photographer muttered. 'Do you think you might be able to smile?'

Alek glanced up from his appallingly lustful stare at her lips to her eyes and amusement flashed between them. He chuckled the same split second she did. And there it was—that soft, enchanting smile he'd not seen enough of. A hot, raw tsunami swept through him at the sight. He wanted more of it.

'Yes!'

Now the photographer sounded far too ecstatic for Alek's liking.

'We'll get changed for the next few shots.' He wanted

to be alone with her. He wanted to make her smile again and he didn't want witnesses.

'Good idea.' Hester bit her lip and walked from the room.

Alek automatically followed her into the bedroom, unbuttoning his shirt as he went. 'What colour are—?'

'Oh!' She started and then stared bug-eyed at his chest.

Her eyes grew so round he almost preened as he shrugged his shirt all the way off.

'Is there a problem?' He couldn't help teasing her. But he was beginning to realise the real problem was all his.

No sex for a year?

'I n-need to get changed,' she stammered.

'So get changed.' With exaggerated civility he bowed and then turned his back to her and unlocked the wardrobe for a fresh shirt.

'This is your bedroom?' she choked. 'I'm so sorry, I didn't realise when we put all the clothes…'

'I don't mind, Hester.'

But it was obvious *she* minded very much. All that efficient poise of hers had vanished and he couldn't help enjoying the moment. It was because of *him*.

'Let me know when it's safe to turn around again,' he offered with a self-mocking smile. He'd prove his 'gentleman' credentials—to *himself* as much as to her.

The following silence was appallingly long. He waited, his new shirt buttoned up all the damn way, for what felt like decades for her to give him the all-clear.

'Um…' She finally coughed. 'Would you mind helping me with the zip?'

Oh, was that the problem? 'Sure.' Smothering a laugh, he turned, only to freeze at the sight of her smooth bare back. A gorgeous expanse of creamy skin was edged by the curling sweep of her voluminous golden brown hair—inviting him closer, to touch. Instead he carefully took the dress in the tips of his fingers so as not to inadvertently touch her skin. To prove his restraint to himself. Slowly he pulled the zip up, hiding her from his hungry eyes again. The desire to lean closer, to touch where he had no permission, almost overwhelmed him. By the time he finished the simple task he could barely breathe. He stepped back, coldly furious with himself. Damn if he didn't need to clear his head.

At that moment she turned and he glimpsed fire gleaming in her eyes. That barely hidden blaze of desire slammed the brakes on his breathing all over again.

'You look…' He couldn't think of an adjective—he could only think of action. Impossible action.

'Let's finish this,' she muttered, quickly turning to leave the room.

'Right.' He'd never been rendered speechless before and it took him several minutes to catch his breath. Several minutes in which he had to look into a camera and smile as if this were the happiest day of his life. And then he just gave up. 'Give us a second.'

He took Hester by the hand and walked her down to the other end of the lounge.

'You get sick of it,' she said.

'Utterly,' he admitted, so happy to see her sweet smile flash instantly.

'It must be intense, knowing absolutely everyone around is watching you all the time.'

'You learn to tune it out.'

'And pretend it's normal?' She glanced away, her smile impish as she took in the artwork adorning the plane's interior. 'As if any of this is normal?'

'Well…' he shrugged '…it is normal for me.' He nudged her chin so she looked back at him. 'It bothers you?'

To his gratification, she leaned a little closer as she shook her head, her gaze locked on his.

'That looks amazing.' A masculine voice interrupted from a distance.

Alek froze. He'd completely forgotten the photographer was still down the other end of the lounge. The startled look in Hester's face revealed she'd forgotten too and the half-laugh that escaped from her glossy pout was the sexiest thing he'd ever heard. Smiling back, he pulled her close on pure instinct. The temptation to test the softness of her lips stormed through his reason. Time stopped as he stared into her eyes, trying to read her soft heat and stillness. Could he coax her into—?

'So perfect,' the photographer muttered.

'Enough,' Alek snapped, enraged by the second intrusion. 'We'll be landing soon.' He dragged in a calming breath to recover his temper.

But it was too late. Hester had already pulled free and that fragile promise was lost.

The photographer quickly retreated to the rear of the plane.

'Everyone will assume this marriage is only because of the coronation requirement.' Her cheeks were still flushed as she sat in the seat and picked up that damn tablet again. He wished he'd never given it to her. 'Do you think it's really necessary for us to try to sell this as a love match?'

'You don't want to be treated as a joke. I have no desire for that either.' Oddly he felt more responsibility about that now. A flicker of protectiveness towards her had surged. 'I think we can pull it off. Who's to say it's not so?'

She hesitated. 'Okay, but the agreement is just between us. Not written down anywhere. I don't want lawyers getting involved and leaking information.'

'You trust that I won't renege on our deal?'

'You have more to lose than I do.' She leaned back into the corner of her chair, still staring at the tablet screen. 'Your reputation actually matters.'

She determinedly studied the information he'd put together for her to do a good job. Yet at the same time, she was determined not to care what anyone thought. Not even him. She seemed to care, yet not.

Intrigued, he studied her. Even in that gorgeous green silk dress, she reminded him of a little sparrow, carefully not taking up too much space in case she was chased away. Only taking crumbs and not demanding anything more. Why was that? Why wasn't she close to her family? Why had she not invited any friends to the wedding? It puzzled him because she was kind. Her friendliness to that feral cat showed that. And more telling, was her relationship with Fi. Fiorella, for all her faults, was a good judge of character. And it wasn't that she hadn't wanted to lose Hester as her assistant. It was that she'd been concerned for her. Was that because Fi saw vulnerability beneath that serenity as well?

The insidious warmth steadily built within him. He could go without intimacy for a year, of *course* he could. But his body rebelled at the thought. He was attracted to her and that attraction seemed to be building by the second. He gritted his teeth, determined to master it, because he was going to have to keep his fiancée close over these next few days and there could be no risk of complicating what should be a perfectly amicable agreement.

'This isn't enough.' She glanced up at him.

'Pardon?'

'I understand more about Triscari's population, economy and geography than I ever thought I'd want to. I know the potted history of your royal family and all that drama with the palace and the castle stuff. But I don't know about *you.*'

A ripple of pleasure skittered down his spine. She was curious about him?

'If I'm to convince people we're a couple then I need to know some facts,' she added primly.

Oh, she just wanted meaningless facts?

'You want my dating profile?' he teased, then chuckled at the glowering look she shot him. 'I enjoy horses, playing polo. My star sign is Scorpio. Apparently that makes me passionate—'

'What are your weaknesses?' she interrupted with a bored tone. 'What do you hate?'

So there *was* a little real curiosity there.

'I hate pickles. And I hate being told what to do.' He stared at her pointedly. 'By anyone.'

She gazed limpidly at him, not backing down. 'What else?'

'You're not taking notes,' he said softly.

'I'm not taking the risk of anyone finding them.'

'Very untrusting, aren't you?'

'Don't worry. I won't forget. *Passionately loathes pickles. And don't tell him what to do,*' she parroted and then shrugged. 'Not so difficult.'

Perversely he decided he wouldn't mind a few commands to fall from her lips. 'Tell me about you. What are your weaknesses?'

Her gaze slid to the side of him. 'I don't have any.'

He chuckled at her flat-out bravado. But it was also a way of keeping him shut out. Ordinarily he didn't mind not getting to know all that much about a woman he was dating, but Hester was going to be his *wife*. And he needed to trust her more than he'd trusted anyone in a long time. Yet she had no hesitation in lying to his face—to protect herself.

'So you expect to learn personal things about me, but won't share any of your own?' He equally pointed out her hypocrisy.

'I've already told you everything personal that's relevant. I told you my parents died when I was a child, that I'm not close to what family I have left, that my life to date has been pretty quiet. There really isn't much else.'

Rigidly determined, wasn't she? That flickering spark within her fired *his* determination. He could quiz her on the meaningless facts too. And he could push for more beyond that. 'Favourite pizza topping?' he prompted.

'Just plain—tomato and cheese.'

'Really? You don't want capers, olives, chilli oil?' He shook his head. 'You're missing out.'

'I don't need a whole bunch of extras.'

'No frills? No added luxuries—just the bare necessities? That's what you'll settle for?' He was stunned and yet when he thought of that dire bedroom of hers, it made sense. 'Tempt your palate a little, Hester. Why not treat yourself to a little something more, or don't you think you deserve it?'

Her jaw dropped. 'It's not about whether I deserve it—'

'Isn't it?' He leaned forward, pleased at her higher pitch. 'Why shouldn't you have all the extras? Other people take them all the time.'

'What if you end up with all the frills and no foundations? Then you discover you've got nothing of substance. Nothing to sustain you.' She put the tablet on the table between them. 'Keeping things simple works for me. The basics suffice.'

The basics? Was that what she considered that soulless cell of a bedroom? But that she didn't even seem to want to *try* something new was interesting. 'Are you afraid to take risks, Hester?'

'Yes,' she said baldly. 'I've fought too long and hard for what I have.'

Her admission surprised him on two counts—firstly, she didn't seem to *have* all that much. And secondly, she'd taken a massive risk with him and she was nailing this with a stunningly cool ability to adapt and handle all the challenges he was flinging at her. 'Yet you said yes to me—to this impulsive marriage.'

'Because it was an offer too good to pass up.' She gazed at him directly.

'You mean the money. Not the pleasure of my company?'

She blinked rapidly but through those glorious lashes she kept her golden focus on him. 'Yes.'

She sounded breathy and he'd like to think she was lying again because he really didn't think she was the materialistic type. He'd bet even more money that this wasn't about what she could buy but what she could *do*. Was this about freedom—so she didn't have to live on campus any more, helping first-year students get their heads around essay requirements and bibliographic details? Was this because she wanted freedom, not just from work, but from being around other people?

'Well, I'm sorry, Ms Moss, but we're going to have to spend quite a lot of time together over the next few days.' He reached forward, fastened her seat belt for landing and flashed a wicked smile at her. 'I don't know about you, but I can't wait.'

CHAPTER FOUR

TRISCARI SAT LIKE a conglomerate of emeralds and sapphires in the heart of the Mediterranean Sea. As if that giant jeweller in the sky had gathered her most prized stones in the cup of her hand and cast them into the purest blue sea in the most sun-kissed spot on the earth. And in their heart, she'd placed treasure in the form of more valuable minerals. It was incredibly attractive, wealthy and secure.

Hester already knew a lot, having researched it when she first found out she'd been selected as Princess Fiorella's safe college roommate and tutor. But now she'd read more closely about the economic success story and envy of all other small European nations. The royal family had maintained their place on the world stage and now, as ruler of a democracy, the King was mostly a figurehead and facilitator, overseeing the rights of all its people. And promoting it as a destination of course. But that was easy given the world had long been captivated by, not only the kingdom's beauty, but the luxury and the lifestyle it offered. Visiting Triscari topped absolutely everyone's bucket list.

Today the sun peeked above the horizon and turned the sea gold, making the islands look like the literal treasure they were. Hester decided she'd entered a dream world. She'd survived her first ever flight—travelling in pure luxury for hours—to arrive in the most perfect, pristine place in the world.

Ten minutes after the plane had landed, Hester followed Alek down the flight of stairs and onto the tarmac. The air was balmy even this early in the morning—the atmosphere radiated golden warmth. She got into the waiting vehicle and gazed out of the window, hungry to take in more. The stunning scenery suppressed her nerves as the car sped along the street. She knew the palace was in the centre of the town while a clifftop castle was at the water's edge. The twin royal residences had been constructed for the King and Queen of four hundred years ago. According to the legends, that arranged marriage had spectacularly failed. The couple had determinedly lived separate lives and set up their own rival courts, vying for the title of 'best'. Both had grand halls and opulent gardens and stunning artwork that had been added to over the ages.

'This would have to be the most beautiful place...' Hester said, her breath taken away by the vista. She glanced at him. 'You must love it.'

'I am very lucky.' His eyes glittered like the night sky. 'I'll do anything for this country.'

'Even get married?'

'Even that.' He nodded. 'Thanks to you.'

'Who'll be meeting us?'

'Senior palace officials.' His expression turned rueful. 'We'll ignore them for the most part, but some things will be unavoidable.'

'You live in the palace?'

'It is where the King resides.' He nodded. 'The Queen's castle is purely for display these days, but the night before the wedding you'll have to stay there. You'll process from there to the palace for the marriage ceremony. People will line the streets to watch. It's the symbolism of unity...no warring with the wife...mainly, it's just tradition.'

The men waiting for them in the vast room were all older than Alek and were all failing to mask their incredibly curious expressions. They watched her approach as if they were judge, jury and executioner in their funereal clothing and they bowed deeply as Alek introduced them.

'Very little is known about Hester and our relationship,' Alek said smoothly. 'I'm aware that where there is a vacuum, the media will fill it with fantasy over fact so we'll fill it. We'll undertake one official appearance to celebrate the engagement. Hester cannot go straight into full-time duties, certainly not right before the wedding. We have a few days but it's not long. She needs time to adjust.'

Hester watched surprise flash over the men's faces.

'Of course, Alek. It is customary for a princess to have attendants to guide her. I thought perhaps—'

'I'll guide her.' Alek cut him off.

'But—'

'We want to be together,' Alek added with a silken smile. 'If we need further support, I'll let you know. I'll meet with you shortly to discuss other issues, but I need to settle Hester into her rooms.'

As the men left Hester turned to face him. 'Do you expect me to speak at this engagement?' The thought terrified her but she was determined to hide that fact. She'd keep calm, carry on.

He glanced at her, amusement flickering in his eyes. 'Only to one person at a time, you won't address a whole room. We will need to do one pre-recorded interview, but I'll be beside you and we'll vet the questions beforehand so you have time to prepare an answer. If you smile, then we'll get through it easily.'

'All I need to do is smile?'

'You have a nice smile.'

'I can do more than smile.'

'Yeah?' His mouth quirked. 'Well, if you could look at me adoringly, that would also help.'

She rolled her eyes.

'And call me Alek.'

'You're quite stuck on that, aren't you?'

'I'm not the one who's stuck.' But his smirk slipped as he sighed. 'I inherited my father's advisors and they're used to things being done a certain way. Change is inevitable, but it's also inevitably slow.'

'Some people find change hard,' she said primly. 'It frightens them.'

'Does it frighten you?' He cocked his head.

'Of course.' She laughed. 'But I'm determined to hide it.'

'Why?' He stepped closer to her. 'You do that a lot, right? Hide your feelings. You do it well.'

'Is that a compliment or a criticism?' she asked lightly.

'Maybe it's just a comment.' His voice dropped to that delicious softness again that implied seductive intimacy—laced with steel.

'With no sentiment behind it?' She shook her head. 'There's always a judgement. That's what people do.'

'True.' He nodded. 'You judged me.'

She stared at him.

'My lifestyle.' He flicked his eyebrows suggestively.

She fought back the flush. 'I never thought you'd be so sensitive to an idle comment.'

'It wasn't idle and you're still judging me right now,' he teased. 'You don't know me, Hester.'

Her heart thudded. 'I know all I need to.'

'A bullet list of preferences that might change in an hour? That's not knowing me.'

'It's just enough detail to give this believability. I don't need to get to know you any more...'

'Intimately?' he suggested in that silken voice. *'Personally?'*

Those dimples were winking at her again. He was so unfairly handsome. And she'd never stood this close to someone in years. Never trusted that someone wouldn't hurt her—with words, or a pinch or a spiteful tug of her hair. So personal space was a thing. Wary, she stepped back, even though there was a large part of her buried deep inside that didn't want her to move in that direction at all.

'I'm going to be your husband,' he pointed out quietly.

'No. You're going to be my boss.'

'Partner.'

'Boss,' she argued. 'You're paying me.'

'You *are* afraid.' He brushed the back of his hand across her jaw ever so lightly. 'Tell me why.'

She froze at his caress, at his scrutiny. She couldn't think how to answer as tension strained between them. She was torn between the desire to flee or fall into his arms. Just as she feared her control would snap, he stepped back.

The dimples broke his solemnity. 'Come on, I have something to show you.'

She traipsed after him along endless corridors with vaulted ceilings and paintings covering every inch of the walls. Even the doors were massive. 'I'm never going to find my way back here. I need breadcrumbs or something.'

He laughed and pushed open yet another door. 'This is your space.'

'My space?'

'Your apartment.'

Her what? She stepped inside and took a second to process the stunningly ornate antechamber.

'It spans two stories within this wing of the palace, but is fully self-contained.' Alek detailed the features. 'You have a lounge, study, small kitchen, bedroom plus a spare, inward-facing balconies for privacy and of course bathroom facilities. You can redecorate it however you wish.'

She couldn't actually get past this initial reception room. 'I have all this to myself?'

'A year is a long time.' Alek circled his hand in the air as he stepped forward. 'I want you to be happy. I want you to feel like it's your home. You can have privacy and space.' He faced her. 'You can build your own library of thrillers in here if you wish.'

Hester stared at the massive room. No one had ever offered her anything like this in her life. When she'd moved to her aunt's house, she'd not been offered the same kind of welcome. And she'd tried *so* hard to fit in. But it had been awkward and they'd made her feel as if it was such a sacrifice to have her take up some of their precious space. She'd felt uncomfortable, unable to change anything for fear of offending them. She'd accumulated nothing much of her very own and that was good, given what had happened. And that minimalist habit had extended to her time at the campus. The rooms were so small, and she'd not cluttered them with anything other than books. So now, confronted with this kind of generosity, emotion choked, not just her throat, but her thinking. It was too much. Everything he'd already done was too much. He'd submerged her in an abundance that she couldn't handle. She gripped her little backpack as her limbs trembled. Frozen and tongue-tied, she couldn't trust herself to move.

'They've brought your suitcase in already,' he said.

She saw it next to one of the enormous comfortable-looking armchairs. She had such little stuff for such an opulent space it was ridiculous.

His eyebrows pulled together and he hesitated a moment before stepping towards the window. 'There's good views across to the ocean and the balcony in your bedroom is completely private. No one will be able to see you.' He paused again and she felt him gazing at her. 'Do you not like it?'

'No.' She could hardy speak for the emotion completely clogging her up. She stared hard at the floor, knowing that if she blinked some of that hot, burning liquid was going to leak from her eyes and she really didn't want that to happen. Then she realised she'd said the wrong thing. 'Not no. I meant… I just…it's fine.'

'Fine,' he echoed, but his voice sounded odd. 'So why do you look like…?' He trailed off and stepped closer than before and there was nothing for her to hide behind. 'You look like you're about to cry.'

She felt that wall of awkwardness rise and slick mortification spread at the realisation he could read her all too easily. Why could she suddenly not hide her feelings? And worse, why couldn't she hold them back?

'I don't cry.' It wasn't a lie—until now.

'Not ever—?'

'Do you?' she interrupted him, forcing herself to swallow back the tears and throw him off guard the way he was her.

He gazed at her intently and it was even worse. 'Hester—'

'I'm *fine*.' She dragged in a breath, but couldn't pull it together enough to keep it all back. 'It's just that I've never had such a big place all to myself.'

The confession slithered out, something she'd never trusted anyone enough to tell before. She didn't want him to think she didn't appreciate the effort he'd gone to. She knew he had insane wealth and property, but he'd thought this through for her. He'd taken time to consider what she might like. No one had done that for her. Not since she'd lost her parents. So she deeply appreciated this gesture, but she really needed to hold herself together because she couldn't bear to unravel completely before him.

She sensed him remain near her for a strained moment but then he strolled back towards the window.

'Personally I think the wallpaper in here is a bit much.' He casually nodded at the ferociously ornate green and black pattern.

Startled, she glanced across at him.

'You have to agree,' he added drolly. 'The word would be gaudy.'

She couldn't contain the giggle that bubbled up, a fountain of pure silliness. As her face creased, that tear teetered over the edge and she quickly wiped its trail from her cheek.

'I'm right, aren't I?' If he'd noticed her action, he didn't comment. Instead he wriggled his finger at the seam where wallpaper met window frame until he tugged enough loose to tear it.

'Alek!'

'Oh, the press are going to love it if you say my name with that hint of censure,' he teased in an altogether different tone.

A shock wave of heat blasted through her. Its impact was explosive, ripping through her walls to release the raw awareness. She'd been determined to ignore it. She knew he was an outrageous flirt, but it wasn't his tone or his teasing jokes that caused this reaction within her. It was *everything* about him. He made her wonder about the kind of intimacy she'd never known. The kind she'd actively avoided. And she'd never wanted to step *closer* to a person before.

'Don't be afraid to ask for what you want, Hester,' he said softly.

She stared at him blankly, her mind going in all kinds of searing directions.

'You can do what you like,' he offered. 'Take out walls, rip up the carpet, whatever.'

Oh. Right. He meant the rooms. Only she hadn't been thinking about the décor and what she feared she *wanted* was far too forbidden.

'Don't worry about the budget. I can just sell one of my horses to cover it.'

'Don't you love your horses more than anything?' She tried to break her unfortunate fixation.

'Other than my crown and my sister?' he teased. 'Or my playboy lifestyle?'

She licked her dried lips and refused to continue along that track. 'Do you have an apartment in here too?'

'Right next door.' He nodded. 'It's best if we're near each other.'

'I understand, it needs to look okay.' She made herself agree. 'Because this is a job,' she reiterated. But it was a lie already. 'It's just an act.'

With no intimacy—emotional or otherwise.

His gaze narrowed. 'I'd like to think we can be friends, Hester.'

She didn't have friends. Acquaintances and colleague, yes. But not friends. Since the rejection she'd suffered after her parents' deaths, she'd not been able to trust people, not got to know anyone well. Not even Princess Fiorella.

But she sensed that Alek expected a little more from her and perhaps that was fair enough. It wasn't right for her to judge him based on the actions of others he didn't even know. Or on the salacious reports the media wrote about him. She had to take him on his own actions around her and so far she had to admit he'd been decent. He'd done everything in his power to make this as easy as possible for her. And it wasn't his fault she was attracted to him like *that*. That element was up to her to control.

'I'm sure we can.' But inwardly she froze, petrified by her own internal reaction to him.

Her brain was fixed along one utterly inappropriate

track. She had the horrible feeling it was like the teen girl's first crush she'd never actually had. The fact was he didn't need to do or say anything but he'd half seduced her already. Could she really be so shallow as to be beguiled by his looks alone?

'It's going to be fine,' she said firmly. 'We have a whole year and most of the time I'll stay safe inside the palace, right?' She moved into the room, faking her comfort within the large, luxurious space. 'Actually I'm happy to stay here while you go to that meeting now, if you like.'

His eyes widened. 'Are you dismissing me, Hester?'

She smiled at his mild affront. 'Are you not used to that?'

'You know I'm not.'

'You'll get used to it.' She couldn't help a small giggle as she echoed his own reassurance.

'What if I don't want to?' He stepped closer.

Hester swallowed her smile and stilled. For a long moment they just stared at each other. Then, once more, he took a step back and the dimples flickered ever so briefly.

'I'm afraid I need you for another few minutes to show you something else.' He gestured towards the door.

'Do I need string?' She grimaced.

He chuckled. 'It's very near.'

She followed him through another doorway and then down a curling flight of stairs and blinked on the threshold of a huge airy space. There was a gorgeous pool—half indoor, half out, surrounded by lush plantings and private sun loungers.

'My father had this built for Fiorella's privacy, but she wanted her freedom. After my mother died, my father became overprotective and the palace became a bit of a prison for her.'

Hester swallowed at the mention of his mother. She'd

not been brave enough to ask him about her at all. 'Was it a prison for you too?'

'I was older. And—as bad as it sounds—I was a guy. He didn't have the same concerns for me as he did for her.'

'Seriously?'

'I know,' he sighed. 'Double standards suck. She was a lot younger though and she'd lost her mother. Everyone needs some freedom of choice, don't they? Fi definitely did.'

'She told me you helped her get your father's approval for her to study abroad,' Hester said. 'That it was only because you promised to stay and do all the royal duties that she could go. And that now your father's gone, you've told her she can do whatever she wants.'

He glanced out across the water. 'She enjoys her studies. She should have the freedom and opportunity to finish them. She's a smart woman.'

Hester's curiosity flared. 'What would you have done if you'd had the same freedom of choice that Fiorella now does?'

His smile was distant. 'There was never that choice for me, Hester.'

Alek's phone buzzed and he quickly checked the message. 'The wedding dress designers have arrived.'

Oh. She'd forgotten about that. But she found herself anticipating the planning—she'd very recently decided that there was something to be said for smoke and mirrors. The look on his face when she'd appeared after her airplane make-over had been both reward and insult. She'd quite like to surprise him some more.

'Is there a particular style you'd like for my dress?' she asked demurely.

He gazed at her for a moment, his eyes narrowing. 'I'm sure you'll look amazing in whatever you choose to wear.'

But his dimples suddenly appeared. 'Though I do wonder if you'll dare to go beyond the basics for once.'

'Feathers and frills?'

'Why not?' He led her back to her apartment where Hester found the women waiting. Hester drew in a deep breath and followed them in.

Four hours later Alek was hot and tired from going through the military-like wedding arrangements with his advisors and answering all their incessant questions. The media had already begun staking out the palace. The news had reverberated in a shock wave around the world. The news channels were running nothing but the photo that had been taken in the plane on the way over and digging deep for nuggets about Hester already. Fortunately her family were already on their way over and unable to comment because he'd ensured Wi-Fi wasn't available on their flight so he still had time to guide their speculation.

Though he'd learned more about her in the small pieces being published as soon as they were written than from her own too-brief mentions of her past. The bald facts were there, but the real truth of her? The depth? He doubted the investigative reporters would get anywhere near it. She was so self-contained even he was struggling and he was the one *with* her. What had happened to her parents? Why was she so alone? What did she keep in that broken little box that she kept nearby at all times?

'Alek?'

He blinked, recalling his concentration. He couldn't waste time wondering what made her tick—what secrets and hurts she held close—he had to run the palace, reply to invitations to tour another country, clarify Triscari's position on a new European environmental accord, and not least decide the next steps for the stud programme at his stables. Too much at the best of times.

Yet he still couldn't help thinking about Hester, concerned about how she was dealing with all those designers and the decisions she had to make, wondering how else he could make her comfortable. He'd liked being able to do something that had truly moved her—seeing her real response pierce her calm exterior had been oddly exhilarating. He wanted to mine more of that deeply buried truth from her and know for sure he'd pleased her.

In the end he called an assistant to check on his fiancée's movements and report back. Five minutes later he learned she'd been cloistered in her rooms this whole time. Stifling a grimace, Alek turned back to the paperwork spread on the vast table before him. The prospect of their impending marriage strangled him, fogging his usual sharp decision-making ability, making everything take longer. Another hour passed and he was almost at the point of bursting in on Hester himself, just to ensure they hadn't accidentally suffocated her in all that silk.

'Enough.' He pushed back when his advisors raised another thorny problem.

He'd been issuing instructions for hours and he was done.

If it were an ordinary day, he'd go for a ride to clear his head. But today wasn't anything like ordinary and he couldn't leave the confines of the palace, what with all the media gulls gathering. Irritated with being even more tightly constrained than usual, he impatiently stalked towards his wing. The tug deep inside drawing him there was desperation for his own space, wasn't it? It wasn't any need to see her.

He gritted his teeth as he reached her door and pushed himself past it. But once he was in his own room he heard soft splashes through the open window. He paused. Was someone in the pool?

He swiftly glanced out of the window. The view all but

killed his brain as his blood surged south. Those utility trousers and tee had done a good job of hiding her figure. So had those two dresses, even, with their floaty fabric and draping styles. Because now, in that plain, black, purely functional swimsuit, Hester Moss was even more lush in particular parts than he'd expected. She truly was a goddess. And maybe this marriage wasn't going to be as awful as he'd imagined. Already teasing her was a delight, while touching her a temptation he was barely resisting.

For the first time in his life he was pleased his father had been so overprotective towards his sister. That he'd ensured the pool was completely secure from prying eyes— beyond these private apartments, of course. In fact, the whole palace was a fortress. No one could see in and, with the air restrictions in place, no helicopters could fly over with cameras on board. He opened the door to his balcony and lightly ran down the curling stone steps to the private courtyard.

She was swimming lazy lengths and apparently hadn't noticed his arrival. It wasn't until she rolled onto her back that she saw him. Her eyes widened and she sank like a stone beneath the surface before emerging again with a splutter. He was so tempted to skim his hands over her creamy skin and sensual curves. He ached to test their silkiness and softness for himself. Except she now hid— ducking down in the blue so only her head poked above the gentle ripples she'd caused.

'What are you doing?' Her gold eyes were huge.

Uninhibited—and frankly exhilarated—he'd undone his shirt buttons before he'd even thought about it. Now he laughed at the look on her face. 'Relax. It's just skin. And it's a pool.'

'You can't swim naked,' she said, scandalised.

'I told you, the pool is completely private. No one can

see us—it's designed so only our private apartments over-look it. Mine, yours, Fi's. And Fi isn't here.'

'You still can't swim naked,' she choked.

'Relax, Hester.' He laughed, amused by her blushing outrage.

'You just do everything you want, don't you?'

'Not all the time. Not everything.'

She had no idea how well behaved he was being right now. Another bolt of attraction seared through him. He kept his black knit boxers on but swiftly dived into the pool to hide the very direct effect she was having on him.

'How'd the fitting go?' he asked once he swam to the surface again. The thought of her in a fancy wedding dress intrigued him. The dresses on the plane had been stunning, but some white lacy bridal thing? He suspected she'd slay it.

'It was fine.'

Of course she'd say that—it was her fall-back phrase to conceal every real thought and emotion. He gazed into her eyes, wishing he could read her mind. Only the softest signs gave her away—her pupils had swollen so there was only a slight ring of colour visible; her cheeks had reddened slightly; her breath sounded a little fast and shallow. But he wanted to provoke a *real* reaction from her—powerful, visceral, *uncontrollable*.

'Alek?' she asked.

Despite the uncertainty in her tone, primal satisfaction scoured his insides, tightening every muscle with antici-pation. He really did like his name on her lips. That small success would be the first of many. And he understood the reason for her uncertainty and slight breathlessness. She had a similar effect on him.

He swam closer, hiding his straining body beneath the cool water. Her eyelashes were so amazing—droplets glis-tened on the ends of a few, enhancing their lushness even more and framing her jewel-like irises to mesmerising perfection. She was every inch a luscious lioness.

'What are you doing?' she muttered as he floated closer still.

'Tell me how the fitting went,' he said softly. 'Tell me something more than a mere platitude.'

'Why?'

'Because I want to know how you're feeling.'

That wary look entered her eyes, but at the same time the water's warmth rose a notch. The tension between them was now half exposed and she couldn't tear her gaze from him any more than he could peel his from her.

'Why?' Her lips parted in a tempting pout—ruby red berries promising delectable, juicy softness.

'Because we're going to be a team, Hester,' he muttered, struggling to focus and to keep his hands off her. 'I'd like to know how you're feeling, how you're coping with everything. We should be able to communicate openly with each other.' He cocked his head. 'I get that you're quite self-contained, but this doesn't need to be difficult.'

Except it felt complicated. Something drew him closer even when he shouldn't. This should be straightforward. Where had this vast curiosity come from? Or this gnawing desire that now rippled through every cell in his body? It hadn't been there yesterday when he'd proposed. But now? Now he wanted to *know* her—and not just in that biblical sense. He wanted to understand what she was thinking and why. Drawing her out was a challenge. It wasn't unlike detangling Fi's glass Christmas tree lights for her when he was younger—careful focus, gentle hands and infinite patience were required.

But Alek wasn't feeling brilliantly patient this second. His heart was thudding too fast. He couldn't resist reaching out to feel for himself how soft she was, placing his hands on her slender waist and pulling her closer to where he stood.

Hester braced her hands on his broad forearms, feeling the strength of his muscles beneath her palms. Her pulse quickened and, despite the cool water, her temperature soared.

'Have you decided to seduce me?' Her voice was the barest thread of a whisper.

He gazed at her intently but said nothing.

Old fears slithered in, feeding doubt and fattening the insecurity that he could never possibly *mean* it. This was just a game for him. He was so used to winning, wasn't he?

'What are you going to do once you've succeeded?' She couldn't hold back the note of bitterness. 'Discard me like disposable cutlery?'

He didn't flinch at her lame dig. His gaze was unwavering and she was drowning in the depths of darkness in his eyes. 'Are you saying I'm going to succeed?'

'A man with your experience is always going to succeed against someone like me.'

He gazed at her relentlessly and something dangerous flickered from him to her. 'You're really not experienced?'

'Of course not,' she snapped as the unfamiliar tension in her body pushed her towards rejection—it was that or something so reckless. So impossible. She'd all but told him back in Boston. 'In your impossible quest for an appropriate bride you've found a virgin fit for a king.' The bitter irony rose within her.

His hands tightened on her waist. 'You're a *virgin*?'

What else did 'not experienced' mean?

'Don't act like you didn't guess already,' she angrily snapped.

'How? And why would I?' He shook her gently. 'You said you'd had a quiet life, but this is…'

'Irrelevant,' she slammed back at him. 'We have an

agreement. You're paying me to do a job. Physical intimacy, other than those two kisses, is off the table.'

But she was finding it impossible to breathe, impossible to tear her gaze from his. And it was impossible to do this 'job' when he kept stripping off and smiling at her all the time.

'Is it, Hester?' he breathed.

Why did he have to be so beautiful? Why did her body have to choose this moment to spark to life and decide it wanted touch? The sort of touch she'd never craved before. Not like this—not with a bone-deep driving need that was almost impossible to restrain.

'Please let me go.' And the worst thing happened—because it wasn't the assertive command she wanted. It was a breathless plea, totally undermined by the thread of desire that was so obvious to her that she knew it was evident to him as well.

But he didn't release her.

'Just so you know, sweetheart, it will not be my "experience" that sees me succeed with you,' he said firmly and then swept her up to sit her on the side of the pool. 'It's not *me* at all.'

He pushed back, floating away from her, leaving her with a parting shot so powerful she was glad she wasn't still standing.

'It'll happen only when *you* decide that I'm the one you want.' He levered up out of the pool on the opposite side and she watched him stride away in all his sopping, masculine beauty. 'You're the one with the power. You're the one who will need to say yes.'

CHAPTER FIVE

HESTER GRIPPED HER new clutch purse tightly. Her dress was suitable, she could walk in her mid-heeled nude shoes, and she'd practised not blinking so she could cope with banks of cameras…it was going to be fine. It was one sequence of appearances on one day—TV interview, public outing and back to the palace. She could manage that. She'd been practising often enough. The last few days had whizzed by in a flurry of meetings and planning. Alek had been with her much of the time but he was constantly interrupted and often completely called away. But she'd hidden in the palace, preparing for the performance of a lifetime, practising the walk down the long aisle of the chapel, climbing into the carriage, then swimming in the pool each afternoon. But he'd not joined her there again.

Now he was already waiting in the corridor. As always her tummy flipped when she saw him, but it was the burn building *below* her belly—that restless, hot ache—that was the real problem. She couldn't look at him without that appalling temptation to slide closer, to soften completely and let him touch… She still couldn't believe she'd made that embarrassing confession the other day. Her virginal status had surprised him and he hadn't denied he was interested in her physically. But he could have any woman he wanted. So she needed to forget all that and remember that this was a *job*.

His appraisal of her was uncharacteristically serious—all jet-black eyes, square jaw and no dimples. She sensed his leashed power; after all, he was a man who could move mountains with the snap of his fingers.

'Your hair's down.' He finally spoke. 'I like it.'

'I'm so glad to hear that,' she muttered, letting her tension seep out with uncharacteristic acidity. 'All I ever wanted was your approval.'

'Excellent.' He smiled wolfishly, soaking up her faux sweetness and ignoring the blatant sarcasm. 'You have it. I knew you'd deliver.'

Gritting her teeth, she wished she wouldn't react to his low chuckle but warmth pooled deep inside regardless. She liked it when he teased her with this sparkle-tipped talk that turned tension into bubbling moments of fun. The kind she'd never had with anyone before.

'Ready to hold hands?' He tilted his chin at her, his eyes gleaming with challenge.

'To stop me running away?' she cooed, then snapped on some seriousness. 'Good idea.'

He took her hand in a firm grip and led her into a vast room filled with fascinating sculptures and books. She could lose herself happily in here for days but she barely had time to blink at all the gold-framed art on the walls because he swiftly guided her to a lamp-lit polished wooden desk. 'Come on, you need to choose something.'

She gaped at the velvet-lined display cases carefully placed on the table before glancing up to see a liveried man with white kid gloves discreetly leaving the room.

'Wow, you've presented so many options...' She didn't quite know what to say. There were dozens of stunning rings—diamond solitaires, sapphire clusters, ruby squares and others she had no idea of.

'I'm hoping one will fit.' Alek's brows drew together as he looked down at her. 'You have small hands.'

'Did you raid all the jewellery shops in a thousand-mile radius?'

'No, these are from the palace vault.' He smiled at her horrified expression. 'There are a number of things in there. You'll choose a tiara for the wedding later this afternoon. We don't have time for that right now and it's supposed to be a secret from me, I think.'

There was a whole vault full of priceless treasure? She stared brainlessly at the tray, stunned yet again by the extreme wealth of his lifestyle—and of his ancient heritage, steeped in tradition. As impossible to believe as it was, she knew all those gleaming stones were real. Just as their impending marriage was real.

'Which do you like?' he prompted.

She shook her head, dazed. 'Any of them. They're all amazing.'

And it was impossible to decide. Still silence followed her comment, but she was frozen with fear and awe and stinging embarrassment.

'Would you like me to help?'

She heard the smile in his voice but she couldn't smile back. 'You can just choose.'

'You should have something you actually like,' he said dryly and then lowered his voice. 'You *deserve* something you like, Hester.' He turned her to face him, making her look up to meet his gaze. 'There's no wrong answer here. You can pick whichever you want...'

It was very kind of him, but way too overwhelming. Pearls, diamonds, emeralds, sapphires, rubies...she was stunned and speechless and so deeply discomfited by his careful concern. It made it worse somehow—that he knew she wasn't used to people consulting her on what she would like, or giving her beautiful rooms to sleep in, or choices of sublime designer gowns and now priceless, beautifully crafted jewels.

'Why don't you start by trying some on to see if they even fit?' He plucked the nearest ring from the tray and grasped her cold hand.

Hester remained motionless as he slid the ring down her finger before removing it again and selecting another with rapid decisiveness. The enormous oval emerald was too enormous. The square ruby's band was too big... As he tested and discarded several options, he kept a firm grip on her hand as if he thought she really might run away if he didn't. Maybe she would've too, because her core temperature was rising and her breathing shortening. He was too near and she was too tense. She just wanted one to fit well enough so this could be done and she could get away from him.

'This makes you feel awkward, Hester?' he murmured, glancing up into her eyes.

Yes, because he was standing so close and it felt too intimate, not the businesslike process it ought to be. Her imagination was working overtime, reading too much into every look, every word—that he was subtly teasing her by lingering as if he knew how much his proximity affected her and he was playing on it.

'Of course it does.' She tried to match his careless confidence but her voice wouldn't get above a whisper. She fell back on practicalities to answer half honestly. 'I'm going to be too scared to go anywhere with something like this on my finger. What if I lose it?'

'You only need to wear it to the events today and the wedding ceremony. The rest of the time, it'll remain safe in the vault.'

Okay. Good. That made it a little better. So she nodded and held still as he tried another that had a too-large band.

'You don't have a favourite colour?' he asked as he cocked his head to study how the next option looked on her small hand.

She shook her head, too embarrassed to articulate anything. It was impossible to think when he was this near to her and holding her with firm gentleness.

'Okay, then I'm going to decide,' he said. 'And you're not getting any say.'

She would've laughed if she weren't so flummoxed by his intense effect on her. With exaggerated movements he angled his body to hide her own hand from her. She felt the sensuous slide of his fingers down hers as he tried a few more rings. But his broad shoulders and masculine body blocked her view. Then he slowed, trying one, then another—then another and taking far longer with one. All the while she stared at the fine stitching on the seam of his jacket.

He turned his head to glance at her, a smile flitting around his lips in a mysterious way. 'I'm done.'

With a flourish, he pivoted to face her, sliding his hold to the tips of her fingers so she could see the ring he'd placed on her.

'What do you think?' he gently prompted.

She just stared. But inside while her heart pounded, her brain was starved of anything useful. It was stunning. One she'd been unable to see at first glance because she'd been blinded by so many gleaming options. It was a fine gold band and a solitary diamond. But the massive stone was cut into a teardrop shape—it didn't glitter brilliantly, wasn't gaudy, but rather the multifaceted cut ensured it gleamed and gave it a depth she'd not thought possible from a mere mineral. She could get lost looking into it. It was exquisite and delicate and moved her unbearably.

'Hester?'

Unable to resist responding to that commanding thread in his voice, she glanced up. Her tongue was cleaved to the roof of her mouth. Her pulse thudded through her body with such ferocity she had to stay completely still to control it—to stop that overwhelming emotion exploding out of her in an ugly mess. It was too risky to reveal anything vulnerable—that something might *matter* to her. But the warmth in the backs of Alek's eyes was different now. There wasn't only that flicker of flirtation and teasing awareness. There was something deeper than both those things and as the seconds passed in silence it only strengthened.

'It's fine,' she croaked.

She knew her response was so woefully inadequate it was almost rude, but no way could she utter the incoherent, incomplete thoughts battling in her head amongst the swirl of confusion. She expected him to either frown or tease, but he didn't. His face lit up and he smiled. Her heart stopped. Those dimples were going to be the death of her.

'Yes, it is.' He curled his arm around her waist and walked her towards the big heavy doors at the other end of the room. 'I'm glad you like it.'

Like it? Total understatement. She couldn't help sneaking peeks at it as she walked with him into a reception room that had been prepared for the interview, but she still couldn't verbalise the hot mess of feeling inside.

The journalist was waiting with only two crew—one for camera, one for sound. Hester perched on the edge of the sofa and hoped her nerves didn't show too much. Alek kept one arm around her and drew her closer to his side while holding her hand throughout. She was so aware of his heat and strength and his smile melted everything and everyone else away until somehow it was over and he was laughing and releasing her only to shake hands with the presenter.

'You did well,' Alek said as he escorted her through the palace maze back to her apartment.

Hester couldn't actually remember a word she'd said in response to the questions, she'd been too aware of him and the slippery direction of her private thoughts. 'Oh, yes, I was amazing. I don't think I said more than three words.'

'Are you fishing for compliments? That wasn't enough for you?' He whirled to face her. 'Ask me for more.' He dared her up close. 'You have no idea how much I want you to ask me for more.' His smile deepened as she gaped at him. 'Oh, you've gone silent again.'

'Because you're a tease.'

'Yeah? Perhaps. But that doesn't mean I don't mean it.' His hand tightened around her wrist. 'Your pulse is quickening.'

'It's terror,' she muttered.

'Liar.' He grinned.

'You're so conceited.'

'Maybe because you've mastered the art of looking at me so adoringly...' He chuckled as she flicked her wrist free of his hold.

'Don't we have to go on this visit now?' She pushed herself back into work mode.

'In an hour, yes.' He leaned closer. 'That's just enough time for—'

'Me to get changed, that's right.' She all but ran back to her apartment to where her stylists were waiting.

'You're nervous?' Alek glanced at her keenly as the car drove them out of the palace gates and through the banks and banks of cameras just over an hour later.

'Is it really obvious?' She worried even more and clutched her bag strap tightly.

'Honestly, I imagine everyone would expect you to be nervous and it's not a bad thing. People like to see the humanity in others.' He reached for her hand and shot her that charming smile.

'They forgive you your sins?' She tried to answer lightly, but beneath it she was glad of the way he rubbed his thumb back and forth over her tense fingers. It was soothing, like when she counted her breathing. But better.

But bad too. Because she didn't want him to stop.

'Nerves aren't a sin.' He laughed. 'They're normal. Everyone has them.'

'Even you?'

'Even me.' He gave an exaggerated nod. 'Does it surprise you that I might feel normal things, Hester?'

That sense of danger as those undercurrents of heat and temptation swirled too close to the surface.

'So this is the paediatric ward visit,' she confirmed needlessly. Just to remember the *job*. Just to stop staring at him. Since when was she so seduced by physical beauty? She'd always tried not to judge people based on their appearance—she knew how it felt to be bullied about things.

'You don't think it's cynical to use sick children to sell us as a couple?' she asked.

'I think that most of these little guys have a really rough road ahead of them, so why shouldn't they get a little joy out of this? I'd far rather spend an hour with them than with some of the captains of industry who don't think I can live up to my father's legacy.'

'You think people don't take you seriously?'

'I'm just the Playboy Prince, aren't I?'

'Wow, I wonder why they have reason to think that?'

'I know, right?' He sent her a mocking look. 'If only they knew I now have a pure and innocent bride to mend me of my disreputable ways...'

'Very funny.'

Except she was revising her opinion on his reputation. It

hadn't taken long to see that Alek considered his country and his people in almost every decision he made.

It seemed there were thousands waiting behind police-guarded barriers and every one held a camera or phone up. As she passed them she was terribly glad of her long dress and the firmness with which her hair was pinned. Alek released her hand so they could engage with the people in the receiving line and she received a small bouquet from a sweet young girl. She heard a child bellowing and glanced quickly to see a small boy being carried away by a nurse but she maintained her smile and pretended she hadn't noticed. There was no need to draw attention to someone else's sensory overload.

Alek compelled attention like a black hole, sucking everyone, everything—all the light—into his vortex and onwards he spun, ever more powerful. But she also felt the people watching her, assessing, judging—she could only hope she passed. After a tour of the ward, they spent some time in the hospital classroom where a few children sat at tables working on drawings. At a table near the back, she could see the small boy who'd been hurried away at their arrival. With the 'freedom' to walk around, Hester gravitated towards where he was, subdued and firmly under the control of the teacher standing beside him. Belligerent sadness dimmed his eyes. Hester didn't make eye contact with the teacher, she just took the empty chair at his table. She drew a piece of paper towards her and selected a pencil to colour in with. The boy paused his own colouring to watch her work then resumed his until they reached for the same emerald pencil.

'I think it's a really nice colour,' she said softly, encouraging the boy to take it.

'It's my favourite,' he muttered.

'Mine too,' she whispered with a conspiratorial smile. 'But don't tell anyone.'

She glanced up and encountered Alek's inscrutable gaze. She'd not realised he was nearby.

'Time for us to leave, Hester,' he bent and said quietly. 'But we'll come back again.'

As they were driven back to the palace he turned in his seat to study her face. She was sure it was only for all those cameras along the route.

'You did very well. Again,' he said.

She inclined her head with exaggerated regal poise to accept the compliment.

He suddenly laughed and picked up her hand, playing with the ring on her finger in an intolerably sweet gesture. 'I mean it. Being able to make someone smile or respond—to make a connection like with that boy who'd been distressed?' Alek nodded. 'That was skilled.'

'Not *skilled*.' Hester shook her head. 'I had no clue. I just tried to give him the time to let him get himself together.'

'Natural kindness, then.' Alek ignored the photographers calling outside the car as it slowly cruised through the crowd. 'You told him your favourite colour. Or was that just a lie to make him feel good?'

She paused. 'It was the truth.'

'So you could tell him something you couldn't tell me?'

She paused, startled by the soft bite in that query. 'Have I hurt your feelings?' She tried to deflect him with a smile.

'Yes.'

She shot him a worried glance. Surely he was joking? He intently watched her—not smiling, not glowering either.

'I just wanted to be kind to him.' She drew in a breath. 'Some people get all the attention, right? The loud ones, or the ones confident enough to smile and call out, and the ones who have the tantrums like him. The ones I feel bad for are the quiet ones—who don't push forward or act out, who are so busy being good or polite or scared...

sometimes they need to know someone has seen them and I didn't today.'

'I did,' he said softly. 'I went around and saw some of those ones.'

Of course he had—because he'd been doing it all his life. Sharing his attention.

'Were you one of those kids?' he asked. 'One who was being so good she became invisible?'

'Good but not good enough?' She wouldn't have minded being that kid. 'No, that wasn't me.'

'I can't see you confidently calling out things in front of everyone.'

'No, not that one either.'

'Tantrums?' He lifted an eyebrow and sent her a sideways smile. 'No? But what else is there?'

In the safety of the car, riding on the success of her morning and the fact the worst of today was now over, she was relaxed enough actually to answer. 'I was the kid who ran away.'

He watched her. 'You really mean it.'

'I really do.' She drew in a slightly jagged breath, regretting the confession.

'Did they find you and bring you home again?'

'They had to,' she replied lowly. 'I was young and they had an image to maintain. But that didn't stop me trying again.'

'Did you ever succeed in running away for good?'

'Eventually, yes.'

She wanted to gaze out of the window. She wanted to end this conversation. But his coal-black eyes were so full of questions that she couldn't answer and so full of compassion that she didn't have the strength to pull back from him either.

'Will you run away if you don't like it here?' he asked.

'No. I'm grown up now and I'll see this through.' She

made herself smile and clear the intensity. 'I think it's more likely that you'll banish me like your ancestor did his rebel Queen.'

To her relief, he followed her lead and laughed. 'I have to banish you to her castle. I'll take you after dinner. It'll be a dark-windowed car tonight. Tomorrow is the glass carriage.'

'The fairy-tale element?'

'Absolutely.'

After another dinner devoted to preparation and planning, this time with several advisors attending and in which Alek refused to release her hand, they were driven to the castle on the edge of the city for Hester's final night as a single woman.

'Welcome to Queen Aleksandrina's home.' Alek spread his arms wide as the enormous wooden doors were closed behind them.

Hester knew the story of Aleksandrina well. Her marriage had taken place after the King's coronation and was such an unmitigated disaster that a law had been passed stipulating that any future prince could not claim the King's throne before being married. Furthermore, at the King's coronation, his bride must bow before him—before all his other subjects did; she was to be prime symbol of deference to his rule. It was appalling, but 'tradition'.

'The rebel Queen who defied her husband and decided to build her own castle at the other end of town?' Hester nodded in approval. 'She sounds *amazing*.'

Alek grinned. 'You know I'm named after her?'

'Really?' That surprised her. She'd thought the rebel Queen was frowned upon. 'And you don't want to live here?'

She hoisted her little backpack on her shoulder and

gazed up in awe at the carved constellations in the vaulted ceiling of the castle's great room. Where the palace was gilded and gleaming, the castle was hand-carved curves and lush plantings. It was softer somehow and very feminine. Carved into the coastline, it had a wild element to it; part of it actually overhung a cliff.

'There's a tunnel to the beach below. I'll show you.' He grinned at her. 'The rumour was it was how the Queen smuggled her lovers in without the King knowing.'

'Lovers—plural?'

'Apparently she was insatiable.'

'And did you say you're named after her?' Hester clarified a little too meekly.

He chuckled. 'My mother always said those rumours were just slut-shaming to steal her powerful legacy from her. The fact was she was a better queen than he was a king and he couldn't handle it.'

Hester stilled at the mention of his mother. She sensed she was an off-limits subject and Hester of all people understood the desire to protect those precious memories. 'It sounds like your mother was quite a woman too,' she said lightly.

'She was.' He turned and headed towards a doorway. 'Come to the ballroom.'

Yes, he wasn't about to elaborate and Hester didn't blame him. 'This isn't the ballroom?'

Two minutes later Hester gazed around the vast, ornate room, uttered moved by gorgeous wooden carvings and low-hanging candelabra. 'I...wow... I just...' She trailed off; her throat was too tight. It was so incredible.

Alek stepped in front of her and brushed her cheek with his hand as he gazed into her eyes. 'You really do struggle to express yourself sometimes, don't you?'

Of course, he saw that. Somehow he was right there, too close. Making her want...too much. Everything she *felt* around him was too strong and so easily he weakened the bonds with which she held herself together.

His hand on her waist was so light, so gentle, she couldn't quite be sure it was even there. But the electricity racing along her veins confirmed it. 'What are—?'

'Practising for our first dance,' he answered before she'd even finished asking.

'You're kidding—we have to dance?' She groaned. 'I can't dance, Alek. I don't know how to.'

'Just relax and follow my lead.' His dimples appeared. 'It'll be fine.'

She put her hand on his chest, keeping him at that distance as he stepped fractionally closer. But the tips of her fingers burned with the temptation to spread, to stroke. And they weren't dancing at all, they were standing still as still, close but not breathing, not blinking either. Somehow time evaporated. Somehow he was nearer still and she'd got lost in the depths of his dark eyes and the current of his energy coiling around her.

'Why try to fight it?' he whispered.

Of course he knew, of course he saw the terrible yearning within her. But self-preservation made her deny it. 'Fight what?'

'The inevitable.'

'I refuse to be inevitable,' she muttered hoarsely, her instinctive self-preservation instincts kicking in.

'There's a saying for that,' he countered with a smile. 'Cutting off your nose to spite your face.'

'You think I'm missing out on something amazing just because I won't fall for your flirting?'

'I think it's interesting that you're making it such a big deal.'

'Maybe I want something meaningful.'

'You think I don't mean it?' A frown entered his eyes.

'Because I do. There's something about you…you're growing on me, Hester.'

'Like a kind of bacteria? Fungus?'

'Not fungus.' Beneath her fingertips she felt the laughter rumble in his broad chest. 'Are you trying to put me off?'

'You know I am.'

'I do.' He shot her a look. 'And I love that you feel the need to try so hard. It makes me think I'm getting beneath that prickly shell of yours.'

'So now I'm a porcupine? And here I was thinking you were supposed to be impossibly charming and irresistible.'

'You know what I think? I think you've decided I'm some big, bad philanderer. And that makes me terrible, for some reason. Sorry for liking sex, sweetheart. Maybe if you tried it, you'd discover it's not so awful. But instead you feel you have to keep me at a distance and not explore the fact that we have quite spectacular chemistry.' He leaned closer. 'Sparks, Hester. Every time we touch. Every time we even see each other.'

She ducked her gaze. 'I just don't think it's wise for us to blur the boundaries. We have a *contract*. That's all.'

'A contract that contains two kisses.' He smiled happily.

Something swooped low in her belly. 'Only two.' And they were both going to be in public so it wasn't as if they were going to develop into anything out of control.

'But you're a lot more fun to be around than I imagined you'd be, Hester.'

'I'm so glad, given I live to please you, my lord.'

He laughed and lightly tapped her on the nose. 'Call me Alek.' He leaned closer and breathed, 'Always.'

Her smile faded. She wished he wouldn't get like this— the combination of playful and serious that was so seductive it shut down her brain and made those dormant secret parts of her roar to life.

'I…don't—' She broke off as a shiver ran down her

spine. She stepped back, seeking distance from his intensity.

He stayed where he was, studying her intently. 'Are you afraid of me?'

'Surprisingly, no.' She was too shaken to lie. She didn't fear him so much as how she *felt* when he was near.

'So you're worried about...?' A frown knitted his brows.

It was easier to talk about everything else other than the riot of emotion he invoked within her. 'The press, the Internet trolls.'

'You're such a liar, Hester. No, you're not. You never would have put yourself in their firing line if you really were. Tell me the real reason.'

'Words *can* hurt,' she argued.

'Maybe. Sometimes.' He nodded. 'Depending on who's doing the talking, right?'

He was very right. And now her voice was stolen by memories she had no wish to recall.

The teasing light in his eyes dimmed and he stepped closer. 'You can tell me,' he assured her quietly. 'I know you're prickly, you won't believe even the littlest of honest compliments. I know you don't let many people into your life.' He paused. 'I know this is an arrangement. I know I'm effectively paying for your company. And I know I tease you...but you *can* trust me. I hope that you might be able to trust me enough to be able to tell me *why* you've built such high barriers.'

She knew she shouldn't let the past constrain her future. And even though she had no real future with him, there was here and *now*. And she didn't want to lie to him any more. 'Because I've had my trust broken before.'

He waited, watching her. She knew she didn't have to explain it to him if she really didn't want to, but he was patient and quiet and somehow compelling.

'You're right,' she growled. 'I'm not really worried

about the cameras or all the crowds or the online commentators. It's my three cousins.' She breathed out. 'I shouldn't have invited them.'

'You don't see them much?'

'I haven't seen them in years.' She didn't want to tell him how weak and vulnerable she'd been. And it wasn't all their fault, right? She probably hadn't made enough effort and they couldn't understand her and it had been too easy for her to shut down.

'I know no one is perfect, but they pretty much are.' She glanced at him quickly, offering superficial detail. 'And I wasn't. I was like a troll in the elven realm. They were a party of extroverted sporting elite. I liked reading in the corner. We just couldn't relate.'

He blinked, his expression perplexed. 'But how did they break your trust?'

She'd forgotten she'd admitted that first. She swallowed. 'With words.'

It wasn't a lie—it was very true. But it wasn't all of the truth.

'They've all accepted the invitation. They're here,' he said after a while. 'I've put them up at the hotel, rather than the palace. I've already issued a personal request that they don't speak to the media but I can't muzzle anyone completely. If they get seduced by the offer of an exclusive with a news agency—'

'I know.' She licked her lips nervously. 'I know you can't control everything.'

Of course they'd accepted the invitations. Who could turn down a flight in a private jet to attend something so high profile in the incredible country of Triscari? Even she hadn't been able to turn down his offer.

'I'm sorry I can't,' he murmured. 'I'm sorry they hurt you.'

She stiffened, holding back that yearning opening

within with every step he took closer towards her. She didn't want his sympathy. She didn't want to think about any of that.

'But I'm not going to do that,' he added. 'I'm not saying anything I don't mean to you. When I talk about our inevitability, Hester, I'm not trying to flatter you. I'm just being honest.'

The trouble was his honesty was so naturally charming, so instinctively seductive. And while he was arrogant and confident, she didn't think even he really realised his potency. He was used to it, wasn't he? Flirting and having affairs. She just wasn't. She didn't think she could handle him.

'There are still only two kisses in our contract,' she breathed, clinging to that flimsy fact.

She had to keep him at that wafer-thin distance. He couldn't change the agreement before they'd even signed the marriage certificate.

'Trust me, I know.' He remained close for the merest moment more. 'And for what it's worth, I think you're going to slay them all tomorrow.'

Truthfully all she wanted was to slay *him*.

Fairy tales indeed.

CHAPTER SIX

HESTER SWAYED GENTLY as the glass carriage carried her along the castle route with its cobblestones and beautiful flower-strewn path to her waiting prince. The fine lace veil covering her face softened her focus so the vast crowds waving and watching blurred, but they were all there hoping to catch a glimpse of her—Prince Alek's mysterious bride.

She'd slept surprisingly well in the large wooden castle. Fiorella had arrived there too late in the evening for them to catch up and then Billie and her team had arrived first thing, along with an army of dressmakers. So she'd had no chance to talk to Fiorella—they were both too busy being beautified for the wedding. This was good because when she'd first spotted her soon-to-be sister-in-law, she'd veered dangerously close to hugging her. And Hester didn't hug anyone.

Before getting ready this morning she'd read only a few of the news stories about her that had been printed over the last few days. They'd not had that much time to dig up too much drama, but there was enough to make her shiver. But, worse, the real truth was there—some whispered of Alek's requirement to marry. That he'd picked someone biddable and shy and inoffensive. 'The bland bride', some bitchy bloggers had labelled her.

The romantics on the other side, however, wanted to believe the fairy tale and drowned out that truth with the fantasy. Their outing to the hospital had silenced many doubters and the body-language experts had had a field day. Apparently their light touch and laughing smiles showed 'intimacy and genuine love' between them.

And her moment with that distressed boy had somehow been leaked—still images taken by a long-range lens through a window while one of the teachers had spoken on condition of anonymity and talked of her natural affinity with the children...while Alek was apparently smitten and protective. Hester had put the tablet down, unwilling to read any more.

'We're almost there. Deep breath, Hester.' Fiorella smiled. 'This is going to be amazing.'

Contrarily Fiorella's soft reassurance sharpened Hester's nerves. Too late she realised the princess had been abnormally quiet all morning. Was she worried—or preoccupied? 'Are you okay Fiorella?'

'Okay?' The princess's deep brown eyes widened and curiously a rush of colour swept into her cheeks. 'You mean about the wedding?'

What else would she have meant? Fiorella's gaze dipped but before Hester could ask more, the carriage slowed and then stopped.

'You're the best person in the world for Alek,' Fiorella whispered quickly before a footman appeared at the door.

Hester was glad of the veil—it gave her soft focus too. She could literally hide behind it.

She climbed the stone steps slowly as instructed, though mainly it was because the silk train of her dress was heavy. Then she saw Alek waiting at the end of the long aisle and was unable to tear her gaze from him. Every step drew her closer to him and revealed more detail of his appearance. He wore full royal regalia—gleaming gold trim, military medals and that scarlet sash of power across his chest and, yes, even one feather. He stood straight and strong and so serious, but as she finally drew alongside him she saw the smile in his eyes and a teasing twitch of his lips.

The ceremony was full of pomp just as he'd promised. There were trumpets, choirs, a cellist…but she barely noticed them. Nor did she really see the beautiful floral arrangements and the stunningly attired guests. *He* sucked all her attention.

It seemed to take for ever, yet passed in a flash. She was vitally aware of him breathing beside her, so close yet distant, and every moment watched by millions. She grew stupidly nervous after reciting her vows. Her mouth dried and she swallowed back her anxiety. Why had she shot down the idea of a practice kiss? They'd probably bump noses, or clash teeth or something even more awkward in front of the world. It was mortifying. And it would be replayed over and over, immortalised in memes on the Internet for ever. The 'world's worst kiss'.

Terrified, she looked at Alek. That knowing glint of good humour in his eyes grew and his lips curved enough to set the dimples free. She couldn't hold back her own impish smile in response. This whole thing? It *was* ridiculous. And suddenly it was fun, this secret contract between them.

He bent nearer, so very slowly. Utterly still, she expected only a brief peck.

It was a gossamer brush of his lips over hers, so gentle that she wouldn't have been sure it had happened if she hadn't seen him. But he lingered and her eyes drifted shut as intimacy was unleashed in that lightest, purest of touches. She yearned to capture it—to stop time and bask in the warmth and connection from such slight pressure.

He pulled back and smiled again right into her eyes as she blinked and returned to the world. The roaring cheers of the crowd seeped through the stone walls and a ripple of audible pleasure ran through the guests present in the magnificent palace chapel. He drew her hand through his arm and escorted her down the long aisle. The noise of the applause boomed tenfold as the church door was opened for them to exit. They stood for a long moment on the top step, smiling at the scores and scores of people—the crowd stretched as far as she could see.

'Hester.'

She heard his soft command and faced him. The wicked laughter in his eyes was for her alone.

'Steel yourself, sweetheart,' he muttered.

She was ready and more willing than she wanted to admit. But he knew, didn't he? She saw the triumph in his eyes as he bent towards her.

This kiss lingered. This kiss lit something else—there was more than a gossamer caress, there was a hint of intent and she couldn't stop her own response—the parting gasp of delight that allowed him in.

But instead he pulled back. She saw his face only briefly but the smile was gone from his eyes—replaced by blazing intensity and an arrogant tilt to his jaw and suddenly he was back. Stealing a third. This last kiss was not chaste. He crushed her lips with his in a too-brief stamp of passion that promised so much more than it ought to—the sweep of his tongue commanding a response that she couldn't withhold. Heat and power surged through her as his hands tightened—holding her firm while promising even more. Still dignified, but so, so dangerous. It was only a moment, but one that changed her irrevocably. Because she'd been the one to moan in regret when it ended. She'd never wanted it to end.

'That was three, not two,' she breathed, trying to whip up some fury but failing. She was too floored, too unstable in containing her feelings.

'So sue me,' he breathed back before laughing delightedly. 'What are you going to do about it standing here in front of the world?'

'Stop it, all the lip-readers will interpret what you're saying and they'll know this is—'

'You stop talking. I'm not even moving my lips. Ventriloquising is a talent of mine. Learned it from a very early age. You do when you're filmed and photographed at every possible opportunity.'

She giggled as she knew he'd intended. 'Is it even a word?'

'You bet. Formal study required.' He turned his head so no cameras could get between either of them and gazed into her eyes; his own were dancing. 'Now seriously, be silent, or I'll have to employ emergency tactics and I don't know that it would be wise for me to do that here and now.'

His voice had an edge and she knew what he meant. He raised his free hand and waved to the crowds, who cheered again, then he helped her down the marble steps and into the glass carriage. He sat close, his arm tight around her while she rationalised that extra kiss. He was pleased with the afternoon's events, that was all. That kiss had been a moment of pure male satisfaction—of pleasure and power.

'Hester?'

'No.' She glinted at him. 'You've had more than your lifetime allowance.' She smiled and waved to the crowd.

'But—'

'You can't ventriloquise your way out of this, Alek,' she scolded. 'You broke the deal.'

'Why, Hester Moss, are you chastising me?'

'I'm no longer Hester Moss.' She flashed her teeth at him in a brilliant smile. 'And I'm putting on a good show, aren't I?'

The woman formerly known as Hester Moss was putting on far more than 'a good show'. She was glittering. And almost flirting. And Alek discovered he could hardly cope. All he wanted was to pull her back into his arms and kiss her again. Again. And again. And ideally everywhere. Instead he had to smile and wave and grit his teeth because there were millions watching them.

In the safe privacy of a palace antechamber, he studied the tablet for the few minutes they'd factored ahead of the formal reception, taking time to settle his own rioting emotions the way he knew Hester did—with distraction and avoidance. But he couldn't deny her radiance—or his primal response to her.

He realised now—far too late—that he hadn't noticed any other woman in days and he *always* noticed women. Now he didn't seem to give a damn. He hadn't even seen them. And it wasn't just about ensuring Hester's comfort in a difficult situation. It was as if she were some giant magnet, while his eyeballs were iron filings. With no will of their own they just kept focusing on her. It was as if she'd obliterated anyone else out of existence. He laughed a little bitterly to himself. Served him right, didn't it? That he hadn't wanted a wife at all, but now he had one and he wanted his wife more than he'd wanted any other woman? And she was so off-limits—she was effectively an employee, she was a virgin, she was clearly vulnerable because she'd been hurt somehow and was isolated now... yes, the reasons why he shouldn't lay a finger on her were probably insurmountable. But that didn't stop his body from wanting her anyway.

'Are you okay?' she asked.

'Oh, I'm dandy,' he mocked himself. And he had to survive spending the night with her in his wing because there was no way they could sleep in separate apartments on their wedding night.

Was it only because she was out of bounds? As if he truly were some spoilt child who was so used to getting everything that he wanted that he couldn't cope the first time he'd heard the word no from a woman?

No. He simply ached to seduce her. He'd been skimming closer to seducing her with every passing day, more deeply intrigued as she'd opened up so fractionally, so slowly. Those sparks of humour, of spirit, fascinated him. He wanted to break her open and bask in the warmth and wit he knew she kept locked inside. And he wanted to test the intensity of this chemistry that made mush of his synapses, made every muscle tense and turned his guts to water.

Instead he had to endure a long celebratory feast in front of hundreds.

He glanced up from the screen and saw her hips and the curve of her bottom and was hit by a rush of lust so severe he had to freeze. No. It wasn't anything as superficial as simply being told he couldn't have something and only then wanting it. He wasn't a child any more. He'd outgrown the pursuit of challenges just for the sake of toppling them. This was all about her. He wanted to see her melt in pleasure. He wanted her to turn to him, to offer him her luscious mouth again. He wanted to coax more of the passion he'd discovered just beneath her still surface.

Instead he glared back at the screen.

The world was absolutely lapping it up—they were trending on all social media sites. Images of them spiralled throughout the web—one picture, just after the kiss, was being shared hundreds of thousands of times a second, it seemed.

When she'd smiled at him, it was like a revelation—all sparkle and beauty. It helped that her dress fitted as if she'd been poured into it—cinched at her waist and flaring over her full hips. It was absolute femininity. She was no rail-thin princess but rather a slim bundle of curves that were almost too sexy for the circumstance. The heels gave her a little extra height but she still barely made it to his shoulder. Her hair had been left mostly loose—all lush, lightly curled beauty—while the fragile tiara with its droplet diamonds added to the overall picture of princess perfection. How had he ever thought she wasn't beautiful?

'What is it?' She stepped over and he tilted the tablet so she could see them too.

She assessed the pictures silently, critically, showing no obvious emotion, but he knew she was thinking and feeling. He craved to know what. His heart still beat horrifically fast. Those two kisses had been the most chaste of his life—yet somehow the most erotic and they'd forced him into stealing that third. That too-brief statement of what he really wanted—to get her alone, away from all the watching people.

As alone as they were now.

He gripped the tablet tightly, resisting the wave of desire ricocheting through him. And the fierce regret. He wanted to start again. To forget the whole damn marriage requirement and instead take the simple pleasure of seducing her slowly and completely. All he wanted was her absolute surrender—for her to be his in the most basic sense of the word. She was the most exquisite temptation—a mystery, as the press had rightly labelled her. But the contract between them imposed rules and boundaries. He wanted to break every one here and now. It was appalling—he'd never imagined that she'd fascinate him so.

'It's amazing what properly fitting clothes and expertly applied make-up can do,' she muttered, oblivious to his turmoil as she swiftly scrolled through the photographs. 'I look okay.'

The dress and make-up merely accentuated the perfection beneath. 'I thought you didn't care what they think.' He managed to push through his tension to half-smile at her.

'Well, I don't want to let you down.'

'So you care what *I* think?' he asked more harshly than he intended.

She drew a slow breath and he knew she was settling her response to him, trying to keep her façade still. 'I care about doing a good job.'

'And that's all this still is to you? Just a job?' He didn't want to believe that. He refused to.

He fought the urge to haul her close—to make her flush, to make that serenity flare in a burst of satisfaction. He ached to see her shudder, to hear her scream as ecstasy overcame her. He wanted her warm and soft and smiling, no more cool, fragile façade. That first kiss had given him the briefest hint of what pleasure they could find together and had seared his nerve endings. He wanted to crack her open and release the warmth he was now certain was at her core.

They'd effectively laughed their way back down the aisle with an intimacy built on something other than physical. It had rendered him unable to resist the need to kiss her the way he'd ached to—stealing that third kiss to feel the heat of her response.

Now she was attempting to rebuild her personal barriers, to hide the fiercely deep feelings she didn't want to express. But she wasn't going to be able to deny them for too much longer. He'd felt the ferocity of her fire.

'I'm sorry about the article,' she said quietly, sidestepping his question.

'Your cousins.' He knew the one she meant. 'They said you ghosted them,' he said. 'That you emotionally shut them out.' He watched her expression stiffen and strove to reassure her. 'Hester, I of all people know not to believe everything I read in the media.'

'But it's true.' She lifted her chin but didn't meet his eyes. 'I did.'

Defensiveness radiated from every pore and his arms ached with the urge to hold her close.

'I'm sure you had good reason to,' he said carefully.

Now liquid gleamed in her eyes and smote his heart.

'It was silly, wasn't it? To have expected them to care for me, just because of blood.'

He took in what she'd said. They hadn't cared for her—they hadn't wanted her. And she'd been so unhappy she'd run away and locked herself in that ivory tower at the university. Quietly assisting students who lived fuller lives and cared less for their studies than she did.

'I didn't think they'd speak to the press.' Her whisper rushed. 'I thought inviting them would...' She shook her head. 'I should have known better.'

'They've gone the "friend of the family" route,' he said, cynically aware of how the media worked. 'So they can say it wasn't them.'

'But it was.' She looked at him directly and he saw the hurt she'd tried to bury. 'I'm sorry if they've caused problems.' She pressed her lips together. 'Do I have to see them?'

'There's a receiving line.' He nodded. 'There'll be other eyes and ears but no cameras. We'll keep them moving quickly. I'll be on one side of you. Fi will be on the other.'

'She's been wonderful today.'

'She understands what it's like.' Alek nodded, but the strain was still etched on her face.

'She said she wants to stay in the States,' she murmured.

He let her lead the distraction, realising she needed it. 'Yes. I want her to do whatever she wants. She seemed distracted, said it's because she's thinking of doing post-graduate study.'

'She's super capable,' Hester agreed softly before turning her gaze back on him. 'What would you have chosen?' She inched closer. 'To do, I mean.'

'The crown chose me, Hester. That's why we're here.'

'But if you were free? If you didn't have to be a full-time royal?'

The wildness clawing inside him soothed a little under her gaze. He'd always wanted Fi to have the freedom he couldn't have. It was the sacrifice he'd made and he didn't regret it. What he regretted right now was the tension lingering around Hester's beautiful eyes. He never talked about all this impossibility; there was no point. But he desperately needed to stop thinking about kissing her. Distraction from difficulty was always good. And he needed to distract her too. Because that was what she was really asking him to do. So he did.

'I wanted to study medicine,' he blurted.

'You wanted to be a doctor?' Her jaw dropped and as she snapped it shut a frown furrowed her brow. 'How was that going to work?'

'I know, right? The idealism of youth.' He shook his head.

'It was a good ideal.' She curled her hand on his arm. 'You would have been—' She shook her head and broke off. 'What stopped you?'

'My father.' He smiled ruefully. 'I didn't ever think he'd disapprove of such a worthy profession, right? Literally trying to save people's lives.'

'You wanted to save lives?'

Dredging this up was infinitely preferable to facing the unrequited lust shivering through him like a damn fever. And thinking of this made him feel nothing but cold.

'I watched cancer slowly suffocate my mother, stealing her vitality and joy. It was horrendous and there was nothing I could do to help her. I hated feeling so inept. I never wanted to feel that useless again.' He glossed over the most painful memories of his life. 'And honestly, I liked science. But my father didn't think I could get the grades—before Mother got sick I'd pretty much mucked around.'

He'd not discussed his mother's death with anyone, ever. Yet it was somehow easier to talk about this than acknowledge the storm of emotion swirling within him. And Hester was in a realm of her own now in his life. Maybe he was a fool but he felt he could trust her. Besides, she'd lost both her parents and that was a pain he couldn't imagine.

'What happened to her motivated me. I wanted to make a difference and I finally got my head together. I was so proud when I got the grades that guaranteed my entry into medical school. I presented them to him. I thought he'd be proud too.'

'But he wasn't?' she whispered.

Her words somehow pushed aside the mocking self-pity to salve the true hurt beneath. He'd laughed it off to himself in recent years, but it had never really been a joke. It had broken his heart.

'He said it would take far too long to study. Eight years, minimum, before any real speciality. I had to devote more time to my country. You can't be King and have a career. Your career *is* being King. Even though I didn't expect to take the crown for a long time.' He shrugged. 'So obviously I couldn't do veterinary school either. Horses were my other passion.' His stud farm on the neighbouring island was world renowned. 'I learned to ride before I could walk.' He made himself brag with a brash smile because he regretted bringing this up.

The lingering empathy in her eyes told him she still saw through to his old hidden pain but then she smiled. 'And what other amazing accomplishments does a prince have to master? Geography, I bet. Languages?'

'Five.' He nodded.

'Ventriloquism being one of them?' Her smile quirked.

'Of course.' That tension in his shoulders eased.

'Piano? Art?'

'Actually I do play the piano but I can't draw.'

'Well, I'm glad to discover you do have an imperfection or two,' she teased. 'So what did you do after he said no to everything you wanted?'

'I went into the military. Always acceptable. I trained with both navy and land-based forces.'

'But not air? You mean even with all your amazing accomplishments you can't fly a plane?'

'I occupied my very little spare time with polo. And other off-field pursuits.'

'Women.'

'I was going to say partying.' He maintained his smile through gritted teeth. 'I was bored and bitter and I felt stuck. I resented him for saying no to every damn thing that I truly wanted to do. So I did my work, but I had frequent blow-outs—and, yes, in part it was to piss him off.' He glanced at her ruefully. 'Predictable, right?'

'I can understand why you'd resent him and want to rebel. It's horrible being denied what you want all the time.'

'It is.' He glanced at her again and smiled faintly to himself. 'I'd wanted to do something meaningful and I wasn't allowed.' He sighed. 'I was angry. I was angry that Fi was so constrained. I was angry that he was always so distant and no matter what I did it was always a disappointment. He disapproved of my straight As, for heaven's sake. What was left to do other than rebel? But then it just became a habit and what everybody expected. It sure kept Triscari in the news—I maintained our high profile. There were just other consequences as well.'

'You were lonely,' she said softly.

'Hester.' He rolled his eyes. 'I was surrounded by people.'

'People who you couldn't really talk to. Your father was distant. Fi was too young and then you helped her get away to study, your mum had gone, there was nothing but party women and yes-men. I think that would get lonely.'

He rubbed his shoulder. 'You're too generous, Hester. I revelled in being the Playboy Prince.'

She studied him. 'You still want to do something meaningful?'

'My only job now is to be a good king for my country. I was angry about the marriage thing but perhaps, now it is done, I can get on and prove that this will all be good.'

'I don't think you need to prove yourself, Alek,' she said. 'I think what you do is very meaningful.'

He had no idea how the conversation had got so sidetracked. He'd meant to distract her from her distress about her family and himself from his desire for her. Yet somehow this had turned heavy and he'd told her far more than he'd intended. And somehow she'd soothed an old wound within him that he hadn't realised was still aching.

He gazed at her—her beautiful leonine eyes were more luminous than ever and how was it he wanted her more than ever? The ache to lean close, to touch her, was unbearable.

Instead he put down the tablet and stalked towards the door, remembering far too late that they had a palace full of people to please. 'We'd better get this over with.'

CHAPTER SEVEN

HESTER WATCHED HER husband charm everyone—hustling the receiving line through while making every guest believe he'd paid them extra special individual attention. She was fascinated by his skill—and so busy contemplating what he'd told her, the depth of his secrets and sadness and sacrifice, that she didn't spot her cousins until they were right there, confronting her with their fake smiles and stabbing eyes.

All the noise of the room receded as Joshua, Kimberly and Brittany stared at her. Hester froze, struck dumb as Kimberly executed a tart curtsey that exuded total lack of respect.

'Thanks for the invitation.' Brittany's faux polite opener was so barbed.

Hester still couldn't speak. They were older yet hadn't changed a bit. And how was it that they could make her feel so inept and small, even here and now?

'Our pleasure.' Alek filled the small silence and extended his hand to Joshua. 'We're grateful you could join us in celebrating our special day.'

In the face of Alek's ruthless charm the three of them were rendered speechless. Hester watched with relief as they continued on into the reception room. It was good they'd shut up, but *she'd* not silenced them. And to her horror she discovered she still cared just a tiny bit too much. But Alek held her hand tightly, glued to her side in an outrageous display of possessiveness and protectiveness that she was enjoying far too much.

'I instructed Fi to spread the rumour that we're sneaking away early,' he muttered near her ear as they took to the dance floor. 'Which we are, by the way.'

'Okay.' It was silly to feel nervous. This wasn't a *real* wedding night, but a charade.

Less than thirty minutes later they walked through the corridors to their private apartments. 'You'll have to stay with me tonight,' he said softly. 'I'll sleep...'

'On the sofa?' she finished for him.

'Something like that.'

'We survived.'

'We did more than survive, we nailed it. Did you see their faces? They loved it.' He threw her a satisfied smile.

'Wonderful.' She'd hardly noticed anyone else. She'd hardly eaten anything at the dinner. And she'd managed only a couple of mouthfuls of champagne.

She glanced around his apartment, taking in the details to divert her thoughts. The set-up was similar to her own, only his had been refurbished in a modern style—no old-fashioned gaudy wallpaper for him.

'I might go straight to bed,' she murmured awkwardly.

'That's what you want?'

She froze. She couldn't even swallow.

His expression suddenly twisted. 'Relax, Hester. It's okay. Take the bedroom, second door on the left.'

She ought to have felt relief; instead hollow regret stole her last smile. But she'd only taken two steps into the bedroom when she realised the problem. Heat beat into her cheeks, but there was no getting around it. She walked back out to the lounge. Alek was exactly where she'd left him, staring moodily at the table.

'I'm going to need help to get out of this dress,' she said.

He lifted his chin and speared her with that intense gaze.

'I'm sewn into it.' She bit her lip, so embarrassed because it felt stupidly intimate and he seemed reluctant to move nearer. 'I'm sorry.'

'No, it's okay.' He cleared his throat and walked over to her. 'Let me see.'

She turned her back, so crazily aware that she held her breath as he ran his finger down the seam of her dress.

'I think I need scissors or something,' he said.

'You could always use your ceremonial sword.' She tried to lighten the atmosphere but it didn't work. Nothing could ease the tension she felt.

'Or my teeth,' he muttered.

She tried to quell her shiver but his hands stilled on her skin. For an endless profound moment, awareness arced between them.

'Come on,' he finally growled. 'I have scissors in the bathroom.'

He meant the bathroom that was en suite to his massive bedroom. Hester hovered on the edge of the room, trying not to stare at that huge bed, while he retrieved the scissors. Then she turned her back to him again.

'I don't want to ruin it,' he said in a low voice that purred over her.

She closed her eyes. 'I'm not going to wear it again—it won't matter if it gets a little torn.'

He worked silently for a moment longer. 'They'll put it on display at the palace museum eventually.'

'Really?' Even with her back to him his magnetism almost suffocated her. She wanted him to touch her more. She wanted another kiss…

'I really need to get out of this dress,' she begged desperately. 'I can't breathe any more.'

'Then let's get you out of it.'

She felt a tug and then he swore. 'I ripped a button off. Sorry.'

'It's fine.'

She heard his sharp intake of breath. And then she heard another unmistakable tearing sound. Her dress loosened, then slipped and she clutched the bodice to her chest. Gripping the silk tightly against her, she slowly turned to face him.

He was so near, so intent, so still. And she could so relate. She had to stay still too or else she was going to tumble into his arms like some desperate, over-sexed...*virgin*.

'Hester...'

She stared up at him.

'Just so we're clear,' he said softly. 'I didn't steal the third kiss for the cameras.'

She didn't move. She couldn't.

'It was pure selfish want on my part. I know I ought to apologise, but I think you enjoyed it as much as I did.'

He was so close she could feel his breath on her skin.

'I want to think you want another,' he said. 'Not on any stupid contract. Not limited.'

She couldn't reply.

'Your lips clung to mine.' Emotion darkened his eyes as he stared down at her, solemn and so intense, pressing his will on hers. 'I think you want me to kiss you and I sure as hell want to kiss you.'

He still didn't move. But he was right. She wanted him to touch her again. She ached to feel the electricity that had sizzled in that too-brief kiss. She wanted to know if it was real or if she'd imagined it. She *needed* to know that. 'Yes.'

'Yes?'

She knew he was warring within himself the same way she was.

'I do.' She whispered a vow more honest than the other one she'd given today.

He swooped down on her instantly. She'd never know how it happened but somehow she was backed up against the wall and he was kissing her and she was kissing him back as best she could because everything she'd been holding back for so long was released in a massive rush. All the want. All the heat. Sensual power burgeoned between them. She could no longer think, she no longer cared about anything other than keeping him kissing her. Keeping him close.

'Tell me to stop,' he groaned, lifting his head to gaze at her. 'Or do you want me to keep going? You know what I want, Hester. And while I'd like to think I know what you want, I *need* to hear it from you.' His breathing was rough but the touch of his hands at her waist was so gentle. 'I need to hear your voice.'

Even though she really wanted to, she couldn't make herself answer. She was so locked inside herself because what she wanted was so huge and she wanted it so much, she was terrified to ask for it.

'Hester?' His hands tightened on her waist.

As she gazed at the restraint in his eyes a trickle of power ran through her veins. And that trickle was enough to make her walls crack.

'I'm stronger than you,' he growled. 'I have you pinned against the wall. I could—'

'It's fine.'

His pupils flared. 'It's *what*?'

'Fantastic,' she corrected in a desperate rush. 'Please, Alek…'

She needed his touch—needed him to take her, *completely*. She wanted all of him for just this one night. Because she was so tired of being alone. She'd not realised how lonely she was until he walked into her life and made her want all kinds of impossible things. Things she could never have for good, but maybe just for now. Just for a night.

'Please what?' he growled, leaning closer. 'Tell me, Hester. I need you to tell me.'

He remained locked before her, waiting—silently *insisting*. His fierce expression forced her own fiery need to burst free.

'I'm *tired* of feeling nothing,' she cried at him breathlessly. 'I want to feel good. *This* feels good. I want to feel more good. Like *this*. With you.'

His eyes widened but he nodded. 'Okay.'

He lifted his hands from her waist to her wrists. She was holding her dress tightly to her chest but she knew what he was about to do. He applied gentle pressure to her wrists; he pulled her arms away from her body, making her beautiful dress slither to the floor. The tight bodice had meant she'd not needed underwear so now her breasts were bared. His coal eyes blazed into hers for a long moment before his gaze then lowered. His tension tripled as he stared at her. Stark, savage hunger built in his expression—an echo of her own. With a muffled groan he bent and pressed his mouth to her—kissing, caressing, caring. Unable to resist, she leaned back against the wall, shuddering with the intensity of the sensations he was arousing in her with every hot breath, each slide of his tongue and tease of his fingers. Her body arched as she was lost in the delight of it. Of *him*. He was so overpowering, so perfect.

'Oh…' She closed her eyes as his hands roved lower.

She was almost scared at how incredible it felt. 'Alek.' She couldn't stand it any more. *'Alek.'*

'Yes,' he muttered, as breathless as she. 'Yes, darling.'

She tumbled into incoherence, into nothing but heat and light, burgeoning sensations of pleasure and want. She arched against him as he slipped his hand beneath her silk panties, writhing until he had to hold her hips still with a hard hand so he could pleasure her, so he could coax her to the very crest of that most incredible feeling. He stroked

her hard until she shook in his arms and screamed out the
agony of ecstasy.

'You are *so* hot,' he said as he picked her up and carried
her to his bed as if she weighed nothing. 'I knew you were.'

She didn't care what he knew, she just needed him
closer. She needed more. 'Alek.'

She pulled him down to her. She'd never been this close
to anyone and she didn't want it to end yet, not now she'd
only just begun to discover him. Her hand slid up his chest,
gingerly spreading her fingers to explore him.

'You can touch me.' He drew a shaking breath. 'Anywhere you want. Anyhow.'

She realised he *wanted* her to touch him. As much as
she wanted him to touch her. This was give and take. Desire and hunger. She slid her hand further and watched him
tense with pleasure at her touch. And then all reticence
fled and she was driven to discover more. She helped him
out of his suit, relishing the slow revelation of his gorgeous body. She caressed every inch of his muscled beauty,
pausing when she ran her fingers over a jagged scar on
his rump—not wanting to hurt him but wondering what
had happened. He smiled, pulling her closer, and she forgot her question in the heat and tease of his kisses. He'd
locked her in a dungeon of desire—hidden deep inside the
heart of the palace, she was a prisoner to the overwhelming lust he aroused.

'Please,' she whispered. Her throat was so dry the word
hardly sounded.

'Hester,' he groaned. 'I need you to tell me what you
want me to do.'

'I thought you didn't like being told what to do?' She
shuddered as he slid his leg between hers.

'I can make an exception for you.' He gazed into her
eyes, his hips grinding delightfully against hers in a slow,
tormenting motion. 'Do you want me to kiss you?'

'Yes.'

So he did—so thoroughly and lushly that she arched, unable to resist the urges of her body. He kissed, not just her mouth, but her neck and her chest. He kissed, nipped and nibbled, working his way lower and lower, kissing parts of her that had never been kissed before.

'Do you want me to touch you?' he breathed huskily against her belly.

'Yes.'

His hands swept over her—more and more intimately teasing and tormenting her until she writhed beneath him and even though he'd made her soar only minutes before, that empty ache inside was utterly unbearable.

And somehow he knew. He lifted himself up above her and looked directly, deeply into her eyes. 'Do you want me inside you?'

She wanted everything. Most of all she didn't want this good feeling to end. *'Yes.'*

But he didn't smile. 'You're sure?'

'This is like a dream, Alek. Just for tonight.'

'A dream?' He shook his head. 'This isn't a dream you can wake up from and take back, Hester.'

Her anger built. She'd not had this—not opened herself up to anyone—ever. And all she wanted was him. Now. And she didn't want him to make her wait any longer. 'Don't say anything more,' she moaned. 'Don't spoil it.'

He tensed.

'And don't stop,' she demanded fiercely. 'Yes. I want you.'

His smile spread across his face and then he kissed her again. Until she arched, until she moaned, until she couldn't form words. For a moment he paused—vaguely she realised he was protecting them both—but then he was back, big and heavy against her, and she revelled in it. He slid his hand beneath her bottom and held her still enough for him to press close. She gasped as she felt his thickness sear into her.

'Hester?' he breathed.

'Yes. Alek.' She wanted this. Him.

As he pushed closer still she trembled. He was so big and so strong and she was suddenly overwhelmed. But he moved so slowly, so carefully and then he kissed her again—in that deep, lush way, as if he'd wanted nothing more in all his life than to kiss her. As if she were the very oxygen he needed to survive. That was when everything melted within her and he slid to the hilt, so they were as deeply connected as they could possibly be. Her need coalesced again into a cascading reaction of movement. He pushed her to follow his sweet, hard, slick rhythm—into a dance she'd never known, but discovered she could do so damn well with him. His breathing roughened as she clutched him back, as she understood more the give and take, the meet and retreat of this magic. Together they moved faster, deeper…until she cried out as he brought unbearable, beautiful pleasure down upon her. As he broke through every last one of her boundaries to meet her right there—where there was light and heat and sheer physical joy.

And finally, when she couldn't actually move, when her body was so wrung out, so limp from that tornado of ecstasy, a small smile curved his gorgeous lips. He rolled but pulled her close, draping her soft body over his. And he kissed her again—a sweet intimacy she was still so unused to, and still so desperately hungry for. So hungry, in fact, that it took only one long, lush kiss to stir her hips into that primal circling dance again.

'Oh, Hester,' he muttered and swept his hands down her yearning body. 'You're magnificent.'

CHAPTER EIGHT

ALEK RESTED ON his side, watching her sleep—half impatient, half fascinated—until she finally stirred. Her gaze skittered away from his as she sat up. For the first time in his life he was unsure how to handle the morning after.

'Sorry I slept in.' She slithered from the bed and swiftly reached for the robe lying across the nearby chair. 'I had an amazing time. Thank you.'

Amazing? She had no idea what amazing was. But he supposed it was better than her telling him it had been 'fine'.

'No regrets?' He pushed for more than this awkward politeness from her.

'I don't think it would be right to regret something that felt that good.' She belted his favourite robe tightly around her waist, hiding her perfection from him again. 'I'll go back to my room now.'

'You don't have to,' he said huskily, rubbing a sore spot he felt in his chest.

Ordinarily he'd be relieved to have a lover leave him with such little fuss, but he wanted Hester to stay. But every ounce of her shy reserve had returned.

'I know…but I…um…' She drew breath. 'My clothes are in there.' She silently sped from the room—as if she daren't leave a mark or a sound.

And he just let her.

He stared into the blank space. Breaking through

her shell had been difficult and this morning it had just bounced back into place. Maybe she needed some time alone to process what had happened? Honestly, maybe he did too. Maybe letting her leave now might mean she'd be comfortable coming back soon.

Just this once.

That was what she'd whispered last night and if he were being sensible, that was how he'd leave this. But he rubbed his chest again as the reality of the situation hit hard. His sexual attraction to her hadn't been assuaged but exacerbated. Worse was his burgeoning curiosity about everything else about her. He wanted to understand it all—her bag and her box and the books she'd not kept. Why did she have so few belongings?

And the emptiness of his bedroom hurt. Suddenly he hated that she'd walked out on him. That he'd made it so easy for her to be able to. He should have stopped her. He should have seduced her. He should have stripped back her protective prickles again and found that hot, sweet pleasure with her.

He gazed out of the window, noting the blazing sun and blue sky. Personal temptation stirred harder. He'd just married for his country—didn't he deserve a few moments of private time?

He phoned his assistant, Marc. 'I know we have meetings this morning, but I plan to take Hester to the stud this afternoon. Make the arrangements.'

'Sir?'

'Two nights,' he repeated. 'Make the arrangements.'

A minute later he knocked on the door of her apartment and turned the handle. 'Hester?'

She'd not locked it and he found her in the centre of her lounge, that wooden box in her hand. He watched as she awkwardly secured the loose lid in place with two thick rubber bands.

'Sorry,' she apologised and put the box on a nearby table. 'How can I help?'

He disliked her deferential attitude and the reminder of that 'contract' between them. Hadn't they moved past that last night?

'Come breakfast with me by the pool,' he invited. 'Then I have a few meetings, but this afternoon we're taking a trip. You'll need to pack enough for a couple of days.'

'A trip?' Hester could hardly bring herself to look at him; all she could think of was what they'd done last night. All night. How good he'd made her feel. 'I thought we had to stay in the city to oversee the coronation plans and practise everything a million times.' She doggedly tried to focus on their responsibilities. 'Do I really have to kneel before you all by myself?'

'All citizens of Triscari do, but especially the King's wife.'

'It's a wonder you don't want me to lie prostrate on the floor,' she grumbled.

'Well, of course I do, but perhaps not in front of everyone else.' He sent her a wicked double-dimpled look. 'We can do that alone later. Anyway, apparently the plans are in hand so we can steal a couple of days for a honeymoon.'

A honeymoon? Her stomach somersaulted. Was he joking? She stood frozen but he bent and brushed his lips over hers briefly, pulling away with a shake of his head.

'No.' He laughed. 'You can't tempt me yet.'

'I didn't tempt you,' she muttered. 'I didn't do anything.'

'Hester,' he chided softly. 'You don't have to *do* anything to tempt me.' He cocked his head and gave her a little push. 'Now, head to the pool. I'll meet you there shortly.'

Hester stretched out on a sun lounger, trying to read, but her brain was only interested in replaying every second of the previous night. Her body hummed, delighting in the recollections. She'd not realised the extent of what she'd been missing out on. No wonder people risked so much for sex. But she knew it would never be like that with just anyone. It hadn't just been Alek's experience or 'expertise'. It had felt as if he'd cared—not that he was in love with her, of course, but that he was concerned for her feelings, for her to receive pleasure. That he desired to see her *satisfied*. She'd not had that courtesy, that caring, from anyone in so long. It was partly her own fault—she'd not let anyone get close in years. She'd not intended to let Alek get close either, but somehow he'd swept aside all her defences. Swiftly. Completely. So easily.

She knew sleeping with her meant nothing truly meaningful to him, not really. This was merely a bonus to their arrangement. She'd consider it that way as well. She could keep her heart safe—not fancy that she was falling for him, like a needy waif who'd never been loved...

But some distance right now was so necessary—which was why this talk of a honeymoon terrified her.

It's just one year.

And last night had been just that once. They'd blurred the lines and perhaps that had been inevitable. While she didn't regret it, she couldn't get carried away on a tide of lust and mistake his actions for meaning anything more than mere physical attraction.

But Alek fascinated *her* far beyond that. She'd instinctively believed he had more depth than he let show and she'd been right. He'd been hurt by his mother's death, frustrated by his father's control over him, protective of his sister. And now of her.

There was meaningful intention in most of his actions. The playboy persona was part rebellion, only one element of his whole. He was also honourable, loyal, diligent and he did what was necessary for his country.

Okay, yes, just like that she was halfway to falling for him.

She swam, trying to clear her head and ease the stiffness in her body. Lunch was delivered on a tray to the table beside her lounger. After eating, she went back to her apartment to pack. But when she went to put her wooden box in her bag, it wasn't on the table where she'd left it. She stared at the empty space, confused. She'd opened it only this morning, but now? She whirled, quickly scanning every possible surface but the box wasn't on any. She broadened her search but it was fruitless. Finally she hit panic point—repeating the search with vicious desperation, tipping out her bag and tearing up the place.

'Hester? What's happened?'

She froze. She'd not heard him knock and now he was in the middle of her mess with his eyes wide.

'It's missing.' She hugged herself tightly, but couldn't claw back any calm. 'I can't go.'

He didn't answer as he slowly stared around her room. Hester followed the direction of his gaze and realised what a mess she'd made of the place. She'd opened and emptied every cupboard and drawer in the apartment and still not found it. Cushions and pillows were strewn across the floor alongside books and blankets.

His focus shot back to her. 'Your box?'

'Yes,' she breathed, stunned that he realised what she meant so quickly. 'Who would take it?' Her anxiety skyrocketed all over again.

'You were going to pack it? You take it everywhere with you?'

'Yes.' She couldn't bear to lose it—it held everything.

A strange expression flashed across his face. 'Wait here. Just wait. Two minutes.'

'Alek?' Confused, she leaned against the wall, her arms still wrapped around her waist as his footsteps receded.

It was more than two minutes before he returned but she was locked in position, blinking back tears. She stared as she realised what he was holding. *'Why?'* Her voice cracked. 'Why would you take it?'

'I thought I could get it back before you noticed it was gone. I'm sorry for upsetting you.'

'Why would you—?' Furious, she broke off and struggled to breathe as she took the box from him and saw it close up. The lid was open while the interior was empty. Heat fired along her veins and her distress grew. 'Where's everything gone?'

'I have it all, just in my room. I'll get them now.'

'Why?' The word barely sounded but he'd already gone.

Hester sank onto the sofa, snatching a breath to study the box properly. She closed then reopened the lid. It didn't fall off any more, while the rubber bands were gone altogether.

Her bones jellified as she realised what he'd done.

Alek returned and carefully set a small tray on the low table in front of her sofa. It held everything she'd kept. All the little things. All her precious memories.

'The lid opens and closes again.' She blinked rapidly as he sat beside her. 'It has a new hinge.'

'Yes.' He cleared his throat. 'I took it this morning after you went to the pool. I thought…' He paused and she felt him shift on the sofa. 'I knew it was precious to you. I knew it was broken. So I—'

'Had it fixed.' Her voice almost failed.

'I wanted it to be a surprise…' He trailed off and blew out a breath. 'I should've asked you,' he muttered roughly. 'I'm so sorry. You probably loved it as it was.'

'Broken?' She shook her head and her words caught on another sob as she was unable to restrain the truth. 'It broke my heart when it happened.'

He gazed at her and the empathy in his eyes was so unbearable, she had to turn away from it.

'I can't even see where the crack was.' She stared hard at the box, refusing to let her banked tears tumble.

'We have an amazing craftsman—he maintains the woodwork in the castle. He's exceptionally skilled,' Alek explained.

'And so fast…' She ran her finger over the lid of the box. How had he done this in only a few hours?

'I talked to him about it before the wedding so he knew the issues.'

'Before the wedding?' Her heart skipped. He'd noticed her box and planned this?

'I wanted to get a wedding gift that you would like.'

Her throat was so tight it wouldn't work. That he'd thought to do this for her? It was more precious than any jewels, any other expensive, exquisite item. And she wasn't used to someone wanting to do something so nice for her.

'I didn't get you anything.' She finally looked at him directly, instantly trapped in his intent gaze.

He shook his head gently. 'You've done enough by marrying me, Hester.'

That was enough? Just that contract? Somehow she didn't want that to be enough for him. She wanted him to want more from her. That dangerous yearning deepened inside—renewed desire for that intimacy they'd shared last night. But he'd let her leave this morning. He'd barely said anything. Horribly insecure, she tore her gaze from his and turned back to the table, taking in the contents of the second tray.

'Did your craftsman put these here for you?' Her heart skidded at the thought. She needed to touch each talisman and make them hers again.

'No. I didn't want him going through your things,' he said softly. 'I took them out before giving him the box.'

Something loosened inside. She was glad it was only he who'd touched them. He'd been thoughtful and kind and suddenly the walls within crumbled and her truth, all her emotion, leaked out—sadness and secrets and sacrifice.

'The box was my father's,' she said quietly. 'Actually it was his great-grandfather's, so it's really old. It was for keeping a pocket watch and cufflinks and things. I loved it as a child and Dad gave it to me for my treasures. Marbles I had, sea glass I found. We found this piece together when I was...' She trailed off as she held the piece in her hand. Memories washed over her as they always did when she opened the box—which wasn't often at all purely because of the intensity of emotion it wrought within her. But it was also why she loved it, why it was so very precious and so personal and she couldn't help whispering the secrets of more. 'The pencil was my mother's.' It was only a stub of a pencil. And the remnant of the thin leather strap from her purse. 'You must think I'm pathetic.' She quickly began putting the other items away. 'All these broken little things—'

'What? No.' He put his hand on hers and stopped her from rapidly tossing everything back into the box haphazardly. Slowly he put one item at a time into her palm so she could return them to their special place.

'Everything around me,' Alek said quietly. 'This palace—my whole life—is a memorial to my family. There are portraits everywhere...everything is a reminder of who I am, where I'm from and who I must be. You don't have that, so you keep all these. There are treasured memories in every one, right?'

She nodded, unable to speak again. Emotion kept overwhelming her and she hated it.

He picked up the white-silk-covered button from the tray and held it out for her to take. 'I'm glad this was something you wanted to remember.'

He'd recognised it? She'd scooped it from the floor on her way out of his apartment this morning. Her fingers trembled as she took the button from her wedding dress and put it into the box.

'I'm never going to forget last night,' she whispered. Just as she was never going to forget anything associated with all her broken treasures. She closed the lid, amazed again at how perfect the repair was.

He watched her close the box. 'How did it get broken?'

She traced the carved lid with the tip of her finger as he'd done that day they'd met. 'It even used to lock. I wore the key around my neck on a ribbon, hoping they couldn't see it under my shirt.'

'They?'

'My cousins.' She shrugged. 'They didn't like it when I went to live with them after my parents died.'

'They didn't welcome you?' He paused.

'My aunt and uncle were sure to publicise that they'd "done the right thing" in taking me in. But they already had three children and none of them wanted me there.'

'So they didn't give you a nice room, or let you make their home your own.'

'No.' She swallowed. 'My uncle sold most of my parents' things, but I had the box. I always kept it near me. I never left it in my room or anything because I knew not to trust them. But the ribbon was worn and one day I lost it. They teased me about never being able to open the box again because I'd lost the key—so then I knew they had it and they knew I knew. That was their fun, right? My helplessness. My desperation. There was nothing I could do and they enjoyed that power.' She shivered. She'd hated them so much. 'So I tried not to show them how much it mattered.'

'I'm guessing you told them that it was "fine" for them to have it?' He rubbed her hand. 'That's your fall-back, right? When you don't want to say what's really going on inside there.' He pressed his fist to his heart.

She nodded sadly. 'My cousin Joshua snatched the box off me, he said he'd open it for me, but he was mocking and mean. He tried to prise it open by force but couldn't, so he got a knife. He broke the hinge and the lid splintered and everything fell on the ground. The three of them laughed at all my things. They said it was all just unwanted rubbish. All broken, with no value. Like me.'

Alek muttered something beneath his breath.

'I ran away,' she confessed sadly. 'There was nothing else I could do, I just ran.'

'I don't blame you.' He gazed at her, his dark eyes full of compassion that she couldn't bear to see, yet couldn't turn away from. 'I would've done the same.'

She shook her head with a puff of denial. Because he wouldn't have. He'd have fought them or something. He was so much stronger, so much more powerful than her. He'd never have let himself get stomped on the way she had. 'I went back hours later, when it was dark and it was all still there on the ground where they'd dumped it.'

'Hester—'

'I knew then that I had to get away for real.' Pain welled in her chest and she gazed down at the box. She'd never understood why they'd been so mean—what it was she'd ever done. Why it was that she'd not been welcomed.

'Were these the cousins who attended the wedding yesterday?'

She nodded.

'If I'd known…' He muttered something harsh beneath his breath. '*Why* did you invite them?'

'It would have caused more harm if I hadn't. Imagine what they'd have said to the media then?'

'I don't give a damn *what* they'd have said.'

'It's fine, Alek. They can't hurt me any more.'

He glanced at her. 'It's not *fine*, Hester. And you know that's not true.'

'Well…' she smiled ruefully '…they can't hurt me as much as they used to. I'm not a child. I'm not as vulnerable. I do okay now.'

'You do more than okay.' He blew out his tension. 'Were these the people who tested whether your eyelashes are real by pulling them out?'

She stared at him, her heart shrivelling at the realisation that he'd seen so much. 'How did you—?'

'No one normal would ever think to do that. You only mentioned it because some cruel witch had actually done it.'

She stared into space, lost in another horrible memory. 'It was girls at school,' she mumbled. 'Pinned me down.'

'At school?'

His horror made her wince.

'I got myself a scholarship to an elite boarding school. It was supposed to be my great escape—a wonderful fresh start away from the cousins.'

'And it wasn't?' He clenched his jaw.

'It was worse.'

She felt the waves of rage radiating from him and opted to minimise what she'd confessed. 'They were just mean. I ran away from the school. I worked. I studied. I did it myself.'

'You shouldn't have had to.'

'It's okay.'

'It's not okay, Hester.'

'But *I'm* okay. Now. I truly am.' And she realised with a little jolt that it was true. If she could handle getting married in front of millions of people, she could handle anything, right?

He looked into her eyes for a long moment and finally sighed. 'My craftsman said he'd fixed the lock too,' he said, drawing a tiny ornate key from his pocket. 'So now you can lock it again and keep it safe.' He held the key out to her. 'And you could put the key on a chain this time.'

She curled her fingers around the key and pressed it to her chest. 'This was so kind of you, Alek.'

His smile was lopsided so the dimples didn't appear and he didn't kiss her as she'd thought he was about to. Instead he stood.

'We need to get going or it'll be too dark.'

'Of course,' she breathed, trying to recapture control of herself, but there was a loose thread that he seemed to have tugged and still had a hold of so she couldn't retie it. 'I need a minute to tidy up.'

'The staff will tidy up.'

'I'm not leaving this mess for them.' She sent him a scandalised look. 'They'll think we had a massive fight or something.'

He grinned as he scooped up an armful of pillows and put them away with surprising speed. 'Or something.'

CHAPTER NINE

HESTER GAZED UP at the double-storeyed mansion set in the centre of green lawns and established trees. 'I didn't think there could be anything more beautiful than the palace or the castle, but this is—'

'Very different from either of those places.' Alek said.

'Yes, it's…' She trailed off, unsure she wanted to elaborate; he seemed oddly distant.

Only then he wasn't.

'What?' He stepped in front of her, his gaze compelling. 'Tell me what you think.'

It was impossible to deny him anything when he stood that close.

'It doesn't seem like a royal residence. It's more like a home.' Admittedly a beautiful, luxurious home—but there was something warm and welcoming and *cosy* about it.

'It was home.' Something softened in his eyes. 'My mother designed it and my father had it built for her before I was born.' His lips twisted in a half-smile.

'You grew up here?'

He nodded. 'She wanted us here as much as possible. School had to be in the city, of course, but before then and every holiday during. It was our safe place to be free.'

Hester was fascinated and honoured that he'd brought her somewhere clearly so special to him. 'Was?'

'My father never returned here after she died.' He gazed across the fields before turning to walk towards the homestead. 'Because she died here.'

Hester stilled. But he strode ahead and clearly had no desire to continue the conversation.

She couldn't catch her breath as she followed him through the living area. The interior of the homestead was much more personal than the palace. Large, deep sofas created a completely different space—it was luxurious and comfortable and she felt as if she was encroaching on something intimate and deeply personal.

'You really love horses,' she muttered inanely when it had been silent too long and because out of every window she saw the beautiful animals grazing in the fields.

He chuckled at her expression. 'You've never ridden?'

'I'm nowhere near co-ordinated enough. I've seen video of Fiorella, though. She's amazing.'

'She likes show jumping. I prefer polo.'

'Whacking things with your big stick?' She smirked.

He eyed her, that humour and wickedness warming his gaze. 'At least I'm not *afraid* of them.'

'They're huge and powerful and they could trample me to death. Of course I'm afraid of them.'

'They'll sense your fear. Some will behave badly.'

'A bit like people, really,' she muttered.

'True.' He laughed as he led her up the stairs. 'Come up and appreciate the view. All the staff have gone away for these couple of nights so we're completely alone.'

His phone pinged and he frowned but paused to check the message.

'It never ends for you, does it?' she asked.

'I imagine it's the same for you,' he replied as he tapped out a quick reply. 'Students pulling all-nighters wanting help with their due essays. Fi's correspondence is mountainous.'

'I like being busy,' she said. 'I always took extra sessions at the drop-in centre.'

'What drop-in centre?' He glanced up and pocketed his phone. 'For the students?'

'No, an advice bureau in the city. I helped people fill in forms and stuff.'

'Is that where you sent that first tranche of money?'

'Yes.' She blushed. 'Something charitable, as you said. I couldn't ignore that.'

But his gaze narrowed. 'I had the feeling it was more than charitable. That it might've been personal.'

'Okay.' Her heart thudded; of course he'd seen that. 'You're right. I've asked the centre to give it to a young mother and her daughter,' she confessed. 'Lucia's on her own. She's trying to make a better life for her daughter. I used to hold the strap of my mum's bag the way Zoe holds Lucia's.'

Alek soaked up the information. The trust blooming in Hester's eyes was so fragile but he couldn't resist seeking more. 'Tell me about her—your mother.' He wanted to understand everything.

She looked at him, her golden eyes glowing with soft curiosity of her own. 'Tell me about yours,' she countered.

His jaw tightened, but at the same time his lips twisted into a reluctant smile. Her question was fair enough. 'Her name was Aurora and she was from a noble family on the continent. Apparently my father saw her riding in an equestrian event and fell for her instantly. She loved her horses so he built these stables for her to establish a breeding programme. It was his wedding gift to her.'

'Wow.'

'Yeah.' He nodded. 'They struggled to have me and it was a long time before they got Fiorella after me. So I'll admit I was very spoiled.'

'Everyone should be spoiled sometimes.' Hester suddenly smiled. 'Especially by parents, right?'

Warmth blossomed in his chest and he took her by the hand and led her to the second-storey veranda.

'My mother passed her love for horses on to me—they were our thing,' he said as he tugged her to sit down on the large sofa with the best view in the world—over horse-studded fields, to his favourite forest and the blue sea beyond. 'She had such a gift with them. Meanwhile, my father was very busy and dignified.' He rolled his eyes but was actually warming to the topic because he'd not spoken of her in so very long. 'She was vivacious—he was the shadow, the foil to her light.'

'They sound like they were good together.'

He stretched his feet out on the sofa and tucked her closer to his side, kind of glad he couldn't see her face, and he watched as the sky began to darken.

'Yeah, they were. She softened him, kept him human. But then she got sick. It was so quick. My father wouldn't reduce his engagements. Wouldn't admit what was happening. Wouldn't speak to me about it. But I was fourteen and I wasn't stupid. I stayed with her here. I'd bring the horses by her window downstairs and we'd talk through the programme...' He'd missed months of school that year.

'And Fiorella?'

'Came and went. She was young and my mother wanted to protect her. So did I. She'd go for long rides every day—she had a governess. And I sat with Mother and read to her. But she deteriorated faster than any of us expected. I wanted to call her specialists, for my father, but she wouldn't let me. It was just the two of us.'

The horror of that morning—that rage against his powerlessness resurged—breaking out of the tiny box he'd locked it in all these years. 'I couldn't help her. I couldn't stop it.'

What did titles or brains or money or anything much matter when you were reduced to being so completely *useless* in a moment of life and death? 'I couldn't do anything.'

He was still furious about it.

'You did do something, Alek,' Hester eventually said softly. 'You were *there* for her. She wasn't alone. Isn't that the best thing anyone could have done? You were *with* her.'

He couldn't answer.

'Nothing and no one can stop death,' she added quietly. 'And being alone in that moment must be terrifying. But she wasn't alone, because she had you. That's not nothing, Alek. That's about the furthest from nothing that you can get.'

He turned. In the rising moonlight her eyes were luminous. This was someone who knew isolation. Who understood it—within herself, and within him. And she was right. A slip of peace floated over his soul, slowly fluttering into place, like the lightest balm on an old sore, a gossamer-thin layer of solace.

He'd never allowed himself to think of that moment. Even the threat of recollection hurt too much. But now that memory screened slowly, silently in his head and for once he just let it.

'And then what happened?' Hester finally asked.

He looked at her blankly.

'Afterwards. Your father, Fiorella, you. How did you all cope?'

They hadn't. None of them had.

'Your father didn't come for you?' Hester asked.

'He never returned here.' Alek coughed the frog from his throat. 'He stayed at the palace and they brought her body to him. He made them bring me too.' He'd never wanted to leave. He'd wanted to hide here for ever. 'I fought to come back from then on because I didn't want the stables to close. People had jobs and there were the thoroughbreds...'

'And it was your mother's project,' she said.

'Right.' He released a heavy sigh. 'She loved it.' How could he let it fall to ruin? 'I didn't want to lose her legacy.'

But it had been hard to come back and see that small room downstairs where she'd spent her last days. Awful to be here alone when she'd gone for ever and his family had almost disintegrated.

'And Fiorella?'

'The governesses kept her away and kept her busy. She was okay. But as my father retreated into his work he became even more strict and controlling over our lives. Over every aspect. I guess it was his way of handling it.'

'And what was your way of handling it?' she murmured.

He flexed his shoulders. 'I didn't have one really.'

'No?'

'You're thinking my social life?' he asked—feeling weary and oddly hurt at the suggestion. 'Maybe. It didn't mean anything.'

'Maybe that was the point,' she said lightly. 'If it didn't mean anything, then it couldn't hurt, right?'

'Not gonna lie—it felt *good*, Hester.'

'Well, wouldn't it suck if it didn't?' She smiled. 'And when things really hurt you'll do almost anything to feel better even for a little while, right?'

He felt raw. Maybe she was right. Maybe it had been more than escape. He'd been burying frustration and grief. But he'd *liked* being the Playboy Prince. He'd liked encouraging zero expectations of him settling down. Only then his father had died. And then that stupid requirement had come into play and he'd been forced to create a relationship he'd never wanted. That he still didn't want—right?

'You don't need to apologise for it,' she said. 'It just was what was, right? I locked myself away. That was my choice. Neither of us were right or wrong necessarily, it was just how we each coped with a really crappy time.'

'Yeah.' He'd not stopped to think about what a really crappy time it had been in so long.

'So now you run the stud.' She looked across the grounds. 'And that was the other way of handling it— building on her legacy. Keeping something that she loved very much alive.'

He swallowed, unable to reply.

'And you freed Fiorella from that royal burden.'

'Of course I did.' He could breathe again. 'That was easy. She didn't need to be stuck in Triscari the same as...'

'The same as you.'

'It's just fate.' He shrugged. 'An accident of birth. I just have to do the best I can.'

'Do you worry about your ability to do the job?' She stared at him. 'Seriously?'

'What, you have dibs on feeling insecure?' He half chuckled. 'Of course I worry I won't be good enough. Being the firstborn Prince means you're going to end up King. It's a full-time job that starts from the moment you're born and it takes up every minute. I'm not saying that to summon your sympathy. I know how privileged I am and I want to do what's right for my country.'

'And you do. They love you. They ask for your thoughts all the time and they trust your answers. Everyone loves you. Everyone knows you do what's best for the country because you care. And as long as you keep caring, then you'll do what's right for Triscari. You're not selfish, Alek.' She paused. 'You've given your life for duty.'

He shot her a look. 'I thought I was a rapscallion play-boy.'

'Maybe you were when you could snatch a second to yourself, but mostly you've done the job forced upon you. And the job you wanted to do for your mother.' Hester realised he couldn't separate his role as Prince from his *self*. It was a career like no other—too enmeshed with his very existence and it brought with it a kind of pressure she'd not stopped to consider. 'You're building on your father's legacy too, by being a good king. But you're more important than just your crown, you know—'

'I know,' he interrupted and reached out to stroke her hair back from her face. 'Don't worry too much, my ego is perfectly healthy.'

She actually wasn't so sure about that. 'But it's isolating, isn't it?' she said passionately. 'Living with grief.'

His eyes widened. 'I'm not—'

'Yes, you are. For your mother. For the life you're never going to be able to have.'

And somehow in the course of this conversation her own loneliness had been unlocked. 'I grieve for the life I might've had if the accident hadn't happened,' she confided in an unstoppable swirl of honesty. 'I was at the library, happily reading and waiting for them to pick me up. They never did and I never got to go home again. I was taken to the police station and after a few hours my uncle arrived and took me. Five hours of flight time later I landed in a place I didn't know, to meet people who didn't want me.'

Alek just stared at her, and this time his eyes were so full of care and compassion and she wanted to share with him—because it wasn't all awful. She'd been so lucky in so many ways.

'My parents were a runaway love match.' She smiled impishly, delighting in the romance they'd had. 'He was the second youngest, destined to uphold their place in society, right? His family were snobs. My mother was new to town, moved into the wrong suburb…she totally wasn't from the right background. They met at school and it was true, young love. But when she got pregnant his family came down so hard and they ran away—living transiently, working seasonal jobs, barely keeping themselves housed and fed, fighting hard to stay afloat and keep me with them. But they did it. They loved each other and they loved me. They decided they couldn't afford more so there was just me and...not going to lie, Alek...' she smiled cheekily at him '... I was spoiled too.'

'Oh, sweetheart,' he said huskily. 'I'm so glad to hear that.'

'Yeah, we had nothing but we had everything, you know? And we certainly never visited his home town. So after the accident when I turned up, all that old bitterness was still real. I didn't fit in—I looked more like my mother than my father. I had her vixen eyes. I was part of who and what stole him away and that made me bad. But they were determined to "do the right thing". Except they had nothing good to say about my mum and they went on about my father's selfishness and weakness. I couldn't tell them how wonderful they really were—they didn't want to listen and they never would've believed me. In the end the only way to get through it was to lock my grief away, shut it down.' She shook her head. 'I put everything into my studies, hoping that would lead to a way out, and eventually it did, but only once I got to university and by then... I was good at keeping others at a distance. I put the treasures into my box and I'd go for long walks.'

'Walks? *That* was your way to feel good?' He half laughed.

'Sure. Mostly...' She smiled more ruefully this time. 'But a couple of times I ran.'

'You shouldn't think running away is something to be ashamed of. Or that it's cowardly.'

'Isn't it though? Shouldn't I have stood up for myself or fought harder to be heard?'

'How were you supposed to do that when there were a

tonne of them and only one of you?' He shook his head.
'I think what you did was actually more brave. Escaping
that abuse, and going out on your own. Lots of people
wouldn't have the courage or the skills to be able to do
that without support.'

Alek hadn't known it was possible to feel supremely
content and disconcerted at the same time. He was both
assuaged and unsatisfied. Most of all he was confused.
This was not the way he'd envisaged this evening going.
He'd thought they'd have been in bed hours ago—that he'd
have stripped her and satisfied them both several times already. Instead they'd shared something far more intimate
than if they'd spent hours having simultaneous orgasms.

And somehow he couldn't stop speaking. 'Tell me
more,' he asked. 'What were their names?'

To his immense relief she answered—and asked questions of her own. He shared old anecdotes he hadn't realised he'd even remembered. Making her laugh over silly,
small things that were too personal to keep back. As the
stars emerged he leaned back lower on the sofa, curling
her closer into his side—soft and gentle and warm and appallingly tired and still talking.

Yet the discomfort was still there. All kinds of aches
weighed down his limbs as he discovered that an old hurt
he'd forgotten had only been buried. It had taken so little
to lift it to the surface. He wanted to resist—to pull free
again. Drowsily he gazed across the fields. He'd go riding
as soon as it was light. He needed to feel that liberation—
the complete freedom as the wind whipped and knocked
the breath from his lungs, racing faster than he could ever
run, jumping high enough to feel as if he were flying for
the briefest of seconds. Yes. He needed that escape. He
needed to ride—hard and fast and free.

CHAPTER TEN

'HESTER.'

Hester blinked drowsily. 'Mmm…?'

'Are you awake?'

Her vision focused. Alek was in the doorway, fully dressed and looking vitally handsome in slim-fit black jeans and a black shirt and gleaming black boots.

'What time is it?' She coughed the question because her insides had turned to jelly.

'Mid-morning.' He leaned against the doorframe and shot her a lazy smile.

Hester gaped—she'd slept like the dead. She didn't even *remember* coming to bed or if he'd even been in this bed *with* her. Disappointment struck. So much for thinking he might want her again or that he'd intended this to be a real honeymoon. She glanced at the table to avoid his eyes. Her box sat in the centre of it and she knew he'd put it there for her to see first thing so she wouldn't fret about it.

'I wondered if you'd like to ride with me,' he said.

'On a horse?' The question slipped out before she thought better of it and her heart hollowed out the second she realised the implication of what she'd said.

'Uh…' He looked diverted but then his smile flashed back. 'Yes. A horse.'

'Um…' She paused, prevaricating while she tried to think of…anything. Ideally a reason or excuse to say no.

But her brain was failing her. She'd not wanted anything from anyone in so long and it was safest that way but now she felt heat and confusion and awkwardness and that *fear*.

'Are you afraid to try something in case you're not good at it?' He tilted sideways to take up residence against the doorframe in that gorgeous way of his.

She gave up on any pretence and just let the truth slip out. 'No. I'm afraid of everything.'

And what she was most afraid of was that what had happened between them wasn't going to happen again. When they'd talked last night she'd felt as if they'd crossed into another level—her heart had ached for what he'd been through. In opening up with him she'd thought they'd forged even more of a connection than the fireworks of their physical compatibility the night before. She'd developed faith in him and every one of her barriers had fallen. She'd relaxed so much in his company that she'd actually fallen *asleep* on him in the middle of a conversation. She'd never been that relaxed with anyone, *ever*.

'I don't believe that,' Alek challenged. 'Not for a second.'

'It's true.'

'Then you're even braver than I already believed.' He cocked his head. 'Because you do it anyway. Even terrified, you get on with what's necessary.'

She willed her brain to work so she could push back her own weakness. 'Yes, but fortunately I don't consider sitting on a massive animal as *necessary*, Alek.'

'But it's so much *fun*,' he goaded with that irresistible grin. 'Come on, Hester, it's just another little adventure and we adventure quite well together, don't you think?'

She gazed at him, sunk already. She couldn't say no to him. She'd never been able to. Not the day he'd made his convenient proposal to her. And not now. 'I'll come watch you.'

'Oh?' Triumph lit his eyes. 'See you down there in five.'

She pulled on jeans and a tee. Downstairs she picked up a pastry from the platter that was on the table and headed out to the beautiful yard. To her relief there was no one there other than Alek. She took one look at the two enormous horses saddled and tethered behind him and almost choked on her chunk of croissant.

'Uh… I'm really not sure.' She shook her head.

'Bess is very old, very gentle,' he assured her, gently patting the chestnut horse.

'And the other one?' She glanced at the jet-black gigantic creature on the other side of him.

'Is mine.'

She didn't need to look at him to know he was smiling and somehow her pride flared.

'Okay.' She drew in a breath and squared her shoulders. 'I'm fine. This'll be fine.'

'Hester,' he said softly.

She looked at him, confused by his gently warning tone.

'Don't hide again. Not with me. Not now.'

'Hide?'

'You've just assumed your calm demeanour. It's the way you keep yourself at a distance. You don't need to do that with me any more. I know the truth.'

'The truth?' Her lungs shivered. He knew how much she wanted him?

'You've already told me you're scared.'

To avoid meeting his gaze and revealing that *other* truth, Hester moved quickly. She could do this. Lots of people got on horses all the time—how hard could it be? She looked at the horse and stepped on the small stool waiting beside it. She held onto the saddle, eyed the stirrup and braced. But suddenly the horse shifted, she missed the stirrup, lost balance and in a flash had fallen. It turned out the ground was hard.

She shut her eyes, utterly mortified as she heard Alek crouch beside her. 'Are you hurt?'

'No.' But she realised she was unconsciously rubbing her rump. 'And don't even think about kissing it better.'

Embarrassment swamped her the following second. What was it with her mouth running off before her brain kicked in? He probably hadn't thought of doing *that* at all. *She* was the one fixated on the thought of kissing—and touching, and everything else.

'Only this would happen to me,' she groaned.

'I can't tell you how many times I've fallen off.' He laughed.

'I didn't even manage to get *on*, Alek.'

'Just sit there for a moment.' He turned his head. 'It's okay.' He raised his voice. 'We're okay.'

Oh, heavens, he wasn't talking to her. 'Are there people watching? They saw that? Great.'

His eyes crinkled at the corners and their coal-black centres gleamed. 'I thought you didn't care what people thought.'

'Of course I do. I mean, I try very hard not to and most of the time that works, but sometimes it doesn't and I... don't know what I'm saying when you're just sitting here grinning at me.' She rubbed her head, feeling so hot and embarrassed while wishing he were closer still and she was still rabbiting on in a way that she never normally did. That 'calm demeanour' he reckoned she had? Shattered. Toasted in the fiery brilliance that was Alek himself.

'Didn't you see my scar the other night? You know, the one on my butt?' He chuckled as the heat spread further over her face. 'I took the most stupid tumble off my pony onto a very pointy stick when I was about seven. Everyone laughed so hard.'

'Everyone?'

'My parents, the staff…' He shrugged. 'It's a good scar. I'm sure you saw it…or do you want me to show you now?'

'No,' she lied, then laughed, then sighed. 'You're going to make me try and get on that horse again, aren't you?'

'I'm not sure anyone can make you do anything,' he teased.

'Don't try to make me feel competent at this when we both know I'm not. It's all right for you,' she muttered quietly. 'You're used to it. You know what to do.'

'It's just practice, Hester.' He reached out to brush her face and whispered, 'What if you ride with me?'

She stared into his bottomless eyes. 'On Bess?'

'No, on Jupiter.' That wickedness gleamed again. 'He's named for his size.'

'Of course he is.' She rolled her eyes. 'If I can't get on Bess, how do you think I'm going to get on Gigantor?'

'Jupiter,' he corrected with another laugh. 'I'll help you.' He took her hand and tugged her to her feet.

She stood nervously as Alek shifted the small stool. His hands were firm on her waist as he hoisted her with ease, ensuring she was safely astride the animal before releasing her. She clung to the reins nervously as Alek vaulted up behind her with superhuman agility.

'You can let go now. I've got him. And you.' Alek's breath was warm in her ear and she heard his amusement as he put his arms around her. He pressed his palm against her belly and pulled her back to lean against his chest.

She drew a shaky breath in because this felt extremely intimate and precarious. They were up *high*.

'Don't worry,' he murmured. 'We'll start slow.'

She closed her eyes for an instant, transported back to that magical night when he'd turned her in his arms and made her feel impossibly good things. But then she blinked as Alek made a clicking noise with his mouth and the horse moved.

She heard his laughter as she tensed. He pulled her back against him firmly again and kept his hand pressed on her stomach. She gave up resisting and just leaned against him. He talked endlessly, telling her the names of the horses grazing in the fields as they passed them but she didn't remember a single one. His voice simply mesmerised her as he pointed out other features of the ranch as Jupiter carried them along a pathway that narrowed as they headed towards a forested area.

'These islands are volcanic,' Alek explained. 'While there's apparently no threat of an eruption any time soon, we do get some interesting geographical features.'

'Really?' She mocked his tour-guide tone. 'Such as?'

'Such as wait and see.'

She felt his laughter rumble again and her stomach somersaulted. Being held in his arms like this just made all her unrequited-lust feelings burn brighter still. It would take nothing to turn her head and press her lips to his neck. It took everything to stop herself from doing it.

Alek pressed his knees, urging Jupiter forward, faster. He wanted to get to the forest sooner. Having Hester in front of him like this was pure torture. He'd been pacing downstairs for hours waiting for her to wake up, yet not wanting to disturb her too soon because she'd obviously been exhausted. And now she was in his arms but not the way he really wanted. The battle within was long lost. He wanted her again and damn any complicated consequences. Yet he still ached. With what he'd told her? What she'd told him?

'I'm sorry we brought your cousins to Triscari,' he blurted.

'I wanted to be a princess for a day,' she said ruefully. 'I wanted to look like I had the fairy tale. Just for that moment. Just for once. Because I do still care, just a little. That's pretty stupid, right?'

'No, I think it's pretty normal.' He totally understood that she'd want to prove herself to them. 'I always wanted *not* to be a prince for a day, so I get it.'

'Does it ever happen? Do you ever get to have a day off?'

'I have one now.'

She was quiet for a while, but he felt her stiffness slowly return.

'When this ends, I want everyone to think I walked away from you. I don't want to be the victim all over again. I'd rather be seen as the evil cow who broke your heart. That it was me who chose. That I had the power.' Slight laughter shook her slim body. 'Can your ego handle that battering?'

'Absolutely.' But he felt choked. He didn't want to think about this ending yet. He didn't want to consider the moment when she'd walk out and not look back. But at the same time he wanted her to feel the power that she sought. He wanted her to know she actually had it already. She was strong and beautiful.

'They'll never believe it, of course,' she groaned. 'But I can pretend.'

'They'll believe it,' he said. 'It wouldn't surprise them to hear I've been a jerk.'

She shook her head. 'You weren't that bad. You just needed to find some fun, right? A blow-out now and then. Especially given you never get a day off.'

He didn't regret his past actions, but he didn't feel any desire to replicate them. The thought of being with anyone else now was abhorrent. Irritation needled his flesh. He didn't understand how everything had changed in such a short amount of time. He urged Jupiter to move faster, taking the excuse to hold her more tightly. Her breathing quickened, but her body moved with his. In the forest it was quiet and felt even more intimate. Through the trees he spied the blue sea and felt that familiar exhilaration and peace. 'The view is amazing, isn't it?' he said.

'Yes.'

'And then there's this.' His very favourite place in the world.

'Is that steam?' Hester asked. 'Is it a thermal pool?'

'Yeah.' He smiled; smart cookie. He guided Jupiter carefully around the large rocks and to the left of the small steaming pond.

'Can we swim in it?'

'Yes. No one else comes here. It's completely private.' It was his.

'And those rocks—they're amazing.'

'Yeah—there's volcanic glass—obsidian—in them. Sometimes I find pieces broken off.'

'It's the colour of your eyes,' she murmured. 'This is your wait-and-see moment.' She was very still against him and her voice was the thinnest whisper. 'It's like some ancient fairyland. It's just incredible, Alek. It's like…a fantasy. There's nothing more, is there? Because what with the palace and the castle and the homestead and now this?'

'This is the best place in the world, Hester.' His chest warmed as she softly babbled on, for once not holding back on expressing anything. And he was happy to confess his own secret love for it. 'I think so, anyway.'

'But am I going to have to get off this horse now?' Her voice had gone even smaller.

He chuckled, tightening his arm across her waist. 'It wasn't so unbearable, was it?'

It had been *completely* unbearable. The raw sexuality Hester felt emanating behind her was making her steamier than the gorgeous-looking thermal pool. She hadn't been able to resist pressing back, indulging in his heat and strength, the security in his hold and the danger in the press of his thighs as he'd guided the horse to a faster pace. The wind had whipped her hair and stolen her breath before it could reach her lungs, exhilarating and liberating. She'd become appallingly aroused and he'd brought her here— to paradise. She never wanted to return to reality.

'Stay there a sec.' He swung and leapt off the horse, landing so easily all the way down there on the ground.

He turned back to face her and held his arms out to help her down. She literally slithered off the saddle and into his embrace—somehow ended up pressed against his chest. His hands ran down her back, pushing her closer against him, and she shut her eyes tightly, savouring the moment before he pulled fractionally away.

'Hester.'

She didn't answer, didn't move, didn't open her eyes.

'Look at me,' he said softly.

Neither her fight nor flight instincts were working. She'd frozen with the worst emotion of all—*longing*.

'Hester.'

She opened her eyes, lifting her chin to gaze at him, pinioned by a riot of yearning. She'd thought—so naively— that once that curiosity had been quenched, it would end. That it had mostly been only curiosity driving her to let him in. Instead, she'd discovered the utter delight of him and she wanted more. There were myriad things she secretly desired to do with him now. To do *to* him. She'd not thought she'd ever want to share any part of herself, ever. But with him?

'You know you can practise your riding skills on me any time,' he said huskily.

Oh, he was just pure temptation.

'What, as if you're some stallion who needs breaking in?' she muttered, but couldn't hide her breathlessness.

His eyebrows lifted and his eyes widened. 'Maybe. While you're the skittish filly who needs a gentle touch to bring her round.'

'Maybe I don't need that gentle of a touch.'

His smile vanished, leaving only raw intensity. 'And maybe I don't need to be controlled.'

The electricity between them crackled. The tension tore her self-control to shreds.

Why should this be difficult? Why shouldn't she reach out and take what *she* wanted? She'd been isolated and alone and denied touch for so long. And while she knew this wasn't going to last, why shouldn't she enjoy everything this arrangement with him could offer?

She couldn't deny herself. She reached for him, tilting her chin to kiss him. His arms swept back around her, pulling her right off her feet. She clung to him as every ounce of need unravelled—forcing her to ensnare him. To keep him close. She kissed him as if there were no tomorrow. But he tore his mouth free.

'I need to…uh… I need to sort Jupiter… It'll just take a moment.' He shook his head and firmly set her at a distance but she saw the tremble in his hands as he released her.

The strongest sense of liberation swept over her as she faced the thermal springs. She stripped off her tee and her trousers, sliding her underwear off too. She wanted to be *free*. She carefully stepped into the narrow pool and then sank lower, letting the silken, warm water soothe her oversensitive body.

'Hester?'

She turned at his choked sound and saw him standing at the edge of the small pond. He was still and intent.

Her awareness heightened and a deeply buried instinct kicked in. She stood, suddenly certain of her own sensuality as she stepped out of the water. She had no designer dress, no make-up. She was just plain, unadorned Hester. Completely bared. But the way he was looking at her? The response that he couldn't conceal?

He believed she was beautiful. He *wanted* her. He ached the same way she did.

Pride and power exploded within her.

For the first time in her life she was *unafraid* to take what she wanted. He could take it—more than that, she knew he willed it for her. For her to find that freedom to explore, to claim, even to conquer. It was almost anger that built within her—a reckless force so fierce and hot she couldn't contain it. That searing need drove her to take what she wanted. And that was simply to get closer to him. To seek that sensual obliteration and satisfaction from him, with him.

She unbuttoned his shirt with a dexterity she'd never imagined possessing. He said nothing but the rise and fall of his glorious chest quickened and suddenly he moved to kick off his boots. But then he was hers again. She unfastened his trousers, freeing him to her gaze, her touch, her total exploration. And she kissed him everywhere.

She pushed and he tumbled. She rose above him, savouring the sensation of having his strength between her legs. She didn't just open up and allow him in, but actively claimed what he was offering. She took, her hands sweeping over him, and she drew on the hot, slick power of him. She couldn't contain her desire any more—it was utterly unleashed and she was hungry. *So* hungry she was angry with it. With the depth of the need she felt for him. The ache that only he filled yet that grew larger every moment she spent with him. She wanted to end it—this *craving*. The sheer ferocity of it stole her breath so for a second she stilled.

He reached up and cupped the side of her face. 'Don't stop. Do what you want.'

'I want you.'

'You already have me. Hester.'

The way he sighed her name was her undoing. She

slid on him—taking him right into her soul. She heard his muttered oath, the broken growls of encouragement as he urged her on, fiercer. Faster. His sighs of pleasure scorched her, catapulting her beyond her own limits. Until she shrieked as he exploded her world.

Dazed, she collapsed on him. She'd felt nothing like this kind of physical exhaustion or satisfaction.

'Hester,' he whispered. 'Hester, Hester, Hester.' He shuddered and his arms tightened again. 'What you do to me.'

Alek sprawled on the ground, holding her close, shattered by the most elemental experience of his life. He wasn't sure his heart rate would ever recover. She was a chaotic bundle of limbs in his arms. He didn't want this fragile connection to be severed—for her to retreat behind her emotional walls again. So he slid his hand beneath her jaw, tilting her face so he could kiss her and keep her soft and pliable and warm. But she shivered. He moved, gathering her properly into his arms and rising to his knees, then feet. He carried her to the pond and carefully stepped in, holding her to him so they were both warmed and soothed by the thermal water. She floated in his arms and he teased with pushing her away only to pull her close and kiss her over and over and over until, impossible as it was, his body hardened with need again and he slid deep into her, locking her close on him, rocking them together until the pleasure poured between them and through them, brilliant and free.

A long while later he lifted her from the water. As he climbed out after her, something dug into his heel. He reached down and picked up the small chunk of obsidian. He weighed it in his palm for a moment. He could give it to her so she could put it in that box of hers and remember this even when she'd walked away from Triscari. When she left him.

He glanced at her—she looked shattered by the passion

that had exploded between them. She didn't speak. Nor did he. For once he had no idea what to say—no smooth little joke or something to lighten the intensity. He'd lost all charm, all calm. It felt as if he were still standing on something sharp and the only way to ease it was by touching her.

So he dressed alongside her in silence, pocketing the stone and swiftly readying Jupiter because he needed to feel Hester resting against him again soon.

They still didn't speak as they rode back to the homestead. He knew they were going to have to address their 'contract' at some point. But that time wasn't now. Now was the time to keep holding her in his arms and pleasuring her.

But that was a fantasy too far. Instead the world was waiting for him. As soon as he saw his assistant together with his housekeeper, he knew duty had come knocking, otherwise they'd still be off-site. He cursed inwardly as Hester stiffened. Of course she understood what the welcome committee meant.

'Your Highness.' His assistant bowed stiffly while looking apologetic at the same time. 'An issue has arisen. We need to return to the palace immediately.'

CHAPTER ELEVEN

ALEK GLANCED AT his watch and grimaced. His eyes felt gritty and he could hardly concentrate on what it was his advisor was asking.

The 'issue' dragging them back after only one measly night away was nothing that couldn't have waited another day or three. It had just been palace officials stressed about his absence and using the smallest drama to summon him back. And that annoyed him. Why couldn't he spend a full day making love to his wife? But now he'd stopped to think about it, that he'd *wanted* to do that was even more of a concern.

It had been Hester who'd solved the foreign dignitaries issue—with a few quiet suggestions to him that he'd amplified to his advisors. She was intelligent and diligent and a damn good problem-solver. He'd selfishly kept her with him as he was consumed by meetings and obligations until he'd seen her losing colour and remembered how tired she'd been. So he'd sent her in the direction of her apartment and continued without her late into the evening. She'd been fast asleep when he'd returned to the apartment and he hadn't had the heart to wake her.

And now he was back there was no escape from the duties, the questions, the decisions that everyone wanted from him. He'd ended up back in conference with courtiers first thing. Which was good. Space from her would shake off that lingering concern, wouldn't it? He'd concentrate on the multitude of tasks at hand and push back that creeping sense of discomfort.

But it felt as if a craggy boulder were slowly and inexorably rolling into his gut, weighing him down further and further as every second ticked by. Those conversations he'd had with Hester at Triscari Stud had been too raw, raising elements of his past that were better off buried. Things he'd not thought of in for ever. Things that, now he'd recalled them, didn't seem inclined to return to that safe stasis easily or quickly.

He'd forgotten so much. And now he'd remembered? That stuff hurt. That stuff wouldn't be shaken. So it was good to lurch from meeting to meeting, to force every brain cell to focus on debates and decisions and stupid, tiny details that really didn't matter.

Except his brain kept returning to Hester. To those moments at the thermal springs. Her unfettered incredible response had been a searing delight. He'd wrapped around her, holding her close—not wanting her to retreat. Wanting no barrier to build between them again.

He stilled, suddenly realising there'd literally been nothing between them physically at all. He'd not used contraception. In that wild, free moment, he'd not stopped to consider *anything* other than getting closer to her. In all his years, in all his exploits, he'd never once failed to use protection. He'd never once risked it. But at the time it hadn't even occurred to him. He couldn't have cared less in his haste to have her.

Which meant he might've got her pregnant. Hester might be carrying his child.

His vision tunnelled. He'd not wanted children. Ever. Even though he knew he was going to have to at some point, he'd figured he could delay it for as long as possible. But now?

Now he had Hester. And she might be pregnant.

He felt as if parts of a puzzle had slid into place without him paying attention. But now he did. If she'd got pregnant would it really matter? Wouldn't they just stay married?

Surprising as it was, that thought didn't horrify him at all. In fact, completely weirdly, that rock weighing on his gut actually eased off. They worked well together—she was skilled and capable. There was no reason why this couldn't become a successful marriage long term. It would answer all their issues, wouldn't it?

She would have the security and safety she'd never had. The viciousness of her cousins and her school bullies appalled him and, while she seemed well free of them now, he didn't want her to suffer like that ever again. He could keep her safe with him. The media might have their moments, but they could shake that off. His life was constricted and that would impact on her—but surely it was better than what she'd had. Surely what he could offer her outweighed those negatives?

He glanced up as the door opened, half hoping Hester might've come to check on him—drawn to him in the same way he was to her. But it was his private assistant who entered.

'I apologise for the interruption, Your Highness, but you requested we update you on your wife if—'

'What's happened?' Alek's instincts sharpened.

'She's walking in the gardens, sir.' His assistant flashed a deferential but reassuring smile. 'But I don't think she realised that it's public viewing time.'

Alek frowned. 'Has she been seen by someone?'

'Her bodyguard believes they might be family members, sir.'

'Damn.' Alek strode straight to the door.

* * *

'I didn't realise you were still here.' Hester remained still, refusing to obey the urge to run away. She didn't have Alek and Fi either side of her, but she could handle the unholy cousinly trinity of Joshua, Brittany and Kimberly now, right?

'The invitation included staying for the coronation,' Joshua said with the faintest edge of belligerence. 'We're looking around the gardens.'

Hester nodded, momentarily unable to think of a reply. They reminded her of crocodiles with their toothy smiles and tough skin and she was instantly cast into freeze mode.

'You look pale,' Kimberly commented with a concern that was a touch *too* solicitous. 'Are you feeling well?'

'Very well.' Hester breathed slowly to regulate her skipping pulse. 'Thank you.'

'I imagine it's been frantic,' Kimberly added. 'Such an unexpected whirlwind wedding, Hester. How *fortunate* he found you.'

'Yes.' Brittany had been watching closely with her sharp eyes. 'You've done so well for yourself, I could hardly believe it was *you* when you walked into that chapel. What an *amazing* dress and make-up job.'

Their peals of laughter reverberated with a cruel edge and Hester all but choked. Because they knew and she knew—it was all a façade, as *fake* as their flattery and smiles were now. Smoke and mirrors.

'And now Alek can be crowned King.' Brittany sent another stabbing look towards Hester. 'But I'd have thought you'd look more like a blushingly happy bride.'

Her cousins had said nothing overtly cruel. Not even they would dare spit bare barbs and bitchiness at her in the palace grounds. No, this was a subtle poison, wrapped in layers of saccharine politeness. But they'd always known where to strike for maximum hurt—mean girls from the moment she'd met them.

Don't reply. Don't give them ammunition.

But that was the old Hester whispering. The one who'd been too afraid to speak or stand up, who'd hidden every reaction, who'd run away...

As Alek had pointed out, there was nothing wrong with choosing not to stick around to be abused. It had taken strength for her to walk out and because she had, she was even stronger now. So she wasn't going to let them chip away her new-found confidence. She'd taken on a huge job here and nailed it. What was more, while Alek mightn't love her, he liked her and he respected what she could offer.

'Oh, I'm very happy,' Hester dredged up enough serenity to assure them. 'Just a little tired from our secret honeymoon. We weren't supposed to go away, what with the coronation so soon, but—' she shrugged and her oh-so-polite tone matched theirs '—Alek's very used to doing and having what he wants.' She paused for a moment to bestow them with a smile as brilliantly fake as theirs had been. 'And he wants me.'

It was true, after all. Even if only for now.

The satisfaction she felt wasn't from seeing her cousins slack-jawed, but from the sudden lightening of her soul. What these people thought of her *truly* didn't matter and she didn't need to bother any more.

'If you'll excuse me...' She stepped past her cousins only to see her security officer standing at a slight distance behind them. Worse, *Alek* was standing beside him.

She froze. She'd been so focused on her cousins she'd not noticed him arrive. Now she saw the question in his eye and knew he'd heard some of that conversation. Her composure began to crumble.

'Is everything all right, Hester?' he asked, his gaze fixed on her.

'Perfectly fine, Alek,' she said clearly, despite her pulse pounding again in her ears. 'But Kimberly, Brittany and Joshua were just explaining that unfortunately they're unable to stay for the coronation. They need to return home tonight.'

'Oh, I see.' Alek swiftly turned to their security officer. 'Could you please escort our guests back to their hotel now and ensure they get on the next available flight this afternoon?'

'Of course, Your Highness.' The security stepped forward with an authoritative air.

Hester watched as her cousins—with furious wordlessness—walked out of her life.

'Are you okay?' Alek asked softly once they were beyond earshot.

She nodded. 'I'm fine.' She flashed a wobbly grin at him. 'I actually mean that. I handled them *fine*.'

'Not fine, Hester.' A chuckle broke his tense expression. 'You eviscerated them.'

Alek watched a raft of expressions cross Hester's face. She was much easier to read now—anger melded with satisfaction, but quickly faded to wispy sadness, to settle on bittersweet relief. It was a mash-up of conflicting emotions that made her so very human. He'd watched, frankly awed, as she'd stood her ground and despatched her former bullies. She'd breathed ice-cool fire.

Those flames within her were so well hidden, but when she let them show? She was incredible. He guided her through the gardens to the terrace and into his private study. He closed the door, determined to be alone with her again.

'I was thinking,' he muttered. 'I don't think this should end.'

'Pardon?' She shot him a confused look.

'Our marriage.' He cleared his throat and discovered

how truly horrible awkwardness felt. 'You realise we had unprotected sex yesterday.'

Her skin mottled and she ducked her head, brushing the swing of her hair back with a shaking hand. 'Oh, I should have told you at the time but I... I wasn't thinking,' she mumbled. 'I won't get pregnant. I'm on contraception for other reasons. I'm sorry if you've been worried.'

'Worried? No.' He needed a moment to absorb the hit of disappointment. It was startling and he had to clear his throat again. 'Well, I think that we should tear up the contract.'

Her eyes widened. 'Tear it up?' she echoed. 'You want this to end already?'

'No. I mean stay married,' he clarified.

'Stay married.'

She seemed to be stuck on repeat.

'That's right.' He nodded. 'For good.'

She just stared at him.

'I will have to have children some day,' he said.

She didn't even blink. 'I thought you had years to figure that out.'

'I think perhaps I've figured it out already.' He watched her closely. 'I'm not going to lie. I didn't think I wanted them. Partly because I don't want to burden them with... everything. But perhaps the sooner I have children, the longer I'll be around to be King, so they can have as long as possible to shape their own lives, have their own careers, their own dreams.'

She was still staring at him, still unmoving.

'We work well together, Hester. We could make a good team.'

Why wasn't she smiling? Why was she staring at him aghast, as if he'd said something insane? Why did he feel as if he'd just tried to run through a boggy field wearing woollen socks?

'You're willing to settle for...' She trailed off. 'Just for that?'

'What do you mean "settle"?' This made sense. 'I don't think I'd be settling, Hester.'

'What about *your* dreams, Alek?'

'My what?'

'Your dreams.'

He shook his head blankly, because that wasn't the point. That wasn't ever the point.

'You don't have any?' she asked softly.

His gaze narrowed as she stepped closer. She'd done a magnificent job of masking her emotions with her hideous cousins, but her façade had truly cracked wide now. Now there was pure golden fire. 'What about *mine*?' she asked.

'Uh...um...'

'You want me to stay married to you?' she clarified. 'To have children with you? So are you saying you're in love with me?'

Hester held her breath, but for once in his life her charming, usually so smooth husband was lost for words.

'Didn't think so,' she muttered. 'You rebelled so much against the control the Crown—that tradition, your father—all exerted over you. Would you really just accept that little now? Really agree to live such an empty life?'

His gaze narrowed. 'Who's to say it would be empty?'

Had he been concerned he'd got her pregnant and decided he'd better offer to make this a permanent deal? Her heart ached because for a second there, just for a second, she'd wanted to believe he meant it for *real*.

'For so long, I've felt like I didn't fit in,' she said.

'You fit in just fine here. You know we could make this work.'

'I want more than to just make something *work*.'

And when he bored of her? What then?

'We're a lot alike, Hester,' he argued. 'You don't really want all that either. You were happy to accept a convenient marriage.'

'Temporarily, yes. But, actually, I *do* want "all that".'

She wanted the whole package—marriage and children, a family built on a foundation of love. The love she'd not had since her parents died. And the irony of it was that it was thanks to the confidence and appreciation Alek had given her that she finally recognised that she could and should.

'I deserve "all that".'

'You could have *everything* here.'

'And what's that? What's "everything"?'

'Security. Safety.'

'That's what you think I need?' She gazed at him. 'Because that's *not* everything. That's not the most important thing to me.'

'Hester, it's what you need.'

'Is that really what you think?' She gazed at him, horrified. Did he think he was 'helping' her somehow? Rescuing her? Trying to fix her life for her because he'd been unable to do that in his past? Because he'd seen her horrible cousins? 'Am I just a win for your wannabe doctor ego?' she asked, hurt. 'I don't want to be that. I don't want your pity.'

'You don't have it.' Arrogance glittered.

She didn't believe him. 'When we first met, you were furious at the fact you had to get married. You thought a marriage of convenience was the worst thing ever and you wanted to fling your own choice in their faces. But now you've decided it's everything you've ever wanted? What, something superficial, some purely contractual, cool paperwork?'

'We're hardly cool paperwork between the sheets, Hester.'

'That's just… That's not anything more than sex for you. You don't want anything actually emotional.'

His jaw hardened and a wary look entered his eyes. 'And you do?'

She looked at him sadly. 'I've not let anyone close to me in a long, long time. Do you truly think I don't feel anything more than just lust for you?'

He stilled and his expression shuttered. 'Hester—'

But she was struggling to maintain her composure. 'I don't want to settle for safety and security. I want it *all*, Alek.'

He pressed his lips together. 'What is it "all", Hester? Moonbeams and fairy tales?'

'Love isn't an impossible fairy tale to me.' She gazed at him. 'My parents loved each other. I think yours did too.'

He'd turned into a statue. But she couldn't stop her emotions from seeping through her once formidable control as in this most terrible of moments her feelings crystallised. Her ability to stay calm—to maintain her mask—vanished.

'And yes, that's the "everything", the "all" I want. Love. And, honestly, I want it with you.'

He looked winded—as if *she'd* sucker-punched *him* instead of the other way round.

'I can't…say the same to you.'

Of course he couldn't. It was the cruellest moment of her life—when she was so close, but so far from the one thing she really wanted.

'It's not you—'

'Don't.' She held up her hand.

'I can't offer that to anyone, Hester.' He overrode her furiously. 'I never have, never will. It's not in my make-up.'

'That's such a cop-out. Why? You're that afraid?'

'It's not about being afraid,' he snapped. 'I just wanted—'

'What? To make me feel better? To make me feel safe?'

He glared at her. 'And what is so wrong with that?'

'I don't need you to keep me safe. I don't need you to feel secure in my life. I just stood up to the worst people ever…and I didn't need you there to do that.'

He swallowed.

'I can do more than survive now, Alek. I can fight for what I want. The irony is that's because of you.' She shook her head. 'You've made me feel like I can.'

He didn't love her. He wanted her, yes, but that wasn't enough.

'And what I want—what I really want—is everything, "all that" and more with *you*. But because you don't feel that deeply for me, you can't understand that you're hurting me without even realising it. That? That you couldn't see that? You might be happy to live such a superficial, safe existence, Alek, but I'm not.'

'You think I'm shallow?'

'I'd hoped you weren't. You're good to your sister. I get that you're trying to be good to me. You don't understand how heartless it really is.'

'Heartless?' He scowled and his control began to slip. 'Would you rather I lied to you?'

'Of course not.'

He was angry. 'Are you going to run away because I can't give you what you want?'

'No. I only run away from abuse, and I know you won't hurt me more now. I made a commitment to you and I won't renege on our contract. But we go back to business.'

'What does that mean?'

'I won't sleep with you any more.'

'No more kissing? No more touching? You really think that's possible?'

He looked so disbelieving it was insulting.

'It's the only way I will stay for the duration until our divorce.'

'You'll need to lock the door, Hester. But not from me.'

'I know I will. But I'll lock the door and I'll throw away the key.'

'If it's going to be that much of a challenge, then why fight it? Why not just accept that we're good together, Hester? There's no real reason why *that* can't last.'

But it wasn't enough for her. She'd told him how she really felt and he still didn't understand.

'You're really not used to not getting your own way, are you?' She gaped at him. 'Listen to me, Alek. I want more. And I'm worth more. And I will never settle for the little you're offering.'

She fled from the room, slamming the door behind her before she stared at him too long and surrendered everything regardless.

Almost all her life she'd not had it all. She'd not felt secure and cared for. She'd not felt safe enough to care for others too. He'd opened her up. She'd allowed herself to fall for someone. To love.

But she wanted to be loved in return. Loved the way other people were. She knew she'd shut down and hidden away, but she'd not realised how entrenched her defensiveness had become. She'd forgotten that she actually had things to offer people. Alek had reminded her. And made her believe she was beautiful. She could open up and share in joy and pleasure. She could engage with people beyond a quick moment in which to help someone in some superficial way. He'd made her feel warmth again—from companionship and closeness and, above all, humour. He'd changed her.

But while she'd changed him—it wasn't in the same way. The adjustment to his offer wasn't enough. And it hurt more than anything.

CHAPTER TWELVE

HESTER STARED AT her reflection, barely recognising the sleek, stylish woman in the mirror as herself. This coronation was more important than their wedding. It was the reason *for* the wedding—so Alek could fulfil the duty conferred on him from birth.

This was what he'd wanted and truthfully it was *all* he'd wanted. Their affair had been a mere cherry on his already massive cake. No doubt he'd have plenty more cherries in the future.

He might've thought they'd make a good team but it would never last. Because what he'd offered wouldn't be enough for her. She'd be hurt more and more and more knowing that she loved him in a way he would never return. When she'd had so little for so long, she couldn't do that to herself.

The teardrop diamond necklace that had been sent to her room earlier hung like an icy noose around her neck, reminding her of the heartbreak she faced. A year was an interminable amount of time. She wished he'd see that there was no need for them to wait that long. But she'd promised him she'd stay. In public, she'd hold her head high and play her part. Thankfully the palace was large enough for her to avoid him at all other times. She would run away to her apartment and survive. Eventually she'd return to the States—or maybe somewhere else entirely. Then she'd start again. She just had to get through this coronation today.

All the years of hiding her emotions were going to stand her in good stead. It was the only way she was going to get through this and do her job. Because that was her one thing—she was damn good at her job.

It was worse than if she'd run away. She was still present, still doing everything he'd initially asked, but she'd become like a will-o'-the-wisp around the palace. He heard her footsteps but never spoke to her. Caught her scent but never saw her. She was incredibly skilled at making herself invisible. Because she knew what she had to do to survive—and for her that meant not seeing him.

That hurt.

And how badly *he* wanted to see her hurt too. When he was with her, he felt good. She'd slipped under his skin and exposed old wounds to sunlight. It had hurt, tearing off those crusted wrappers. But the salve was Hester herself.

He'd not given anyone real meaning in his life in a long time because it hadn't been a risk he'd been prepared to take. He hadn't even realised how hurt he'd been. He'd not seen the truth. He'd accused her of being prickly and defensive when he was the one holding back. He'd thought he was whole and happy. But he'd been a heartless coward.

But she'd asked him what his dreams were. No one had asked him that, ever, he didn't think. And he hadn't thought he had any. Until now. *She'd* ignited new dreams, enabling him to imagine beyond merely passing personal pleasure. She'd made him realise the emptiness in his life that he'd have denied he felt only a few short weeks ago.

She'd wakened within him the possibility of a future that held more than duty. The prospect of private happiness—of laughter and fulfilment for himself. He wanted—

ached—to inspire that in her. He wanted to be the one *she* dreamed about in the way he dreamed about her. He actually wanted this marriage—with her. And children—with her. He wanted to be the father he'd not had—one who was there. One who *listened*.

She made him want everything he'd deluded himself into believing he dreaded—one woman. Children. Love.

He'd been so wrong about her. He'd thought her shy— she wasn't shy; biddable—where she was intractable, and dutiful—when she could be so defiant it made his blood sing. He'd been unable to admit how much she'd come to mean to him—not to himself. Not to her. Which mean she was right and he was a coward. It took strength to leave a situation, to speak up for what you wanted. He'd been weak in offering less than what either of them wanted or deserved. And in not opening up properly—in not allowing himself to be vulnerable the way she had—he'd hurt her. And he couldn't stand to know that.

The solution had dawned on him early this morning— after another long, sleepless, heart-searching night.

Now, as she slowly made her approach towards him in front of millions again, he realised she'd retreated further behind her walls than ever before.

Her ball gown was of epic proportions—it was the colour of the ocean surrounding the islands while the scarlet regal sash crossed her breast. This time her hair was swept up high. Long silk gloves hid, not just her fingers, but her wrists, right to her elbows. It was impenetrable armour.

But while her face was beautifully made up, he saw through to the emotion-ravaged pallor beneath. He saw the tearful torment in her eyes for that snippet of a second before she looked to the floor again. She was so formal. So correct. So dutiful. And he hated it.

He'd hurt her too badly and the knowledge gutted him. He curled his hands into fists, barely containing the self-directed anger building within him. Barely restraining his urge to run to her and haul her into his arms and beg her forgiveness.

He had to do this properly.

He didn't want her to kneel in front of him. He wanted her to stand beside him. He *needed* her beside him. She strengthened him and he hoped he could strengthen her.

For so long she'd been able to hide behind those walls. Self-contained and in control, masking her emotions, trying to bury everything so deeply so nothing and no one could hurt her. But he knew her walls were built with the thinnest of glass now and with one false move of his, they'd shatter. He didn't want to do that to her. Not here, not now. He'd hurt her too much already. He'd never seen anyone as brittle and as fragile. Or as determined.

So while he was filled with pain for hurting her, he was also consumed with pride and awe. Because she walked towards him smoothly, hidden courage lifting every step. She was loyal and considerate and frankly loving, even when he didn't deserve it.

He was determined to deserve it. And he was determined to show her how much she mattered.

Hester couldn't hold Alek's gaze. He looked so stern it scalded her heart. The last thing she wanted was to walk towards him in front of the world. This packed room was enough, but this was being broadcast again to millions over the Internet. But she had to lead the way for the rest of the citizens in his kingdom. Tradition dictated she display deference before him. Before all of them.

Her blood burned as she kept her eyes on the floor. Slowly she walked to the edge of the dais on which he stood in his cloak and crown. She couldn't look at him even then. The media would probably interpret her body language as submission and that was fine by her. Because she didn't want anyone to guess that it was pure pain and hopeless love.

Slowly she knelt before him. There was a moment of complete silence, then she heard movement as all those people behind her lowered to their knees as well.

She couldn't bear to look at him. It was all just a pretence anyway—just the part she'd promised to play. She'd grit her teeth through the final act and in a year's time she'd leave and, fingers crossed, never see him again.

'Hester.'

His soft call was a command she had to obey. Looking up, she saw he'd moved closer, right to the edge of the dais. But his solemn stare still left welts on her heart.

'I will not let you kneel before me.' His harsh whisper rasped against her flayed skin, stinging like salt rubbed across raw cuts.

She stared at him blankly.

He bent and took her hand and tugged, but she frowned and didn't move. With an impatient grunt he put his hands on her waist and physically lifted her to her feet, pressing her against him for the merest moment.

'What—?'

'Not long and we'll be alone, Hester. Trust me until then, okay?'

It was the quickest whisper in her ear so that no camera could capture the movement of his lips and no distant microphone could amplify the secret speech.

Why was he insisting she stand? Why he was going so far off-script of this massive pantomime they'd been preparing for?

Murmurs rippled across the crowd behind her. The courtiers and guests had remained kneeling, but they were looking up. Alek had stepped to the side briefly but now turned. She saw he held a crown in his hands—a smaller one than his but no less ornate.

He met her gaze for only a moment before looking beyond her to his wide-eyed citizens.

'Allow me a moment to explain,' Alek said. 'I am proud of Triscari's traditions and I will honour them but I also look forward to building new ones.' His face was ashen and his smile so faint. 'I do not wish for my most important partner to bow before me.'

Another murmur rippled across the crowd, but Alek kept talking and they silenced.

'It is a bittersweet time, this coronation, because it only happens because we have lost my father and he was a great king. He was devoted to our country and you, his people. But he was also a lonely man after my mother died. As my sister is, my mother was intelligent, progressive and loving. Losing her was very difficult for us as a family. We do not speak of her enough. I will confess, I thought the requirement for the monarch to be married was archaic—that it was a constraint and a form of control. It is only recently that I've realised it was never for the country's benefit, but for my own. To find a partner, a woman with whom I could share everything—riches and rewards, hope and dreams, and also the weight of this crown. So it is my honour, my privilege, to bow before *you*. To offer my life in service to my people, my country. And finally to offer my love to my Queen—Hester.'

Vaguely she heard cheering through the stone walls— the crowds outside were shouting his name over and over again. Not just his name. Her name too.

'Alek and Hester!'
'Alek and Hester!'
'Alek and Hester!'

Now he was staring straight at her, willing her to move. She couldn't ignore him, yet it hurt, this public display of unity that was so false. But his intense, unwavering gaze and the emotion emanating from him were all-encompassing. Surely it was something she had to reject?

But she couldn't. Not because of the crowds watching, but because of *him*. He compelled her to move with just that promise in his eyes. And even though she couldn't trust it, she couldn't deny him. So she stepped forward and took her place on the dais beside him. He turned and placed the crown on her head—the fine-wrought gold the delicate mate of his.

To her amazement, he then bowed before her. Without prompting, without even thinking about it, she dropped into a curtsey before him. They rose together and he reached out to take her hand. This was good because the air was rushing around her and she felt faint. To the beat of those chanting voices, they walked the length of the grand hall and out to the balcony. Time sped crazily as they stood in front of the gathered crowds and the clicking cameras and listened to the hum of reporters broadcasting their commentaries.

Eventually he turned and guided her back into the palace and into the nearest escape room.

'We need a few minutes.' He shut the door in the face of the palace official seeking to follow them.

Keeping her back to him, Hester stepped further into the room to gather herself.

'You…' She trailed off, realising she couldn't speak about anything too personal without losing it. 'That was an amazing spectacle,' she said harshly, indescribably angry all of a sudden. 'You really nailed it.'

His muttered oath sounded suspiciously close.

'Hester, look at me.' His hands were on her shoulders and he spun her to face him.

His eyes blazed with an emotion she couldn't hope to analyse and couldn't bear to face.

'It's wasn't a *spectacle*,' he said furiously. 'It wasn't

some show for public consumption. I meant it. Every word. Not for them. For you.'

She stared up at him, stunned into rigidity.

'I don't want to do any of this without you. I was a jerk. I'm sorry. I was never more serious in my life than when I said you are my Queen. *You're* who I want by my side, always.'

She got that he thought they were a good fit. That she could complement him. But it wasn't enough. She shook her head. 'I can't—'

'I know what I offered wasn't enough for you, Hester. I thought I understood, but I didn't. It wasn't until we were apart these last few days that I realised just how hollow my words were. How stupid.'

Her mouth dried.

'I had my walls too, Hester, I just didn't realise. All those women? It was avoidance. I didn't want to get close to anyone and never stopped to think why. You helped me— you opened me up and I realise I never dealt with any of it: the ache of losing Mother of watching Dad retreat into isolation and control. And that I'd done the exact same thing in my own way. I thought I was so clever when, actually, I'm a coward.' He huffed out a powerful sigh. 'I thought you were the one who was shut off—and you were. But you're braver than I've ever been. You realised what more you really need and you decided to fight for it.'

'That was only because you got through to me. *You* made me realise how much I was worth. And how much I really want.'

'How much you *deserve*.' His chest rose and fell. 'I know it's all been too fast but give me a chance, Hester. Give *us* time. We're amazing together.'

Amazing together? She blinked.

'Hester, I've fallen in love with you.'

She stared at him fixedly. 'That's not possible.'

'Why?' That old smile twitched. 'Haven't you fallen for me?'

She swallowed. 'Yes, but—'

'The only problem was I couldn't admit it to *myself*. I couldn't admit how much *you* mattered. I was able to keep anyone from mattering much for a very long time. But you slid into my life and suddenly everything was up-side down and inside out. Me, *I'm* inside out—I'm unable to exist the way I used to. Because it isn't enough for me any more either. I want you right with me. I can't stand the thought of losing you. I hate this distance we've had.' He was shaking. 'I know it's a lot to ask. I know my life comes with a whole lot of pressure and complication. But you belong here—this could be your home. Stay with me, Hester. Please.'

'You didn't really want me to before. Not like this.'

'Because I was an idiot. Because I didn't know how to handle my own feelings. Because I was afraid. Losing someone you love hurts, Hester. I didn't realise how much I was avoiding letting myself love someone. But the fact is, I can't stop myself and I don't want to any more. I love you. And I want you to let me love you.'

She shrivelled inside. Not believing him while at the same time wanting to.

'Is it so hard to believe that I could love you?' he asked.

'It's been a long time…'

'I know.' He brushed her cheek with the backs of his fingers in the way that made her feel *precious*. 'But I think a lot of other people are going to love you, if you let them. A whole country full.'

That scared her, a lot. 'I don't want all that…' she mumbled. It felt like such pressure and all that mattered to her was him. 'I just want you.'

'And you have me.' He drew in a deep breath. 'You're

so beautiful.' He leaned closer. 'You're loyal and brave and funny and kind and so very organised.'

She almost smiled.

'But if you don't want to stay here, we can work something out.' He glanced at her. 'I don't quite know—' He broke off.

'Of course I want to stay, Alek.' Of course she would stand beside him, do anything she could to help him. Just as she was beginning to realise that he would for her. 'I want to be with you. To work with you.'

His hands swept to her waist to hold her still, but it was the look in his eyes that transfixed her. She didn't notice their finery; the gold and jewels faded into insignificance because all that mattered was the emotion shining so clearly in his eyes.

'I have something for you.' He unfastened the top two buttons of his jacket and reached into the inside breast pocket. He pulled his fist out and unfurled his fingers in front of her. A small shard of obsidian sat in his palm. 'It's from that afternoon at the springs.'

'You took a piece?'

'At the time I thought...'

'Thought what?'

'That you might put it with that button in your box.' He gazed into her eyes, his own a little shy. 'But *I* wanted the reminder, that's why I didn't give it to you then. And now I know we should collect more memories *together*.'

Little treasures from little moments that meant so much more than any precious jewels ever could.

He put the obsidian in her palm and locked his hand around hers. What he'd given her was beyond precious— it was access to his heart, his soul. And she would always keep it safe. Just as he was offering to keep her heart safe in his hand too.

He was here for her. He wanted her. He loved her.

Her eyes filled as he swept her into his arms. But he kissed the tears away. He pressed her close against him as if he were afraid she'd disappear if he didn't; his grip was almost painful. But she revelled in it—rising to meet his mouth with hers. To pour every ounce of soaring emotion back into him. She loved him. And he loved her.

'I should've known when I realised I wasn't terrified by the thought of you being pregnant,' he confessed with a breathy laugh. 'I never thought I wanted kids, now I can't wait. I want to see you cradling our babies. I want to see a whole bunch of miniature Hesters curled up in a big chair and reading their favourite books.'

She laughed through her tears. 'While mini Aleks will wow everyone with their ventriloquism?'

'Something like that.' He pulled her close again. 'You believe me?'

She rested her head against his chest and wrapped her arms around his waist, needing to feel him against her and know he was solid and real. 'I will.'

'I know, we need some time together alone.' He sighed. 'But right now we have to go in there for a while. Can you handle it?' He sounded apologetic.

She lifted her face to smile up at him. They'd have their time alone together soon enough and she couldn't wait for that magic. But she understood that right now Alek had the obligations of that heavy crown upon him. It was a burden she'd gladly help him shoulder.

His answering smile reflected the joy rippling through her veins. She rose up on tiptoe to kiss him and whisper her absolute truth.

'I can handle anything when I have you beside me.'

EPILOGUE

Two years later

'COME RIDE WITH ME.'

Hester glanced up and registered the heat of intent in her husband's eyes. 'I thought you had meetings all afternoon?' she asked, faking cool serenity. But she put down the book she'd been reading and quickly stood.

'Finished early.' Alek smiled knowingly.

She knew that smile so well and every time he sent it her way, it hit her right in the solar plexus. He didn't just love her, he *adored* her—making her feel beautiful inside and out. And with him at her side, she didn't just handle everything—all the good and the bad—that life had to offer, she *revelled* in it.

So now she drank in the sight of him in the black trousers and shirt he preferred to ride in. Sensual attraction fluttered as she felt ruthless desire emanating from him. Their need for touch hadn't dissipated in the two years since their mad, quick and convenient marriage—in fact it had increased.

After the coronation they'd had to escape—stealing a full month of a real honeymoon at the stud, replying to any arising issues via phone and emails. And even then, upon their return, it had been a challenge to concentrate for longer periods of work again.

Together they'd formed their alliance. She'd accompanied him more on engagements and she'd found a purpose of her own in reinvigorating the city's literacy programmes. Then, just this year, she'd opened the children's library of her dreams—using a room in Queen Aleksandrina's castle, to bring life and love and laughter back to the place, so that more people could take time out there and appreciate the beauty built by an untameable woman who'd refused to fit in.

And every weekend they could, they came back here to Triscari Stud to oversee the breeding programme and take some time for themselves. So now Hester walked with him to the yard. Jupiter was saddled and waiting not quite patiently. They always rode together when staying at the stud even though Hester had learned to ride on her own and actually found she wasn't just getting better, she enjoyed it.

Today Jupiter carried them both. Alek steered him in the direction of the clifftop forest that they'd gone to on her first visit here. Hester's heart sang as, sure enough, they went to the hot springs where they'd come together again in that desperately passionate way. She treasured that piece of obsidian that rested safely in her box. But today it wasn't only the striking rock formations and steaming water that caught her attention. A circular white tent was set up near the pool and a small sofa actually sat outside in the warm sun, smothered in plump cushions and rugs.

'What's this?'

'Our anniversary escape.' He tightened his hold on her. 'Or did you think I'd forgotten?'

'I didn't think you'd forgotten,' she murmured. 'I

thought you were probably planning something for later. I figured your meeting was a cover.'

'Were you planning something?'

She smiled coyly and leaned back against him. 'Of course.'

She loved dreaming up nice things to show she cared. Small things, to treat him, and he did the same for her—slowly building their own language of care and love and collecting the trinkets to put in their shared memory box. But this time she had the most perfect secret to surprise him with.

She slipped down from Jupiter and walked towards the tent. Fairy lights were wound around the wooden poles while the interior was filled with fresh flowers and a pile of soft-looking wool throws artfully strewn on a bed. There was a small table with a wicker basket beside it that she knew would be filled with their favourite picnic food.

'Going for comfort this time?' she teased him.

'Going to stay the whole night.' He nodded. 'Maybe even two nights.'

She curled her toes with delight. There was nothing better than stealing time for just the two of them. She'd never known such fulfilment and happiness.

'So...' He leaned back to look into her eyes. 'Has my bringing you here caused any problem for what you had planned?'

She shook her head. 'My plan was vague but portable.' Her heart pounded and to her amazement tears formed, bathing her eyeballs in hot acid that spilled before she could speak any more.

Alek's eyes widened. 'Hester?'

She nodded quickly. 'I'm fine.' All the emotion clogged her throat so she could only whisper. 'I'm better than fine. You know...'

He still frowned but a small smile curved his mouth

and his hold on her tightened. The contact strengthened her. She trusted him completely—knew she could expose herself, reveal her greatest vulnerability—because he always caught her. He always listened. He cared.

'I'm pregnant,' she blurted.

He stared, frozen for eternity before his expression exploded with intensity. 'Say it again.'

'We're having a baby.'

Because this was *them*, together, and their little unit of two was going to become three.

A huge rush of air hissed from his lungs and she felt the impact as relief and joy and incredulity radiated from him.

'It's been hideous keeping it from you these last couple of days.' She lifted her hands to frame his beloved face. 'But I wanted to save it just long enough to tell you today.' She rose on tiptoe and pressed her tear-stained mouth to his.

They'd decided to delay trying for a little while after their wedding so they could discover and delight in each other and solidify the intense connection they'd forged so quickly. But a few months ago they'd discarded any contraception. And now? Now her joy was so fierce, it burgeoned, encompassing him too.

'Not going to lie—I'm terrified. But I can't wait, Hester.'

He pressed her to him and she felt his strong muscles shaking.

'We can still make love? Is it safe—?'

'There'll only be danger if we don't!' She laughed and growled at the same time. 'I need to have my way with you, my King.'

'Well, you are my Queen and I will always bow before you.' He didn't just bow, he dropped to his knees, his hands firm on her hips as he gazed up the length of her still-slim body. 'I can't wait to meet our child, Hester.'

'Neither can I.' She dropped to her knees too—desperate to feel again the pleasure that was only theirs.

With him she was free and utterly unafraid to reveal everything—her body, her soul, her secrets—all the things that scared her, all the things that delighted her. He didn't just accept them, he embraced them, and he shared his own so together they were stronger still.

'Alek…' she breathed, enraptured by the fantasy world into which he'd cast her.

'I'm here, Hester.'

And he was.

Because beneath it all—the crowns, the diamonds, the palaces and castles…everything—their love was real.

* * * * *

COMING SOON!

MILLS & BOON

Coming next month

REVELATIONS OF HIS RUNAWAY BRIDE
Kali Anthony

'This marriage is a sham.'

In some ways, he agreed with her. Yet here he stood, with a gold wedding band prickling on his finger. Thea still held her rings. He needed her to put them on. If she did, he'd won—for tonight.

'You're asking me to return you to the tender care of your father?' A man Christo suspected didn't have a sentimental, loving bone in his body.

Thea grabbed the back of a spindly chair, clutching it till her fingers blanched. 'I'm asking you to let me go.'

'No.'

Christo had heard whispers about Tito Lambros. He was reported to be cruel and vindictive. The bitter burn of loathing coursed like poison through his veins. That his father's negligence had allowed such a man to hold Christo's future in his hands...

There was a great deal he needed to learn about Thea's family—some of which he might be able to use. But that could wait. Now it was time to give her something to cling to. *Hope.*

'You'll come with me as my wife and we'll discuss the situation in which we find ourselves. That's my promise. But we're leaving now.'

She looked down at her clothes and back at him. Her liquid amber eyes glowed in the soft lights. 'I can't go dressed like this!'

No more delays. She glanced at the door again. He didn't want a scene. Her tantrums could occur at his home, where any witnesses would be paid to hold their silence.

'You look perfect,' he said, waving his hand in her direction. 'It shows a flair for the dramatic—which you've proved to have in abundance tonight. Our exit will be unforgettable.'

She seemed to compose herself. Thrust her chin high, all glorious defiance. 'But my hat… I told everyone about it. I can't disappoint them.'

'Life's full of disappointments. Tell them it wouldn't fit over your magnificent hair.'

Thea's lips twitched in a barely suppressed sneer, her eyes narrow and glacial. The look she threw him would have slayed a mere mortal. Luckily for the most part he felt barely human.

'Rings,' he said.

She jammed them carelessly on her finger. *Victory*. He held out the crook of his arm and she hesitated before slipping hers through it. All stiff and severe. But her body still fitted into his in a way which enticed him. Caused his heart to thrum, his blood to roar. Strange. Intoxicating. All Thea.

'Now, smile,' he said.

She plastered on a mocking grimace.

He leaned down and whispered in her ear. 'Like you mean it, *koukla mou*.'

'I'll smile when you say *that* like you mean it, Christo.'

And he laughed.

This second laugh was more practised. More familiar— like an old memory. But the warmth growing in his chest was real. Beyond all expectations, he was enjoying her. For his sanity, perhaps a little too much…

Continue reading
REVELATIONS OF HIS RUNAWAY BRIDE
Kali Anthony

Available next month
www.millsandboon.co.uk

LET'S TALK

Romance

For exclusive extracts, competitions
and special offers, find us online:

f facebook.com/millsandboon

🐦 @MillsandBoon

📷 @MillsandBoonUK

Get in touch on 01413 063232

For all the latest titles coming soon, visit
millsandboon.co.uk/nextmonth

MILLS & BOON
DARE

Sexy. Passionate. Bold.

Sensual love stories featuring smart, sassy heroines you'd want as a best friend, and compelling intense heroes who are worthy of them.

our DARE stories published every month, find them all at:

MILLS & BOON

THE HEART OF ROMANCE

A ROMANCE FOR EVERY KIND OF READER

MODERN

Prepare to be swept off your feet by sophisticated, sexy and seductive heroes, in some of the world's most glamourous and romantic locations, where power and passion collide.
8 stories per month.

HISTORICAL

Escape with historical heroes from time gone by. Whether your passion is for wicked Regency Rakes, muscled Vikings or rugged Highlanders, awaken the romance of the past.
6 stories per month.

MEDICAL

Set your pulse racing with dedicated, delectable doctors in the high-pressure world of medicine, where emotions run high and passion, comfort and love are the best medicine.
6 stories per month.

True Love

Celebrate true love with tender stories of heartfelt romance, from the rush of falling in love to the joy a new baby can bring, and a focus on the emotional heart of a relationship.
8 stories per month.

Desire

Indulge in secrets and scandal, intense drama and plenty of sizzling hot action with powerful and passionate heroes who have it all: wealth, status, good looks…everything but the right woman.
6 stories per month.

HEROES

Experience all the excitement of a gripping thriller, with an intense romance at its heart. Resourceful, true-to-life women and strong, fearless men face danger and desire - a killer combination!
8 stories per month.

DARE

Sensual love stories featuring smart, sassy heroines you'd want as a best friend, and compelling intense heroes who are worthy of them.
4 stories per month.

To see which titles are coming soon, please visit

millsandboon.co.uk/nextmonth

JOIN US ON SOCIAL MEDIA!

Stay up to date with our latest releases, author
news and gossip, special offers and discounts, and
all the behind-the-scenes action
from Mills & Boon...

 millsandboon

 millsandboonuk

 millsandboon

It might just be true love...